EVERY THOUGHT TAKEN

LAKE LAVENDER SERIES

PERSEPHONE AUTUMN

BETWEEN WORDS PUBLISHING LLC

EVERY THOUGHT
TAKEN

LAKE LAVENDER SERIES

USA TODAY BESTSELLING AUTHOR
PERSEPHONE AUTUMN

BETWEEN WORDS PUBLISHING LLC

Every Thought Taken

ISBN: 978-1-951477-65-3 (Ebook)

ISBN: 978-1-951477-66-0 (Paperback)

ISBN: (Hardcover)

Editor: Ellie McLove | My Brother's Editor

Proofreader: Rosa Sharon | My Brother's Editor

Cover Design: Abigail Davies | Pink Elephant Designs

BOOKS BY PERSEPHONE AUTUMN

Lake Lavender Series

Depths Awakened

One Night Forsaken

Every Thought Taken

Devotion Series

Distorted Devotion

Undying Devotion

Beloved Devotion

Darkest Devotion

Sweetest Devotion

Bay Area Duet Series

Click Duet

Through the Lens

Time Exposure

Inked Duet

Fine Line

Love Buzz

Insomniac Duet

Restless Night

A Love So Bright

To my younger self—the girl that just wanted to be loved and accepted. To my current self—the woman that still battles depression on occasion. To every person out there that lives with depression, a dark cloud that never really leaves your side.

I see you. I hear you.

You are strong. You are beautiful. You are loved.

It's okay to not be okay. It's okay to ask for help.

TRIGGER WARNINGS AND AUTHOR'S NOTE

Every Thought Taken is a contemporary romance story. Graphic content, depression, self-harm, bullying, attempted rape (off page), and death of a parent (off page) in certain scenes may trigger emotional distress in some readers. If you are sensitive to the listed triggers, this story may not be for you.

Please use your own personal judgement before proceeding.

If you or anyone you know has depression, suicidal thoughts, or self-harms, please seek help. If you are not able to seek help online or by phone, but know someone who can, please push them to do so. And never give up the fight.

Suicide & Crisis Lifeline

- https://988lifeline.org/
- In the US, dial 988

Find a helpline in your country at https://findahelpline.com/

Dear Reader,

Some may know while others are unaware that I am a suicide survivor. Depression has been part of me for more than 30 years. Some days are great, others the complete opposite. I compare it to internal battle that never ends, but is simply managed on a day-to-day basis.

If depression is something you struggle with, please contact your country's crisis helpline, speak with someone you trust, or seek professional help locally.

You matter. You are wanted. You are loved.

I love you.

Persephone

PROLOGUE

ANDERSON

Far back as I can recall, not a day exists when I haven't loved Helena Williams. In my younger years, my love for her was more familial or akin to friendship. But as the years passed, something changed between us. The unrequited love I had for my sister's best friend was reciprocated. Like the seasons, our love fluctuated. Like the moon, some nights were dark and cold while others were bright and warm.

I loved her.

I *love* her.

Nine years ago, I broke in two. She said goodbye, and I tried to let her go. She moved on and I did unthinkable things.

With her gone, I fell apart. I let the darkness take over. Let myself drown. The dark was familiar. Comforting. Guaranteed. Constant.

But now, I am ready to breathe again.

Being on the road for years, I dissociated from reality. From the heartache she brought to life. From the cracks in my relationship with my parents. On the road, I was free. Free to think and feel without guilt or shame. Free to express myself, even if only to myself, without skirting around the shadow attached to my soul.

It took years for Helena to not be my first thought each day. It took years to love myself. To feel something other than disgust or indifference. Though my self-love is still question-able, it exists. Flickers to life when the darkness clouds my vision.

And like my darkness, I linger.

Across the street, I hover near the entrance of the Lake Lavender Cinema. The crowd of movie-goers cloaks my unabashed surveillance of Always Classic. Her boutique. Where she stands near the window and futzes with the street-side display.

The backs of my eyes sting as I stare after her. As I watch her go about life. Breathing with ease. Existing without restraint.

A customer pushes through the black-framed glass door and she spins around, a bright smile on her face as she greets them. She resumes her task in the window as the customer steps farther into the store, and I don't miss how fast her smile fades.

"What saddens you, my love?"

I wade through the crowd and move closer. People shuffle past, but I never lose sight of her. Never miss a beat as I suck in a deep breath and cross the street. My pulse whooshes loudly in my ears with each step forward. My breathing jagged as I reached the opposite side of the street. And when she looks out the window and sees me standing on the sidewalk, my rib cage constricts.

Tears rim my eyes as I stand there, waiting.

Damn, she stuns.

Helena has always been beautiful. The girl I fell in love

with years ago, I still see pieces of her as I stare at the woman in the window. Her hair is different. Shorter. Straighter. Her face thinner and hips curvier.

As I absorb and catalog each change in her appearance, my gaze drops to her hands clasped at her waist. My brows twitch and vision blurs as she twists the ring on her right ring finger. I *know* that ring. Thin, gold double bands with a small baguette-cut sapphire at the heart.

Fire blazes in my lungs, and I force myself to take a breath. Wetness coats my cheeks as she backs out of the display. The fist around my heart tightens as she moves toward the door. I can't move, can't breathe, can't think as she opens the door and steps out. I clench my fingers into loose fists as my limbs tremble.

In seven heart-pounding steps, she stands within arm's reach. Her sweet rose and amber scent hit my nose and my eyes close. A flood of memories rushes in. Swarm my thoughts and blanket my heart. More tears spill over as I meet her gaze.

"Hey, Ander," she whispers.

"Hey, North." The nickname I gave her scratches my throat.

I don't miss the flinch of her brows. The shift in her stance as she glances over my shoulder and loses focus. With each passing breath, her eyes glass over more. Red rims her green irises. A slight wobble takes over her chin. And when our eyes meet again, her tears match my own.

"Missed you," she chokes out. Her head falls forward as she twists the ring on her finger.

"You did?"

She straightens her spine. Her eyes dart between mine as her brows pinch tight. Lips trapped between her teeth, she nods.

Without a second thought, I reach forward and take her hand. Press my thumb to the ring on her finger. Suck in a sharp, shaky breath as tears pour freely down my cheeks. With one touch, everything I felt for her rushes to the surface. With one touch, I flaunt my vulnerability.

Years ago, Helena knew me better than anyone. Then life got flipped upside down. She left. She split me in two. And with her absence, I detached from the world. From her. Though we are practically strangers now, the throbbing ache in my chest begs to differ. Pleads with me to not let go. Implores me to hold on tight. Tighter than before.

And I want to. I want to get lost in her. Get lost in what we might be now.

But if the past has taught me anything, it is that I need to guard my heart now more than ever. I need to shield my soul. Because she is the only person that can shatter both. And I wouldn't survive the blow. Not this time.

With one last stroke of her ring, I take a deep breath and inch closer. "Missed you, too," I confess and pray the words don't come back to haunt me.

PAST

CHAPTER 1
HELENA

Summer — Sixteen Years Ago

"Ow!" I rub my forehead in an attempt to soothe the sting.

Laughing under her breath, Lessa jogs around the flat tent and knocks my shoulder. "You okay?" She snickers a little louder as she inspects my face. "That's going to leave a mark."

I roll my eyes at her and tilt my head so my hair falls forward. "Not like anyone will see it." I wave a hand at the dense forestry. "Well, except for everyone here." With a shrug, I bend down, swipe up the brown nylon, and grab the offensive tent pole. "Help me, please. I'd like to not get smacked again."

She fights another laugh as she goes to the opposite side of the tent and picks up the other end of the pole. The pole she tried to anchor too early, which then sprang from my grip and whacked my face. It was an accident, but I may have to exact revenge before our camping trip ends.

As we anchor the final corner of the tent, Dad sidles up to me and inspects our handiwork. Hands on his hips, he hums his approval. "Good work, Bug." He hooks an arm around my shoulders and hugs me to his side. "I'll make an explorer out of you yet." With a kiss to my crown, he releases me and wanders back to his and Mom's tent.

Every summer, we go on our annual camping trip to Seaquest State Park. The summers before kindergarten, it was me, Dad, and Mom. We pitched one tent and soaked up nature for a long weekend. Then I met Lessa and Mags, and our camping trips took on a whole new meaning.

This is our sixth year camping as a group. Me with Mom and Dad. Mags and her parents, Maria and Jacob. Lessa, her little brother, Anderson, and their parents, Joan and Sam. It took a heck of a lot of convincing the first summer to get our three families to take the same vacation. But after days of sad eyes and moping, the parents coordinated and agreed to the joint excursion. Each summer that followed, it got easier to convince them. And now, the annual vacation is booked a year ahead.

"Did you hear Trudy from Mr. Pembrooks's class got her period last week?" Lessa whisper-asks as she unzips our *girls-only* tent.

She steps inside the tent, and I follow. As I sit and crisscross my legs, Mags enters then zips up the screen door. She parks next to me and mimics my position.

"What are we talking about?" Mags looks to Lessa.

"Trudy got her period last week," Lessa repeats.

Mags winces. "How do you know?"

If there is news or gossip to be heard, Lessa is all over it. She isn't one to spread the details beyond our small group, but she makes a point to keep us up to date. Which is why I don't share the embarrassing details of my life with her. Like the time I tripped during PE and face-planted in the dirt. She wouldn't have told anyone except Mags, but she probably would have teased me about it for months.

A brief, sharp hiss fills the air and we turn to see Anderson unzipping the tent screen.

"Hey, Baby A. Your tent all set up?"

Aside from the dads, Anderson is the only guy on our summer trips. More than once, I wanted to ask if he had a friend he would like to bring along. Someone from his class or a neighborhood buddy he hung out with. But I never asked.

It is a rare day if Anderson smiles—really smiles—but the week we spend here each year, there is a lightness in him I don't see back home. And it is the lightness that keeps me from prying.

Anderson enters the tent and rezips the screen. "Yeah." He hands us sleeping bags, then parks next to Lessa.

Most girls our age have a hate-love relationship with their siblings. Mags and I are only children, so we have nothing to compare it to except Anderson. With three years between us girls and him, you'd think he would irritate us. But he doesn't.

Anderson joins us most days. He and Lessa have always been close and it feels natural to include him. Most of the time, he sits and listens. Keeps to himself and stares off in the distance. I don't know if it is because our topics are of no interest to him or he doesn't understand. Either way, he sticks around. Sometimes, it seems as if he prefers our company and nothing more.

Lessa sets her sleeping bag aside and turns her attention back to me and Mags. "About Trudy... I saw it on her profile."

My jaw drops. "She shared that online?"

Some people our age are brave. Not in an *I fought a bear and won* kind of way. More in an *I openly share everything about my life and don't care what anyone thinks or says* way.

I am not one of those people.

Though I haven't started my period yet, there is no way I will broadcast the news online when I do. I am not embarrassed by it. Periods are a part of growing up. But what happens to my body is private. It's bad enough girls in my grade already have boobs and my chest is flatter than a CD. You won't catch me telling the world I wear a training bra just to feel included.

Mom sat me down last summer, before fifth grade, and talked about the changes I would soon see in my body. She did her best not to use medical terms but couldn't help it when I asked questions. As the primary nurse at the Lake Lavender Community Clinic, Mom educates me on the things school teachers aren't able to because of curriculum changes. Thankful as I am, I keep our talks private. The only exception is if Lessa or Mags needs answers only she has.

"Yep." Lessa pops the *P*. "And half the school liked it."

"Ew," Mags says. "So weird."

"Anyway…" Lessa turns her attention to Anderson. "Want to hike while the parents sit around the fire and talk about grown-up stuff?"

At this, Anderson perks up. "Sure. Let me grab my pack and some water."

Anderson dashes from the tent, forgetting to close the screen. On the way to his tent, he tells the parents we are going for a hike. As expected, Dad stops stacking wood in the firepit and heads in our direction.

"Knock, knock."

"Come in," I answer.

Dad ducks his head in the tent and peers around. Mags stashes her sleeping bag in the corner while Lessa unrolls hers. Our backpacks and clothes are still in the truck—something we don't usually sort out until after dinner on the first night.

"Anderson said you all want to go on a hike."

"Mm-hmm," I answer with a nod.

His eyes scan the tent as he mulls over the idea of three ten-year-old girls and a seven-year-old boy hiking without adult supervision. Not like I plan for us to go far or unprepared. I have my Swiss Army knife and bear spray. We will also pack water and snacks and matches.

Some of the girls at school teased me because Dad taught me *boy stuff*. I told them to shut up. It isn't *boy stuff* to carry a knife for protection. It isn't *boy stuff* to know how to read a compass and track animals or people in the woods. And it certainly isn't *boy stuff* to build a fire and learn how to survive in the woods if you get lost. Knowing life and survival skills is smart, not *boy stuff*.

Stupid, prissy girls.

"Make sure everyone has permission before you take off."

"We will, Daddy."

"You have your knife, Bug?"

I stand up and pat my front pocket. "Yep."

"And your spray?"

I point in the general direction of the truck. "In my pack."

"That's my girl." He backs out and straightens. "Before you go, come see me. I want you to take a walkie with you."

Thrill courses through my veins. *He's actually letting us hike. Without a parent.* I hoped he'd say yes, but wasn't certain.

Not only had we gone camping every summer, but Dad also taught me about nature. What to look for and how to react in specific situations. Though we do plenty of fun daddy-daughter activities, there is no stopping his park ranger persona when we set foot in the woods.

"I will. Thanks, Daddy."

CHAPTER 2
ANDERSON

Helena twists the stick holding her marshmallow, flipping it so the other side gets toasty. The perfect golden brown, exactly how she likes it. My marshmallow, on the other hand, is charred, just the way I like mine. Something about the crispy outside and gooey inside makes it taste better. That hint of smokiness is an added bonus.

"Want to make a s'more?" she asks, shaking a small container filled with graham crackers and chocolate.

I shake my head. "No, thanks." I bring the marshmallow close and blow on it. "Maybe tomorrow."

While she neatly stacks the graham crackers and chocolate, I take my first bite. Sweet and woodsy with a hint of bitter from the char. Perfection.

As I stab another marshmallow with my stick, she takes the first bite of her s'more. Before burning my next marshmallow, I stare at her as she eats hers. Stare at her stuffed cheeks and big eyes. Space out as she laughs because her s'more is falling

I like my sister's best friend—one of my only friends—so I won't ask. Asking will make me sound like a dummy. Like I am the only person who doesn't know why it's funny when your food falls apart.

"Are you excited for third grade?"

Blinking, I look up at her. "Huh?"

"Third grade," she repeats, licking chocolate off her finger. "Are you excited?"

I hate school. No one is friendly, not with me anyway. My sister, Helena, and Magdalena don't count. While most kids in my grade are friends and talk with each other, I sit still and keep to myself. It is hard to make friends when people whisper in your direction and point fingers at you.

"No," I say only loud enough for her to hear. Last thing I need is for Mom to know how I feel.

"Wish we'd still be at the same school."

I peek at her from the corner of my eye and see a bit of sadness on her face. The downturn of her lips makes me feel weird. Seeing her upset makes my belly cramp. Helena never looks sad. Not that I have noticed.

"Me, too."

By the time she finishes her next s'more, I have eaten two more marshmallows. On the other side of the fire, her dad and mine talk about the storms last winter and how it made work harder. Mr. Bishop sits with them and listens, nodding every once in a while. Magdalena and Ales lie on their bellies on a blanket, flipping through the pages of some teen girl magazine with pictures of famous boys.

Does Helena look at the boys in those magazines?

I have never seen her look at the same magazines Ales does. Maybe Helena thinks like I do. That geeking out over famous people makes no sense. That fawning over a famous person's every move is creepy. So what if they sing on stage or act in movies? They are just people. Regular people that are good at what they do.

Nobody gets excited to see me. Ever.

Mom gets up from the picnic table where she and the other moms have been talking. She steps up next to me and pats my shoulder. "We're headed to bed. You kids should do the same."

When I tip my head back and look up, she stares at me with a half smile. It's a smile I know all too well. This is her quiet way of saying she means *I* should go to bed, but the girls can stay up longer. I may be younger, but I am far from stupid. Everyone—well, almost everyone—treats me like I am brainless, but my teacher said I am smarter than other kids in my grade. That I read and write and understand math better than most fourth and fifth graders.

Mom knows this and still treats me like a baby. She doesn't care this is vacation. She doesn't care I won't fall asleep for hours. All she cares about is routine and looking good in front of the other moms.

When she doesn't look to the girls, signaling they should go too, I stand from my camping chair and shove it back. Without a word, I stomp off for my tent. At least I get my own tent this year. It'd be ten times worse if I had to sleep with my parents.

"Anderson Gregory," she snaps and I ignore her. If she wants me gone, then here I go.

I unzip my tent, step in, rezip it, and secure the two zippers with a paper clip. Kicking off my shoes, I open my sleeping bag and lie down, not bothering to undress or blanket myself with the top.

Until the fire no longer lights the vents at the top of the tent, I listen to everyone outside. Listen to the girls chat about what they want to do while we are here. Listen to the dads talk about fishing and the great steaks they bought and new trails they want to explore this trip. And listen to the moms—who obviously lied about going to bed—talk about Magdalena's dance class, Helena dressing less like a tomboy, and Ales's excitement over the café we stopped at on the way here.

The one thing I notice, the one thing that hurts most... no one mentions me in their conversations. No talk of me in extracurriculars or school. No mention of including me in any activities during our trip. Nothing. As if I don't exist.

Sometimes, I wish I didn't.

CHAPTER 3
ANDERSON

Winter—Fifteen And A Half Years Ago

Giggles erupt in the next room, my sister's laughter louder than the others. Mumbled words bleed through the wall, followed by more chuckles.

Eyes glued on the ceiling, I huff in exasperation. I fist the comforter with both hands. Grind my molars and pray my sister and her friends will quiet down soon. Most days, I ignore their snickers and whispered gossip. Most days, I get lost in my own thoughts and brush off their constant blather.

For whatever reason, tuning them out tonight is impossible.

On the next laugh, I groan loud enough for them to hear me through the shared wall. I shoot up from the bed, stomp across the room, fling open the door, and bolt down the hallway for the living room. On the way, I flip off all the lights my parents left on before they went out for date night.

I drop onto the couch, reach for the remote, and power on the television. I drown in endless channel options as I surf for something mildly entertaining to watch. With Mom and Dad not home to police what I watch, I skim the premium cable channels. I hit Showtime and see a season marathon for *Dexter*. After reading the show description, I start episode one, turn the volume up, and lie longways on the couch.

"What are you watching?"

I startle and push up on my elbow to see Helena standing near the couch arm. In her favorite cream-and-brown flannel pajamas, she narrows her eyes at the television. Her arms wrap around her middle as she stares at the screen. I sit up farther and scoot to one end of the couch in silent invitation.

"Some show called *Dexter*." I shrug. "Want to watch it with me?"

She twists her hands together and looks toward the hallway. When she turns back to face me, she gives a halfhearted nod. "Yeah. Okay. But I need a drink and a snack."

I press pause on the remote and follow her into the kitchen. Turning on the light over the stove, we squint at the sudden brightness. While Helena goes to the pantry, I open the fridge and scan the drink options.

"Pepsi, Dr Pepper, Sierra Mist, or Mountain Dew?"

Helena peeks out of the pantry and taps her lips with a finger. "Hmm. Sierra Mist, please. Any snack requests?"

I shake my head as I grab two cans from the fridge.

She exits the pantry with several bags and boxes, a guilty smile on her face. "Couldn't decide."

For the first time in months, I laugh. It hurts and feels good. "Bring them all."

We shuffle back to the living room, open the cans, bags, and boxes. I scoot the coffee table closer. Offer her one of the throw blankets on the couch arm. We stuff our faces and watch the rest of the episode. Just as the episode ends, Ales and Magdalena come out.

"Movie night?" Ales asks.

I press pause as the next episode starts, open my mouth to answer, but Helena cuts me off.

"Um, not really." She side-eyes me for a second. "It's some new show about a serial killer that kills serial killers." Her forehead wrinkles. "It's... strange."

I flinch but don't think she notices. Her use of the word strange is a swift kick to my back, to my stomach. Only one episode in, I feel the opposite about the show and character. Calm and somewhat indifferent. Maybe it will change the more I watch. Maybe not.

"Not sure that's a good show to watch, Baby A."

I roll my eyes. "Don't care. Mom and Dad aren't home and I'm watching it." I gesture to the empty space on the couch next to Helena. "Stay or don't. Either way, I'm watching."

I press play, sit back, and toss a blanket over myself. Ales and Magdalena shuffle past the table and plop down next to Helena. She scoots closer and her leg brushes my leg. For a moment, I ignore the television.

Wouldn't say I am anti touching, but it isn't often I sit this close to anyone. Hugs happen even less. Not because no one loves me or is opposed to hugging me. I tend to avoid them. Physical affection makes me uncomfortable. Like I owe the person something other than a hug or kiss on the cheek. Like I need to thank them or say something after. Tell them I love them.

Ales is the only person I hug. The only person I say I love you to. It doesn't feel forced when I say it to her. And she doesn't guilt me if I don't tell her. Our shared affection has always been easy, unlike with our parents.

Although I don't love her, Helena makes me comfortable too. Safe enough to be close or talk. She is my sister's best friend, but also my friend. We have known each other for years. Most of all, she doesn't make me feel less important or unworthy.

Bags crinkle as we crunch on chips, pretzels, and other snacks. Halfway through the episode, snores filter through the quiet parts of the episode. I lean forward and see Ales sleeping on Magdalena's shoulder and Magdalena asleep on the couch arm. Helena is awake, a small smile on her lips.

"I always fall asleep last," she whispers.

I sit back and sink farther into the couch. "Me too."

She inches closer and leans in. "Do you like this show?" Her warm breath hits my cheek. Out of the corner of my eye, she twists her hands in her lap.

I shrug. "So far, yes." Taking a deep breath, I consider how to explain why. There is no perfect answer. "His reasons for killing killers make sense."

"You don't think it's wrong he's a killer? Even if he's taking out killers, he's one too."

"Yeah. But it's better than him killing good people."

Helena jerks back and stares at me, her brows pinched. She studies me a moment and I shrink inside. Her stare isn't cold, but it is similar to Mom's look of disapproval. And I hate this look on her face. I disappoint enough people already. Letting down friends... not sure I can handle that.

She pats my leg with a hand. The simple touch is familiar, like something Grandma Everett does when she is proud of my vocabulary quiz grade. It is also different, but I don't know how.

"Killing aside, what else do you like about the show?"

Her hand is still on my leg. Warm and... nice. I close my

eyes, mentally shake it off, and focus on her question. The deeper I dig for an answer, the more I wonder if she wants to hear it. Because it isn't normal… like me.

"He isn't scared to be himself. He knows darkness exists in him and chooses to accept it. People call him weird and he doesn't care."

The corner of her mouth tips up. "That's a very specific and smart answer." She knocks my shoulder with hers. "Sometimes I forget you're younger." Her face softens. "You act more mature than most boys—in your grade and mine." She lays her head on my shoulder and whispers, "It's one of my favorite things about you."

CHAPTER 4

HELENA

A shiver wakes me and I tug the blanket to my chin with a groan. Clangs and mumbles in the distance wake me further. I crack an eye and see Mags next to me on the floor, curled into a ball in her sleeping bag.

How did I get to bed?

Memories of my talk with Anderson last night begin to surface. I was confused by his answer about why he liked the show. Last I remember, we started the third episode with my head on his shoulder. I'd never been so physically close with Anderson. He was Lessa's little brother and, in some ways, mine too.

When he spoke of darkness and fear and brushed off negative comments as if he related to each, instinct took over. I wanted to comfort him. Take away every hurt he has known. Steal every dark thought he ever had.

Last night, he laughed for the first time in a long time. I may not see Anderson every day like I do Mags and Lessa, but we spend a lot of time together. Enough for me to pick up on the small changes in his smiles and laughter and attitude. Often, I consider asking Lessa if he is okay. But I resist butting in. It isn't my place. He isn't technically my family.

If something is wrong, his family has to know. Right?

Unzipping my sleeping bag, I sit up and look past Mags for Lessa. Her sleeping bag is empty. I twist and scan her bed. Empty. I stretch my arms then consider waking Mags but decide to let her sleep.

I tiptoe to the door and twist the handle, peeking over my shoulder as the hinges creak. Mags doesn't move. Hints of sweet and savory and smoky hit my nose as I step into the hall and shut the door. I use the bathroom and brush my teeth then head for the kitchen.

As I round the corner, Lessa and Anderson come into view. Their backs to me, they stand at the stove. Lessa flips pancakes while Anderson stirs scrambled eggs and turns over bacon on the griddle. Without a word, I slide onto one of the stools at the breakfast bar and watch. The timer buzzes and they step back. Anderson grabs a hot mitt and opens the oven door.

"Hey," Lessa greets then turns off the burners.

"Morning," I say as Anderson sets a pan of homemade biscuits on a trivet.

Footsteps echo down the hallway seconds before Lessa's parents enter the kitchen. I don't miss the slight slump in Anderson's shoulders. I also don't miss the way that one move twists my stomach.

"Good morning, kiddos," Mr. Everett says with enthusiasm. He steps up to Lessa, wraps her in a tight hug, and kisses the top of her head. "Thank you for making breakfast." He passes Anderson, pats his shoulder, and goes to the coffee maker and starts a pot.

Mrs. Everett wishes us a silent good morning with a wave and halfhearted smile then goes to the cabinet to grab plates. She stacks them at the end of the kitchen island then goes for the utensils. Before I get the chance to offer to help, she has forks and knives on napkins on the dining room table.

My mom isn't as loving as my dad, but she has this warmth incomparable to anyone. As I watch Mrs. Everett move around the kitchen and dining room, I don't catch an ounce of the warmth most moms have. The instinctual drive to nurture and safeguard their children. It's… odd and disarming.

Lessa and I have been friends since the start of kindergarten and not once did I see Mrs. Everett in this way. Robotic and detached. Uncaring.

Maybe she didn't sleep well.

The creak of Lessa's door steals my attention. Mags shuffles down the hall in fuzzy socks with a blanket wrapped around her shoulders. She walks up to me and playfully shoves my shoulder.

"Why didn't you wake me up?"

I shrug. "You were cozy." I shift my attention back to the tray of biscuits and my stomach grumbles. "And I haven't been up long."

She tightens the blanket around her shoulders. "Did you see it snowed?"

I shake my head.

"We should go out after breakfast," she suggests.

"Only after you check in with your parents," Mrs. Everett says before I answer.

With my back to her, I scrunch my face. "We will," I say without looking her way.

I have never once disrespected parents—mine or my

friends'. It bugs me that the first thing Mrs. Everett says to any of us this morning is sharp, as if we disrespected her. Yes, I am a child. From time to time, I may talk back, but my parents taught me to respect adults and my peers. To be thoughtful. To consider other people's feelings when I speak. Words can hurt. Sometimes more than anything else.

But shouldn't adults do this with children too?

We may be young, but we aren't stupid. We feel and think and hurt too. And harsh words from someone who should love you unconditionally hurt the worst.

"Let's eat, call our parents, then go see the snow," I say as I stand.

We pile our plates with pancakes, eggs, bacon, and biscuits. I fill a glass with juice and sit on the far side of the table. Lessa takes the spot across from me, Mags next to her. Anderson's lips flatten in a line as he takes the empty seat on my side. After Mr. Everett stacks his plate high, he sits at the head of the table.

And it isn't until after I drown my pancakes and bacon in syrup that I notice Mrs. Everett hasn't grabbed a plate. Instead, she rushes around the kitchen, wiping counters and huffing as she washes dishes.

Lessa bolts out the front door and runs for the now-buried sidewalk. Mags hurries behind her with a little less enthusiasm but a wide smile on her face.

"Come on," Lessa groans out. She plants her gloved hands on her hips, taps her foot, and gives me and Anderson a pointed stare.

"Just go. We'll meet you there," I suggest.

Her brows shoot up and her hands drop. Then she shrugs, grabs Mags's hand, and speed walks down the street. "We'll probably have a snowman built by the time you make it," she hollers over her shoulder.

"Whatever," I yell back.

The Everetts' house is just over a mile from Lake Lavender Elementary. Every winter during break, the neighborhood kids go to the playground and field to enjoy the snow and get out of the house. For years, the principal told parents to not let their children visit school grounds when school was out. Neither the parents nor kids listened, and the principal had no way to stop anyone unless someone patrolled the school at all hours. Eventually, they gave up. At the next town meeting and each school event, they told parents the school isn't liable for accidents or injuries.

No one has been hurt over the years. And visiting gives us all something to look forward to as snow blankets the ground.

Anderson and I walk down the street, Lessa and Mags nowhere in sight. He hasn't said a word all morning; his eyes down and posture slumped. Before his parents entered the kitchen, his lips started to curve and he almost gave me his sad smile. But then it fell away. I didn't like it. At all.

"Hey," I say, bumping his arm with mine.

His steps stutter as he looks at me. "Hey," he mutters, then shifts his eyes back to his feet.

I hate prying into people's business. Mom says if people want you to know about their life, they will share the details with you. So, I tend to keep things to myself and don't ask others to share.

With Anderson, though... he hasn't been himself. His sadness has me worried.

"You okay?"

He stops a step back. I spin around and return to his side, watching as his expression twists. As he mulls over the simple yet difficult question. He lifts his head and stares past me down the sidewalk.

Our breaths fog the cold, spruce-scented air. I curl my fingers in my mittens, wishing I had on two pairs instead of one. A door across the street slams as a woman chases a little boy. He looks like a starfish in his stiff layers as he laughs uncontrollably.

I turn my attention back to Anderson, his blue eyes rimmed with tears making my chest hurt. I want to hug him. Tell him everything is okay.

But I have no idea what is wrong.

"If I tell you something," he chokes out. "Will you promise not to tell anyone?"

That is a hefty oath to keep considering I don't know the secret. What if what he tells me is bad and an adult needs to know? Can I keep something terrible a secret? I hold his stare and ask myself this over and over. Either way, whatever it is, it's happening. Better he has someone to confide in than no one at all. For Anderson, I will keep his secret.

"I promise."

He nods and takes a step toward the school, and I fall in step beside him. Our pace is slow and over the next several minutes, Anderson tells me about the bullies harassing him at school. Ugly words said about his clothes and how soft he speaks. Pranks played on him before, during, and after school. Boys knocking over his tray in the cafeteria. Girls teasing him over his haircut and skinny arms and legs. The whispered conversations that stop when he gets too close. The shoving and name-calling when no teachers are around.

"I hate them," he states as we walk through the playground gate. "I... I..."

Grabbing his arm, I stop him before we get close to Lessa and Mags. "Wish I had a way to help." But if he wants to keep this secret, there isn't much else to do.

Without hesitation, I hug him. And for a moment, he hugs me too. I let go and step back, my eyes doing a quick sweep of the playground. Last thing either of us needs is Lessa asking why we hugged.

"Sometimes, I think about hurting them."

At this, I inch back and furrow my brow. "What do you mean?"

"They make me so mad. They say and do mean things and then laugh. They make other people laugh too. And... and... I just want to hurt them. Hit them. Cut them. Show them what it feels like. Watch them cry and then laugh at them."

"Anderson..."

Teary eyes hold my stare. "No," he croaks out. "You don't get to talk to me like I did something wrong." He looks away. "I didn't do anything." He hangs his head. "I never do anything." His chin wobbles as he lifts his head and stares at me with empty eyes. "No one likes me. No one cares. Maybe if I was mean like everyone else, I'd fit in."

"I like you," I whisper, taking a step in his direction. "I care."

Anderson is the little brother I never had. A friend. Someone to have fun with when Lessa is a brat. He isn't a backup choice, he is just not the first person I think of when I want to hang with friends.

A tear falls down his cheek and he wipes it away. "Well, maybe you shouldn't." He sniffles. "Maybe there's a good reason why no one likes me."

"Nope." I shake my head. "I don't believe that."

He takes a step toward the playground. Then another. He stops, peers over his shoulder, and shrugs. "Doesn't matter what you believe. I don't like me, so why should anyone else?" And then he walks off.

CHAPTER 5

ANDERSON

Late September—Fourteen Years Ago

Birthdays are this asinine commemoration of the day you leave the womb. With each passing year, they get more over the top. Parents attempting to make their kids' party better than little Johnny's or little Jane's.

In my opinion, celebrating my birth is a waste of time. As of now, the only person that appreciates my existence is Ales. And I think Helena and Magdalena. Dad cares more than Mom, but it bothers him that I am not like other boys my age. I don't beg him to throw a football or ask for a basketball hoop or want to fish on the lake.

I am the family disappointment.

When Mom asked what I wanted to do for my birthday and I responded with "sleep in and stay in my room," a big frown took over her face. She said, "It's your special day. We have to party." So this entire display—colorful balloons and cheery banners, a large cake and tub of ice cream, games and noise makers and loud music—is for everyone except me. Because *she* wanted this party.

I am not opposed to parties. But being the center of attention makes my skin crawl. Especially when I said no.

Dozens of kids from ages eight to thirteen roam the backyard. Mom got this *wild idea* to celebrate my and Helena's birthdays at the same time. I foresee this becoming an annual thing—not that I mind sharing the stage with Helena. At least she wished me happy birthday when she and her family arrived. Other than Ales, she is the only one.

Three years and eleven days separate us. It wouldn't surprise me if sharing her party with a young boy embarrasses her. Her middle school friends are probably weirded out by the younger kids here—some of which have kicked me or given me wedgies in the bathroom, and others have called me names like stupid or creepy or smelly or ugly.

I have no real friends in school. My only friends are my sister and her friends, which is pathetic.

"Anderson, come over here," Mom calls from across the yard.

With a heavy sigh, I push up from the chair on the far side of the yard and walk over to the patio. She and Helena's parents hover over the shared birthday cake decorated with different-colored flowers. In the center, it reads *Happy Birthday Lena & Anderson*. Helena's mom, Hannah, stabs twelve pink candles in while Mom adds nine blue candles.

My brows tighten as I watch them. "This is weird," I mutter.

Mom stops her candle placement and looks up. "What was that, Anderson?"

With a shake of my head, I say, "Looks nice."

A smile brightens her face as she nods. "Yes, it does."

Yeah... nice for Helena.

Minutes later, everyone is beckoned to the table. Helena and I are told to stand opposite our mothers while everyone sings, "Happy Birthday." Each candle is lit and the unharmonious song starts.

My eyes drop to my feet for two breaths before an arm hooks with mine. I shift my stare to the arm then up to Helena, who smiles and leans closer.

"Is it just me or our mothers losing it?" she whisper-asks.

At this, I smile. I like that she knows how to make me smile. "Definitely," I whisper back.

With her mouth close to my ear, she says, "When they finish singing, let's switch sides. You blow out my candles and I'll blow out yours." She leans back, looks me in the eyes, and raises her brows in question.

Mom will hate the idea. Will probably say I ruined the party or made her look bad in front of the other parents.

I nod. "Yes," I mouth.

As the last line of the song ends, she unhooks her arm from mine and gives me a fresh smile. With a nod, we switch positions and blow out candles. Everyone cheers and whoops. But when I stand up straight, I spot the slight grimace on Mom's face.

I don't care, I scream in my head. *It's Helena's and my birthday, and we'll do whatever we want.*

The cake is cut into squares and slapped onto plates with a scoop of Neapolitan ice cream. The backyard quiets as everyone takes a seat and devours the sugary treats. I go back to my chair at the farthest point in the yard, away from everyone. Shade from the tall evergreens on the other side of the fence blocks the sun and hides me from some partygoers.

After I scrape all the icing off my cake, I stab a corner of the vanilla-chocolate marble cake and shove it in my mouth. Dry and too sweet, but made by Mom's friend. *"Gina makes the best cakes in Washington."* I shove the square aside and decide to eat only ice cream.

Halfway through the ice cream, Helena parks a chair beside mine and sits. Not far behind her, my sister and Magdalena walk our way with chairs and loaded plates.

"This cake is gross," Helena states just above a whisper. Her eyes shift to my plate. "Guess that's why you're not eating it too."

With a nod, I say, "Yep. Maybe next year, if our parents do this again, we let your mom be in charge of cake."

She leans into me and bumps my arms with hers. "Agreed. Bad enough we have to smile as we eat it. No one else should be forced to eat it too."

Ales and Magdalena set down their chairs then sit. The four of us eat ice cream and toss napkins over the unfinished cake on our plates. Ales sparks a conversation about some guy at her school who smiles at her during lunch every day. I aim my eyes to the clouds between the branches and zone out.

While Ales and Magdalena chat, Helena turns her chair more in my direction. "How's school?"

One question and the ice cream in my stomach sours. With a slight turn of my head, I widen my eyes at her and silently say, *"I'm not talking about that with other people around."*

She closes her eyes for two breaths then softens her gaze in apology. "Did you get Mr. Talbot or Ms. Higgins?"

"Talbot," I mutter.

Her shoulders sag and she smiles. A small thank you from her for me not being mad. "We had him too. Wait until he starts science." She smiles bigger. "He's such a science nerd."

The way she says it doesn't come across as mean. More like she is amazed someone loves science so much.

"I'll let you know when he does."

"Present time," Mrs. Williams hollers, her balled fists shaking with excitement in front of her chest.

I groan and rise from the chair. "Not like I got gifts," I mumble.

We leave our chairs and return to the patio. We toss our plates in the trash and take a seat at the table next to each other. Helena has a mountainous stack of gifts. Boxes in varying sizes, wrapped in soft, colored paper and ribbon. As for me, I have five. The wrapping paper is lackluster in comparison to Helena's gifts and I suspect they are all from my parents, Helena's parents, Magdalena's parents, and my sister.

Not a single one of my classmates brought me anything. Not even a card. Color me not surprised.

Helena unwraps her gifts first. Pretty tops. A new purse. Sneakers and dress shoes she has had her eye on. Hair accessories and a bottle of perfume. A denim jacket. Books with people hugging on the cover. And last, a gift Mom bought from all of us, a Polaroid camera with film.

"Thank you, everyone." Her eyes scan the party. "These are all wonderful."

An uproar of "you're welcome" and "so glad you love it" flood my ears. I close my eyes and take a moment to breathe. To prepare myself for all the eyes that will be on me as I open the less-exciting gifts.

"Alright." Mrs. Williams claps. "You're up, Anderson."

At least she sounds excited. I wish my mother cheered me on the way Mrs. Williams does.

Grabbing the first box, I read the tag. *From Mom and Dad.* I tear into the brown paper and open the box. Jeans and T-shirts and flannels. And socks.

A few snickers echo across the table and I internally groan. *This will be the next reason I get picked on at school. Great.*

"Thanks, Mom." I meet her waiting eyes and smile. It feels forced, but I try to soften it so it looks the opposite. "Thanks, Dad."

"You're welcome, son," Dad says. "We'll exchange whatever doesn't fit."

I nod and move to the next gift, reading it is from Magdalena and the Bishop family. Making quick work of the black-and-gold-foil birthday paper, I open the box and see a new pair of hiking boots. The good kind. Taped to the top of the box is also a gift card for the sporting goods store for fifty dollars.

Holy crap.

Tears blur my vision, but I shove them away as I look to the Bishops. "Thank you. So much. I love them."

As much time as we spend outdoors, especially in the summer, these boots will be handy for at least two years. Having new boots also gives me another reason to go out on weekends. Less time at home, less time listening to Mom and how unhappy she is with everything I do.

I pick up the next present, this one from Mr. and Mrs. Williams. The box is small and wrapped in shiny, dark-blue paper with a clear and colorful bow. I tug at the flaps, rip apart the paper, and gasp. The threat of tears hits harder.

This is expensive. Really expensive.

With my head down, I blink back the tears and will myself to look up. When my eyes meet their happy stares, the backs of my eyes burn and my stomach flips.

They bought me an iPod Nano. The new one that came out days ago.

"I… I don't know what to say," I declare, fumbling over my words.

"How about you thank them, Anderson," Mom bites out.

Her sharp words stab at the joy bubbling in my chest. "Yes. I'm sorry. Thank you, Mr. and Mrs. Williams. I… this is… wow."

Mr. Williams steps around the table and comes to my side. He lays his hand on my shoulder and gives it a squeeze. "You get to put your own music on there and listen to the radio. It has some other cool features we can look at later." He squats down next to my chair and leans closer. "There's also a small gift card to get your collection started," he says only loud enough for me to hear.

I should say more than thank you to them. This is so much. Too much. More than I deserve.

Mr. Williams straightens his legs but stays close to my ear. "We love you, bud. And whatever you're thinking, stop. We wanted to get you this."

"O-okay."

He goes back to stand with Mrs. Williams and they both smile.

The next gift is from Ales. I side-eye her as I peel away the brown paper with doodles all over it. Inside the box is a leather sleeve with a gold metal flashlight. I slide the flashlight from the holder and turn it over in my hand. Along the battery housing, it is engraved with *So you're never in the dark.*

My eyes shoot to Ales's and I question what she knows. Did Helena spill my secrets? Does my sister know I have dark thoughts? Does she know I spend more time in the dark than in the light?

"It's perfect," I say. "Thank you."

She gets up from her chair, comes to my side, and hugs me tight. "You're welcome, Baby A," she whispers in my ear. "Don't know why you're sad, but I'll always be here. For whatever." She gives me one last squeeze then lets go. "Always," she repeats.

I nod. "Love you."

"Love you, too." She ruffles my hair then takes her seat.

One last present. Did a classmate buy me something? All the family gifts have already been opened.

With a buzz of excitement in my belly, I pick up the last box. The package is small. A little bigger than my palm. I tear off the dark-green bow and ribbon. *No tag.* Then I peel back the gray paper. Lift the lid on the blank white box and open the tissue paper flaps. A brown leather pouch with a gold snap in the middle sits nestled in the box. It matches the leather case for the flashlight. I remove it from the box and open the pouch. Stare down at the hinged gold circle with a button and loop.

With a press of the button, it pops open. Inside is a compass. On the inside of the lid is another engraved message. *When you're lost, find true north.*

"Do you like it?" Helena whisper-asks.

My eyes shoot to hers as my vision blurs. Slowly, I nod. "My favorite," I choke out quietly. "Thank you."

Her gift is practical. Something no one would ask questions about. But the message… is generic enough to not raise brows or stir uncomfortable conversations. But it also says I am not alone. There is always another path to take. There is always hope if you go in a different direction.

A bright smile lights her face. She reaches over the arms of our chairs and wraps me in her arms. I close my eyes and let her peace fill me up. Let her light shine on some of my darkness.

She straightens in her chair and gives me a smaller smile. "Happy birthday, Ander."

No one has ever called me Ander, but I like the way it makes me feel. Like I belong.

"Thanks, North."

Her smile grows.

"Happy birthday to us."

CHAPTER 6
HELENA

"Thanks for coming."

I wave and smile as the last of the partygoers get in their car. When the car's taillights vanish, I drop my hand and relax my expression. Inhale a lungful of air and hold it for three, two, one. On the exhale, the rest of me relaxes. Peace loosens my muscles as the quiet warms my soul.

Crowds don't bother me, but I do prefer smaller groups of people. The more familiar the people, the better. Aside from Mags and Lessa, I do have friends. But I have never wanted to spend time with anyone outside of school except them. My best friends. My sisters.

Fun as the party was, it would have been more enjoyable with less. Mom and Mrs. Everett went a bit over the top. The constant entertainment and stimuli. The endless checking in with people rarely spoken to.

Anderson avoided the kids from his grade more often than not. And I didn't miss their quiet laughter when he opened the gift from his parents.

He said he didn't have friends at school. That he was

bullied. Come Monday, the kids that laughed today will pick on him for his new clothes. And dang it, I wish I could be there. I wish I could get in their faces and yell. Shove them away and give them a dose of their own medicine. Make them feel an ounce of what Anderson does when they mess with him.

But it isn't my battle to fight. If Anderson wants my help, he has to ask. For now, so long as he isn't injured, I will be there for him. However he needs me to be. If it is just to listen, then I will listen.

Going back inside the Everett house, I head for the living room. Mom and Dad are still here, hanging out with the other parents in the dining room. Dad has one arm around Mom's shoulders, his hand rubbing the top of her arm in slow circles while he talks with Mr. Bishop. When his hand stops, Mom leans more into him, her silent way of telling him she loves the small touch.

I drop down on the couch between Lessa and Anderson and blow a lock of hair out of my face. "Ugh. Parties are exhausting."

"I like parties," Lessa says. She sits up straighter and twists to face me better. "What's not to love? Special snacks and dessert. Soda and loud music. Time with my friends." Falling back into the cushion, she sighs. "I want a cool party on my birthday."

The room falls silent as we digest her glee in our own way. I prefer smaller gatherings. I get to be more myself, more comfortable. Though no one bugs me about what I wear or how I look, I am a girl. And like most girls, I care what other people think about my appearance. I care about clothes and acne and fitting in.

Some days, I wish I didn't care about such trivial things. Some days, I wish no one did. We would all be happier.

"Maybe our parents can give you the fancy birthday instead," Anderson mutters under his breath. "You can have them all."

I knock his arm with mine. "I'll agree to this under one condition."

His eyes widen as he gives me his attention. "What condition?"

My lips kick up in a small smile. "No one shares a birthday with you except me. Ever."

For the briefest of seconds, he smiles. A genuine smile, not the forced one he usually gives everyone. I memorize this gentle, carefree smile and store it away. Lock it up tight, swearing to only bring it out when he has a dark day.

"Still think birthdays are stupid, but yeah. Sure. I'll never share a birthday with anyone else."

I pat his leg then hop up from the couch. "Be right back. Going to change." I walk toward the hallway. "You guys pick a movie."

"You seriously like this?" Anderson asks.

Mags pushes up on her elbow from our spot on the floor and looks past me to Anderson and Lessa, who giggles on the other side of him. Her eyes narrow, as if daring him to make fun of her movie choice. If I were him, I'd tread lightly.

"Yes," she says with bite. "I do. And so do your sister and Lena."

I turn my head to look at him. Head on a pillow, eyes on Mags, he scrunches his brow in confusion. "Why?"

Mags huffs, sits up straight, and pauses the movie. "Because it has adventure and excitement and young love. It makes me smile and dream about happy stuff. It makes me feel good."

Anderson clamps down on his lips and gives a slow nod. "Oh," he whispers.

Satisfied with his short acceptance, Mags lies back down, grabs her bag of Twizzlers, and hits play on the movie. On the screen, Jessica is telling Bella who all the Cullens are, talking about each with envy but acting as if she couldn't care less.

Part of me wonders if high school will be like it is in movies or shows. It seems so boring and routine—except for the drama they add for effect. Middle school has been somewhat dull. The only difference from elementary school... pettiness and jealousy. Almost every day, someone is upset about something. How someone talked about them or didn't give them the time of day. How someone has the latest and greatest, but they don't, so they spread rumors to make themselves feel better. Girls are meaner now. Guys are somewhat the same, some a little mean.

Boring would be nice.

I lift the box of Sno-Caps and dump some in my hand. "Want some?"

Anderson purses his lips and takes a few from my hand. "Thanks." Besides sharing the same birthday month, we also both love the same movie snack. On occasion, we share a tub of popcorn, but one of us always has Sno-Caps.

I toss the rest in my mouth. "Mm-hmm." After I swallow, I lean in close and whisper, "Never talk bad about *Twilight* around Mags." I inch back and slash my fingers across the front of my throat.

This makes him smile for the second time in a single day. A lightness fills my chest at the sight.

He nods. "Promise I won't."

We watch the rest of the movie, Mags hanging on every word and moment while Anderson, Lessa, and I pay more attention to our snacks. When the ballet studio scene comes on, I peek at Anderson out of the corner of my eye. Watch him while he watches the movie. Although this isn't the darkest movie or show, there is a dark undertone. And if I pick up on the darkness, Anderson definitely will. The last thing he needs to believe is love and darkness go hand in hand.

Wanting to distract him, I reach between me and Mags for my new Polaroid. I inch closer to him and lay my head on his pillow.

"What are you—"

I hold the camera over us. "Take a picture with me."

His brows pinch together. "You're weird."

I chuckle and Mags shushes me into silence. "So are you."

Before he says another word, I press the button. A small rectangle pops out of the camera and I hand it to him. Holding the camera higher, I press the top of my head to his temple, make a face, and take another picture.

"Will you stop," Mags huffs out. "The flash is messing with the screen."

I pinch my lips between my teeth to not laugh. "All done."

I remove the second picture and wave it back and forth to develop faster. Little by little, the picture replaces the black rectangle and our faces become more defined. I stare at the goofy face I made and swear no one but the four of us will see this photo. Then I look at Anderson in the picture. The corners of his mouth are tipped up slightly. Most people wouldn't notice the faint smile, but I do.

And after seeing it, I promise no one else will see this picture. Only me and him.

Anderson is like my little brother and I will protect him within my means. Sharing his smile is his decision, not mine. He gifts it to me because I care for him. Because I make him comfortable. Because, in some ways, we are family.

But it is the most offbeat thing... the feeling in my chest. It is warm and a little buzzy. Like summer with a hint of thrill. Maybe this is what you feel when you care for someone. When you want them safe and happy. When you want them to smile more.

I turn onto my side and wiggle a little closer to him. "Thanks for being weird with me, Anderson," I whisper.

"Any time."

CHAPTER 7
HELENA

Thirteen Years Ago

"I hate him," I yell between sobs.

Lessa hooks my arm with hers as Mags takes my other arm and does the same. We shuffle down the sidewalk from Lake Lavender Middle toward the elementary school. Students pass us, some peering over their shoulder to see the crying girl.

Take a picture already!

"Grant is a jerk," Lessa states. She leans into my side and squishes me between her and Mags. "Don't know what you saw in him anyway." Her grip on my arm tightens. "He's not cute."

I sniffle and wish away the tears Grant Michaelson provoked with his harsh words. He doesn't deserve my tears or a single second of my thoughts. Not after today.

As my friend, Lessa will knock Grant down to lift me up. Call him names. Cheapen his looks. Find some random details about his life that will embarrass him the way he did me in the cafeteria two hours ago.

"Yeah, I agree," Mags chimes in. "His new haircut…" She giggles. "I don't care what he says, it's not a new trend." She laughs harder. "That's just his excuse for the hack job. I mean, who does he think he's fooling? Uneven and half-buzzed haircuts are not a trend."

At this, I snort. A faint smile tugs up the corners of my mouth.

For months, my crush on Grant blinded me to his true self. I've been oblivious to what everyone else saw. The boy with an ugly personality. The boy that thinks he is better than the rest of us.

Now, I see him for who he really is. A cruel boy surrounded by people just as awful.

"Thank you," I mutter as we approach the elementary school. I squeeze Mags's arm, then Lessa's. "It doesn't wipe away the hurt, but it helps."

At the far end of the school property, we wait near the trunk of an evergreen for Anderson. For years, this has been our spot. The place we met after school to walk home together. Our houses aren't on the same street, but when our parents allowed us to walk home from school, we went to the closest house. The Everett house.

Most school days, Mags and I are at Lessa's for two to three hours before our parents pick us up. We do some homework—don't want to upset the parents—watch TV, listen to music, or hang out in her room. Sometimes we talk about boys—today is one of those days—and other days, we talk about the future. High school, summer vacation, what we want to do when school ends. Daydreams and aspirations.

I plop down and tug a blade of grass free. "Do you think people believe him?"

Lessa reaches for my hand. "Are you talking about Gross Grant?"

I peek up at my friend and shrink at her expression. Raised brows, wide eyes, and lips in a tight, flat line. Wincing, I nod.

"No, Lena. No." She shakes her head. "If people believe him, they're not anyone you should be friends with." Angrily, she plucks her own piece of grass and tears it apart. "Don't let him get in your head."

It is difficult to ignore the most popular boy's opinion. There is no way I am the only girl with a crush on him. His haircut may be strange, but he is otherwise attractive. Well, in my opinion.

Weird as it is, don't most people act mean or strange to people they like?

Years ago, Mom told me about this boy in high school that always said mean things to her. He'd call her names, make fun of her choice of clothes, no matter what she wore, and tug her hair in the halls. This went on for more than a year. The entire time, she never acted any differently. She continued to smile at him. Would say things like, "Good one," when he came up with a creative name to call her. Showed him kindness when he did anything but.

Midway through her junior year, he asked Mom why she had been so nice to him. Her answer was simple.

"Sometimes, one smile is what gets you through the day."

This guy was Mom's first serious boyfriend. That one day changed everything between them. A fast friendship formed and she'd figured out why he'd said and done those things. He was lonely. His parents worked countless hours and spent little time with him. The time they did spend together, he was often reprimanded for his less-than-perfect grades in school or how well he did his chores. Mom dated him for a little more than a year. The only reason they broke up was because he and his family moved to Virginia.

So my question about people believing Grant doesn't feel unreasonable to ask. "It's difficult not to."

As I mutter the words, I spot Anderson across the lot. His hands fist his backpack straps at his shoulders as he weaves through the crowd. Eyes downcast and back hunched, he ignores his surroundings. He darts past people and cars as if they don't exist, as if no one will knock him down or run him over.

Would a smile help Anderson get through his day?

He lifts his head when he reaches us and I smile. With one action, I let him know I am happy to see him. Although my day sucked, smiling at Anderson eases the sting Grant left with his words.

"Hey, Baby A." Lessa rises to her feet and pulls him in for a hug. "How was your day?"

Shrugging, he says, "Same crap. New day."

Lessa has no idea what *crap* he goes through, but I do.

Mags and I stand up and shrug on our backpacks. Without another word, we trudge toward Lessa and Anderson's house. When Mags and Lessa spark a conversation about algebra, I slow my stride and fall in step with Anderson.

"Hey, Ander." I bump his arm with mine. "Bad day?"

His eyes dart to Lessa, concern heavy on his brow. A few steps pass before his expression smooths out. He fists his backpack straps tighter and nods. "Yeah."

"Want to talk about it?"

"Not now," he says with a subtle shake of his head.

"'Kay." I clasp my hands at my waist and squeeze until it hurts. "I had a bad day too," I whisper.

He locks in place and I stop a step ahead of him. His face twists in pain as he releases his backpack straps and curls his fingers into tight fists at his sides. Anger like I have never witnessed pours off him. I open my mouth to tell him it is okay now. But before I get a word out, his sneakers pound the pavement.

I rush forward to catch up with him. Reach out and clasp his arm. Slow his stride to match our previous. "Didn't mean to upset you."

"I know." He nods, but the deep lines in his expression disagree. "Want to talk about it?"

I loop my arm with his and sigh. "Maybe later."

Mags and Lessa may be my best friends, but something different exists between me and Anderson. Friendship for sure, but also more. A nameless feeling. A familiar yet indistinguishable connection. A bond sealed with trust and solace.

I like time with Mags and Lessa. I like time with Anderson too.

"Whenever you're ready, North."

The crook of my arm hugs his tighter. "Thanks, Ander."

CHAPTER 8

ANDERSON

If my sister says the word jerk one more time, I might punch a hole in the wall. The walls in this house are too thin. Or I need to move my bed so it doesn't butt against our shared wall.

Since walking through the front door an hour ago, Ales has gone on and on about some guy at their school. And since hers is the only voice I hear, I assume no one else wants to talk about him.

"Gah! Can't believe he was such a jerk. In front of everyone," she says for the umpteenth time.

And that is my cue.

I dog-ear my page in *The Hunger Games*, drop it on the bed, swipe up my iPod and shove it in my pocket, and head for the door. As I pass Ales's door, I hum to drown out her endless rant about some stupid boy.

Is that why Helena had a bad day? Because my sister won't shut up? I would too.

In the kitchen, I grab a Dr Pepper and chips. Just as I

consider zoning out to mindless television, my sister turns up the volume on her verbal attack.

"I hope Gross Grant the jerkface gets never-ending acne and a rash he scratches constantly," she hollers loud enough for the neighbors to hear.

"I wish you'd shut up," I mutter as I head for the sliding glass doors.

With a soft *swish-swoosh* of the door, I step onto the back patio and sigh into the silence. Breathe easier as my eyes roam the trees and mountains. Relax more as I escape reality for a time.

Dragging one of the loungers into the yard, I park it beneath the tree at the farthest point from the house. I plop down, crack open the can, and dig into the chips. As each second passes, I feel more at ease. More comfortable.

I close my eyes and let my other senses take over. The soft rustle of leaves in the light breeze. The distant bird calls as they soar the sky. Inhaling deeply, I let the crisp, piney air fill my lungs as goose bumps prickle my skin.

And for a blip in time, I feel *something*. Alive, maybe. More than just another person existing for someone else's benefit. More than a shadow or nuisance as I mentally scream into the silence.

We are the best of friends—me and silence. Have been for several years. Silence has never been a bother. Silence has never mistreated me or let me down. If anything, I crave silence. Solitude. Peace. If I am lucky enough to get silence outdoors, I bask in it.

Until recently.

There is only one exception to the silence. One I don't fully understand. One I want to hold close.

The back door opens and Helena steps out, cheeks red, chest heaving, and eyes glassy.

I sit up straight, ready to go to her and ask why she is upset. But before my foot swings off the lounger, she spots me beneath the tree. Without hesitation, she crosses the yard and stands at my feet. Her brows pinch together as she rolls her lips between her teeth.

"Hey. Can I?" She looks up and loses focus in the tree foliage. Inhaling deeply, she closes her eyes. Clasps her hands at her waist and wrings her fingers. Minute-long seconds pass before she levels her gaze and swallows. "Can I sit out here with you?"

Why was that so hard for her to ask?

Scooting over, I pat the small empty space. "Sure." I give her what feels like a smile. "You never have to ask, North."

The corners of her mouth tip up slightly. "Thanks." She plops down, stretches out her legs, crosses her arms over her chest, and sighs as she leans into the back cushion. "Can today end already?" She huffs with a shake of her head.

Earlier, she said today was bad. Annoying as my sister's rant is, it is foolish of me to assume her unending blather over some guy is what has Helena upset. Helena isn't the bubbliest person I know—that award goes to Ales—but she is a ray of sunshine in my dark world. For her light to be dimmed, it has to be something closer to her heart.

Soon as the thought hits, I mentally slap myself.

Helena is upset. Ales won't shut up about how much some guy sucks. And I am an idiot for not putting the pieces together sooner.

I may be young and somewhat oblivious to girl drama, but I am no fool. Weird as it is, people my age hang out as more than friends all the time. Kissing and groping and bragging about it when the adults are out of earshot. It is all so... uncomfortable.

Not to say I would never kiss anyone. More like I wonder who would want to kiss me. No one wants the dorky kid with messy hair, oversized clothes, and a black heart. And if by some miracle someone did want me for me, I wouldn't blab about us to other people. What I do is my business.

"If only it were so easy," I say wistfully.

"Lessa means well. I know she does." She turns her head so we are face to face. "But her rant is making it worse." She closes her eyes and sighs. "I want to forget it happened." Her eyes open and stare into mine. "I don't want it to steal my happiness."

I want to hurt anyone who steals her happiness.

"Sorry for whatever happened. I know you want it over with and probably don't want to talk about it, but it may help." I nudge her leg with my knee. "Promise not to call whoever a jerk a thousand times."

Light laughter spills from her lips and warms my chest. I like that I can make her feel somewhat better.

"She needs to learn new descriptors," she says, tipping her head back and staring at the late afternoon sunlight as it filters through the tree branches.

Minutes pass without a word. I mimic her and get lost in the dancing sunrays. Breathe easier as we sit in the stillness together.

Existing in the quiet with Helena is nice. Noninvasive. Calm. Content.

Does she enjoy this too? Do I soothe her hurt?

Her arm brushes mine before she leans into my side and drops her head on my shoulder. My eyes fall shut as I try to remember the last time someone else was this close. The last time I received more than a brief hug or pat on the shoulder or back.

Too long to recall.

"A boy in my grade said some nasty things about me today."

I start to inch back, wanting to look at her. But she fists my arm and holds me in place.

"Stay like this. Please," she pleads, her voice soft and almost inaudible.

Maybe she feels less pressure or embarrassment to talk without my eyes on her. No matter the reason, I respect her enough to do as she asks.

I drop my head on hers and nod. "'Kay."

"This boy, Grant... I kind of had a crush on him," she confesses and I stop breathing.

She lays a hand on my thigh. Picks at the frayed denim near a tear in the fabric. Gives me more of her weight. And the moment I exhale, she continues.

"At this point, I don't know why I liked him. We never talked. He never looked in my direction. We shared one class together last year." She pauses and shakes her head. "Guess I thought he was cute." She shrugs, her fingers still working at the frayed material of my jeans. "But I never saw the *real* him. Not until today."

Is it weird to ask why she thought he was cute? Probably. But I want to know.

Obviously, it isn't his attitude or personality that won her over. Is it the way he styles his hair? The clothes he wears? Maybe she liked his eyes or the shape of his face. The way he smiled.

No girl wants a guy that doesn't smile. No girl wants a boy like me.

"What'd he do?"

She sucks in a deep breath, holds it a moment, then trembles on the exhale. The small shudder says a lot. Tells me it hit her hard. Harder than maybe she wants to admit.

"We were at lunch. Everyone in our grade was in the cafeteria. Lessa, Mags, and I sat at a table in the middle, where we always eat lunch. Out of the blue, Grant sat at our table. A few spots down, on the opposite side, he and Marissa Lasko—the most popular girl in our grade—ate and smiled and talked."

She tugs harder at the frayed denim of my jeans. I don't interrupt or ask her to stop.

"He caught me looking at them. I wasn't staring. Much." She sighs. "Guess I zoned out. Lost in my thoughts. Wondering what made Marissa so popular. Asking myself what attracted a guy like Grant to a girl like Marissa."

Involuntarily, I shrug. "Attraction is subjective."

Helena leans away. "That's pretty profound."

A half smile tugs the corner of my mouth up. "Thanks, I guess." My face relaxes. "Haven't I told you?"

Her brows pinch in the middle. "Told me what?"

I tap my temple. "Supersmart."

She playfully slaps my leg. "Shut up." Tugging me toward her, she rests her head on my shoulder again. "Already knew you were smart," she whispers.

Silence blankets us once more. I know there is more to her story, but I won't push. I may not offer the best advice, may not be the one to smother her with uplifting words, but I am a good listener—which is what she needs.

"He called me a fugly prude," she says, a breath above a whisper.

Every muscle in my body locks up. Fire burns my veins. Pain lances the center of my chest as my breaths come in short, quick bursts. Fingernails dig into my palms as I clench my fingers tighter and tighter.

I want him to hurt. More than he hurt her. And I want to be the one who hurts him. A fist to the face, over and over until I break his nose. A swift kick in the dick, then to the stomach while he is down, again and again, until he apologizes and takes back his nasty, untrue words.

I hate him and every guy like him.

Who the hell does he think he is? What gives him the right to say such vile things?

Does he even know her? Obviously not. If he did, he wouldn't be such an asshole.

Her fingers spread on my thigh before she squeezes. "Whatever you're thinking," she whispers, dragging in a shaky breath. "Please stop."

I slam my eyes closed, take a deep breath, and hold it. Like I have done countless times, I count to ten and try to refocus my thoughts. Try to exit the dark tunnel my mind entered.

Each number I tick off in my head, I pair it with something positive. Tangible. A happy memory or thought.

Ales's breath-stealing hugs. Summer camping trips at Seaquest. Hikes in the woods or by the lake. The smell of rain and the feel of it on my face. Movie nights with Ales, Helena, and Magdalena. The hours between school and when my parents get home. Snowball fights with the girls. Birthdays with Helena—minus the big party. The compass from Helena. Moments like this, where it is just me and her and comfort.

I unfurl my fingers and exhale. Open my eyes and take a steadying breath.

"Better?"

"Yes." Not completely, but better.

Her fingers toy with the ripped denim of my jeans once

more. "What he did is beyond unacceptable. I gave in to my fury and devastation after school when no one would see." She releases the string, twists onto her side, and hugs my arm with hers. "Now…" She takes a deep breath, her hand slipping beneath the sleeve of my shirt. "He gets none of my energy. None of my thoughts. Nothing."

I want to wish away my darkness the way she wishes away this guy. Life would be easier. People would want to spend time with me, befriend me, care about me and my opinion.

If only it were that simple.

"Since you made peace with it, so will I." At least, I will try.

"He doesn't deserve any of our thoughts—good or bad."

Silence falls between us once more. It isn't loaded with questions or tension or hurt. Instead, the contentment from before our talk returns. Forms a bubble around us. Protects us from the Grants and Marissas and asshole bullies of the world.

I like this bubble.

"I never want to fall in love," she whispers into the breeze. "I will never give some stupid boy the chance to break my heart. Never again."

And just like that, the bubble pops.

CHAPTER 9
HELENA

Twelve Years Ago

"Yes, girl," I say as I clasp my hands together and bring them to my lips. "Red is definitely your color."

Lessa holds the fire engine red V-neck top to her chest as she assesses herself in the mirror. "Yeah?"

Mags sidles up to her, arm draped with several tops and dresses to try on. "Absolutely."

With our reassurances, Lessa scurries into a dressing room, Mags taking the one next to her. I drop into the cushy chair and wait for the fashion show to start. To no one's surprise, Lessa has something from each rack in the store. And we will get no less than a dozen outfit changes before she decides what to buy. Mags's pile of maybes is the same size as mine. Small.

Though I love new clothes, I only get a couple new tops and bottoms at the start of a new school year. Over the past two years, I haven't grown much. Not enough to donate my current wardrobe and start fresh. Which makes me fortunate enough to add new pieces here and there. And since we ski the mad rush to buy new clothes before the school year starts, we don't end up with the same stuff as half the school—which isn't big to begin with.

The curtain whooshes open and Lessa steps out, a huge smile brightening her expression. "I love this shirt." She walks over to the mirror and twists from side to side. "It makes my boobs look bigger."

My cheeks heat as my gaze falls to my lap. Locks of hair fall forward as I drop my chin to my chest. I use the momentary privacy to glance at my own chest. Frustration and self-degradation simmer beneath the surface as I take in my lack of boobs. My lesser femininity.

A year ago, I swore off boys. Swore off pricks who would break my heart. But just once, it would be nice if a boy stared. It'd be nice for one of them to say I'm pretty.

Taking a deep breath, I straighten my spine and lift my chin. "That top was made for you," I say with more confidence than I feel. "Should definitely get it."

Mags walks out in a knee-length cream-and-floral sundress with half sleeves. The neckline dips between but doesn't flaunt her small breasts. The material hugs her body enough to show her slight curves but not restrict her movement. Flowy, yet snug.

"And you should say yes to that dress," I declare.

Mags runs a hand over where the bust meets the skirt. "It's not too tight?"

I rise from the chair, take her hand, and haul her to the mirror. At her side, I grip her shoulders and stare into the mirror. "Nope. You look more woman and less girl."

Her lips curve up in a soft smile. "If you haven't decided on a college major yet, fashion should be at the top of the list."

I jolt back and furrow my brow. "College? We started high

school a month ago." One step after another, I back away until my legs bump the chair. "And I haven't thought about what happens after." My gaze meets hers. "At all."

She and Lessa crowd the chair, Mags's hand on my shoulder while Lessa strokes my hair.

"Didn't mean to freak you out," Mags says, a frown turning down her lips. "Just saying you'd be good at it."

With a sigh, I nod. "Thank you." I reach for her hand, then Lessa's, and give them both a quick squeeze. "Love you both."

"Love you back." Lessa releases my hand. "Now, let's try the rest of these on." She pats her stomach. "Don't know about you two, but I'm starving. And Dad said he was picking up pizza at five."

I check my watch. "Best get moving." I tap the watch face. "Thirty minutes."

"Crap." She darts for the dressing room, tugging up the shirt as she goes.

I laugh as she and Mags change into the next piece. Neither step out to show me anything new. They simply veto or approve them without further opinion.

While they pick and choose, I stare around the small boutique. In Stitches is the only all-feminine clothing store in Lake Lavender. On the outskirts of town is a shop with general clothes for all ages. Target, the sporting goods store, and the mall are about twenty minutes outside of town. We only venture there when necessary.

Could I work in a place like this? Recommending shirts and dresses and selling clothes? I have a keen eye for fashion and decorating, but that doesn't mean I'll be good at selling it.

Either way, it isn't something I need to worry about today. I'd much rather focus on the present, on the fact that Grant Michaelson moved away over the summer and will no longer torment me in the halls. His snide remarks and loathsome smile are a thing of the past.

This year, I get to start fresh. This year, I don't have a dark cloud named Grant looming nearby.

This year, maybe I'll become the pretty girl.

CHAPTER 10

ANDERSON

"**P**izza is here," Dad hollers as the front door closes with a loud thud.

I stare at the ceiling above my bed until Ales's door opens and the girls shuffle down the hall. Sitting up, I swing my legs off the bed and take a moment to prepare for the onslaught of questions or comments to come.

Meals and forced time together are when I see my parents most. Dad is cool. He doesn't pry and ask for specifics about my day. He doesn't tell me I need to do more of this and less of that. And he doesn't try to dictate every breath I take. Mom... well, she is the complete opposite.

"Where's your school journal? Mr. Tran sent an email saying there's a note in your journal."

"Why didn't you eat lunch today? Your father and I work hard so you have good lunches."

"Where's the paper for your science project? It's not due until February, but you'd best start working on it now. You'll forget around the holidays."

"You got a B on your math test? You said you studied. Maybe I need to watch you study."

Usually it's one question per meal, but my lackluster answer is what riles her up. Not that I care. I gave up caring or trying to make her proud long ago. If I were more like Ales, maybe Mom would love me more. If I were more like my sister, maybe I would be happy.

Planting my feet on the floor, I push off the bed, amble out of my room and to the dining room. No one pays me any attention as I enter the room. Cancel that. Helena meets my gaze and smiles. The second her lips tip up, Mom twists in my direction and scowls.

"What took you so long? You've kept everyone waiting," she scolds.

"Joan," Dad admonishes. "He's fine. I still need to grab plates and napkins." We cross paths as he goes to the pantry. His hand lands on my shoulder and rubs twice before he pats it. "You're fine, son. Take a seat."

"Thanks," I mutter.

I sit in the seat next to Helena and she bumps my shoulder.

"Hey," I say, giving her a brief, restrained smile.

"Hey," she says, a breath above a whisper. "Sorry we didn't meet you after school." Her eyes shoot to Ales and roll. "Someone couldn't wait until tomorrow to buy clothes."

Ales sets her drink down and purses her lips. "What if we went tomorrow and they had nothing I liked? Then we'd have to drive out of town and spend the day at the mall. At least now we have the weekend to do whatever we want." She does some weird tilt twitch with her neck then points a finger at Helena. "You should thank me."

Instead of gifting Ales with gratitude, Helena laughs with a shake of her head. "Not happening."

Dad hands out paper plates and napkins, putting a stack between the pizza boxes on the table. He opens the first box and Ales grabs two slices of pepperoni. Mom takes one before Dad swaps the box for the one underneath. Mom, Helena, and Mags grab cheese slices. Then Dad and I dive into the last box —half supreme, half veggie.

Conversation quiets—my favorite part of dinner—as we eat. But it doesn't last long.

"Mom, you should see the outfits I got today," Ales says between bites. "I wasn't sure about a few, but Lena convinced me to try them on." She smiles at Helena. "One day, she'll design my clothes."

"Pssh. You're ridiculous," Helena says.

"Glad you found something you like, sweetheart." Mom looks at Ales like she can do no wrong. Then her attention shifts to Helena. "And don't discount your talents, Lena. If fashion is something you're interested in, I'm happy to show you the basics."

Mom's sweet disposition with Ales, Mags, and Helena makes fury and euphoria surge through my veins.

With them, she smiles. Displays excitement and interest. Gaiety. With them, she is a different mom. Not *my* mom. And I love that they aren't the brunt of her irritation.

In the same breath, I want what they have. A mother joyous over their presence. A mother delighted over their individuality. A mother with open arms, ready to embrace me when I've had a bad day.

I love how she loves them. I also hate how she loves them.

I envy the one thing it appears I will never receive from her.

"Thank you, Mrs. Everett. But it was more Lessa's idea than mine."

Mom wipes her hands with a napkin then lays one on Helena's forearm. The simple touch is a match to the detonation cord connected to my dynamite-packed heart.

"Well, my needle and thimble are available if you change your mind."

My fingers ball into knuckle-bleaching fists beneath the table. I grind my molars as I stare down at the half-eaten slice of pizza on my plate. Focus my attention anywhere but on the saccharine sound of my mother's voice, the tone she uses with everyone except me.

As if she *feels* my pain, Helena lays a hand on one of mine beneath the table. Her thumb rubs my clenched fingers in slow strokes. And with each pass, I loosen my grip. Straighten my fingers. Relax my jaw. Breathe easier.

I peek at her from the corner of my eye and soften at the small smile on her lips. A smile for me, not my mother.

She threads our fingers and hugs my hand with hers, not an ounce of space between our palms. My heart pounds in my chest for a new reason. A loud whooshing in my ears.

"I appreciate the offer, Mrs. Everett. I'll keep it in mind."

The rest of dinner goes by in a haze. Helena keeps our hands latched, carrying on as if nothing has changed. As if nothing is different.

But it is different. *We* are different.

Coffee table shoved aside, I sprawl out on the empty blanket in front of the television. Swiping up the remote, I surf through Netflix in search of something to watch. Earlier this year, Dad decided to cancel cable to save money. Now, it is either Netflix,

Hulu, or DVDs. Nine times out of ten, I watch reruns or DVDs now.

Nothing stands out, so I crawl across the floor and sift through the DVD shelf. I land on *Harry Potter and the Sorcerer's Stone* and remember the final movie comes out on DVD next month.

"*Harry Potter* marathon it is," I mutter as I take out the first disc and pop it in the player.

I return to my spot on the blanket and press play on the movie. When the room goes dark, I shift my gaze to the sliding glass doors. Everyone is outside—talking and laughing and smiling, without me.

No shock.

After dinner, Mags's and Helena's parents came over. In a matter of minutes, Dad, Mr. Bishop, and Mr. Williams grabbed a bottle of beer from the fridge in the garage and went out back. They pulled out chairs at the table, sat down, and haven't moved since. I suspect their conversation is about work or fishing or sports. It always is.

Mom played the gracious, artificial hostess inside for a few minutes, then suggested the ladies go out too. Start a fire, catch up, and roast marshmallows.

Not once did anyone offer to include me. Again, no shock. More often than not, I am a ghost among the families. Among my peers.

With everyone except her.

And tonight at dinner, she threw me a lifeline. She took my hand in hers and pulled me back to the surface. To the light. To her.

She held me with gentle strength. She quieted the violence in my thoughts. More than anything, her simple touch told me she cared. Told me I had someone. Told me I was not alone.

Rising from her seat near the fire, Helena says something to Ales then walks toward the door. Paper plate in one hand, she opens the sliding glass door with the other. Loud conversation filters in and drowns out the movie for a moment before she closes the door.

"Brought you something." She gives the plate a light shake before she glances at the television. "*Harry Potter*?"

I shrug. "Nothing else on. Figured we can do a marathon this weekend."

She parks next to me on the blanket, folding her legs and crossing them. Holding the plate out, she offers, "Marshmallow?" The corners of her mouth kick up. "I burned them just for you."

I sit taller and survey the blackened marshmallows. No chocolate or graham crackers, just marshmallows. Exactly how I like them.

"You didn't have—"

"I wanted to." She pushes the plate closer. "Hope I made them right."

I take the plate from her and smile down at the charred sugar. Warmth blooms in the middle of my chest. "They're perfect," I whisper before meeting her waiting gaze. "Thank you."

She leans her head on my shoulder and hugs my arm. "You're welcome."

Half the movie plays before Ales and Mags join us with more sugary and salty snacks and fresh drinks. By the time the parents come in, we are almost to the end of movie two.

We pause the movie to say our goodbyes. Helena is staying the night, but Mags is leaving since she has dance class early tomorrow. With all the farewells and hugs given, we settle back on the floor.

"Not too late," Dad says, then pats my shoulder. "Maybe turn it down a notch. Please." He gives me a crooked smile and I nod.

Ales falls asleep ten minutes into movie three, her soft snores background noise to the movie. But Helena is wide awake, her head more on my arm than shoulder now. Eyes on the screen, but not really watching.

I rest my head on hers. "Everything okay?"

Her arms around mine shift and tighten. "Yeah. Was going to ask you the same?"

I peek over at Ales and double-check she is asleep. Mouth slightly open, eyes shut, steady breaths. Yep, she is out.

"Same crap, new day," I answer.

"What about school?"

I hate talking about school and the imbeciles I can't seem to shake. It shouldn't surprise me. Starting middle school doesn't mean I don't have the same classmates. Curse of a small town. But I'd hoped maybe some of the idiots would have grown up over the summer.

Wrong.

"School is a joke." I laugh without humor. "I'm smarter than most of the student population, bored out of my mind, and subject to fists and boots and more."

She sits up and waits for me to look at her. "Not that I expect you to, but have you told anyone? Aside from me."

"No."

"Maybe they—"

"No," I repeat, firmer. I take a deep breath and shake my head on the exhale. "I like that you want to help." I take her hand and thread our fingers like earlier. "But no one understands. Not like you." My eyes drop to our hands and I stare at her thumb as it strokes my skin.

"You're my best friend," she whispers.

The movie becomes white noise to my ears. My brows pinch at the middle, the backs of my eyes stinging as I absorb her words. *Best friend.* Feels like we are much more. Something beyond friendship. Something more than this simple life.

I swallow and level my gaze with hers. "Best friend," I croak out, testing the words on my tongue and lips. They don't hurt. But they do feel lacking. Nowhere near enough. Weak.

She nods. "Not like Mags and Lessa." Her hold on me tightens. "Different." Her eyes dart between mine. "Feels like I can tell you anything, and you won't judge or tease or hold it over my head for years."

Unsure how to respond, I simply nod.

"Remember the mean guy I told you about last year?" she asks.

How could I forget? "Yeah."

Her weight shifts and we lie back how we were before the conversation started. She hugs my arm, our hands still connected. Then she exhales a heavy sigh.

"He moved away over the summer."

"Good. He was a twit."

A soft chuckle leaves her lips. "Agreed." She snuggles more into my side, her eyes on the television but not watching the movie. "And now things are better at school. No one points and repeats his ugly words. Everyone smiles when I pass them in the hall." She pauses and I feel her jaw work against my arm. "And some of the guys... notice me."

I stop breathing. My mind blanks as I try to figure out what to say or do or think or feel. Pain stabs me in the chest and jolts through my limbs. I hate it. Hate that I care. Hate that I want her to look at me and think I notice her too. Because I do.

Maybe not the exact same way the guys in high school do, but I notice her.

But I can't tell her. She's my best friend. My sister's best friend. And if I lost her, I'd lose so much more.

I can't lose her.

I *won't* lose her.

So, I do the same thing I have done for the past eleven years of my life. I suck it up and keep going. The only other option is…

"That's"—I clear my throat—"that's great," I choke out.

It is the complete opposite of great, but I refuse to tell her otherwise. Her happiness keeps me alive. Her happiness gives me something to look forward to.

"Thanks, Ander," she whispers, hugging my arm tighter. "Means a lot to hear it from you."

I close my eyes and swallow. Remind myself of all the positivity she brings into my life. Remind myself she is the proffered hand and constant light in my darkest moments.

Better to have her as a best friend than nothing at all.

I kiss her hair then rest my head on hers. "Always, North."

CHAPTER 11
ANDERSON

Eleven Years Ago

I miss her. Damn, do I miss her.

High school changes people. High school has changed her. Not all the changes are bad. If anything, Helena has discovered herself. Though still less exuberant than my sister, she has developed this subtle, quiet confidence. A strength I envy. A coveted resilience.

And as she blooms, I wilt.

A little more than a year ago, Helena claimed me as her best friend. Every day since her declaration, I see less of her. High school and appearances and boys have stolen her attention. She spends time with Ales and Mags, but more outside of the house, at the town's cinema or park on Main Street.

The girls no longer include me in their plans to hang out. I get it. Who wants to socialize with the sad, unstable younger brother? I wouldn't want to rub shoulders with me either.

Now they invite new friends to gatherings. The few girls I've met in passing seem flighty but nice. The guys…

Nausea rolls in my stomach as I grind my molars. "None of them are good enough," I mutter to myself.

Life has been shit. More than usual.

The day my sister started dating, I bore witness to Helena's green monster. The glassiness in Helena's eyes as he hooked his arm around Ales's shoulders. Helena's slumped frame as he whispered something in Ales's ear and she laughed. With each act of affection my sister displayed with a guy, Helena's cheeks flushed. Her frame stiffened. She dropped her gaze to her clamped hands.

Helena wanted what Ales had. The affection and attention from a guy. And it wasn't long before she landed someone. A smug asshole with pretty hair and a letterman jacket.

I hate him.

"I will never be worthy." Not compared to pricks like him.

Self-deprecation spreads through my veins like toxic poison. Infecting my cells and burrowing deeper in my bones. Years ago, I hated the vile sensation. The chill, the queasiness, the suffocation. It swallowed me whole with no promise of letting go. Now, I close my eyes and bask in the familiarity. Give in to the intimacy I share with the dark. Let it consume me until I am numb to the world.

The dark never fails. The dark never forgets. And it is in the dark that I feel most myself.

I strip my pants and boxers. Sit on the edge of my bed and open the top drawer of my nightstand. Take out the worn copy of *American Psycho* and thumb through the tattered, high-lighted pages. Stop midway through and stare down at the dull metal rectangle nestled near the binding.

With a stuttered breath, I pluck the razor from the pages and toss the book aside. The blade lost its shine months ago when I stole it from the box in the garage. Dad wouldn't notice one missing razor from a box of many. Not when he had no reason to count them.

I widen my legs and push my limp dick aside. Bring the edge of the blade to my skin beneath several lines scarring my flesh. Press the sharp metal down and hiss as it breaks the surface. And for a brief moment, I bask in the sensation, the pain, the euphoria. I revel in the fact that I feel *something* other than numbness.

When the rush fades, I do it again. And again. And again.

Staring down at the inflamed, bloody marks, my heart beats viciously in my chest. My dick hardens for the first time in weeks. The sight, the sensation, and the act arouse me, but I refuse to touch or relieve myself. I don't need to jerk off. I don't need to come on my sheets or a dirty T-shirt. Not when I have this.

I wipe the blade's edge off on the dark comforter rumpled at the foot of my bed. Tuck it back in the book and stow it in the drawer. Fall back on the bed and close my eyes. Lie naked from the waist down and savor the last of the adrenaline.

When the rush dissipates, the self-loathing seeps back in. Consumes another piece of my soul.

"Just end already," I whisper. "Just make it stop."

Why won't it stop?

Loud pounding echoes down the hall from the front door as someone bangs on it and I bolt up. As I yank my boxers on, Ales yanks her bedroom door open. She thunders down the hall as I pick my pants up off the floor. I tug my pants up and wince as the denim seam chafes my thigh. But my pain goes out the window the second I hear sobs in the distance.

Helena.

I pad across the room, unlock my door, and fling it open just in time to see my sister and Helena pass. Mascara-stained tears bleed down her blotchy cheeks from puffy, veiny eyes. Her body shakes as Ales hugs her side and guides her into the bedroom next to mine.

The second the door shuts, I take a step back and close my own. Press the heel of my hand to my chest, close my eyes, and beg for her pain, her suffering. I will gladly take it to give her relief. To free her from her burdens.

I move to the wall separating our bedrooms, press an ear to the drywall and listen. Helena talks between sobs, but her words are muddled as they travel from her lips to my ear.

After minutes of unintelligible words, I step away from the wall and go back to my bed. Lie on my back and stare up at the ceiling. Zone out and beg the universe to give Helena peace. Happiness. Whether it is with me or not.

Her joy is what matters. *She* is all that matters.

CHAPTER 12
HELENA

Mags hugs me tighter as Lessa rummages through the kitchen. She left the room with a promise to return with food that will cheer me up. Whatever that means.

I sniffle and wipe at my cheeks. Upset with myself and my obvious naivety. Angry at Scott Tomaski and his trickery. "Idiot," I choke out. My sobs from an hour ago are gone. Now, I exist in the aftermath. Misery and humiliation. Doubt and confusion.

How did I not see this coming? How did I miss the signs?

Easy. Boys like Scott are used to getting what they want. I wasn't his first girlfriend. Like a fool, I hadn't questioned the fact he'd had his arm around at least five other girls since the start of freshman year. Sure, we are young and none of us expect to fall in love at fifteen. Had I not been so swept up in the idea of one of the most popular boys in our sophomore class wanting to be my boyfriend, I might have thought with my head instead of my hormones or my inexperienced

"He is the idiot," Mags says as she pets my hair. "His loss, not yours." She inches back and locks me with a reassuring gaze. "You hear me?"

My brows tweak at the middle before I give a slow nod. "Yeah."

She pulls me back into a hug. Squeezes me tighter.

"Thanks," I whisper.

Several minutes of silence pass before Lessa waltzes back into the room with a loaded tray. Mags's arms fall away and I straighten. My eyes roam the pile as she sets the tray on the bed. Sour cream and onion chips. Macaroni and cheese, still in the pot, with three forks. Chocolate candies and red licorice and gumdrops. A tube of chocolate chip cookie dough with spoons. Grilled cheese sandwiches cut into quarter triangles. Cans of soda.

The backs of my eyes burn as my vision blurs. "You did all this?" I shift my gaze to her. "For me?"

She nudges my arm playfully and rolls her eyes. "Duh. You're one of my best friends. My sister. Of course, I did this." She plucks a chip from the bag and pops it in her mouth. "You'd do the same, so would Mags, in a heartbeat." She leans across the bed and gives me a lung-crushing hug. "Boys come and go, but we're forever."

I grab a forkful of macaroni and cheese, shove it in my mouth, and nod. "Boys suck," I declare, words garbled.

"Hear, hear!" Mags holds up a piece of licorice. "To sisters over misters!"

We scarf down carbs and cheese and sugar for the next hour, and it helps ease the heartache. A little.

And while Lessa and Mags talk about the biology test today, I lose focus. Let my mind drift to the next room. To my other best friend. The one I've basically ignored for the past year. The one I'd rather be bingeing empty calories with.

Anderson.

Through thick and thin, he has been there. Lent me an ear or shoulder or warm embrace. And in my quest to explore life and love, I abandoned him. Not completely, but more than acceptable.

That changes tonight.

I miss him. Fiercely.

Shame on me for waiting until my rose-colored glasses cracked to realize what I had done. To realize I fractured our friendship. All for a stupid guy.

Never again.

Muted words fill the room as an episode of *The Vampire Diaries* plays. After Lessa took the almost empty tray to the kitchen, she returned with DVDs of the most recent season. We love the show and often watch new episodes when they come on, but I wish she would have chosen something different. Watching two guys pine over one girl… I didn't want mushy. She meant well, but *Mean Girls* would have lifted my spirit more.

Sandwiched between Mags and Lessa on her full-size bed, I itch to get out of here. I peek to my left. Eyes closed, Lessa's mouth hangs open slightly. Her chest rises and falls in time with her soft snores. I shift my attention to the right, where Mags faces me with a throw pillow hugged to her chest. She, too, is asleep.

Thank goodness.

I love these girls, but I need a breather.

Inch by slow inch, I worm my way to the foot of the bed. When my knees hit the edge and bend, I sit up and drop my feet to the floor. Rise and tiptoe to the door. Turn the handle slowly and ease the door open, wincing when the hinges creak. I glance to the bed, but neither Lessa nor Mags have moved.

I slip out of the room and close the door. Take a deep breath and pad down the hall to the next door. Grip the handle, count to five, then twist.

Unlike Lessa's room, his is blanketed in darkness and silence. I close the door behind me and shuffle across the room, my feet brushing clothes and books and shoes. With each drag of my feet, my eyes adjust to the lack of light. Mere feet from his bed, his head turns and I stop.

"North?" he whisper-asks.

"Hey," I croak out.

He sits up and spins to face me, hand extended. "You okay?"

I shuffle forward and take his hand. Scan his silhouetted profile. Though I can't see them, I *feel* his eyes on my face.

I drag in a ragged breath and shake my head. "Not really."

Yanking me forward, he bands his arms around my waist and presses his cheek to my chest. Startled by the action, it takes me a moment to register his embrace, his affection, his comfort. The second it clicks, I hug his shoulders and cry. He doesn't interrupt or let go. No, he holds me tighter.

We stay like this for hour-long minutes. And when the tears simmer down, he loosens his hold, inches back, and guides me onto the bed.

In the pitch black of Anderson's room, I let him haul me to his chest. I fist his hoodie and tangle my legs with his. Rest my head on his shoulder while I lean into the crook of his neck.

Being with him like this doesn't feel uncomfortable or wrong. If anything, it feels as if I can breathe for the first time in hours.

One hand pins me in place while the other strokes my back and toys with the length of my hair. His touch is hypnotic and tender and complete comfort.

He inhales deeply and presses his lips to my hair. "Want to tell me what happened?"

"Yes. No," I mutter into his chest. "Yes."

Soft laughter shakes his frame. "Whatever and whenever you want, North."

My fingers shift to the strings of his hoodie. I hold them like a lifeline as I close my eyes and mentally prepare myself to share. He won't like what I say. He won't like that someone hurt more than just my feelings. What happened today... my trust in guys has tanked—with the exception of Anderson. He won't like it, but I need someone to know.

Earlier, I shared a fraction of the story with Lessa and Mags. I wanted comfort more than an endless rant on how shitty Scott is as a human. I am fully aware now. So, I gave them a watered-down, generic version.

Anderson will get the full story. Not because I love Lessa and Mags less, but because he won't flash me pitiful stares after I tell him. He won't go on an endless tirade.

"Until today, I've been dating this guy, Scott."

His body stiffens and his hand in my hair freezes. He takes a deep breath then resumes fiddling with the strands. "Mm-hmm."

My heart beats a vicious rhythm in my chest, its theoretical fists pounding against my rib cage. I inhale a shaky breath and wish away the frenetic energy whirling beneath my lungs.

"During lunch, he asked if I would help him study after

school. Said he wasn't doing so great in algebra and knew I was a whiz."

I shift my hands down his hoodie and tuck them in the front pocket. Anchor myself as I work up the courage to continue. As if he senses my anxiety, Anderson hugs me impossibly closer. One hand on my hip and the other at the nape of my neck.

"Got you, North," he says with a conviction I've not heard before.

Sawing my lips between my teeth, I nod. After another deep breath, I force out my confession.

"He tried to force himself on me." The words burn my tongue and steal my breath. Anderson vibrates as his arms secure me closer to him. "I said no," I whisper. "And he wouldn't stop." Tears spill from my eyes and dampen his hoodie. "He pinned me to his bed, shoved my shirt up, and started unbuttoning my pants." I sniffle and twist my hands in his hoodie pocket. "If his mom hadn't walked in the room unannounced, things would've ended differently." I shiver from head to toe. "When she saw the tears on my face, she slapped him. I grabbed my things and ran." Tears soak my cheeks as I sob into his chest. "I was so scared, Ander."

Warm lips press against my hair as he holds me in place. Comforts me with his strength and love. Brings me back to the here and now. With him.

"It's over." He kisses my head again. "He won't hurt you." He massages my neck and cocoons me in warmth. "I won't let anyone hurt you."

The promise is bold yet firm. I want to believe it. Want to believe I won't know heartache or fear again. But it is a difficult pill to swallow. For now, though, I let myself indulge. Convince myself his words are law.

"Sorry I haven't been around much."

"No." He kisses my crown. "Don't apologize. Sure, life sucks more when you're not here, but your world doesn't revolve around me."

I untuck my hands from his pocket and tip my head in an attempt to look at him. He shifts and meets my gaze, forehead scrunched in concern. And I don't know what it is about the dark, but boldness takes over as I reach up and cup his cheek.

"Don't do that," I whisper.

Ever so slightly, he leans into my touch. "Do what?" he asks, his voice scratchy.

"Diminish your feelings to appease mine." My thumb strokes his cheek once, twice, before my hand falls away. "Your feelings are valid." I swallow past the sudden lump in my throat. "It's acceptable to admit I've been a shitty friend for months."

He tugs on the end of my hair and drops his forehead to mine. "I've missed you, North." His eyes close. "A lot."

"Promise it won't happen again."

The room quiets as we curl into each other again. My eyelids grow heavy with his slow, lazy strokes along my spine. In his arms, I am at peace. In his arms, I am home.

Just before sleep takes me, I whisper into his chest. "My wish... is for someone like you."

CHAPTER 13
ANDERSON

Ten And A Half Years Ago

"You should've seen her face," Helena says from across the table. "Brave and outgoing should be her middle names." She chuckles with a shake of her head. "But leave it to the varsity quarterback to make Lessa falter."

The corners of my mouth tip up. My sister shocked into silence… not something I imagined possible. "Did he ask her out?" I lean forward and sip my soda. My eyes drop to the table momentarily as Helena shreds her napkin and rolls the bits into balls.

I meet her gaze as she shakes her head. "No, surprisingly." The hint of jealousy in her voice is a hot blade on my skin. "Just said he'd see her after summer."

"Why does that bother you?" I blurt out before I lose the nerve.

Helena's head jerks back an inch, her brows tugging at the middle. Her light-green irises turn a hint darker as they roam my face. Then her expression softens, the harsh lines smoothing out as she takes a steadying breath and sits straighter.

"It doesn't bother me," she says, her words lacking conviction.

I swipe up a few fries from the plate between us and dip them in mayonnaise. "You feel some sort of way about it." I point the fries in her direction. "When you know someone as long as we've known each other, you pick up on these things." Shoving the fries in my mouth, I sit back and lean into the booth.

Summer break kicked off two weeks ago. Hours without adult supervision. Hikes on the local trails. The occasional fries or onion rings and soda float at the Lake Lavender Diner. Time away from the school imbeciles and their incessant bullshit.

Summer is a breath of fresh air. So is spending most of my days with Helena. Though it isn't always just me and her, I relish the time when it is only us. Over the past few months, we have grown closer. Our conversations are more frequent, deeper. Sure, we talk about lighter stuff too, but nothing surface level or generic. When she hangs at the house, she wants me in the room with her—unless Ales or Mags requests otherwise.

This summer, life is more sunshine than shadow. And it is all because of the girl across the table. The girl that makes me smile more. The girl I look forward to seeing every day.

Helena Williams. North. *My North.*

"Fine," she huffs out with a roll of her eyes. "It bothers me a little." She lifts her hand and brings her thumb and forefinger close together for emphasis. "But not how you think."

My brows shoot up. "And how do you think I mean it?"

Her lips flatten into a line as she stares at me with a *really?* look. "Playing dumb doesn't become you, Ander."

The corner of my mouth twitches. "Touché."

"I'm not jealous of *him* liking or flirting with her if that's what you're thinking."

"Okay," I draw out.

She snatches a fry from the plate and stabs the end into the BBQ sauce cup before shoving it in her mouth. I remain tight lipped and give her time to mull over what to say. How to express what it is she feels about the whole Ales-attracting-popular-boys situation.

When she finishes the fry, she takes a long pull from her soda. As her cup hits the table, an audible sigh fills the space between us.

"It's more envy than jealousy. Not that they're much different." Her hands fall to her lap and I know what I'd see if I looked underneath—her hands tangled together, knuckles bleaching as she wrings her fingers. "Next to Lessa," she whispers. "I feel small. Unseen. Like a nobody." She hangs her head and shakes it once, twice, before sitting up straight. "I love her. Mags too. But sometimes, I wish I was as noticeable. That I didn't disappear with her in the room."

"Hey," I say, a bite in my tone as I lay a hand on the table. I wait until she holds my steady gaze. "You don't disappear."

She opens her mouth, ready to disagree. I see it in the lines of her face. The slight twitch of her eyes. The faint blush on her cheeks.

I slap the table, garnering the attention of a few patrons. I ignore them and focus on Helena. "You. Don't. Disappear."

"How?"

I lick my lips and swallow. "Because I always see you."

After the heavy conversation in the diner, Helena suggests we do something fun. Something that requires less thought. I agree with her. My mind veers toward hours in front of the television with too much sugar, salt, and caffeine. Maybe a comedy to lighten the mood.

I agree far too soon and learn a little too late Helena has other ideas.

"Please, Ander," she begs, hands slapped together beneath her chin. "Pretty please with Sno-Caps on top."

My eyes lock on the package on the vanity and lose focus while my mind conjures up some way to say no. To shut down this idea. Tell her it is too *girly*. That I don't need to—my vision clears—exfoliate and hydrate and nourish my face.

But when I lift my gaze to hers, the argument on my tongue fizzles out.

Hope brightens the lighter part of her green eyes. A soft pout pushes out her lips. And with each passing second, that pout transitions into my favorite sight. Her smile. My heart rattles in my rib cage and I swallow at the odd carbonated sensation in my chest.

"Ugh." I tip my head back and sigh. "Fine."

"Yes," she says with too much enthusiasm. She balls her hands into loose fists and bops her head side to side while the rest of her does some type of jig.

"But…" I hold up a finger and she stops dancing. "This will not be a regular thing."

She playfully shoves my shoulder. "Whatever." Swiping up

the package, she tears it open. "Just wait. When you peel it off, you'll change your mind."

I roll my eyes. "Seriously doubt it."

The next few minutes are spent with me on the toilet seat lid while she applies the mask. Eyes closed, I focus on her touch. The light graze of her fingertips as she pats and shifts the semi-stretchy material. The warmth and tingle from her touch as she presses the seams around my mouth. My fingers twitch in my lap when her breath caresses my exposed skin.

"There," she whispers and I open my eyes. Inches away, she licks her lips and swallows. "All done."

God, I want to reach out and touch her. Rest my hands on her hips and pull her closer. Band my arms around her waist and kiss her.

But I won't.

Reading signals isn't my forte. Definitely a skill I have screwed up more often than not.

Helena's proximity is probably one-hundred-percent inno-cent. A closeness shared between friends. Best friends. Her feeling something for me is natural but undoubtedly platonic. If I open my mouth and spew warm and fuzzy declarations, I will scare her. Push away the best person I know. Ruin the only true connection I have in my life.

I may be enamored with Helena Williams, but I won't break us with immature words of juvenile adoration.

With a slight upward curve of my lips, I say, "Thanks."

She blinks a few times and nods.

I break eye contact and look at the other mask on the counter. "Need help with yours?"

Stammering back, her hands wriggle at her sides. Thumbs moving restlessly over her curled-in fingers. She shakes her head and steps farther away. "No," she croaks out then clears her throat. "No," she repeats with more confidence. "But you should watch." A brow quirks up as this devilish smirk lights her face. "Then we can do our own together next time."

I rise from the toilet and inch closer to her. "Hey," I say, leaning a hip against the counter. "I said this won't be a regular thing."

The tension from seconds ago fades to the background as her smirk softens into a smile. She rips open her mask and pulls it out. I watch her every move as she prepares it for application. Then she lines it up on her face and presses down on her forehead, the apple of her cheeks, nose, and chin. Once those places stick, she goes about setting the rest of the mask.

Once finished, she twists to face me and I can't help but chuckle. "We look like aliens."

A wicked grin plumps her cheeks.

I point at her face. "Uh… what the heck is that?"

"Be right back."

Before I get the chance to ask anything else, she exits the bathroom and dashes down the hallway. I creep toward the door and peek around the corner. Thankfully, no one else is home right now. Ales is with Mags at her dance class. Mom and Dad are at work. So I am less concerned about anyone seeing me in full facial mode.

Helena waltzes back down the hall. My gaze falls to her hand and I freeze.

"No." I hold up both hands and vehemently shake my head. "Nuh-uh. Nope. Absolutely not." I spin around, give her my back, and dash down the hall.

"Oh, come on." Her feet thump on the floor in an attempt to keep up with me. "Please."

I peek over my shoulder and chuckle. "What is it about the word no you don't understand?"

"For me, Ander," she whines. "Please."

Rounding the sofa, I zigzag toward the kitchen and loop around the island. "Why?"

She huffs and I laugh. "Memories."

"Can we just remember it happened? Without photographic evidence."

She halts and plants her hands on her hips. "I won't show it to anyone." She draws an X over her heart. "Promise."

The vow and gesture form a fissure in my resolve. Create an inkling of acquiescence. The longer we stand here, holding each other's stares, the more I consider caving.

Because this is Helena. *My North.* And dammit, I'd do anything to see her smile.

I tip my head. "Ugh," I cry out to the ceiling before leveling my gaze. "Fine," I grumble.

"Yay!" She claps animatedly.

Closing the distance between us, I point a finger at her. "No one, and I mean *no one*, sees this."

She pins her pinkie down with her thumb and holds up three fingers. "Scout's honor."

"Uh, that only works if you're an actual Scout."

She waves off my comment. "Whatever." Holding out an arm, she beckons me closer with the wiggle of her fingers. "Get over here."

I step into her side embrace and teeter from one foot to the other.

What do I do now? Do I put an arm around her? Hug her to my side?

God, I want her in my arms. More than just a casual embrace. I want to feel how perfectly she fits with her front to mine. Her head on my shoulder or against my chest. Hands fisted in my shirt. Comfortable. At ease. At home. With me.

My pulse shoots into overdrive. Pounds a vicious rhythm in my chest at the idea of cradling her in my arms. Of feeling *wanted* by my favorite person.

That's probably too much to ask right now. Too close for us —physically and emotionally.

But how close is too close?

Where do I put my arm? Maybe around her shoulders. That's a safe zone. At least, I think it is. What if I put an arm around her waist? Warmth spreads through my chest at the level of intimacy such a simple hold would possess. If I were to curl my fingers and grip her hip, would it freak her out?

I close my eyes and count to five. Shake off the unrealistic thoughts brewing in my head.

When I open my eyes, I spot Helena watching me from the corner of hers. She hooks an arm around my waist and crushes me to her side. "We're taking two."

I groan.

"Shush, you." She pinches my side and I jump. "As I was saying," she continues with a roll of her eyes. "We're taking two. One with smiles and the other with goofy faces."

My arm between us circles her waist and I mentally sigh. *Perfect.* "Fine," I say with more curtness than I mean. Pretenses and all. "But if you want these pictures, you better take them already."

She lifts the Polaroid and holds it as far away as possible. "Smiles first." Her finger finds the shutter button. "One, two, three."

The flash blinds me temporarily as the photo ejects from the top. I blink a few times as she waves the picture back and forth. Slowly, the image of our masked faces comes into view. And if I am honest with myself, I really like the picture. More than I thought I would.

"Alright, time for the funny shot."

"Gimme," I say, stealing the camera from her hand.

"Hey." She reaches for it and I hold it higher.

"My arms are longer. We'll get a better shot."

Her free hand slaps her leg. "You have a point."

I lengthen my arm and aim the lens at our face. "Goofy face in three, two, one." Our faces contort and I press the button. Picture two spits out of the top and, as she yanks it out, I snap another.

"What the—"

"That one's for me," I say, grabbing the picture and tucking it in my pocket.

"You could've said something. I would've taken another."

"Yeah, I know. But what's the fun in that?" I pat my pocket. "This one's more in the moment. Spontaneous. No posing involved."

She rolls her eyes and takes the camera from my hand. "I swear, if I look stupid in that picture…"

I wait for her to finish, but she doesn't. "No way you look stupid," I say. "Not possible."

She drops her chin as she waves the second picture, a hint of pink on her cheeks. Once the photo develops, she holds it up. For a moment, I stare at the two of us. Me with pouty lips and crossed eyes. She with puckered lips, eyes heavenward, and a slight tip of her head in my direction. We look happy and carefree and… more than friends.

"It's perfect," she proclaims. Then, without warning, she kisses just beneath the angle of my jaw. "Thank you."

Before my brain or lips form a response, she wanders back down the hall and disappears into Ales's room.

She kissed me.

CHAPTER 14
HELENA

"This is it," Mom says with a stern expression as she hands me cash. "Don't spend it all on junk."

I playfully roll my eyes. "What's the fun in that?"

She lays her hands on my shoulders and shakes her head. "Get at least one thing that isn't complete garbage. Like trail mix without candy." She pulls me in for a hug. "Don't need you sick from malnutrition."

"I'll be fine. And I promise to pick one good thing."

"Thank you."

Mom walks off and joins the other parents. This is the first summer the kids and parents are shopping separately for camping food supplies. Each of us got a wad of cash and I bet if we combine it we'll make out like bandits.

"How much did you get?" Lessa asks.

I sift through the bills in my hand and count. "Thirty

"Uh… yeah." I hold the bills up and show everyone. "What about you?"

Lessa puckers her lips then shifts them sideways. "Dad added ours together"—she motions between her and Anderson with a finger —"and gave us thirty total."

"Cool." I look to Mags. "Whatcha got?"

Mags waves two tens and a five. "Twenty-five."

Lessa claps her hands and we all jerk back momentarily. "Alright. That's eighty-five total. We need a game plan. What matters most and what we can cross off if need be."

Lessa pulls her cell phone from her back pocket and opens the notes app. We toss out our favorite foods and prioritize them. The parents said they'd buy all the breakfast, lunch, and dinner foods. Unless we want something specific to go with meals, we are free to spend the money however. Well, except Mom wants me to get one healthy snack.

Anderson fetches a shopping cart from the corral, does a short run, and hops on the foot bar, gliding through produce until he reaches us at the bakery.

Eyes on me and a smirk on his lips, he says, "Hop in."

I scan the other patrons in our small-town grocery store and wince. "Um." I nibble at my bottom lip. "Not sure that's such a good idea," I say when I spot Mrs. Wrigley, one of the grumpiest teachers ever. She'd probably stomp through the store and tattle on us to our parents.

Anderson follows my line of sight and scoffs. "Don't worry about her."

I twist to meet his gaze and tilt my head slightly.

He collapses the child seat and bangs the metal basket. "C'mon, North. Hop in. We have shopping to do."

"Just get in the basket, Lena," Lessa encourages. "Who cares what people think."

"In or out?" Mags chimes in. "I have a hankering for peanut butter cups and Cap'n Crunch."

"Fine," I concede. "But if I get in trouble, you're all going down with me."

I step on the bottom rail of the cart, grab the edge of the basket, and swing my leg up and over, climbing in. Short as I am, it is crampy and uncomfortable sitting up straight. It also leaves next to no room for food. So, I scoot my butt to the middle of the basket, lift my legs up, and dangle my feet over the end. Still nowhere near cozy, but better than before.

Lessa claps again. "Alright. Let's do this."

One aisle at a time, we weave through the store. Mags, Lessa, and Anderson toss items in the basket without care. The occasional box corner jabs me in the belly, but otherwise it's no big shake. Gummy worms, Sour Patch Kids, and Cap'n Crunch. Cheez-It crackers, Chex Mix Muddy Buddies, chocolate bars, Reese's Peanut Butter Cups and Reese's Pieces. Three flavors of Pop-Tarts—frosted, of course.

We reach the cookie aisle and Mags pipes up. "Important question." All eyes look in her direction. "Do we get graham crackers for the s'mores, like usual? Or do we get chocolate chip cookies to use instead?"

From my spot in the cart, I peer up at everyone and take in their uncertainty. "Lessa?"

"Yeah?"

"Where we at with the total so far?"

She stabs at her phone screen for a moment then looks up. "We have about thirty dollars left. But we should leave wiggle room for tax."

I shift my gaze to Mags. "Get both. We have the money."

Both get tossed in the buggy and we move on to the next aisle. We pass the parents near the endcap, wave, and keep going. After a handful more items, we reach the end of the chips aisle and head for the checkout.

One by one, we load everything onto the belt. The older cashier gives me a forced smile while the younger guy bagging our heap of salt and sugar stifles a laugh. As the last items get put on the belt, I look to my right and see individual portions of trail mix for under a dollar.

"Hey." I tip my head back and look up at Anderson. "Add one of those, too." I point to the blue package. "Without the candy."

He chuckles, grabs the mix, and tosses it on the belt. "Your mom would've never known."

"Probably," I say as he pushes the cart forward. I hop out of the basket, stretch my limbs, and crack my neck. "But knowing my luck, she'd actually check."

With two dollars to spare, we pay the cashier, exit the store, and steer the cart to the cars. The parents meet us minutes later and we load everything up. Mags and Lessa opt to ride with the Bishops, while Anderson and I ride with my parents.

Miles pass as we head for our summer camping getaway at Seaquest State Park. Leaning into Anderson, I drop my head onto his shoulder and close my eyes. He rests a hand just above my knee, his thumb stroking my skin slowly.

The simple touch is anything but simple. His hand on my skin is hot and electric and makes my heart race. I never want him to stop. I never want the buzzing energy to end.

And for the rest of the trip, we sit like this. Connected. Together. More.

"C'mon, North. You got this," Anderson encourages as we traverse a new trail.

I trudge up the incline, winded, as I grab roots and limbs to help heave me forward. Several feet back, Lessa grumbles under her breath about her brother picking the worst trail possible. Mags, on Lessa's heels, watches her footing every few steps then looks around the woods with a smile.

"How far in are we?" I ask as I reach him. Planting my hands on my thighs, just above the knee, I take a few deep breaths.

"Almost to the lookout point."

"Thank god," Lessa wheezes out as she and Mags catch up to us. She rests a palm over her heart and points a finger with her free hand at Anderson. "You don't get to pick trails anymore."

Anderson laughs and I can't help but stare. Take in the creases at the corners of his mouth and eyes. The bob of his Adam's apple. The carefree delight in his current state.

Not many have witnessed Anderson's easygoing side. The gentle, wondrous boy with an incredible smile he shares with very few. I see it from time to time, but only when it is the two of us. I love this side of him. Uninhibited with a spark of delight and mischief.

Much as I wish more people knew this side of him, I am glad he doesn't give it to everyone. It makes each laugh and smile and twinkle in his eyes that much more potent and special.

"If you say so," he taunts. "Might change your mind when we reach the lookout."

"Doubt it," she grumbles. "How is there not an easier route to the lookout?"

"I'm glad we're taking a new trail," Mags chimes in. "Think of it as an adventure, Lessa."

Lessa narrows her eyes on Mags. "I can't be the only one thinking I'll have heart issues after this." No one responds to her nonquestion. "Ugh. Whatever." She stomps past us. "Let's just get this over with already."

We hike to the lookout in relative silence, Anderson at my side while Mags treks alongside Lessa. Every now and then, I point out birds or small animals or the occasional insect as they wake for the day.

Leaving for a hike at dawn was Anderson's idea. Lessa groaned last night throughout dinner, dessert, and before we drifted off in our tent. Though I knew we'd be tired, I'd been excited. The world is a different place as the sun rises. There is a gentleness not often seen as your part of the world stirs to life.

"Thanks for this," I say.

I feel his eyes on me as we approach the turnoff for the lookout. "For going on a hike?"

With a shake of my head, I meet his gaze. "For picking a new trail. For getting us up early." I shrug. "Tired and grouchy as some of us are—"

"You know I can hear you, right?" Lessa looks over her shoulder and rolls her eyes.

"Anyway," I say, loud enough for her to hear before lowering my voice to continue. "Thank you. We'd probably miss an incredible view had you not thought of this."

Anderson inches closer. "You don't need to thank me, but you're welcome. Just wanted to see the morning sun with you." He swallows as a faint dusting of pink colors his cheeks. "Who knows how many chances we'll get to see it here."

Something about his admission warms me head to toe.

Blankets me in the summer sun long before it graces the sky. I welcome the sensation. Let it consume every inch and root itself deep in my bones. Allow it to take over my thoughts.

No one knows Anderson the way I do. No one else gets to see the complex angles of his mind or heart. I love that he considers me special enough to get this piece of him. In the same breath, it saddens me that he keeps this side of himself hidden from everyone else. Intentionally locked away and sheltered from the world to guard and protect himself.

I peek at him from the corner of my eye as we walk a more level part of the trail. Almost the same height as me, Anderson is lithe with sharper angles. A black hoodie hangs loose on his thin frame, wisps of his blond hair peeking out from the hood on his head while his hands sway at his sides. Charcoal cargo shorts stop just beneath his knees. White socks barely peeking out of the hiking boots on his feet.

He is still the same Anderson I've known more years than not. Yet, he isn't the same person.

Anderson Everett is no longer a boy, yet not quite a man. He's somewhere in that in-between. The place where we try to figure out who we are and what we are meant to do in the world. Were he not wise beyond his years, he'd be cracking corny jokes and playing silly pranks with other boys his age. But he isn't the type to do either and I like that about him.

As we reach a bend in the path, he shifts to look my way. When he sees my eyes on him, the smile he gives only me makes an appearance.

"What's up, North?"

My eyes shoot straight ahead, my cheeks heat, and I shake my head. "Nothing."

A short, muted chuckle fills the air between us. "Mm-hmm." He inches closer and I feel the heat of him through the sleeve of my shirt. "I'll let it slide. For now." He takes my hand in his. "But only because we'll reach the lookout in a minute."

Perspiration dampens my skin despite the cooler, early morning temperature. My heart thumps brutally in my chest while my breaths come in stuttered gasps. Neither has anything to do with the hike and everything to do with the guy holding my hand.

For months, Anderson and I have grown exponentially closer. He is my best friend. More than my best friend. He is the one person I think of when I have a bad day. The first person I want to share happy news with. We have always been close, always had a different connection, but this...

I zero in on where our hands connect and close my eyes for one, two, three steps. A zing of energy whirls in my chest and makes me swallow. The sensation is exhilarating and over-whelming, pleasant and familiar. A touch of comfort and home. In the same breath, it's scary and worrisome.

Without a doubt, I care for Anderson. Deeply. But what if I feel things for him that he doesn't reciprocate? What if his hand holding mine is purely out of friendship? A simple connection between two people that have known each other for years and are nothing more than at ease with one another.

I don't believe it, but what if he does?

"Holy shit," Lessa says, her voice echoing in the trees.

Beside me, Anderson laughs without inhibition. "Told you it was worth it," he mutters only loud enough for me to hear.

I tighten my grip and tug him forward, eager to see what has Lessa awestruck. As the trees thin and the path opens up, a boardwalk over a body of water comes into view. My steps falter as I scan the horizon and take it all in. The sun barely brightens the sky, but I see everything. The mountain in the distance. The scattered trees lining the endless boardwalk and beyond. The scraggly grass plants in patches in the water where birds wait for fish to swim past.

Stepping up to the rail, I lean over and stare out at the open landscape. His hand still in mine, I take a deep breath and let the cool, piney air fill my lungs. In one breath, my muscles relax and my mind quiets.

This right here, right now, is perfect.

Most girls my age wouldn't be caught dead in the middle of nowhere. They are more concerned about hair and makeup and fashion. I am not opposed to those things. They have their place and time. But being out in the thick of nature, there is just something so real about it. Out here, you get to disconnect from the crazy and reconnect with yourself. Out here, you get to let everything else go.

Shades of pink and orange smear the sky. I don't dare move from my spot. Don't dare to look away and miss a second of the view.

"Thank you," I whisper, giving Anderson's hand a squeeze. "Best camping memory yet."

We remain rooted in place as the sky slowly morphs into a cloud-covered light blue. He never lets go and neither do I. For a beat, the world is quiet. Peaceful. Harmonious. I close my eyes and bask in the moment. The solace and warmth and endless buzz in my chest.

Then the bubble pops when Lessa hollers for us to catch up.

I don't miss Anderson's irritated huff. Nor the short, soft stroke of his thumb on my hand. And it's in this single blip in time that I *know* what I questioned earlier isn't true.

Anderson holding my hand... it isn't just friendship. It's so much more. But what exactly, I don't know.

CHAPTER 15
ANDERSON

No time in my life compares to now. To this summer. To countless moments with her.

I don't question our bond. Don't ask why she is the only person able to lift me up and shine a light on my darkest hours. Whatever the reason, I am lucky to have her. Helena Williams. My best friend. My only real friend.

Years ago, it saddened me to say I had no friends. No one, other than my sister and her friends, cared about me, which is different than friends of your own. Now, things are different. With the exception of a few, I still lack genuine people in my life. But this fact no longer tugs me down or whispers insecure thoughts in the back of my head.

Because I have her.

Chin somewhat tucked, I survey everyone around the campfire. The parents are off in their own world, as usual, after dinner. The dads sit in collapsible chairs closer to their tents and talk about having a dads-only camping weekend. The moms are parked in their usual spot at the table, Mrs. Bishop praising her daughter, Mags, and her skill as a dancer. When my eyes scan our group, everyone seems lost in their own thoughts. Glum over our last night at the park. Can't say I blame them.

With our chairs nearly touching, I nudge Helena's knee with my own. "S'more?"

She blinks a few times and turns her head to face me, half her profile shadowed and half illuminated by the fire. "I'm sorry. What?"

I hold up the almost empty bag of marshmallows. "Want a s'more?"

Her eyes hold mine for two of the slowest breaths before she swallows and nods. "With cookies."

I hand her the bag. "I'll get the cookies if you prep the marshmallows."

"Deal."

Rummaging through the snack bin, I fetch chocolate chip cookies, the last chocolate bar, and a sleeve of graham crackers. Plopping back down in my chair, she hands me my speared marshmallow and smiles. I pin the skewer between my knees and open packages. After a quick check of my marshmallow and a flip, I hand Helena two cookies. While she smooshes her lightly browned sugar cube between the cookies, I break off a piece of chocolate and snap a graham cracker.

"Going to miss this," she mumbles around a monstrous bite.

I stifle my laugh so only she can hear. "Uh, what?"

She playfully slaps my arm, finishes her bite, and gives me a pointed stare. "I said I'm going to miss this." She waves a hand to nothing in particular. "Being here. Hanging out." Picking at the edge of the cookie, she tears a small piece off and sticks it in her mouth. "So much is different now." Her eyes dart to mine. "In a good way," she rushes to say. "But it feels like the last summer we'll get to be like this."

My brows pinch together. "The last summer?"

While I assemble my s'more, she nibbles at hers. I mull over her words. Look for things left unsaid. Our annual camping trip has happened without fail every year since I was three. Not that I believe we will have them forever, but why wouldn't we be here next year? The thought alone drags me into the dark recesses of my mind.

As if she hears my inner downward spiral, she rests a hand on my forearm. That simple touch, her skin on mine, stop all the swirling mental chaos. It grants me room to breathe.

"Sorry," she mutters. "Didn't mean to upset you."

"You didn't—"

She holds up a hand. "Don't lie to me, Ander. I see it on your face."

"Fine. Whatever." I yank my charred marshmallow from the fire, smash it between graham crackers and chocolate, and toss my skewer aside. "Why do you think this is our last summer?" Then I shove the s'more between my lips.

"Again, I'm sorry," she says then sighs. "It's just that next summer will be busy. I'll have to start studying for the SAT. Maybe I'll have a job." She takes a small bite and barely chews before swallowing. "I don't know why." Glassy eyes hold mine. "Something about this summer feels like the end. Not of this place or us, but something else."

Much as I wish our lives could remain like this, I am not foolish enough to believe things won't change. I start my second year in middle school. Helena, Ales, and Mags start their sophomore year in a week and a half. Life has been nothing but big changes for years. Although high school gets more intense each year, she will handle them with grace.

"You got this, North." I nudge her elbow. "And if you need someone to lean on"—I point to my shoulder—"I got you."

"Right back at ya."

I hate the dark cloud looming over her. The idea that this trip will be our last gnaw at my happiness. But something in her words fit. Change, especially one that involves her or us, makes my stomach flip. Change is inevitable, I know. Doesn't mean I have to like it.

One by one, everyone says good night and goes into their tent until only Dad and I remain. He sits in the chair beside me and we stare at the dying fire.

"Everything okay, son?"

Heart-to-heart conversations aren't really my thing, with the exception of Helena. When Dad sparks a talk, though, I don't ignore it. Otherwise, Mom steps in, and I'd rather not deal with her.

I shrug. "Fine. Why?"

He shuffles his booted feet in the dirt. "You seem better than usual but still unhappy."

Great.

"There's a long list of things that upset me, Dad." I tip my head back and stare at the stars. "Being here isn't one of them."

"Do you want to talk about the other things?"

On an audible exhale, I level my gaze with the fire. "Not tonight and never here." I turn to look at him. "I'd rather not ruin this place."

He nods as if he gets it. "Okay." Rising from the chair, he taps my shoulder. "Don't stay up too late. Make sure the fire is out." Sticks and leaves crunch as he takes a few steps then stops. "When we're home, I think we should talk more."

Every meager ounce of happiness inside me wilts at his words. "Sure thing, Dad," I mumble.

Once alone, I put out the fire. Wandering to my favorite spot, I drop down to the ground, lie flat on my back, and stare up at the dark sky. Scattered stars break up the black and subtly brighten the night. And for the first time since my bleak talk with Helena, I take a deep breath.

The rustling of leaves grabs my aural attention, but I don't move or acknowledge the sound. Seconds later, someone drops to the dirt beside me and lies down. Without looking, without a word, I know who it is. Because only she knows where to find me in the dark.

My North.

CHAPTER 16
ANDERSON

Two weeks after school started, Dad came to me again. Initiated the conversation he was so desperate to have. A conversation he undoubtedly regrets now. A conversation that probably costs him a lot of time and money.

"I just want my happy boy back," Mom says as Dad gives her the CliffsNotes version of our talk.

Badly as I wanted to ask her the last time she thought I was happy, I refrained. Instead, I went along with my parents' decision to send me to therapy. To send me to a psychiatrist. A woman, maybe in her early fifties that wears her graying hair in a studious bun on top of her head. The few appointments I've had, she is always in some pantsuit or skirt suit.

Dr. Rose Flowers.

Really? How the hell am I supposed to take this woman seriously? Her parents must have been hippies.

"Tell me about school, Anderson."

She also never asks a question. Everything is phrased as a statement. Something she wants an answer to, even if it isn't an actual question. It gets under my skin about as much as the slight tilt of her head every time she wants me to share all of my secrets.

Do I share pieces of my life with her? Yes. If I remain tight lipped, it will only cause more problems.

Client confidentiality is still a thing between me and the good doctor, but since I am a minor, not everything is as private as it would be if I were an adult. So I participate in the charade. A little. Give her snippets. Enough to get things off my chest, but not enough to turn my entire life into a therapy session.

Let's be real for a minute. It would take a lifetime to unpack years and years of bullying, parental degradation, depression, and self-harm. The latter two have faded somewhat or fallen away as Helena and I grow closer.

"Not much to say, Dr. Rose. Kids are assholes."

"Language, Anderson," she admonishes, her voice soft and even.

"Sorry." I roll my eyes. "They're donkey holes."

She writes something on her notepad. "You're an intelligent young man, Anderson. Please find other colorful words to describe things or people that are less crude."

"Okay."

"Thank you." A soft smile dons her face. "Tell me what these kids do that makes them such… blockheads."

Blockheads? Is that an actual word?

I picture all the assholes at school with cinder blocks for heads. The mental image has me biting the inside of my cheek. I mean, they are about as smart as cement, so it fits.

For the rest of our session, I skirt around the truth and tell her how cruel kids in my school are without directly saying what it is they do to me for *fun*. Last thing I need is the good doctor or my wishy-washy mother talking to the counselor at school.

One by one, the dominoes will fall and create more issues than resolutions. More *blockheads* will join the brigade. Cruelty and name-calling will morph into something much worse. Current pranks will be child's play compared to what they do once provoked. The occasional hit in the gym or halls will turn into full-on attacks when teachers are nowhere in sight. Obviously, I will lash out. Hurt someone in the process of standing up for myself.

And at the end of the day, only one person will be punished. Me. The loner kid that seems *troubled*, even though I am the victim, always shoulders the penalty.

So, I keep the horrendous acts inside. Don't tell her or my parents that I don't shower during gym class anymore because someone will cut or beat or laugh at my naked body. Or worse, steal my clothes. I don't tell them about the notes taped to my locker door every day. Notes with words like *worthless* and *freak* and *kill yourself*. And I don't tell them about the bruises and scars—visible and not.

There is only one person I trust enough to share those painful truths with, and I shield her too.

CHAPTER 17
HELENA

I thrust back in the chair and toss my pencil on the table with a huff. "In what universe do I need to know gastrocnemius is the main muscle of the calf?"

Beside me, Anderson chuckles under his breath as he scribbles on notebook paper. Knowing his supersmart brain, he is probably writing an essay for English class that surpasses *my* level of English class. Or maybe he is working on his history project.

All I remember of my middle school history project is the stress. With the project being fifty percent of the final period's grade, I wanted it nothing short of perfection. I took the easy route and chose a popular name in history. Someone I'd easily find stories about online or in the library.

Anderson, on the other hand, never takes the easy way out. Who will he choose? Knowing him, he will avoid the popular choices. Dig deep online or scour the pages of dusty books in the school library. Pick a lesser-known person that advocated for communities throughout the country. And then he'll write a brilliant paper. He'll make sure people his age know about this person and what they accomplished. He'll give them a fresh voice and stir conversations about stories of the past.

Me… I'll be in this chair, staring at this too-thick textbook on human anatomy, questioning why I thought taking this class was the best science choice this year.

"Do you know what you want to do after school?" He sets his pencil down and takes a sip of cola. "Maybe you'll be the town's physical therapist." He shrugs. "You'd need to know muscles for that."

I roll the idea around in my head for three breaths then shake my head. "Nope. Not a zing of interest."

"Maybe you'll follow more in your dad's footsteps," he says. "Be a park trail guide instead of a ranger."

"What does that have to do with learning muscles?"

"If someone hurts themselves on the trail and you have to radio for help, wouldn't it be helpful to know bones and muscles?"

He must be joking. He has to be. In what world would I be a trail guide? Don't get me wrong, I love the outdoors. But I love doing my own thing—by myself or with select people. With strangers, though… Nope. Still no interest.

I meet Anderson's gaze and open my mouth to respond but snap it shut when I see the fierce hold his teeth have on his lips.

He's mocking me. Saying stupid shit to get a rise out of me or throw me off. That little punk.

Two can play this game.

"You know, you're right."

He releases his lips as his brows tug together. "I am?"

"Mm-hmm. I do love hiking and being in the woods. Should probably talk to Dad about my next steps." I bring a hand to my chin and tap my lips with my forefinger. "Do you know if there's a park ranger school? Or should I look for books? There's probably a beginner's manual online. I mean, how hard can—"

"North," Anderson interrupts my fake tangent, his eyes wide. "I was joking."

Tilting my head, I plaster on my best fake confused face. It lasts only a few seconds. Laughter bursts from my lips and I slap the dining room table. Tears blur my vision, but I don't miss the narrowing of his eyes or pucker of his lips.

"You weren't serious, were you?" he asks, tone slightly accusatory.

I wipe my eyes and cheeks. "Not at all."

He reaches for my side, fingers digging at the base of my rib cage. "You little—"

The front door opens and the clap of shoes on wood echoes through the house. *Lessa and Mags.* Anderson rips his hands away and straightens in his chair. He picks up his pencil and tries to look more studious than either of us has been for the last fifteen minutes.

"Baby A? Lena? You guys here?" Lessa calls out as she rounds the corner and trudges our way. "Oh, hey!" She sets down her backpack in one of the free chairs, Mags mirroring the action with the chair beside it. "Maybe joining clubs was *not* the best idea." She steps into the kitchen, opens the fridge, grabs two cans of soda, then goes to the pantry for chips. Handing a drink to Mags, she plops down in the chair with a huff. "Now I'm too tired to do homework that I can't skip. Ugh."

"Mine wasn't that bad," Mags chimes in.

Lessa cracks her can open. "Yeah, joining the dance club when you dance regularly isn't a challenge."

Mags sticks out her tongue. "Should've picked something easier. Like the gossip circle instead of cooking."

"Ha ha." Lessa gives Mags a playful shove then turns her attention across the table. "How's homework?"

The easy comfort Anderson and I share is nowhere to be seen. He doesn't necessarily shy away from me when Lessa and Mags are around, but he puts up a wall. I know him well enough to know it isn't out of embarrassment or concern. More like he wants to safeguard our bond.

My leg grazes his under the table and his writing pauses long enough for me to notice. I like the pause.

"Mister Smarty-Pants has no homework issues," I tease and point to Anderson. "As for me"—my gaze toggles between Lessa and Mags—"I'm questioning my curriculum choices."

Mags lifts the corner of my textbook to see the cover and winces. "Not sure my chemistry class is any better."

"But at least you get to play with chemicals and fire occasionally."

"True."

After busting open the chips bag and eating a few, Lessa and Mags fish out textbooks and notes for their homework. The table falls into a familiar, comfortable silence we all share this time of year. The hours between school and parental time.

The four of us... we're our own little family. Bonded for life.

Under the table, Anderson leans his leg against mine, but he doesn't otherwise shift his posture. He remains hunched over his paper, scrawling in his notebook, a hint of a smirk on his lips. I peek across the table from under my lashes, where neither Lessa nor Mags take their eyes off their own studies.

A tornado of warmth and energy swirls in my chest and I

stop breathing. No matter how often I feel this with him, his touch always affects me the same. Like each press of his leg or grip of my hand or stroke of my skin is new. Unique. A first.

A big part of me wants many firsts with Anderson. We've shared so many already, but none of them have felt like this. Potent. Powerful. Something more than friendship.

Is that what we are now? More than friends. Is that what I want? What he wants? I honestly don't know.

But I am willing to find out.

CHAPTER 18

ANDERSON

"Ugh." Ales slurps the last of her root beer float. "I'm bored already." She shoves the tall glass mug to the side, plucks several french fries from the shared plate in the middle of the table, dunks them in ranch, then devours them on a moan. "Can we please do something?" she asks with a hand over her mouth.

Next to her in the booth, Mags sips hot cocoa. "The cinema has a movie marathon in one of the theaters." She looks at Ales then across the table to Helena. "Buckets of popcorn, boxes of candy, some liquid sugar, and ten hours of the *Twilight Saga*." Fishing through her purse, she pulls out her phone and taps a button to light the screen. "Started thirty minutes ago, but it's not like we haven't seen the first movie a gazillion times."

Helena grabs a fry from the plate and slathers it in barbeque sauce. She pops it in her mouth then elbows my side. "You up for a day full of teen angst, vampires, and were-wolves, Ander?"

I have zero feelings about the movies. Truly.

Until a few years ago, I'd been somewhat oblivious to the

franchise. That's when the first two movies hit our small town in Washington. That's when every school-age girl in Lake Lavender went gaga over Robert Pattinson, including my sister and Mags. Helena showed excitement for the movies, but not to the same degree as Ales and Mags. Those two earned their Twihard title all on their own.

Although I have no desire to spend my entire day watching the saga, I will say yes. I will sit in uncomfortable seats, listen to every girl in town talk over the movies, and pretend like I'm interested. All because of the girl next to me in the booth.

"Yeah. Sure." I drink the last of my Dr Pepper. "Probably should let the parents know."

Ales whips out her phone and taps the screen with quick fingers. "On it." She pauses and looks up. "Anyone need money? I have enough to pay for me and Baby A."

Helena digs into her front pocket while Mags riffles through her purse.

"Been saving my allowance and still have leftover birthday money. I'm good," Helena states.

"Me too. Since it's fall break, Mom gave me play money," Mags says.

Ales claps and startles us all. "Let's go."

We settle the check and leave the diner. We weave through the crowded sidewalk on Main Street and I instinctively reach for Helena's hand. Lace my fingers with hers and breathe easier from the simple contact. I tell myself it is so I don't lose her or let her get trampled by people shopping for Thanksgiving.

Those are half-truths.

If I am honest with myself, I want her hand in mine more often than not. Holding her feels right. Perfect. Like home. Her touch, innocent as it is, revives my heart. Chases away my demons and warms me in ways I never thought possible.

Does she feel the same? A constant desire to be close, just the two of us. A magnetic pull when we exist in the same space. An unmatched level of comfort. If I were to spill all my secrets, it would be with her. Is it the same for her? Or does she hold my hand for a different reason? To appease my need to touch her. Out of pity, to ease my sadness. She doesn't have a boyfriend that I know of, and I am familiar and easily accessible. Like family. A brother.

The tightening of her fingers in mine snaps me out of my introspection. I drop my gaze to our hands for one, two, three steps before I meet her waiting eyes. The light green of her irises is darker, edged with concern. Her lips part, voiceless words on the tip of her tongue, then she snaps her mouth shut.

I stroke the pad of my thumb down the length of hers. "What is it?"

She freezes on the sidewalk and I jerk to a stop. Looking up the street, Ales and Mags are a few storefronts ahead of us. If we don't catch up before they reach the cinema, they will wait.

"Did I do something wrong?" Helena asks.

My attention swings back to her. Uncertainty wrinkles her brow. The fingers of her free hand fidget with the front pocket of her hoodie. And her eyes... she won't look up.

I step into her, crowd her, a death grip on her hand. "No." Her eyes still downcast, I inch impossibly closer. Invade her every breath. Bring my other hand to her chin and lift her gaze until we are eye level. "No," I repeat, tone firmer. "Never."

"We don't have to watch—"

"I want to," I say, cutting her off.

"It's just that..." Her eyes dart between mine in search of answers. Then they drop to my lips, only for a second, but long enough that I notice. "What's changed since we left the diner?" She fists the cotton of my hoodie, anchoring me to her. "You seem… different."

Releasing her chin, I tuck loose strands of hair behind her ear. I love my fingers in her hair. So soft. Pretty. Delicate. I like it more in the colder months when she wears it down.

"Sorry," I whisper, my eyes following the path of my fingers. "Sometimes, I get lost in my own thoughts and spiral." I tug on the end of her hair. "Just how my mind operates."

She eliminates the breath of space between us, wraps her arms around my middle, and lays her head on my shoulder. My arms band around her waist and shoulders. Hug the breath from her lungs as I hold her in a way I never imagined possible.

"Ander?"

I close my eyes and take a deep breath. Commit every second of this moment to memory. How she holds me with unrelenting strength as her warm body molds mine. The sweet floral and earthy scent of her perfume. Our stuttered breaths mixed with the rapid beat of my pulse and hers. The din of town patrons as they move around us. But most of all, the amplified thrill in my veins.

"Yeah, North?"

"I'm here," she says, barely audible. "Always will be."

I want to counter her last words. Tell her no one can make such a steep promise. No one can swear forever and keep their word. Instead, I keep the thought to myself.

"Thanks, North." With one last deep breath, I straighten and inch back. "Should probably catch up." I point toward the cinema. "Before Ales freaks out."

She tugs on my hoodie strings, then drops her hand to

mine and weaves our fingers once again. "Yeah, I'd rather not start our week off with her wrath."

We hurry down the sidewalk and come face-to-face with an irritated Ales. I open my mouth to apologize, to tell her I caused the delay. Before I get the chance, Helena comes to the rescue. Tells her she saw cute fall decorations in a window display her mom might like.

And just like that, subject dropped.

At the concession stand, we buy two large popcorns and sodas to share among the group then our individual sweets. We wander into the dark theater and wait for a brighter scene to illuminate the seats. Ales points to empty seats and we duck and shuffle our way through the theater.

Soon as we settle, Helena flips up the armrest between us and lays her head on my shoulder. For hours, we stay this way. Connected. Content.

And I can't help but wonder what happens next.

CHAPTER 19

HELENA

Y ou can't predict the future. You can't know what will happen today that might change your tomorrow.

Days before Thanksgiving, the guy Mags had been seeing broke up with her. She cried for hours with me and Lessa. Told us she thought everything between them was going well. Confessed she lost her virginity to him, which shocked us more than anything. Not that she'd lost her virginity, but the fact we had no idea she was ready to take that step with her boyfriend.

Sure, high school has changed us. Driving us in different directions while somehow keeping us together. But I hate that big steps like this got pushed aside until monumental moments arrived.

Sadly, Mags's lost virginity and recent breakup are a blip on the heartache radar. At the time, they seemed monumental and all we thought about.

But the worst had been right around the corner.

A week ago, Mrs. Bishop was in a car accident on her way home. From what Mom and Dad told me, the other driver swerved into her lane and hit her head-on. She didn't make it.

A week ago, we lost a family member. One of our moms. Mags's mom.

I don't know what to do or say or think or feel. I don't know how to talk with my friend. Don't know how to console her. Not a chance in hell I will tell her everything will be okay. Falsehoods won't bring her mom back. Falsehoods won't change what happened. She will never be the same, and that is the only thing that is okay.

For obvious reasons, Mags started winter break early. She and Mr. Bishop have holed up in their home. Mourning and making preparations for the service. Lessa and I stopped by a few times with food, which they accepted graciously, but they asked for more time alone.

I get it. If my mom passed away suddenly, Dad and I would be basket cases. We wouldn't leave the house or remember to eat either.

It feels wrong staying over at Lessa's house without Mags. It feels wrong for the world to keep moving forward while our friend's life is stuck in this horrific moment. And it definitely feels wrong to celebrate anything—holidays included —right now.

"I don't have anything to wear," I mutter.

Lessa sifts through her closet in search of anything black. Considering her preference for brighter colors, her wardrobe choices for tomorrow are slim. Not that I think anyone in attendance at Mrs. Bishop's service will care if our attire is dark enough or matches.

"We'll figure it out." She yanks a black top from its hanger, followed by a dark-gray top. Holding both up, she spins to face me. "If you have pants or a skirt, I have tops."

"I'm sure I do."

She stuffs the tops into a bag and shoulders it. "C'mon. Let's go look. Then we'll be ready for tomorrow."

Death is strange. Not the actual moment but how people react to it.

Mags has been inconsolable since the day her mom died. Mr. Bishop, too. I wouldn't be able to stop crying if either one of my parents died. Every teenager has a rebellious streak, a time when we think we hate our parents but really don't. It's the rules we dislike. But even in my angriest moments, I still love my parents. I still want them in my life. Still want their hugs and I love yous.

Losing those moments... how do you breathe?

I scoop a bite of mystery casserole onto my fork and survey the room. Scan the sea of faces in the Bishops' home for the wake. My stomach twists as I take in some of the townspeople, chatting and smiling like everything is... normal.

Appetite gone, I find a trash can and toss the small plate of food. I crack open a bottle of water and drink a third of it before screwing the cap back on. Warmth lands between my shoulder blades and I sigh at the familiar scent of Anderson.

"Holding up, North?"

I hook my arm with his and hug his side. "Trying to. For Mags."

"Make you a deal."

Brows pinched, I look up at him.

"I'll hold you up while you support her."

The backs of my eyes sting as my throat swells. I swallow past the lump and nod. "Okay," I croak out.

He pins me to his side and moves us through the crowd. "Is she in her room?"

"I think so."

Anderson weaves us through the tightly packed house. We locate Lessa with Mr. and Mrs. Everett, grab her hand, and make our way to Mags's room. After a soft knock, I twist the knob and step inside. Lessa closes the door behind us as we kick off our shoes.

And without a word, we crawl onto her bed and hold our friend. Silently tell her we are here. To hug or cry with or talk to or scream at. Whatever she needs, we are here when she is ready.

CHAPTER 20

ANDERSON

The past few days have been strange. Since the service for Mrs. Bishop, my parents now have a new outlook on life. Dad spends more time with Mom, me, and Ales. Mom is less grouchy, especially with me, and slightly more affectionate.

The change is nice but weird.

With every halfhearted smile, I question the validity of her behavior. Question if she genuinely loves me or simply feels guilty for treating me like the family leper most of my life.

Death changes people. It's sad that it took my mother losing a dear friend to make her kind.

"You guys want pizza?" Mom hollers from the kitchen.

With the exception of Mrs. Bishop's service, winter break has been spent in front of the television. Ales, Helena, and I curl up on blankets in front of the couch and get lost in fictional movies and shows. Movie marathons we don't have to focus on. Serial bingeing of shows we previously watched, so we don't feel bad if our attention drifts.

Lying on my back, Helena on one side and Ales on the

other, I lose focus as we watch *Gossip Girl*. Helena inches closer, rests a palm on my chest, and snuggles into my side. My eyes fall shut as I wrap an arm around her and pin her in place.

In a time of loss, I shouldn't feel anything other than sadness. That's what my thoughts suggest. But I can't ignore the zing of delight in my veins as Helena turns to me for comfort.

"Sure, Mom," Ales answers.

An odd sound of delight echoes from the kitchen and my forehead wrinkles. I have always wanted to belong, to feel like my mother loves me, to feel like I matter, but not like this. The sudden flip in her behavior puts me on edge. Makes me itchy. Her joy is inappropriate. Disturbing. Disgusting.

Do I prefer this side of my mother? Of course. She hasn't berated or curled her lip at me in days. Hasn't looked at me as if I ruined her idea of the perfect family. Instead, she smiles and hugs and speaks in gentle tones. Asks if I need help with my winter break homework. Seems genuinely interested in *me*.

Only took her thirteen years and the death of a friend for her to care.

Close to an hour later, there is a knock at the door. Dad answers the door, thanks the delivery driver, and wanders into the dining room with three pizza boxes. My stomach grumbles when the scent of baked cheese hits my nose.

I comb my fingers through Helena's hair, press my nose to her crown and inhale deeply. "We should eat," I say, though I'd rather not move.

On a subtle nod, she scoots up to a seated position. "'Kay."

We shuffle to the table, grab a couple slices, then return to our spot on the blanket. Mom and Dad eat in the dining room and talk in hushed tones. It isn't long before the leftover pizza is stashed in the fridge and they retreat to their room for the night. I discard our trash and grab us all drinks.

Halfway into the next episode, Ales rolls onto her side, her back to me as soft snores spill from her lips. I move her drink to the table, drape a blanket over her, and kiss her forehead. She hugs the blanket tighter but otherwise doesn't stir.

Resituating in my spot on the blanket, Helena curls back into my side. I close my eyes, wrap my arm around her shoulders, and bask in the comfort only she provides.

"She asleep?"

Tingling warms my chest as I caress her arm with measured strokes. "Mm-hmm."

Aside from the faint sound of the show, the living room is quiet. Helena stills in my arms, her cheek on my shoulder and hand on my chest. When the episode ends, I open my mouth to ask if she has fallen asleep. Just as the words form on my tongue, I freeze.

Her hand drifts across my chest until it wraps around my waist. The warm tingle in my chest from minutes ago expands to a wildfire. I don't move, don't breathe, don't speak as I wait for what she will do next. Inch by slow inch, her hand wanders to the bottom hem of my hoodie and beneath the cotton. The second her fingers graze my skin, I suck in a sharp breath.

"Sorry." She starts to pull her hand out, but I stop her.

"No," I whisper, holding her hand in place. "Don't stop." I twist to look down at her and our eyes meet. "Unless you want to."

For a moment, neither of us moves. My heart swells in my chest, beating with unimaginable force against my rib cage. My lungs burn and beg for deeper breaths. And this eddy of inexplicable energy expands in my stomach.

And then her hand coasts up the side of my torso. Her

fingers map my skin as she tucks herself impossibly closer. I tighten my hold on her as I remind myself to breathe. Fingers splayed on my pec, she tilts her head. The heat of her breath blankets my neck and sends my pulse into overdrive.

"Is this okay?" she asks, her voice barely a whisper.

I swallow past the nervous lump in my throat. "Yeah."

We lie like this for hour-long minutes. Her fingers drawing lazy circles on my chest. Her breath hot on my neck. My arm pinning her to my side while my fingers brush her skin.

And then she shifts again. The tip of her nose grazes my skin. Followed by her lips.

Fire licks every inch of my skin as my breathing shallows. My lips part as all my blood rushes south and I swell in my pants. I pinch my eyes tight and wish away my erection. Wish away the embarrassment soon to hit us both.

Then her lips are more than brushing my neck. There is more pressure. Softness. A new kind of fire as her lips move closer to my ear and the angle of my jaw.

"North," I whisper-groan.

She freezes on my nickname for her. "Yeah?"

I lock on to her and twist until my chest presses against hers. I shimmy down a few inches and hold her green eyes illuminated by the television. For three breaths, I don't speak or move. We stare at each other in the dim light and I silently wonder if this is what she wants or if it's a reaction to all the recent events and heightened emotions. I pray for it to not be the latter.

"Are you sure?"

I assume nothing. Expect nothing. But I have to ask if taking any step beyond friendship is what she wants. Kissing and more... changes relationships. If she isn't sure, I don't want to risk losing her.

I may be young, but I'm no idiot. Though I haven't kissed anyone—or done anything else—I am not oblivious to the lead-up. Ales probably had the boys-and-sex conversation with Mom or Dad years ago. Me? Since school sex education is a joke and my parents are blasé when it comes to me, I learn from the internet. My research isn't extensive, but I know enough.

Her nails lightly scrape my skin beneath my hoodie. "Yes."

Bringing my free hand to her hair, I brush it off her forehead, tuck it behind her ear, and trail the length of it down her back as I hug her to my chest. In that single move, my lips press hers and her body sighs.

Her hand on my chest drifts around to my back, clinging and clawing softly at my skin. The kiss is soft. Sweet. A rush of heat and energy. A jolt of life to my soul. There is no tongue, no groping. Just lips and tastes and stuttered breaths in the air.

This moment... I will never forget it. The moment we became more.

CHAPTER 21
HELENA

J anuary to May has been a blur.

Although Mags will never be the girl she was prior to losing her mom, she and Mr. Bishop have slowly begun stepping out of the house more. Family gatherings will never be the same, but we meet as often as time allows and treasure every minute we get with each other.

As for me and Anderson…

Six months ago, we kissed for the first time. We've kept the shift in our relationship between us. Neither of us is embarrassed by the other, but we agreed that keeping it quiet is probably for the best. With the gray cloud still looming over our families with Mrs. Bishop's passing, plus not knowing how Lessa or our parents would feel about us being more than friends, there is no good time to talk about it.

Our kisses have intensified since that cold winter night, but we haven't explored much beyond that. No hands beneath my bra or down the pants. Physically, I know we both want more. The bulge in his pants and the way he grips my neck and holds me in place as we kiss is all the evidence I need

I want those steps with him. I want his hands in places without barriers. Want to feel his lips and tongue and teeth in other places on my body.

When the time is right.

Every time I consider the next step, a warning bell goes off in my head. This a silent reminder that, although I am sixteen and our birthdays are around the corner, Anderson is only thirteen. His body might be ready for more, but are his mind and heart? I can't be sure. Intellectual maturity is much different than emotional maturity.

I twist the thin ring on my right ring finger. Drop my eyes to the twin thin bands with a small, rectangular sapphire at the heart. Shortly after our first kiss, Anderson gifted me the ring. When I asked how he paid for it and why he bought it, he said he used his Christmas money and some saved birthday money because he thought it was the perfect gift.

Since slipping it on my finger, I haven't taken it off.

The final bell of the school year rings and cheers erupt throughout the classroom. I stop doodling the compass in my notebook and stow it in my backpack. Shouldering my bag, I wave to the teacher and head for the front of the school to meet Lessa and Mags.

"Don't know about you two, but loaded fries and a root beer float from the diner are calling my name," Lessa says as I approach.

"I need to call Dad first, but okay," Mags says as she pulls out her phone.

"Sounds good. We should swing by and get Ander, too."

For a split second, Lessa narrows her eyes. "I'd never forget Baby A."

What was that look? Does she know something is going on with us? Or is the suspicion in her expression all in my head?

I don't have time to dwell. Mags joins us and we trek toward the middle school. I contemplate messaging Anderson and letting him know we are going to the diner, but then I think better of it. If I message, he won't be surprised when Lessa brings it up. Then she will have another reason to give me or him the stink eye.

Anderson meets us soon after and we weave our way toward Main Street. With today being the last day of school, the diner is packed when we arrive. Luckily, we don't wait long for a table.

Soon as the loaded fries and onion rings hit the table, our conversation halts. Lessa moans uncontrollably as she devours fries. Mags is a bit quieter as she slowly eats. Anderson and I are somewhere in the middle as we dunk and eat while slyly holding hands under the table.

"We should do something different this summer," Lessa declares after a sip of her float.

Beside her, Mags wilts.

Without a doubt, summer will be the hardest for her. Which is why we should spend more time together. Do things we can look back on and smile at in the future. Losing Mrs. Bishop taught us all how precious every moment is. How much each second counts. Sure, we are young and should be out doing wild and adventurous things. Living in the here and now. Breaking rules and experimenting with life. But we should also do things that make us happy and stir up the good memories.

I shrug. "We can, but I like our summers. Diner days, movies, hiking." I swallow as a memory from last summer pops up. When I told Anderson last summer that it felt like it was the last year we'd all be together. Initially, I'd said it because of studying and some of us possibly getting jobs. But I was so far from the truth. "It won't be the same, but we should camp too."

Mags twirls her straw in her drink. "I don't know…"

"Maybe we can do something for Mrs. Bishop at the park. Like our own tribute." Anderson circles a finger around the table, pointing at us all. "Mark a spot for her or watch a sunrise."

The corners of Mags's mouth curve up slightly. "Mom would like that idea." She sips her drink. "I'll talk to Dad about it."

We finish at the diner and walk in the direction of Lessa and Anderson's house. Mags calls her dad on the way. As per our new normal, Anderson and I walk a few steps back from Lessa and Mags. He hooks a finger with mine as we turn off Main and into the neighborhoods. And then, on the public sidewalk where anyone can see, he leans in and presses a chaste kiss to my lips.

This summer will be one I'll never forget.

CHAPTER 22

ANDERSON

A light mist of rain coats my face as we hike a trail near the town's namesake lake. Helena walks a step back at my side while Ales treks slower at the rear. I love my sister but hoped she'd want to sit out on today's hike. No such luck.

"I need five," she says when the trail levels out.

Pausing, we drink water from canteens and munch on snacks. I pull up the trail map on my phone and find our location. Roughly a mile in, we aren't far from the first lookout point—a wooden platform jetting over the cliff and with a panoramic view of the lake and mountain. The second lookout —another mile north on the trail—is a three-story tower with a more unobstructed view of the mountain and lake.

Tossing my canteen and trash into my pack, I cut our break. Ales grumbles under her breath and I can't help but laugh.

"No one forced you to tag along," I say over my shoulder.

"Yeah, but I wasn't leaving Lena alone with you."

Her comment throws me and my foot catches on a root, causing me to trip but not fall. I recover in a couple steps and focus on the ground as I trudge forward. "What's that supposed to mean?" My tone harsher than intended.

"Chill, Baby A. Just didn't want her bored without me. That's all."

I jerk to a stop and Helena pauses at my side. She reaches for my elbow and gives a gentle squeeze as her eyes widen. A silent plea to let it go.

"Thanks," Helena says to Ales.

In turn, my sister throws me a smarmy smile. But before it has the chance to grate my nerves, Helena continues.

"I would've been perfectly fine with Ander." She turns her bright smile in my direction, leans into me, and hooks her arm with mine at the elbow. "No one else I'd rather get lost with." She rests her chin on my shoulder. "Not that we'd get lost."

The corner of my mouth kicks up for a split second. I love her sweet reassurances. Her easy touches and candid words. The subtle actions and sentiments we exchange around others that no one questions.

With a simple turn of my head, my lips would brush hers. Soft and warm and perfect. Right here, in the middle of the woods, in front of my sister, I could kiss her. Could get lost in the feel and smell and taste of her. Let her kiss rob me of breath and jump-start my heart.

With her in my arms, life is more stable. More desirable. Worth it.

But we aren't there yet. We aren't ready to let others in on our relationship. Tell them we are more than friends.

"You'll never be lost with me, North."

Ales rolls her eyes. "You guys are weird." She stomps past us. "Let's go. It's getting hot."

I silently count to five, double-check Ales's attention isn't on us, then twist and press a chaste kiss to Helena's lips. "Better catch up before she freaks out further."

With a lick of her lips, Helena nods. "Agreed."

We hike to the first lookout and stare beyond the railing a while, soaking in the view. Ales and Helena take pictures with their phones before Helena pulls out her Polaroid. She huddles us together and snaps a pic with the lake and mountain behind us.

Almost an hour later, we reach the second lookout. Ales jogs up the stairs and I take advantage of the momentary privacy with Helena.

Taking her hands in mine, I close the space between us and press my lips to hers. I sweep my tongue over the seam of her lips. Lips parting, her tongue tangles with mine. She releases my hand and fists my shirt. Drags me closer and shifts slightly, deepening the kiss.

As I snake my arm around her waist, the loud thump, thump, thump above us has me breaking the kiss and inching back. "Over here," I mutter, dragging Helena toward the rail.

Ales reaches the bottom level seconds after we reach the rail. "The view's much better from the top." She steps up to the rail beside Helena and nudges her shoulder. "C'mon."

On the top level of the tower, elbows on the rail, we stare out at the wispy clouds almost close enough to touch. Take in the white-capped steel-blue mountain and the tall, lush evergreens blanketing half the hillside, thinning just before the rocky shore of Lake Lavender.

Inhaling deeply, I close my eyes and get lost in my senses. Goose bumps flare up on my forearms and climb my biceps. Earth and pine and a familiar, unnamable wild scent drift up my nose. I grip the rail and let the rough bite of wood ground me as I mentally float with the clouds.

In the woods, in the thick of nature, a strong sense of freedom inhabits my soul. Out here, I am alive. Out here with Helena, I am free.

We sit on the wood deck near the rail and take out sandwiches, chips, and water. Over the next hour, we eat and talk and laugh feet below the clouds. More pictures are taken—most of scenery, but a few with some version of us.

All too soon, we pack up and head down the trail. The walk home is quiet and quick.

Ales drags Helena to her room and I am left wondering how to spend the next hour or two until they emerge. Plopping down on my bed, I unlock my phone and tap on the photos icon. I scroll through today's pictures, staring a little longer at the images of Helena or the two of us.

"Who would I be without you, North?" I whisper into the fading light of day. "No one. Without you, I'd be no one."

CHAPTER 23
HELENA

Mom and Dad joined us at the Everetts' for grilled burgers and side salads for dinner. The first ten minutes they were here, Mom droned on about me never being home. I blamed it on summer, getting older, and wanting to hang out with friends.

What I keep to myself is wanting to spend time with my boyfriend. If either of our parents catches wind of our new relationship status, all our unsupervised time together goes out the window. And that is not happening.

While the parents drink and chat around the patio table, we kids surround the small firepit in the backyard and follow a summer tradition—roasting marshmallows.

"I miss Mags," Lessa says, twirling her skewer.

"Same," I state, pulling my marshmallow from the flames and inspecting it. "But she and Mr. Bishop need some time away. Just the two of them."

"They went to her grandparents?" Anderson asks.

I lower my marshmallow into the flames, deciding it's not

quite golden yet. "Yeah. Her mom's parents. They live in Smoky Creek."

Lessa's marshmallow catches fire, and she yanks it from the flames, blowing on it. "Damnit."

"Language," Mrs. Everett shouts across the yard.

"Sorry, Mom." With her back to the parents, she rolls her eyes. "Still edible," she adds with a smile and picks apart the outer crust. "Think she'll be back for the camping trip?"

"Doubtful," I say, taking a bite of my marshmallow. "But you never know."

We sit around the fire until the flames are all but extinguished. Mom and Dad leave just before eleven, making me promise to spend some time with them tomorrow or Sunday. Mr. and Mrs. Everett walk my parents to the door and don't return to the backyard afterward.

Dousing the embers with water, we head inside and down the hall. Lessa mentions watching a movie in her room and I all but pout that Anderson won't be there. We watch movies in the living room most of the time, but every once in a while, Lessa wants it to be just the girls.

I can't argue with her. She is one of my best friends. Denying her girl time would be wrong. And if I said anything against the idea or suggested Anderson hang with us, it may draw unwanted attention or prompt questions.

"Be right back," I tell her. "Going to change and brush my teeth." *And talk to Anderson a minute.*

She grabs a tank top and sleep shorts from the dresser. "I'll load the movie." She lifts a hand to her mouth and stifles a yawn.

An ounce of thrill floods my veins. Call me selfish, I don't care. I may love my friend, but I also want alone time with my boyfriend. Alone time tonight involves sneaking out of Lessa's room and tiptoeing into his.

Once I'm in my pajamas, I brush my teeth and wash my face. Before returning to Lessa's room, I poke my head in Anderson's room and let him know I'll be in once she falls asleep. In a quiet rush, he pads across the room to the door and kisses me chastely.

Back in Lessa's room, we lie in her bed and watch *The Perks of Being a Wallflower*. She won't admit it, but I think the main reason she wanted to see this movie when it came out is because of Emma Watson. We all love the *Harry Potter* movies, but she always stood up for and boasted about Hermione.

Not even thirty minutes into the movie, soft snores spill from her lips. Every other minute, I inch away from her on the bed. When I reach the edge, I slowly swing my legs out from the covers and rise from the bed. I let the movie play and cover any noises I make on my way out.

Stepping into the hall, I twist the knob, close her door, and exhale the breath I am holding. After a few deep breaths, I pad over to the next door, push it open, creep in and quietly close the door behind me.

It takes my eyes a moment to adjust to the dark as I tiptoe across the room. A foot from the bed, Anderson extends his arm in my direction, inviting me to lie with him. I ease onto the bed and snuggle his side. He covers us with the sheet and blanket, wraps me in his arms, and molds me to his frame. We lie like this, unmoving, for who knows how long.

Eyes closed, I listen to the steady rhythm of his heart. Feel the rise and fall of his chest with each breath. Inhale the distinct blend of campfire and earth that always reminds me of him.

And then his hand moves. Fingers coasting over the cotton of my tank top along my spine. His lips press and remain against my hair. His fingers trail up to the nape of my neck and massage the muscles at the base of my skull. I tip my head back and kiss his throat, the hard line of his jaw, and his chin until I reach his lips.

The kiss starts slow. Soft and innocent. Warm with a hint of temptation.

Then his tongue sweeps over my lips and I open up. Invite him in. Shift on the bed to press my breasts to his chest and change the angle of the kiss. His hand trails down my spine, over my hip, and stops at my knee, hooking it up and over his leg.

With that single move, the kiss goes from paced to frantic. Our hands clasp and grope and feel parts we have yet to explore. Arms banded around my middle, he rolls onto his back. Pins me to him with a hand in my hair and one on my lower back. My arms bracket him like parenthesis, my fingers in his hair, curling and lightly tugging at the strands.

His hands drift down and grip my hips as he rocks his. The feel of him, hard beneath me, has me gasping and breaking the kiss. And then I am on my back. His lips are on my throat, the curve of my neck, my shoulder as he pushes the strap of my shirt aside.

"Is this okay?" he whispers against my skin.

Is this okay? Are we ready for this? The next step—sex—is a big deal.

Every nerve in my body is on edge, antsy. Doubt wriggles its way into my mind for a split second. Makes me question whether or not now is the right time. We are young yet mature. Sex for us isn't the same as it is for people our age. Anderson isn't just my boyfriend. He is my best friend. Someone I trust and love.

I mentally shake my head at the last word.

Love?

Maybe.

Bringing a hand to his face, I stroke his cheek with my thumb. Eyes on his, I lift off the mattress and press my lips to his. The kiss is tender and too brief.

With a nod, I say words I never thought possible at sixteen. "I love you, Ander."

His eyes dart between mine, searching. Fingers toying with loose strands of my hair, his eyes glaze over as he swallows. "Love you too, North."

When his lips meet mine again, his kiss feels different. More powerful. Exhilarating. Alive.

In the dark hours of a late-June night, we give in to our unbreakable connection. Express our love in a new way. With clumsy moves, muffled sounds, and sweat-slicked skin, we become each other's first in a new way.

CHAPTER 24

ANDERSON

Has the world always been this bright? This colorful? Undoubtedly, someone will argue today is no different than any previous day. But I beg to differ.

Walking the halls of the English quad, my eyes roam rows of lockers and peers as they swap textbooks or folders or check their hair before the next class. I meet the occasional glare or curled lip as some look up, but their callous disposition and cruel hearts don't faze me as I pass. Not today. Not this year.

I have no false ideas about friendship with any of my class-mates. No assumptions they will change and become bigger or better people. Plain and simple, they are trashy humans. Fixing the way they think doesn't happen overnight. It takes a grand act to correct such malice and disrespect, like the loss of a loved one. A deed outside of their control that shifts every future step forward, like a car crash or fall that leaves them less whole than before.

In the past five-plus years, I have put up with their bullshit. Let them push me around, call me names, degrade and humiliate me in front of my peers. Clothes stolen during gym class. Head shoved in toilet bowls while they flush and laugh and carry on as if their actions will never bear consequences. Whispered words harsh enough to slice skin and leave scars no one else sees. The outstretched foot as I walk to my desk in the classroom or locker in the hall. Ugly words written in Sharpie on bathroom walls.

I don't know what tipped the first domino, what one thing made the *Anderson Bully Brigade* come to life, but I refuse to let them knock me down anymore. Refuse to be the scapegoat for whatever hurt wounds them that they choose to pass my way.

This year is different. This year, hope and love and a need to kick back are on my side.

"Oh, look," an all-to-familiar voice says. "Someone let the psycho come back." He crumples a sheet of paper into a tight ball, throws it across the room, and hits me in the temple as I reach a desk and sit. "Another year, another round of fun."

When it comes to Charles Bates, I never engage. I let him blather on with all his fake and brutal words. Let him spill falsehoods with his imaginary pitchfork and garner groupies to join his attack.

But this year… fuck him.

Twisting to face him, my lips curve up in a mischievous smile. "Nice to know you've missed me, Chucky." I scoop the crumpled paper off the ground and smooth it out. The page has random doodles, nothing of importance. But my guess is no one else knows that fact. "Aw, Chucky," I say with false sweetness as I pretend to read the blank lines before meeting his eyes again. "Mommy hopes you have the best day at school. Says she'll reward you if you're a good boy." I wince. "Sounds like Mommy loves you a little extra."

"Shut up, fuckwit," he says with too much volume as the teacher walks in.

I face forward in my seat, stare straight ahead, and smile bigger as the teacher points at dear ole Chucky. "Detention..." he declares then trails off.

Charles groans. "Charles Bates."

"See me after class, Bates." The teacher sifts through papers on his desk before scanning the room. "Before we get started, let's clear something up. I do not tolerate profanity, slander, bullying or degradation. Not in my classroom or presence anywhere in the school. Many of you lack maturity but not intelligence. This is a high school–level class and I expect more from everyone present. If you're incapable of treating others with the respect they deserve, I am more than happy to schedule an appointment with administration to resolve the situation." He grabs a marker from the silver tray lining the dry-erase board and removes the cap. "And if you don't understand a word I just said, I implore you to study harder or speak with your guidance counselor about your current schedule."

The marker squeaks over the board's surface as he writes *Mr. Otis Georgiou or Mr. G.* Beneath his name. He scribbles *Advanced English 8* and underlines the title.

Capping the marker, he sets it back on the tray, swipes up a stack of papers, rounds his desk, and passes pages to the student at the front of each row to pass back.

"This is your syllabus for the semester. Familiarize yourself with it now. Make a plan to finish your classwork within your rigorous schedule. This class will not be easy. It will test you and make sure you're ready for what comes in high school. Now is the time to figure out if the workload is too much. If you're in more than one advanced or honors class, you won't have time for much else—including extracurriculars." He sits on the edge of the desk, drops his eyes to the sheet in his hand, and hums. "Everyone take out a pencil and paper. Let's get started."

"Hey," Helena says, a cheerful smile plumping her cheeks as I approach her, Ales, and Mags. "How was the first day?"

"Surprisingly, good. What about you guys?" I sidle up to Helena as we trek down the sidewalk toward home. "Junior year," I say with exaggerated enthusiasm.

Ales spins around and walks backward. "Junior year sucks, Baby A. Feels like I'll never get to enjoy life. Ever."

I chuckle. "Can't be *that* bad."

Mags looks over her shoulder and rolls her eyes. "You're such a drama queen, Lessa. Besides, we have zero plans for the next few weeks."

Helena giggles under her breath and I can't help but smile.

"I'll make you a deal," I suggest.

Ales stumbles then regains her footing, still walking backward, backpack straps clutched in her hands. "I'm listening."

"You do my homework and I'll do yours."

I have no clue what my sister's curriculum entails—she is smart, yet lackadaisical—but I doubt it is heavier than my own. There are four required books on the English syllabus. It is also *encouraged* we read two or more books of our choosing to discuss during the year. And math... I suspect we are taking the same level.

She nibbles on her bottom lip and mulls over the idea, but not for long. "What teachers do you have this year?"

Smart, sister. Very smart.

"Georgiou, Clenford, Wilkes, Ferguson, Muñoz, and Mann," I rattle off.

Spinning around to face forward, she shakes her head. "Nope. No deal."

Knew she wouldn't take the bait. Without a doubt, her schedule and workload are lighter than mine. Ales is smart, but she prefers a good blend of work and play. She rushes through schoolwork so she can venture into town, hang out with classmates in front of the cinema or grab fries and a drink at the diner. The older she gets, the more I see her desire to be out of the house, to do something other than mingle with her little brother.

Ales loves me, she always will, but she also wants to explore life. So long as she doesn't steal Helena away, she can do as she pleases.

My hand brushes Helena's fingers as we turn onto our street. With Ales and Mags paying us no attention, I hook my finger with hers. Drag her close enough our arms touch. Lean in and press a swift kiss to her cheek before shifting my lips to her ear and whispering, "Love you, North."

She tightens her hold on my finger. "Love you, Ander." Her eyes dart to Ales and Mags for one, two, three seconds before she places a hurried kiss on my lips. "Glad you had a good day."

I want to tell her nothing can sour my mood, nothing can rob me of the thrill in my veins, nothing will take away the light she brought into my life. But my tongue and lips refuse to form the words. Refuse to give them life.

Instead, I wrap an arm around her shoulders and haul her

to my side. Relish the warmth she radiates and the love she gives effortlessly. Breathe in her earthy floral scent and press my lips to her hair.

This is all I need.

"Me too, North." And it is all because of you.

CHAPTER 25

HELENA

"What the hell are you wearing?" I stare at Lessa as she slips on the skimpiest Halloween costume I have ever seen. *Does it actually cover anything?*

She picks the package up from the bed and holds it in my direction. "Aphrodite." Tossing it back on the bed, she walks over to the full-length mirror in the corner of her room and finagles the thin, barely there fabric. "I think I look hot."

My eyes roam the costume and take it in with fresh eyes. Without question, Lessa looks good. Hot. That's nothing new. Out of the three of us, Lessa is queen extrovert and the most comfortable in her skin. And as I stare at her, she adjusts her boobs in the bust of the dress, lifts them and exposes more cleavage.

"You do," I say after a beat of silence. "It's a great costume."

She spins around, a bright, wide smile on her lips. "Thanks, Lena." Crossing the room, her eyes examine my costume. "And you'll catch a few stares in this freaky nurse outfit."

I drop my chin and scan the body-hugging candy striper

dress. Intentional slashes in the fabric expose parts of my ribs and lower belly. The skirt stops inches below my butt and the bust shows off more than I feel comfortable showing. Fake blood splatters the dress. A thigh garter snug on my skin just below the skirt holds a fake knife slicked with more fake blood.

Typically, I wouldn't choose such a gory or provocative costume, but Anderson wanted to have similarly themed outfits. Me, the crazed candy striper, him the psycho surgeon.

The idea is brilliant. Gross but still brilliant.

"I'm not looking for attention."

All I want is to spend a night out with my boyfriend without it being weird. A night out in the world, just the two of us, without questions or strange looks. I want normal with him.

We agreed to keep our relationship a secret, and I still think it is for the best, but the longer we are together, the more I want everyone to know he is mine as much as I am his. I want to hold his hand in the open without worrying who is nearby. I want to kiss him in front of others without hearing gasps or snide commentary.

One day.

"Either way, you look hot too."

"Thanks." I clasp my hands at my waist and squeeze until my knuckles burn. "Should we head over to see Mags first?" I ask in the hopes of shifting the attention elsewhere.

"Yeah." She steps back up to the mirror and does some final touches to her makeup. "Sucks she won't be out with us, but I understand why."

Not a year has passed since we lost Mrs. Bishop. Holidays were her favorite, and now they feel less without her. Mags and Mr. Bishop stick together more often than not now. They make each day and holiday count more than ever. Mags still spends time with us, but it isn't like before. Can't say I blame her.

"Same." I slip on the short heels that go with my costume. "I'll go see if Ander is ready."

She twists in the mirror, looks at her outfit from various angles, then starts futzing with her hair. "I'll be out in a few."

Perfect.

I exit her room and head to the next door in the hall. Twisting the knob, I step into Anderson's room and shut the door. A few minutes alone isn't enough, but I know we will get more time later when Lessa finds guys from the party to distract her.

Anderson is sprawled out on his bed, book in hand, as he lounges in his bloody and slashed blue scrubs. And for a beat, I wordlessly take him in. His darker blond locks purposely messy with product and splashes of fake blood. One of his long legs is stretched out before him while the other is bent at the knee.

I study his face, his neck, the hollow spot at the base of his throat. In the past year, the contours of his face have sharpened some. Become more defined. His cheekbones, the angle of his jaw, the bow and plumpness of his lips. Lips he slowly kicks up into a smirk as I regard him.

"Whatcha doing, North?"

I swallow, take a deep breath, and cross the room to his bed. Sit on the edge of the mattress as he marks his page and sets the book aside. Toy with the bottom hem of his scrub top, watching the small action as his gaze heats my face.

"Checking to see if you're ready." I lift my eyes to meet his. "Lessa needs a few more minutes."

He sits up, bringing his chest and face and lips within

inches of mine. I suck in a sharp breath but don't move. With his breath hot on my lips, my pulse whooshes in my ears as my own breath comes faster.

"Been waiting for you." He leans forward, closing the breath of space between us, and presses his lips to mine. "Not sure I'll be able to keep my hands to myself tonight," he says when he breaks the kiss. "You look..." He shakes his head. "*Damn*."

My cheeks heat at his flattery, my heart hiccuping in my chest.

I've never been the girl who truly knows or owns her beauty. Sure, there are days I feel pretty, believing the compliments of others. But more often than not, I don't see what they do. I don't look in the mirror and see the "hot" or "beautiful" girl they call me in my reflection.

Anderson lays a hand on my exposed thigh and gives a subtle squeeze before his hand drifts beneath the hem of my dress. "You steal my breath, North." His thumb strokes the inside of my leg where my thighs touch. "Make me lose focus." He presses a chaste kiss to my lips. "Drive me wild with need." His hand inches higher, the tips of his fingers brushing the fabric of my panties before he leans in and steals a deeper kiss. "Love you, North," he whispers against my lips. "God, do I love you."

I rest my forehead on his and close my eyes. "Love you too, Ander." Tilting my chin, I press my lips to his again. "So much."

A knock at the door has us jumping apart seconds before Lessa walks in. My heart hammers in my chest, my vision a touch wobbly. I focus on quieting my heavy breathing and pray my friend doesn't notice our distressed state.

When I peek up at her, she's wiping her hands over her

outfit. "Ready?" Her bright eyes meet ours. Before either of us answer, she spins on her heel and exits the room. "C'mon. I don't want to be the last to arrive."

I rise from the bed, tug down my dress, and extend my hand to Anderson. "Party time, psycho surgeon."

He slips his hand into mine, swings his legs off the bed, and stands. Not an inch of space between us, he brings a hand to my neck, his thumb stroking the line of my jaw before he tips my head back and kisses me with hungry lips.

"Party time, crazy candy striper." Something in his tone warms my lower belly.

I lace my fingers with his, lick my lips, and nod as I drag him from the room. *Party time.*

I am so over this party.

The past hour plus has been nothing but a terrible mix of booze and immaturity. The jocks vie for everyone's attention as they run through the house in togas that barely cover their bodies and try to convince random girls to do body shots. *Bleh.* Half the girls present are trashed already, their costumes covering less and less of their bodies.

And we lost Lessa in the throng of people shortly after we walked through the front door.

Anderson tugs my hand and weaves us through the crowd toward the backyard. We step outside, away from the crowd, and I take my first full breath since arriving.

"Thank you," I say as Anderson guides us away from the clusters of people outside.

"Always."

We stop next to a tall evergreen and spin to face the party. Bottles, cans and cups litter tables, chairs, the pool, Jacuzzi, and the ground. Peeled-away costumes decorate bushes and the ground like additional holiday decor. People make out in the Jacuzzi while others skinny dip in the steaming pool.

I really don't want to leave Lessa here, but I also don't want to stay another minute. Pulling out my phone, I type a text to her.

HELENA

Where are you? I'm thinking of heading out.

"You message Ales?"

Staring down at the screen, I nod. "Yeah. Don't know about you, but I'm ready to leave."

He wraps an arm around my shoulders, his thumb stroking the exposed skin of my arm. "Was ready to leave the moment we got here."

I glance up at Anderson just as the gray bubble dances on the screen. "Why didn't you say something sooner?"

"Didn't want to ruin your fun." He shrugs.

Dropping my eyes back to the screen, I mumble, "I would've left earlier had I known." As the words leave my lips, Lessa's message pops up on the screen.

LESSA

I'm staying a little longer. You leaving with Baby A?

HELENA

Sure you're okay if we leave? You'll be okay? Yes, leaving with Ander.

"Lessa wants to stay but says she's cool if we go."

Anderson scans the crowd, his lips in a harsh, thin line. "I know she's a big girl, but I don't know if I'm okay leaving her." He points to my phone. "Ask her to come outside and say goodbye. Just want to make sure she's okay."

I type out another text asking her to meet us out back then hit send.

LESSA

I'm good. Be out in a sec.

Holding up my phone, I show Anderson her message. After reading it, he lifts his gaze to the glass doors leading from the house. Less than a minute passes before he raises a hand and waves Lessa down.

Cheeks flushed and temples sweaty, a smile dons her face as she steps up to us. "Seriously, you can leave. I'm good."

Anderson narrows his eyes as he studies his older sister. "How much have you had to drink?"

A crease forms between her brows. "I'll have you know I haven't had any alcohol." She shoves his shoulder. "Jerk."

"Not trying to be a jerk. Just want you safe." He scans the crowd. "Please walk home with someone. And text before you leave."

Like the smart-ass she is on occasion, she salutes him. "Yes, sir."

With a roll of his eyes, he softens his voice as he says, "I'm serious, Ales. Things are getting out of hand. I want to leave, but will stay if I need to."

"It's fine. *I'm fine*, Baby A." She lays a hand on his upper arm and gives it a squeeze. "Promise I'll be okay."

"Just keep your clothes on. And don't drink from cups you didn't pour."

She chuckles with a shake of her head. "Uh, yeah. That's a

given. No drunk-people sex or roofies for me, thank you very much."

"Ew." My lip curls in disgust. "Okay. We're going." I wrap my arms around Lessa and hug her tight to my chest. "Please call or text if you need us," I say only loud enough for her to hear. I release her from the hug, hold her at arm's length, and narrow my eyes.

She draws an *X* over her heart. "Promise."

Anderson hugs her just as fiercely and kisses her forehead. "If you need someone to walk home with—"

"Go!" She waves her hands at us as if shooing off a needy pet. "You both worry too much. I'll text before I leave." Then she turns and walks off, waving a hand high and dismissing us.

"I love her, but sometimes your sister is annoying," I say on a laugh.

Anderson snort-laughs. "Taking your side on this one." His hand finds mine, our fingers threading. "C'mon." He juts his chin toward a gate on the side of the house. "Let's go."

CHAPTER 26

ANDERSON

After washing all the shit out of my hair, I peel the scrubs from my body and toss them on the floor before tugging on sweats. Helena is in Ales's room, changing into something more comfortable. And thankfully, my parents are out with friends.

We have the house to ourselves for an hour or two and I've never felt so energized being alone with Helena.

I head to the kitchen for snacks and drinks, grabbing a few of our favorites before heading back to my room. Dumping everything on the bed, I grab the remote, turn on the television, and browse Netflix for Halloween movies. I opt for *Nightmare on Elm Street* and get situated on the bed.

As I tear into a bag of chips, Helena walks in wearing leggings and one of my hoodies and I can't take my eyes off her. *Damn, I am a lucky bastard*. I swallow past the lump building in my throat as she closes the door and flips off the light. My heart bangs in my chest as she pads across the room toward the bed. My breathing stutters as she crawls on the

"Hey," she says so softly I almost miss it.

"Hey."

I lean in, cup her cheek, haul her closer, and kiss her. Soft and slow and just lips. Then her hand is on my chest, fingers fisting the cotton of my hoodie, a timid moan in her throat. That little sound mixed with her proximity sparks a fire in my veins.

I suck on her bottom lip as my arm bands around her waist and I tug her closer. She tosses a leg over both of mine, straddles my lap, and frames my face in her hands. Her tongue swipes the seam of my lips as she gives me more of her weight. My hands find her hips, my fingers kneading at her flesh as my tongue tangles with hers.

The television goes black and blankets the room in darkness. Her hand falls from my face and grips mine on her hip. Inch by painful inch, she shifts my hand under her hoodie.

She breaks the kiss, her breath ghosting my lips. "Touch me, Ander," she says, voice raspy.

Sliding down the bed, I roll us over. Hover a breath above her. Stare down at this incredible girl I get to call mine. I drop my mouth to hers, kiss her chastely once, twice before skating my lips along her jaw to her ear. My hand skims beneath her hoodie, grazing her soft skin as I pepper her neck in kisses.

When I reach the bottom of her breasts, I expect to find a bra. But there is nothing. I push up on my elbows and lock my gaze with hers, silent questions passing between us.

Is this okay?

Are you sure?

How far is this going?

Helena and I have had sex. Several times. But I made a promise to myself to never assume with her, to never make decisions about sex without her consent each time.

"I need you, Ander." Want and hunger lace her words, her plea. She lifts her hips and rocks them against mine. "Please."

I brush the hair off her cheek. "I need you too, North."

And beneath the cloak of darkness, we lose ourselves in each other.

My bedroom door cracks open and Ales pokes her head in. The television illuminates the room as she looks to the bed and sees Helena curled into my side beneath the comforter. I lift my free hand and press a finger to my lips then point to Helena.

Ales tiptoes into the room and around the bed. She bends over and presses her lips to my forehead before dropping them to my ear. "Want me to wake her? Or you can bring her to my room."

My first thought is, *Hell no, you're not waking her*. My second thought is, *Like hell is she leaving my bed*. But I can't say either to my sister.

Instead, I shake my head. "She's beat," I whisper. Beneath the covers, my fingers stroke the exposed bare skin of her lower back. "I'd rather not move her."

Ales narrows her eyes at me before shifting her gaze to Helena. When her eyes meet mine again, I see it. Realization, maybe? I should be worried, should be freaking out that my sister is puzzling out the extent of my relationship with Helena.

But not an ounce of panic fills my veins. Oddly, all I feel is relief. Contentment. Happiness. If anyone were to know our secret, Ales is the person I'd want to know.

"Okay." Eyes still assessing the situation, she nods. "If you need me…" she whispers, not finishing the thought.

With a subtle smile, I nod. "She'll be fine." My fingers continue to caress her skin. "I've got her."

Without a doubt, Ales will mull over those three words. She will flip them over in her head for days or weeks as she watches how we act around each other. And she will figure out they are more of a proclamation than simple sentiment. A promise carved in stone. Because I will always be there for Helena. Every step going forward, I will be by her side.

Ales tiptoes back to the door, grabs the handle, then peeks over her shoulder at me, at us. "Be good to her."

I swallow at the seriousness in her voice. Pull in a jagged breath and nod. I want to open my mouth and tell her I love Helena. I want to tell her Helena loves me in return.

Instead, I purse my lips, keep everything to myself, and give her a curt nod.

She twists the knob and slowly opens the door. As she steps into the hall, she spins to face me one last time. "This year has been busier, but you know I'm always here. To talk about *anything*." A soft smile tips up the corners of her mouth as her eyes drop to Helena for a beat. "I'm happy that you're happy, Baby A. Love you."

"Love you, Ales," I whisper back, emotion pooling in my mouth.

The second the door closes, I exhale the breath I've been holding. *She knows. The way she assessed us… she knows.* Ales, possibly knowing the truth, is surreal and extraordinary and exhilarating… and terrifying as hell.

Grabbing the remote, I turn off the television and bask in the darkness for a moment. One breath at a time, I release every shred of worry. We kept our relationship secret to ward off family criticism—more from our parents than Ales. Much as I'd love for everyone to know, Ales just changed my mind. For a little while longer, I only want me and Helena in this bubble. Our bubble.

Closing my eyes, I haul Helena impossibly closer. A soft moan fills the room as she hikes her leg higher over mine. Her arm under my hoodie bands around my waist and hugs me to her. She nuzzles my neck, sighs, and drifts back to sleep.

This is all I need. Her and me and no one else. Just us and our bubble.

CHAPTER 27

HELENA

"What happened?" Dad asks as he waves my most recent report card between us. "Is your workload too heavy? Are classes more difficult?"

Shrugging, I push a piece of broccoli around my plate with my fork. "Yeah, I guess."

"You guess what, Bug?"

A loud clatter fills the room as I drop my fork. I cross my arms over my chest with a huff. "Things are harder," I say, harsher than I intend. Dropping my chin to my chest, I close my eyes and take a deep breath. A bit calmer, I meet his waiting and worried eyes across the table. "Sorry." I unband my arms and lay my hands in my lap. "There's more work and some classes are harder this year."

The corners of Dad's eyes soften as he looks from me to Mom. "We've been there, Bug. School is tough." Dad sets down the slip of paper with two *D*s, three *C*s, and one *B*—my worst report card. "If you need help, it's okay to ask. Mom and I might not be able to help you with some stuff, but maybe we

"No." The two-letter word shoots out of my mouth immediately.

Dad looks to Mom again and she nods, a silent conversation between them I'm not privy to.

He drags in a deep breath, exhales, then says, "If you don't want a tutor, that's fine." My body sags with relief. Too soon. "Your mom and I have already discussed alternatives."

My eyes dart between them. "Alternatives?"

Dad sets his fork down, wipes his mouth with his napkin, and sighs. "Bug, you need to pull up your grades. Until you do, no more hanging out with your friends."

Every muscle in my face tightens as my skin heats. "I'm grounded?" I ask in disbelief. "The first two bad grades in my life and I'm grounded. Really?"

"Bug…"

"I'm not a bad student."

"No, you aren't. And we want it to stay that way." He reaches across the table and lays his hand near my plate. "Harder classes mean more studying, and that's difficult to do if you're not home, Bug."

"Can I study with my friends?"

He winces for a split second. "Only if it's at home and one of us is home."

I push back on my chair, the legs scraping the floor with an angry groan of wood on wood. "This is bullshit."

"Helena Ann," Mom admonishes my use of expletives, more so toward them.

I spin around, plant my hands on my hips, and widen my eyes. "Sorry, but it's true." Tipping my head back, I stare at the ceiling and blink back the sting behind my eyes before leveling my gaze. "Sorry I'm not the star student anymore. Sorry I don't understand trigonometry or remember all things related to the human body." I lift my hands up, then drop them in a slap against my thighs. "But take away my freedom because of two Ds? I promise I'll bring them up. I'll study more. Ask the teacher if I can do extra credit. Whatever it takes."

Mom tilts her head as she silently asks Dad his thoughts. "Maybe we can come to a compromise."

Relief creeps its way back into my chest. "What kind of compromise?"

Dad and Mom have another silent conversation as I look between them. Finally, Dad pipes up. "You can study with your friends, but it still has to be at home. Aside from daily homework, I want to see extra study time. Three weeknights and one weekend day for at least a couple hours. That's the best you'll get until your grades improve."

Option two still sucks, but it's better than feeling like a lonely prisoner and living in my textbooks. "Deal."

"Mom and I expect to see your work every night. We'll also be in touch with your teachers."

Deep breaths, Helena. It could be a hell of a lot worse.

"Fine."

"And we need to know who's here studying with you."

Damnit. A ball of nervous energy expands in my belly. "I only study with Lessa, Mags, and Ander." I say his name last in the hopes they don't think too much of it.

"You study with Anderson?" Mom asks with another tilt of her head.

Play it cool, Helena.

"Yeah. He's in a bunch of advanced classes. Some of them are pretty close to the curriculum in ours."

Mom studies me with narrowed, unblinking eyes. The harsh scrutiny has me borderline nauseous. How she eyes me, examining every line and twitch of my face for confessions left unsaid. I don't move or breathe as I try to relax my expression. Hour-long seconds pass as my skin heats further and a hint of perspiration dampens my face. She is searching for any hint of a lie. Thankfully, nothing I said is an actual lie. Omitting Anderson is my boyfriend… that is a topic for a different day.

"How's he doing in his classes?" Mom asks.

I shrug. "He makes dean's list or honor roll, but I didn't ask after school today."

"Fine," Mom says. "You're allowed to study with Anderson, but only if Alessandra or Magdalena are here too."

Shit. She suspects. Keep it cool.

"Okay," I reply with a nod. "Thanks, Mom, Dad."

"We just want the best for you, Bug."

I can't argue with that. "I know. Sorry for being mean earlier. It's just I'm already upset about the grades and it felt like I was being punished for not being good enough."

Dad rises from his seat at the table. A second later, he stands a foot away. He yanks me forward and crushes me to his chest. "This is new to us too, Bug. But we'll get through it and everything will be better soon." He strokes my hair. "We got this." He releases me and holds me at arm's length. "Okay?"

I nod. "Yeah." I peek over at Mom. "Okay."

"This sucks," Anderson mutters as we walk with Lessa to my house after school.

"Yep," I say, popping the *P*. "Not like I had a better option."

Anderson jerks to a stop and twists me to face him. "Hey.

I'm sorry." He tips his head back, stares at the dismal winter sky, takes a deep breath, then levels his gaze. "You have every right to hate this more than anyone." He toys with my fingers twined with his. "But please, don't hate me." Bending slightly at the knees, he lowers to my height. "I want to help. However I can."

I tighten my hold on him and tug him forward down the sidewalk. "Sorry I snapped at you. The whole situation has me frustrated."

He leans into my side and presses his lips to my temple. "I get it. We'll get you caught up and this will be behind us."

I nod but say nothing further. Anderson is right. With a week or two of aggressive study sessions, I will be back on track. My grades will return to honor roll status in no time. Though I have a new routine, at least I still get time with Anderson. We may not be alone, but I will take any time over none at all.

"C'mon, North." Anderson tugs me until we all but jog through the thin layer of snow to catch Lessa. "We've got a study date."

Light laughter spills from my lips, but I feel no joy. A strange new pressure sits in the middle of my chest. A pressure that formed when my parents put their foot down and enforced better study habits. The heavy-growing weight isn't strictly about school and improving my grades. No, there is something else mixed in with that tension. Something I can't quite make out. Something itchy and uncomfortable and bitter.

I shove down the sensation. Push it aside for another day.

Only one thing matters right now. Doing better. Being better. Because failing isn't an option.

CHAPTER 28

ANDERSON

"I can't tomorrow, Ander," Helena huffs out over the phone. "Or any other day this week."

When I walked out of school this afternoon, the smile I'd worn for several months fell away. Ales and Mags stood on the sidewalk, arms wrapped around their middle, a small bounce in their stance as they waited for me to arrive. Helena, on the other hand, was nowhere in sight. I asked Ales where she was and she gave me the saddest smile before saying, *"Her parents told her no more study dates and to come straight home after school."*

The entire walk home from school, I sent text after text to Helena. She ignored them all. Probably because she was studying and I was nothing but an interruption. After a fifth unanswered text, I stashed my phone in my pocket and told myself she would text after she was done studying.

Hours passed without any response. Focusing on my own homework had become a challenge. I checked my phone too many times to count. When I still hadn't heard from her by the end of dinner, I decided to call her.

"You're upset, I get it."

"Do you, Ander? Do you get it?"

The irritation in her tone isn't for me specifically. She is just angry with the situation. Angry that her parents got reports back from her teachers and her grades had barely improved. Angry that they're choosing to put her on lockdown until her grades get better.

I love Helena, but it isn't fair for her to put her rage on my shoulders. I will gladly share the burden, help ease her through her pain, but I won't be her punching bag. I've been in those shoes at home all my life. I cannot bear being that person with her too.

"Actually, yeah," I say, harsher than intended. "It may not be my grades that my mom attacks me for, but I get it. I've had a target on my back all of my life. Nothing I do is good enough for anyone. So yeah, Helena, I completely understand."

"Ander..." My name on her lips is an apology laced with pity, and I hate it.

"Maybe you have the right idea."

A storm brews in my chest. Fury and hurt and heartache swirling in a vicious tornado beneath my sternum. All it does is fuel the bad, the dark, the wrong ideas. The pain is bitter on my tongue but familiar. Comfortable. An old friend.

"What are you talking about?"

"You're busy. You need to focus." I close my eyes and grind my molars. "So here's me letting go. Here's me relieving you of another burden. Here's me setting you free... of me."

"Ander, no."

I ignore her protest. "It's done." *I'm done.*

She sniffles on the other end of the phone. "That's not what I want." Desperation laces her tone. "Please don't do this,

Ander. I love you." The sentiment is a whispered plea on her tongue.

The backs of my eyes sting. "Love you, too." I inhale a deep, shaky breath. "But I'd rather love you from afar than be your hurt."

Pulling the phone away from my ear, she says something else I don't hear before I end the call.

White hot pain sears my chest. I press the heel of my hand to my sternum, trying to stave off the hurt. All it does is burn hotter, intensify with each beat of my heart, grow exponentially bigger and spread like cancer throughout my body.

Jerking forward, I sit up, grab my phone, and launch it across the room with a thunderous scream. I curl my fingers into a fist, my nails digging deep into the flesh of my palms. The small cuts a reminder I still feel *something*. A reminder of the only feeling that never lets me down. Pain.

I open the drawer in my bedside table, fling notes and photos and false promises across the room, searching for an old friend buried deep in the back corner. I unearth the book, yank it out, and flip through the pages until I hit the one I'm searching for. Shoved in the middle of the book, the metal catches the light and glimmers with an all too familiar promise.

My lungs heave as I stare down at it. My heart hammers in my chest as I brush the worn pages. I take the blade in my fingers and study the sharp edge as memories of all the times I pressed the shiny metal to my skin flood in. The initial sting. The hiss from my lips as it split my skin and released all the hurt in the form of blood and tears.

I close my eyes, hands trembling as I swallow down the idea of adding new scars.

"No," I whisper to no one as my eyes peel open. "No," I rasp out with less confidence.

I set the blade back in the book, place the book in the drawer, and slam it shut.

This phase with Helena won't last. She said hurtful things, I said hurtful things, but neither of us meant them. I am not the source of her pain, but I happened to be in her line of fire when she exploded. Lashing out is all it is from both of us.

This will pass. Things will get better. *We* will get better.

We *have* to get better.

Knuckles rap on my door, but I don't respond. The light squeak of the knob twisting echoes through the room as the door opens. I already know who walked in. The same person who's been checking on me several times a day for weeks. The only person I can count on.

"Baby A, you awake?"

I don't answer. Don't move. Don't acknowledge my sister's presence in the room, like every other time.

This never stops her. If anything, my silence, my absence, my slow shutdown push her more. Forces her to seek me out and speak to me more often.

She worries. If I were her, I'd worry too.

Stepping around the bed, she sits next to where I'm curled loosely in the fetal position. She brings a hand to my face, brushes her fingers over my cheekbone, my temple, through my hair. I don't meet her eyes. Don't lean into her touch. Don't blink.

Concern bleeds from her pores and covers me like a

blanket of anxiety. I hate it. Hate her worry. Hate her pity. And if I did meet her gaze, I'd hate the unshed tears I know are there.

"Dinner's ready."

Again, I don't answer. I have no plans to eat with my family. Mom will bitch the entire meal when I don't come out. She will speak loud enough for me to hear her through the walls, to hear her disappointment. Then, after she bitches for thirty minutes, she will wrap my uneaten food with plastic wrap, put it in the fridge, and tell Dad how hard she worked on a dinner I didn't eat. How I have no respect for her or the effort she puts into making meals.

Eventually, when all the lights are out and everyone falls asleep, I will leave my room and eat enough to barely satiate my growling stomach. Drink enough water to keep me going.

"She misses you," Ales whispers as her fingers ghost my forehead.

A knife pierces the center of my chest at her words. *She misses you.* Wish I believed her. Wish I believed anyone could miss me. But I know the truth. No one misses me. No one cares.

Ales leans into me, wraps an arm around my twisted form, and kisses my forehead. A sniffle sounds in my ear as she hugs me tighter. "Love you, Baby A." Then she releases me, rises from the bed, and leaves my room.

The second the door clicks shut, I curl into a tighter ball. Hug my knees to my chin and free an ounce of the pain. Release a little of the hurt as tears leak from my eyes.

She misses you.

And I forget how to breathe without her.

CHAPTER 29
HELENA

Four and a half painful months. Were they worth it? Yes and no. It was lonely and dreadful and harrowing, but I managed to pull all my grades up.

I stare down at the report card in my hand, at the A's and B's printed on the small scrap of paper. Pride blooms in my chest at the accomplishment. Right beside pride, though, is this unending emptiness. Dark and hollow and cold. A place that was once warm and bright and filled with love and light and laughter. A place reserved solely for Anderson, who I haven't seen or spoken to since late January.

He hasn't walked home with us from school for months. Hasn't responded to any of the texts or calls or notes I sent via Lessa. After my regretful blowup, he shut me out.

Can't say I blame him. If our roles were reversed, I can't say I wouldn't have done the same.

Although I deserve his silence, I pray he will forgive me for my heat-of-the-moment outburst. I pray he will give me

The bell rings and I swipe up my backpack, beelining for the door. People wish me a great summer as I pass, but I don't stop to return the sentiment or spark conversation. No, my only goal is to leave school on swift feet and make it to Anderson's school before he bolts.

"Lena," Lessa yells through the throng of bodies as I exit the hallway.

I don't stop for her. I push forward and slow jog to the sidewalk lining the front of the school. A minute later, my muscles burn as I switch from a jog to running. My pulse whooshes behind my ears, my lungs begging for more air as I eat up the distance.

Then I see him, already on the sidewalk near the opposite end of the middle school campus. His gait is wide and his stride is quick and determined as he trudges forward.

I open my mouth to yell his name, but my voice won't come. So I push harder, run faster, chase after him. And just before he turns the corner, I catch up to him, grab his arm, and yank him back as I skid to a stop.

My lungs tighten in my chest. My heart beats an uncontrollable rhythm beneath my breastbone. The muscles in my legs are on fire and ready to buckle. But none of that matters because he is here.

"Ander." I wheeze and hold up a hand. "Please." I lift my arms in an attempt to ease my breathing. "Wait."

He doesn't say anything as his eyes roam my face. The muscles in his jaw flex a moment before he looks away.

As I wait for my breathing to settle, I take him in. After eighteen horrendous weeks, I scan his face. A face I have missed.

The first thing I notice is his sunken cheeks, the tightness of his skin on his bones. Dark marks rest below his dull blue eyes that refuse to meet mine. He tucks his hands in the front pocket of his hoodie, the hood over his head. Even with the baggy material concealing his body, I see his slender frame. The weight he has lost.

"Ander," I say more confidently as I reach for him.

He flinches and takes a step back. The small move is a slap to the face. A hit I deserve.

"Hey," I say, a touch softer. "Please." I pull my hand back and clasp both together at my waist. "Can we talk?"

At this, his eyes finally meet mine. The single glance is loaded with agony and rage and distrust. All of which I earned.

"Why?"

I hate the sharpness of his single-word question. Hate that I made him want to question why I would want to speak or spend time with him. But I created this wound, and it is up to me to heal it.

"Because I have a lot to say, starting with an apology." I glance down the sidewalk and see more people filing out of the school. "Can we go somewhere? Please, Ander."

He looks past me with a shake of his head. I see the war brewing inside him. Two sides of the coin, each begging to be the victor. As much as I don't deserve a yes from him, I want it. I want him to agree if only for a few minutes, to listen.

"Please," I whisper with desperation on my tongue.

Glassy eyes meet mine for a beat before he starts walking. "Fine."

Instead of going to his house, he guides us toward the park in the center of Main Street. It isn't private, but the benches and tables are quiet as most kids and teens go off to celebrate the end of the school year elsewhere.

He unhooks his backpack from his shoulders and tosses it to the ground near the base of a tree. Dropping down next to it, he leans back against the tree and hugs his knees to his chest, closing me out. I set my backpack on his and sit at his side, my arm brushing his as I mirror his posture.

"I panicked," I say, a breath above a whisper. "My parents basically grounded me for months and I panicked. I was angry with them. Yelled at them every day for weeks. Said things to them I now regret. All because they want me to succeed." I swallow past the thickness in my throat. "Most of all, I hate how I treated you. How I spoke to you last time we talked. How I lashed out and hurt you." Hesitantly, I lean to the side and lay my head on his shoulder. "I was an asshole to you, and you didn't deserve my cruelty." My eyes fall shut as I breathe in his earthy scent. "Sorry is nowhere near enough for how I feel, Ander, but I am so sorry."

We sit unmoving against the tree. Hour-long minutes pass in the most deafening silence. As each second ticks by, I question if my apology is too late. Question if my explanation is not enough. Pray that he is simply mulling over my words, processing them all and figuring out how to respond.

Without a doubt, I own how horribly I treated him these past months. I own the wretched decisions I made to please my parents. When I finished my schoolwork each night, I should have texted or called Anderson. Should have made an effort to be a better girlfriend. He would have supported me regardless of disliking the new boundaries in place.

Instead, I punished us both. I busted ass on my classes, pulled up my grades, and lost myself and my friends in the process. It didn't help that my parents were breathing down my neck. The constant reviews of my homework. The unending questions about college applications and what major I plan to apply for. In the heat of one of many arguments, I barked out how pressured I felt. That I didn't want to go to college, so I definitely didn't care about a major.

For weeks, our conversations were vicious circles of me yelling and them putting their foot down. Though I am proud of the hard work I put in, the college applications I filled out, I still ask the same question.

Was it worth it?

Because right now, Anderson's silence tells me it may not have been. How can it be worth it if I lose him?

"Can't do that again," he mumbles, voice scratchy. I feel his head shake before he continues. "I get that shit went sideways, but I won't be your punching bag."

Stab. One I rightfully earned.

"I promise."

He sniffles and lifts an arm to his face, dragging the sleeve of his hoodie across his nose. "Not gonna lie. I've been pretty fucked up since the last time we talked."

I didn't have all the details, but after a few weeks of my house arrest, Lessa told me Anderson had shut down. He didn't leave his room. Hardly ate or drank. Maybe spoke a word or two to her on occasion, but nothing more and to no one else.

And with each fresh detail, all I thought was how it was my fault. He didn't react the way he did to gain attention or inflict pain in return. But the wound I created grew deeper, gnarlier each day I didn't see him after school, each time he refused my call or didn't answer my texts.

I formed the wound with unkind, false words. Now it is time to heal the wound.

"Lessa didn't tell me everything, but she told me plenty." I twist into his side, curl my arm around the bend of his, pressing myself to his side. "I will never be sorry enough for how I treated you." I tug down his hood and press my forehead to his temple. The backs of my eyes sting as tears blur my vision. "Wish I could take it all back. Wish I could go back and say something else. Do something other than what I did. I was angry at my parents and I took it out on you." Slowly, I drop my chin and press a kiss to his sallow cheek. "God, I missed you. Missed this. Us."

To my complete surprise, he twists and shifts his arms. In a swift and unexpected move, he drops his legs, grabs my hips, picks me up, and drags me into his lap, my legs straddling him. He bands his arms around me in a suffocating hug as he nuzzles my neck. My arms weave around his shoulders as I fold into him. Hug him with every ounce of love I own.

And just as I close my eyes, he begins to shake beneath me. Not a light tremble of fear. No, this is a full-body, no-holds-barred tremor. His arms and legs quake uncontrollably. Dampness hits my skin where my shoulder and neck meet. His limbs constrict more and more with each shuddered breath he takes.

"God, I'm so sorry," I whisper against his skin.

He squeezes me painfully, but I don't dare tell him to let up. If anything, I mentally beg for more. Beg for him to release every ounce of hurt I inflicted and return it to me tenfold.

Not sure how long we sit like this—quiet and completely engulfed in each other—but as the sun shifts behind the trees in the park, I suggest we leave. Go to my house or his. Go somewhere to spend time together, alone. To just lie around in each other's arms and ignore the outside world a little longer.

And as we leave the park hand in hand, I send a silent thank you to whoever listens.

Thank you for him. Thank you for his forgiveness.

CHAPTER 30

ANDERSON

Things are better with Helena, but they still feel *off*. With her college applications in and her grades better, her parents thought it was a great idea to get a summer job. I'm not so keen on the idea. Don't get me wrong, I'm happy she enjoys the fifteen hours a week she works at the local clothing boutique. But it sucks to see her less. Again.

So, I take it upon myself to frequent the store on the days she works. The owner isn't there most days when she works, but I get a few strange looks from the women in the store. Which I completely understand since the store doesn't hold a single piece of attire I'd wear.

"We should go hiking this weekend," I suggest as I sift through colorful sundresses. "Since you're not working, and you'll probably miss the annual camping trip, we should get away for a couple nights. Hike and camp one of the trails nearby."

She folds a shirt on the front display table and straightens others that are out of place. "I like this plan." Moving to the accessory rack near the wall, she peeks over her shoulder. "Friday and Saturday? Then back early Sunday?"

God, just the idea of being completely isolated with Helena makes my skin buzz. Months apart damaged both of us in different ways. But a weekend away together... damn, I can't think of anything better.

"Sounds perfect. Think your dad will be cool about it? Just the two of us camping with no adult supervision."

She organizes the hair accessories then shifts to the jewelry. And for a beat, I simply watch her move. The sway of her hips as she somewhat dances to the music in the shop. Her delicate, thin fingers as they pluck a necklace from the wrong hook and place it on the correct one. The occasional bop of her head as she hums to herself.

Helena Williams isn't just beautiful on the outside, she radiates love and charm and everything good from within. We may have had hiccups and bad days in our relationship, but every couple does. How do you love the good days if you don't know what a bad day looks like?

"After second semester, I've earned a weekend away without criticism. Dad will probably freak out at first"—she looks across the shop where I sit—"but he'll get over it. I mean, he knows you. Has known you for twelve years. What is there to argue about?"

Her question is rhetorical, but I answer anyway. "Uh, let's start with the fact that I'm your boyfriend. Then there's the whole thing about dads not wanting their daughters to spend time alone with boys."

She finishes straightening the jewelry and makes her way across the shop, dropping down in my lap and wrapping her arms around my neck. She presses a chaste kiss to my lips then straightens.

"Ander, you're not just any boy. We've spent plenty of time alone together over the last however many years. We've camped together every summer since I was five. You've seen me in my bathing suit, held my hand in public, called me a nickname no one else does for years."

I hug her close and inhale her sweet, earthy fragrance. "And your dad thought I was just a friend during all those moments." I sit back and look up at her. "We've been more than friends for longer than they realize." Once her dad learns this, his mind will scour every single moment we have spent together.

The bell over the door jingles and Helena bolts from my lap. "Welcome to In Stitches. Anything I can help you find?"

Two ladies weave through the clothing racks and head for the swimwear. "No, thank you."

I rise from the chair and straighten my shirt. Taking her hand in mine, I kiss Helena's cheek. "See you in a bit. I'll tell my parents I'm camping, but I'm leaving you out of the equation. Mom gives me enough shit as is, I don't need more."

A soft pout plumps her lips. "I'll talk to Mom and Dad tonight. Maybe have dinner at my house and we can talk with them together?" She phrases the last part more like a question.

Mr. and Mrs. Williams have always been nice to me and my family, but I have to wonder if they will see me differently if they know I am more than Helena's friend. And which of them will be worse? Dads can be pretty fierce when it comes to their daughters, or so I've heard. But from what I know, all the wrath comes from mothers.

"Dinner would be nice. Text me when to come over."

She lays a peck on my lips. "Love you, Ander."

"Love you too, North."

"Are you out of your mind?"

"Dad…" Helena admonishes. "Can you not be a jerk? Please."

I stab a piece of chicken on my plate and shove it in my mouth. Sitting across the table from Helena, I nudge her foot under the table. At least, I hope it is her foot. Her eyes meet mine a second later and I sigh in relief.

"So let me get this straight. You and Anderson want to go camping this weekend? Alone. For two and a half days."

I swallow the bite in my mouth and take a sip of water. Helena's cheeks are pink as her dad gives her questioning eyes. Taking a deep breath, I decide to speak up, even though Helena said she wanted to do all the talking.

"Yes, sir."

His bold stare slams into my eyes. "Boy, I've known you almost your entire life. Still doesn't mean I'm okay with you spending a romantic weekend away with my seventeen-year-old daughter. Hell, you're only fourteen. What do your parents have to say about the idea?"

This is where I gauge exactly how much to say, how much to divulge. It isn't common practice for people to share the worst parts of themselves. And like most people, I doubt my mother is forthright about how she talks down to her son. Dad isn't as bad as Mom, but he sure as hell doesn't stand up and tell her to stop.

"Sir, I wish my parents cared about what I did as much as you and Mrs. Williams care about Helena."

At this, his eyes soften. Not in pity, but the type of sadness any parent should feel if a child is treated unfairly or poorly. And the longer we sit in silence, the more he digests my words, the more he sees a different side of the boy he thought he knew.

He works his jaw back and forth as he mulls over his indecision. It'd be easy to open my mouth and prattle off all the ways I will keep Helena, his only daughter, safe. Pocket knives and bear spray. My knowledge of the outdoors might have impressed him if he knew nothing about me, but a lot of what I learned over the years was from him. As the only boy during our annual camping trips, all the dads circled around me with outdoor survival skills. Some I retained, most of them from Mr. Williams.

"I still don't like the idea," he mutters under his breath.

Across the table, the corners of Helena's mouth curve up the slightest bit. She knows he will say yes.

"Anderson, dear?"

My attention shifts to the opposite end of the dinner table, where Mrs. Williams studies her daughter. "Yes, ma'am?"

Green eyes so similar to Helena's meet mine. "How long?"

My brows bunch in confusion. "Only a couple days. Promise we'll be back Sunday afternoon."

"No." She gives a subtle shake of her head before setting her fork down. "How long have you and Helena been dating?"

"Mom…"

Why didn't I expect this question? I should have known one of her parents would ask. But the idea of finally having time, real time, with Helena again clouded my normal thought processes.

My attention drifts to Helena for a beat, a soft smile on my lips, before I sit taller in my seat and return my gaze to Mrs. Williams. "Officially, it's been almost a year—minus the past few months. But we've been close for years." I swallow to quell the nervousness building beneath my diaphragm. I hold her gentle stare as I say the next words. "She's my best friend."

A strange silence surrounds us as no one responds. And it's odd, the comfort I feel sitting at this table. Telling Helena's parents I am more than her best friend's little brother or just a friend wasn't on the slate when I walked through the front door. But now that the confession is out, now that our relationship is a little less secretive, all I feel is relief.

"We love you, Anderson," Mrs. Williams says, and my body sighs at the simple but powerful sentiment. Warmth blooms in my chest. "But we can't allow what happened this past school year to happen again." Though her voice holds no malice, all the warmth from seconds ago bleeds away. "If Reg is okay with this weekend, then you have my blessing." She picks up her wineglass and takes a small sip. "But things will be different the rest of the summer and next school year. I hope you understand."

Beneath the table, I curl my fingers into fists. Dig my nails into my palms as I take slow, deep breaths. Tell myself it isn't something I specifically did. She doesn't disapprove of *me* or my relationship with Helena. She is simply concerned for her daughter. Wants her to succeed. Wants the best for her, just as I do.

Whether or not that includes me remains to be seen.

"Yes, ma'am," I say, relaxing my fingers in my lap. "Next year will bring big changes for us all." I look to Helena. "Senior year for Helena, Ales, and Mags. Freshman year for me." I pick at my thumb cuticle a second before clamping down on the digit with my other fingers. "I hope we can all help each other."

Those last words are a subliminal plea, a desperate petition for her or Mr. Williams to not rob me of time with Helena. Not like before.

A soft smile plumps her cheeks, but it doesn't touch her eyes. "We'll see."

With those two words, a touch of the darkness slips back in. A niggling of doubt eats away at the happiness I regained. And I hate how easily it settles in my bones and chills my core. A chill that never lets go.

CHAPTER 31

HELENA

It's a true miracle we convinced my parents to be okay with this trip. I thought Dad would put his foot down, a throaty *no* on his lips. But it was Mom's opinion that held more weight. Embarrassing as it was to sit there and listen to her and Dad ask Anderson question after question, relief washed over me that it all happened in one shot.

After serious deliberation, they conceded… with stipulations, of course.

When this weekend trip ended, I had to spend more nonworking hours studying. As the end of the school year approached, all juniors were handed a list of books to read over the summer as well as topics to research. Mom and Dad took it a step further and requested summer assignments to keep my mind fresh and in study mode.

Thankful as I am that they love me and want nothing but my success, I despise what they have stolen from me by piling constant work on my shoulders.

"Burgers or chicken?"

Snapping out of my thoughts, I watch Anderson riffle

through the cooler. For a moment, I simply stare in silence. Study his slender build, his black shirt a little loose on the lean muscles of his arms and chest. His cargo shorts baggy on his hips and covering most of his slim legs.

Bulky guys have never garnered my attention. The slight muscles Anderson has have come from years outdoors, hiking through the woods and walking around town. And personally, I prefer his lithe frame to that of jocks.

"Chicken," I finally say.

He peeks over his shoulder and narrows his eyes. "Were you checking out my butt, North?"

I push off my camping chair and join him at the cooler. Give his butt a quick slap and squat at his side. "What if I was?"

He chuckles. "I'd tell you to carry on."

I playfully slap his arm. "You're ridiculous." I turn toward the nonperishables and stare down at the minimal food we brought. "What can I help with?"

He points to the frying pan. "Hand me that and I'll start on the chicken. Want to cut up potatoes?"

"On it."

Years of camping have taught us a lot. We may not be chefs, but we have basic cooking skills. We also know how to make something from next to nothing. The simplest of meals made over a campfire can be pretty damn good.

I get to work on the potatoes, cutting them into small chunks so they cook quickly. Anderson adds a pat of butter to the pan over the fire, then adds precut strips of chicken to the pan, sprinkling them with herbs. Sizzling fills the air, the pungent aroma of the herbs hitting my nose.

A minute after he flips the chicken, he pushes the chicken

to the outside of the pan and leaves enough open space in the middle for the potatoes.

"Done?" he asks and I nod. "Toss 'em in."

Once the potatoes are in the pan, I sprinkle in more herbs and some garlic powder. He reaches for the tote next to the cooler, grabs the roll of foil, tears off a piece, and tents it over the pan.

While dinner finishes cooking over the fire, we clean up our mess. The entire time, I peek at Anderson from the corner of my eye. Watch his every move. Notice how he doesn't second-guess what to do next. Think how easy it is to do this with him—not camping, but existing.

Anderson has always given me a level of comfort no one else provides. We move with ease around each other. We don't always need words to convey how we feel. As if we just know what the other feels or thinks or wants. I love our muted moments as much as the ones when he whispers words of love or adoration.

Our months apart earlier this year were nothing short of torture. I detested my parents for tearing me away from life, from my friends, from Anderson. Yes, I appreciated them for loving me enough to want nothing but the best. But being isolated had damaged so much. Not just Anderson and our relationship but with me too.

The more I lost touch with everyone, Anderson especially, the more anxiety crept in. I questioned everything and every-one. Lost trust in my intuition. After weeks of not talking with Anderson, I panicked more often than not. His dark days wiggled their way into my memory. Planted seeds and night-mares in my mind. Nightmares I couldn't shake because he refused to talk or respond to my countless messages. Were it not for Lessa and her daily reports at school, I would've defied my parents and gone to him.

Part of me wishes I would have done it anyway. With his sunken cheeks and starved frame on the last day of school, I should have done something sooner. Somehow, I should have tried harder.

Thankfully, that is behind us now. And I have no intention of going back.

"Food's ready," Anderson says, folding the foil and setting it aside.

I grab plates and hold them near the fire as he portions the chicken and potatoes between both. He sets the pan on a small rock pile to cool as we park in our chairs and dive in.

I moan around the first bite. "So good." Something about food cooked over a fire makes my mouth water. Grilled meats and vegetables are good, but there is magic in cooking campfire meals. The food and methods are simple, but they have something you just don't get from home.

Anderson nudges my elbow with his, a smirk on his lips as I turn to face him. "Never heard you moan for anyone else's chicken and potatoes."

"Yours is the best." I take another bite and moan again. "Duh."

"Noted." He chuckles. "But I also don't think our parents would appreciate their children moaning." He points his fork in my direction. "Not like that."

My cheeks heat as I stab another piece of chicken and potato on my fork and shove it in my mouth. This time, I refrain from my appreciative sounds.

We finish the rest of dinner in silence, cleaning our dishes afterward. And then the first dose of apprehension kicks in.

We're alone. Together. In the woods. Not a soul for miles.

I have zero fear of being alone with Anderson. We have spent countless hours and days together, just the two of us. Movie nights, summer days at the town diner, hikes on previous camping trips.

But this... this is different.

There is no chance of anyone interrupting us. No one will join us or pull one of us aside. We aren't surrounded by familiar faces or restaurant patrons. This isn't our annual camping trip, and there won't be any parents in a few hours to tell us to go to our tent.

"Walk to the lookout?" Anderson reaches for my hand, lacing my fingers with his.

On a trail just outside of town, we set up camp in a small alcove. Dad let me use his truck for the weekend, and I drove us to the trailhead, parking in the small lot. Aside from the gear on our backs, we brought a small cooler, a tub of nonper-ishables and dishware, and jugs of water. We hiked close to a mile before we set up camp, the alcove providing some shelter and protecting our back side.

I didn't worry about hikers nabbing any of our belongings. It's the animals whose habitat we shared that I worried about breaking into the cooler or wrecking our tent.

As if reading my thoughts, Anderson gives my hand a gentle squeeze. "Everything will be fine." He points down the path. "It's maybe a quarter mile to the lookout." He pivots, brings a hand to my chin, and lifts my gaze to his. "You, me, the sunset." He drops his lips to mine. "Then we'll come back."

I melt under his touch. How the hell can I say no to that?

"'Kay," I rasp out.

We walk the path without hurry, breathing in the rich scents of earth and pine. His thumb strokes the length of mine every few steps, his eyes on the trail ahead. I peek up at him from beneath my lashes, study the slope of his nose, the now sharper angle of his jaw and chin, and the light dusting of blond hair on both. But my eyes stay on his lips the longest. The perfect cupid's bow, his lips not too thin or full.

A smile ghosts his lips as we reach the lookout point, but his eyes remain forward. "Thinking about kissing me, North?" When I don't answer right away, his smile stretches wider as his eyes meet mine. "It's okay, you know."

I lift a brow and shake my head. "Yeah, Ander, I know." I chuckle. "And what if I was?"

Arm on the wood rail, he inches closer, his breath warm on my ear. "I'd say act on it. God knows I always think about kissing you."

Heat blooms in my chest, trickling through my limbs, up my neck, and low in my belly as he kisses the line of my jaw, stopping just before my lips. My pulse whooshes in my ears with his lips a breath from mine. But he doesn't lean in to seal the kiss. No, he hovers and waits and tortures me with ragged breaths and desperation.

I fist the cotton of his shirt, suck in a sharp breath, and close the space between us. His smile falls away as I take his bottom lip between mine, as I lick the seam of his lips, as I dip my tongue inside and taste him. He moans and I swallow down the sound. And then we're moving, my back pressed against the rail as his hands frame my face and he deepens the kiss further.

The kiss feels obscene, an indecent display out in the open. Our touches or kisses have never been this... hungry in public. Then again, we have never been so completely alone in public. No watchful eyes. No town gossips or school blabbermouths.

I've never felt more free—on my own and with him.

And just as the thought crosses my mind, he breaks the kiss and rests his forehead on mine. Our ragged breaths mingle with the warm summer breeze, his fingers toying with my hair as mine tighten their hold on his shirt.

"Love you, North. So damn much." He drops a chaste kiss to my lips.

"Love you, Ander."

"Much as I want to keep kissing you, I want to watch this sunset with you too." Soft laughter leaves his lips and I can't help but do the same.

"Fine," I huff out in a tease. "But once that sun's down…"

"Say no more."

CHAPTER 32

ANDERSON

After pink and orange danced across the sky, Helena and I walked back to the campsite, her arm hooked around my elbow. The entire time, all I thought of was her lips and the heady kiss we had shared not long before.

Now that we are back at camp and settling in for the night, nervous energy floods my veins.

Intimacy is nothing new with us. Hand-holding. Cuddling in dark places. Sweet and indecent kisses, more so in private than public. Sex.

The three-letter word suddenly makes me sweaty. Has my fingers twitchy and eyes darting to her more often than not. Has me finding unnecessary things to do before we enter the tent and close ourselves off from the world all night.

The tent. Our two sleeping bags are situated to make one large bed. Is it stupid of me to assume we will have sex while camping? It's hot and a little muggy out. Will she wear her usual pajama shorts and tank top? Or sleep in less? Maybe she just wants to lie together and cuddle all night. Maybe she wants to sleep on her own.

Argh!

"Hey." She fills my line of sight, her hands cupping my cheeks. "What's wrong?"

I blink a few times in an attempt to clear my rampant thoughts. Take a deep breath, then another. "Nothing," I rasp out, and I almost believe myself.

"Ander." Her thumbs stroke my cheekbones. "It's me. Just me." She presses her lips to mine for one, two, three beats of my heart before inching back and holding my gaze. "What's wrong?"

This is Helena. I can tell her anything.

I lick my lips and swallow past any residual unease. "Started thinking about our sleeping situation and kind of spiraled."

Her brows pinch at the middle, confusion marring her expression. "Why?"

Good question. I shrug.

"Ander." My name rolls off her tongue like a litany. "It's me. Just me," she repeats her words from a moment ago. "It's us." Her hands drift north, combing through my hair, her nails grazing my scalp. "You never have to worry when it comes to us."

I want to believe those last words, that I never have to worry about us or our relationship. But then I flash back to the tail end of winter and all of spring. Remember what it was like to not see her, touch her, or love her for months. Remember the emptiness, the darkness I existed in.

"I'm here, Ander," she whispers, the fading firelight dancing on her skin. Then her lips are on mine. "I'm here." Her hands trail down my neck, my chest, my abdomen before her fingers hook in the belt loops of my shorts. "I'm here."

My eyes roll back as I deepen the kiss. *She's here.*

She tugs me forward, her tongue tasting mine as she inches me off the chair. "I'm here." And then she rises to her feet, pulling me up with her. Fumbling us toward the tent, our lips glued together until we duck inside and zip out the world.

Piece by piece, we slowly strip off our clothes. With each kiss, each gentle touch, we rediscover each other. Memorize curves and scars. Caress peaks and lips. Moan names and beg for more without interruption.

In a small alcove on a ridge outside Lake Lavender, I fall deeper for Helena Williams. And I never want to come back up.

CHAPTER 33
HELENA

I read the same sentence for the fifth time, huffing in annoyance at my lack of progress.

"Everything okay?" Anderson asks, his fingers brushing softly on the bare skin of my thigh.

Not really, I want to say but keep to myself. Saying such things will only stir up more questions. And the last thing I want to tell Anderson, my boyfriend, the guy I love and who loves me equally, if not more, is that his constant touch is distracting me from summer homework. Bad enough I have to read a book I don't want to read. No sense in making the situation ten times worse.

"Fine." I slip my bookmark between the pages. "Just having trouble getting into the book."

Anderson bookmarks his own page and sets his book down on the side table. When I told him earlier in the week I needed to catch up on my summer school assignments, he suggested doing so on the loungers on my back patio. A little summer sun to make it less daunting.

Yesterday was a snap. I breezed through several chapters

before we stopped for lunch. Then I read a few more. But yesterday, we hadn't had this constant contact. Yesterday, I hadn't been thrown off by his touch on my skin.

And for some unknown reason, today I don't want it. Today, I want solitude. To dive headfirst into this book and get it over with. To be done with all this excessive work.

Does that make me a bad person? A bad girlfriend? The twinge in my gut says it does.

"Talk to me." His words are soft, consoling. A desire to help.

His offer shouldn't rub me the wrong way, but it does. I should be grateful. That I'm not is grating my irritation further.

I push up from the lounger and away from him. An invisible bubble forms around me, heavy and suffocating. A constant pressure, reminding me of all the things I haven't done, all the people I need to please. Mom and Dad mean well, but every time they *check in* on my schoolwork, every time they ask if I've heard back from my college applications, this unbearable weight presses on my chest. Add Anderson into the mix and I feel like I'm being pulled in ten different directions.

None of this is his fault, but something needs to give.

"It's nothing. Just stress."

Anderson looks off in the distance, his eyes glazing over as he searches for what to say. "How long have we known each other?" Eyes still unfocused, he continues without me answering. "It's rhetorical because we both know the answer." Rising from the lounger, he walks to the rail lining the edge of the patio and stares out into the trees beyond the property. "Things are shitty, I get it. Your parents, school, work... me."

The muscles of his jaw flex, irritation darkening his expression as he looks at me over his shoulder. "But don't lie. Not to me."

Nausea rolls in my belly and I swallow past the thickness in my throat. I ball my fingers into fists at my side before relaxing my hands once more. One foot in front of the other, I step closer to the edge, closer to him, stopping a few feet away.

"Ander..."

He shakes his head. "Don't say something just to appease me."

I inhale deeply. Once, twice, a third time. My brows pinch together as the nausea in my belly slowly climbs up my throat. The last thing I want is to hurt him, but my honesty will do exactly that. I love him more than anything, but I feel so torn.

"I've been struggling."

With my admission out in the open, he turns to face me fully. "How so?"

Now it's my turn to lose focus in the trees. To mull over how to explain the stress I've felt these past months. Without hurting him.

"Ander, I literally have no clue what to do."

His eyes sear my profile, but he doesn't say a word.

"Every night around the dinner table, my parents harp on me about school. They want to know what my plan is for senior year. What I'll do to keep my grades up. Questions about college applications and if I've decided on a major yet." I suck in a sharp breath, praying for an ounce of relief, but it's nowhere near enough. It never is. "It's like I'm one of those carnival acts. The performer balancing plates on several sticks. They keep spinning and spinning, and all I can do is watch and wait for one to fall."

Anderson takes a step in my direction, his hand on the rail, ready to reach and comfort. To take away some of the hurt. But this can't be swept aside with soft words and warm embraces.

"Sorry I'm taking this out on you." My green eyes meet his blues. "But every time I try to get ahead"—I point back to the loungers—"like reading books I have no desire to read, something throws me off."

He inches closer, his fingers gripping the rail as he nods. "And today, I distracted you." Though inches away, he sounds distant.

I swallow past the truth crawling up my throat. "Yes," I whisper.

Silence engulfs us as we stand there, me looking at him, him staring off into the distance. With each passing breath, I see small, subtle shifts in his demeanor. A hardening. A wall erecting.

Bile climbs my throat and dances over the back of my tongue because I know what this is. Anderson won't throw in the towel on us, not fully, but he will sacrifice his happiness. He will give me the solitude I need but won't dare ask for. He will stand on the sidelines and fade away so I can flourish.

The worst part... my mouth refuses to form the words to stop him.

With a nod, he releases the rail, takes a step back, pivots, and walks back to the table beside the loungers. He swipes his book from the surface, pauses, and looks over his shoulder, his eyes on the ground. "Let me know when you have free time."

A knife pierces my heart at his words, the blade twisting left then right as he takes one step then another and disappears from view. Seconds feel like minutes as I stare at where I last saw him. Disbelief splinters my chest while an insufferable ache expands beneath my breastbone.

What have I done?

Much as I want to chase after him, much as I want to tell him there has to be another way, I remain rooted in place. All it will do is make him run faster and farther. I may not have said I needed space, but everything I *did* say indicated as much. And like the selfless person he is, Anderson does exactly that. Gives me space.

But should I let him? And for how long? I fear there are no right answers.

CHAPTER 34
ANDERSON

The parents canceled the annual summer camping trip.

"If the girls can't be there, I don't see the point."

Maybe if I'd been born with a vagina, Mom would like me more. Maybe she would consider how badly I need the time away. Or maybe Dad should have piped up and declared a boys-only trip.

None of the above happened, and by no means am I surprised. Because no one gives a fuck about Anderson. No one gives a fuck about what I want or how I feel or how much those trips away from town mean.

No one. Fucking. Cares.

So, I loaded up my gear, told Dad I was camping on my own and I'd be back soon.

Fuck them all.

Hands over the fire, I rub them together in an effort to stave off the relentless chill. A chill that settled in my bones two weeks ago when I left Helena's house. A chill I can't shake no matter what.

A persistent pang singes my chest like a branding iron that won't quit. It sears and scars and taunts me with false promises of recovery. False promises of better days to come. Promises I so badly want to believe.

"She just needs time," I mutter, my words catching on the breeze and floating away.

Every day, I say the exact same words. Every day, I pray it is the day she texts or calls and says she wants to see me.

But every night, disappointment slaps me in the face. Every night, I take another step into the darkness. Because at least in the dark, I know what to expect. I know what is waiting there. I know what monsters lurk in the shadows.

In the darkness, no one lets me down.

Twisting away from the fire, I grab my pack and riffle through the front pocket. My fingers land on a small mints tin and I pluck it from the pocket. Crossing my legs on my sleeping bag, I lift the lid on the tin. Light from the fire glints on what lies inside. Shiny metal stares back with promises to never let me down.

I remove the thin blade and drop the tin at my side. Turning it over again and again, I focus on how the razor's edge glitters in the firelight. How it calls to me. How it vows to give me solace from the pain in my heart.

Shoving a sleeve up, I lift the blade to my skin and sigh when it pierces my flesh.

The burn reminds me I'm alive. The euphoric rush reminds me I still feel. But it's the trail of red spilling down my bicep that says the most. That not all pain is permanent.

CHAPTER 35
HELENA

"Senior year," Lessa says on a sigh. Her gaze shifts to me, a smile brightening her expression before she looks to Mags. "This is it. This is the end." She wraps an arm around each of us and walks farther into the school. "After this, we get to explore and conquer the world."

Exploring sounds incredible, but conquering… I'll leave that up to her.

"All I want is for it to be over," I admit. Yes, college is just another round of school, but at least we get to choose our path.

Lessa releases us and skips ahead, spinning around to face us. "I see it all so clearly." She walks backward, waving a hand in front of her. "I'll own the cutest restaurant in Lake Lavender. People will drive here from all over the state to sit in my dining room."

I chuckle. "Oh yeah?"

With a purse of her lips, she nods. "Yep."

Wagging a finger between me and Mags, I ask, "And what about us?"

She taps a finger on her lips. "Hmm." After a few steps, her eyes light up. "Mags will run a dance studio in town."

I don't miss Mags's wince at the mention of dance. Since her mom passed, she hasn't set foot in the ballet studio or slipped on her pointes. She may love dance, but it was a love she shared with Mrs. Bishop.

Lessa drones on, oblivious to her discomfort. "And you, my dear Lena, will be the fashionista people all over the country talk about." This dreamy look comes over her. "Since you started working at In Stitches, I've seen the changes. Your style is on point. And you always give the best recommendations in the shop."

Over the summer, I grew to love clothes and accessories. But being a fashion designer... One, I can't see it. And two, my parents would probably lose it if I went to college to design or sell clothes. Neither Mom nor Dad has said exactly what they expect from me with college and degrees, but I doubt it's retail.

I open my mouth to retort Lessa's obvious compliment but get cut off when someone shoulder checks me and keeps walking.

"What the hell, Baby A?"

My mind swirls as I stare at the back of a black hoodie and process Lessa's words.

That was Anderson?

Before I register what I'm doing, my legs pick up the pace and usher me down the hall. Faster and faster, my muscles burn as I weave between the crowd to catch up to Anderson. Passing another cluster of lockers, I get within arm's reach, clutch his elbow and yank.

He whirls around, ripping out of my hold and raising his hand. When he sees it is me, he lets it slap against his thigh.

"What?" Jaw tight and lips in a thin line, the single word is severe on his tongue. Sharp. Cruel.

I narrow my eyes. "Did I do something wrong?"

With a shake of his head, he laughs without humor. "Nope." He steps closer, his face inches from mine. "You've done *nothing*."

And before I process the sting of his words, he spins on his heel and walks away. Just like he did a month ago.

"Catch you guys later," I say to Mags and Lessa, jogging toward the front of the school.

Not that I love school, but the entire first day was shit after the run-in with Anderson this morning. His words echoed in my ear over and over. They tormented me throughout English class. Ate away at my sanity during math. Had me on the cusp of vomiting during lunch. By the end of history class, I'd been ready to scream.

I never said I wanted to break things off with Anderson. Never said I didn't want to spend time with him.

What I did need was a way to balance it all. This is my last year. My grades and actions this year account for much more than any of the previous years combined. I can't fail. I can't let my parents down.

Unfortunately, finding a new rhythm also means having to make changes. Big changes. Changes that impact more than me.

Does it make me selfish to focus on my future? No. But it does make me callous to not think of how my decisions may hurt others. I chose to be with Anderson. I made him promises, some of which I failed to uphold. That *is* on me. But shouldn't he also be happy for me? If he loves me, shouldn't he want what's best? Even if it involves less time together.

I jog through the lot of the school, stop and scan the thinning crowd. Just as I'm about to give up, I spot him near the sidewalk. Taller than most, hood still on his head, he walks away from the school on fast feet.

Fisting my backpack straps, I run in his direction. I open my mouth to call out to him but think better of it. If he doesn't want to see or speak to me, he'll take off at the sound of my voice. Cramps pinch my side as I close the distance between us. After minutes of running, I finally reach him, shoulder checking him as I pass and whip around.

"What the—" His words cut off when his eyes meet mine. He opens his mouth to say something else but snaps it shut before taking the next step and walking past me.

"Really, Ander? Is this what we're doing now?"

At that, he stops. Hands at his sides, he curls his fingers into fists, his chest heaving. I stare at his back, silently begging him to turn around. Begging him to give me something, anything besides his anger. He tilts his head, his fingers straightening before they cinch tight again. With a slow twist of his hips, he spins around. Eyes downcast, he worries his bottom lip. Relaxes his hands. Shakes his head then swallows.

"I can't keep doing this." His words come out in a staccato. Broken. He lifts his gaze and all I see is pain. Heartache. Devastation. Dark bruises rest beneath his eyes. His cheeks are sunken in again. "I can't be at your beck and call. A romantic convenience only when *your* life is good."

"Ander..."

I take a step in his direction and he takes one back. The

backs of my eyes sting as pain ripples through his features. *I did this. I hurt him.*

"I'm sorry," I choke out. Emotion pools in my mouth and I swallow it down. "I-I didn't mean to—"

Dull blues hold my greens, and in them, I see layer upon layer of agony, of suffering, of concession. The shadow that hovered over him for so many years, the one that disappeared when he was with me, is back. But it isn't just a shadow anymore. Now it's a storm. A violent tornado, sweeping in and stealing every good and loving piece of him.

And it is all my fault.

"What can I do? How can I make this right?" I point between us.

His lips bunch as irritation consumes his expression. "I'm not some fucking project, Helena."

Helena. Not North.

"I'm not some sad little boy that needs someone to swoop in and rescue him." He takes a step in my direction. "I loved you," he bites out, tears welling in his eyes. "I love you," he says, a breath above a whisper. His eyes fall shut, his jaw working back and forth as he takes methodical deep breaths. Then his eyes open and bore into me with unmistakable force. "But my love isn't enough." A sad smile turns up the corners of his lips. "Never has been for anyone. I get it now." He takes a step back and swallows. "So, please, either say you'll stay and actually follow through or let me go."

Bile climbs up my throat, licking the back of my tongue. I open my mouth to say something but can't seem to find the words. I want to tell him I love him too. That I will always love him. I want to tell him I will make this work, that I will find a way. But try as I might, my tongue refuses to form the words. My voice refuses to make a sound.

"That's what I thought," he says, giving me his back and taking a step away.

I lurch forward and grab his arm. "No," I shout, yanking him back. I step into him, crowd him, lift my hands to his face and cup his cheeks. "No," I whisper.

Heartache mixes with fear as he holds my gaze. "Don't say it if you don't mean it." He shakes his head. "Don't you dare."

"I love you, Anderson," I breathe out. "But I'm scared." Tears well up in my eyes and blur my vision.

"Of me?"

I shake my head, a tear spilling down my cheek. "Of doing the wrong thing. Of not being enough—for you or anyone else. Of following my path and hurting you still." Inching forward, I press my forehead to his. "I'm so tired, Ander. So tired. And no matter what I do, no matter what choice I make, someone gets hurt." I worry my lips between my teeth. "How do I decide who to hurt?"

He rests his hands over mine and closes his eyes. For a moment, we simply breathe each other in. Then his thumbs stroke the tops of my hands. His breath warms my lips. He leans in a little closer and gently presses his lips to mine.

I melt under that kiss. Every ounce of uncertainty I felt over the last month vanishes.

Then his lips are gone and he pulls back. Drops his hands to his sides and straightens his spine. "We may love each other, but it's not enough." He shakes his head and steps back. "Not right now."

"Ander, what are you—"

"I'm giving you an out. Giving you the chance to do what you need to do."

Tears flood my vision once more, spilling in parallel lines

down my cheeks without care. "No," I choke out in disbelief. "No." I shake my head. "I love you, Ander."

He takes another step back. "I'll always love you, North. But it's not our time." He shrugs. "Not sure if it ever will be."

"Please don't do this." My words are desperate as I reach out for him. "Please…"

He adds more distance between us. "It's the right thing to do."

"For who?"

"For you. Always for you." He swallows. "And that's all that matters."

"I don't want the right thing if it doesn't include you."

A tear rolls down his cheek. "I'll remember that. One day down the road, I'll remind you."

Before I get another word in, before I drop to my knees and beg him to stay, he spins around and runs.

Not sure how long I stand there. I don't know how many tears I shed. But by the time Lessa and Mags catch up, tears coat my cheeks. A chill soaks me to the bone. And I can't seem to shake this horrible feeling in my gut.

I want to run after him. Run away with him. Right every wrong and rift I created between us. But he won't let me. Not now. Maybe not ever.

CHAPTER 36

ANDERSON

The past eight and a half months have been pure hell. I've spent less time at home and more time in the middle of nowhere. Mom spends most days complaining about how ungrateful I am. That I will flunk out of school if I keep avoiding life. Tells me she worries every time I leave the house because sometimes I'm gone for days.

But I don't care.

Though I'm passing with flying colors, school is a joke. *Life* is a joke. No one actually cares where I am or what I'm doing. If they did, I'd be locked in my room. Dad would've scoured every inch of forest around town when I left without so much as a word. Someone would have done something.

No one came looking. No one did anything. And it comes as no surprise.

My parents are too busy with work and socializing with friends to seek me out. Ales, Mags, and Helena have been bogged down with senior year activities, preparing for graduation and leaving for college.

College. The word is bitter on my mental tongue, but I still swallow it down. I have no choice.

Throughout the school year, while I did every possible thing to avoid Helena, she moved forward. With too much ease, if I am honest. And like my sister, she is packing up her life to drive hours across the state for college tomorrow.

Part of me wants to beg her to stay. Part of me wants to run away and follow her. But neither will happen. We haven't spoken since the start of the school year. More than anyone, I avoided her. Skipped classes or school on days when I feared bumping into her. Left the house when I heard her in Ales's room. Marred my flesh more days than not just to feel something other than sadness.

But it's never enough.

I am not enough.

Before I darted from the house yesterday, Dad caught me. Asked me, practically begged, that I be home to say farewell to Ales when she leaves for college in the morning. Much as I want to dodge Helena, I can't not say goodbye to my sister, the one person who's never actually let me down. Sure, she is busy. But she'd stop everything if I reached out.

Without Ales at home, nothing and no one will stop Mom from unloading her frustrations. And I don't think I'll be able to stand strong against her long. Not alone.

"Anderson," Dad bellows across the house. "Get out here and help see your sister off."

Begrudgingly, I push off my bed and shuffle out of the room. Ales's bossy words load the air as she directs Dad to grab the last box. Another thing I will miss, her need to direct the room.

I follow everyone outside, where Dad crams the box in the back of Ales's car, her SUV packed to the brim.

"Don't think you girls can fit anything else," Dad huffs out as he whips his arm out and slams the hatch. He winces as the box shifts and presses the rear window.

Ales jogs over to him, wraps her arms around his middle, and hugs him tight enough to crack a rib. "Thanks, Daddy. I love you."

"Love you too, sweetheart."

I take a step forward, ready to go to Ales and wish her luck at college, when a voice locks me in place.

"You almost forgot your—"

I peer over my shoulder and see Helena with a hair curler in her hand, her mouth stuck open and words lost. Her brows twitch for a split second before she swallows and walks past me to my sister.

"You almost forgot your curling wand." She opens the passenger door and tosses it into the back seat.

Her eyes find mine, but I look away and start for Ales on the driver's side. I wrap her in my arms and squeeze her with undeniable strength.

"I'll miss you," I say only loud enough for her to hear, the backs of my eyes burning. "A lot."

She tightens her hold around my middle, a sniffle hitting my ear. "I'll miss you too, Baby A." Releasing the hug, she inches back and holds my gaze. "Call or text. I don't care what time it is. If you need me, I'm here."

I swallow down her words. Swallow down that my biggest ally is leaving. "I'll be fine." My vision blurs as the lie rolls easily off my tongue. "Promise."

Her eyes dart to the side then back to me as she whispers, "It's okay to not be okay." She squeezes my biceps in her hands. "Just because I'm not *here* doesn't mean I'm not here for you."

I nod before pulling her into another fierce hug. "Love you, Ales."

"Love you too, Baby A."

Mom and Dad give Ales another round of hugs as I back away, moving to the front porch. I lean against one of the posts and watch as goodbyes are exchanged. I peek over at Helena as she wrings her fingers.

I heard Mr. and Mrs. Williams here hours ago, but I assumed Helena left with them. That she'd be with her own family until it was time to leave. Being out of the loop, I didn't know Helena was leaving from our house with Ales. I also didn't know why her parents were gone now.

As if she hears me thinking about her, she takes a few tentative steps in my direction. With each step forward, I erect the walls around my heart. Shut down the part of my heart dedicated to her.

"Hey," she says as she reaches the bottom of the steps.

"Hey," I mutter.

She takes a deep breath. "Ander, I..." Her eyes drop to the ground, her expression scrunched in confusion. "I miss you," she says, a breath above a whisper before lifting her gaze to mine.

I want to return the words. Want to tell her how much I've missed her, how shitty life has been without her, how I still love her.

But I won't. I can't.

For her, I will gladly fall apart, be less of a person, be nothing, so she has all the happiness life has to offer. For her, I will be nothing more than her best friend's little brother.

I nod, my only show of agreement. "Have a great time at college." The generic words sound all wrong. "Do amazing things."

Green eyes hold my blues, tears rimming her lids. I see everything left unsaid in the breaths that pass between us. I see every ounce of sadness she won't admit, a way to shield her own heart.

"Yeah," she whispers. "Sure." Then, to my complete surprise, she takes the steps up onto the porch and wraps her arms around my middle. "I love you, Ander. No matter what, I love you." She releases me, presses a kiss to my cheek, and walks away.

Seconds later, she and Ales hop in the car, wave through the windshield, and drive off. I reach up and hold my cheek, the burn of her kiss still hot on my skin.

I love you, North.

But love isn't always enough.

CHAPTER 37

ANDERSON

I glance left then right, not a soul in the aisle as I stare down at the small box in my hand. I peek up at the curved mirror in the corner, noting none of the store clerks are in sight. Head down, I shove the box in my pocket and bolt for the exit.

Each step forward, my breaths come in jagged bursts. Each one is another splinter in my heart.

I can't do this anymore. I don't want to do this anymore. I'm tired. So damn exhausted. And I just… can't.

In a matter of minutes, I reach home and step through the front door. Blissful silence greets me with Mom and Dad still at work for the next several hours.

I enter the kitchen, grab a soda from the fridge, then walk down the hall to my bedroom. Switching the lock in place once the door closes, I peel my hoodie off and drop it on the floor. My shirt and jeans join the hoodie. I dig into the pocket and retrieve my loot.

Dropping onto my bed, I cross my legs and stare down at

the blue letters on the white box. On a deep breath that does nothing to relieve the constant ache in my chest, I peel the box open and remove the bottle inside. I crack open the can of soda, take a sip, then set it on the nightstand. With a slow twist of the cap, I line up the two small arrows on the bottle and rub the pad of my thumb over them again and again, the ridges harsh against my skin.

With a small pop, the cap falls onto the bed, a wad of cotton stuffed inside to keep the pills from rattling. I dig out the cotton and throw it aside. Turn the bottle over and dump the pills on the bedding.

Thirty-two blue tablets.

The box says to take two for a restful sleep.

But what if all I want to do is sleep? What if I don't want to wake up?

I reach for my drink, scoop up some pills, pop them in my mouth and drink enough to make them go down. A hint of peace blankets me as the pills move to my stomach and I close my eyes.

More. I need more than just peace.

Opening my eyes, I grab another fistful of pills and swallow them down. With each swallow, I feel inches closer to the serenity I crave. And when the pills are gone, I sigh.

I set down the can and lie back on my bed. Close my eyes and let my mind drift. Soon enough, the darkness will come. The darkness that doesn't end. The darkness that frees me of pain, of obligation, of every wrongdoing.

Tears sting the backs of my eyes. "I love you, and I wish it was enough," I whisper to the one person I want here. "Wish I was enough."

My stomach churns then cramps. I swallow as my body

sends every signal it's about to throw up. Take a deep breath as my closed eyes grow heavy. Bile claws up my throat, but I shove it down with another swallow.

No.

I lift an arm, the limb heavy as I cover my mouth. Everything in me swirls, my body off-kilter as the sleeping pills break down and seep into my system. My stomach clenches, vomit hitting the back of my throat. Sweat blankets my skin, a shiver rolling up my spine and skittering over every inch of my body.

Rolling onto my side, I hug my knees to my chest. I shiver as vomit claws its way up my throat. And before I can swallow it down, everything grows heavy, darker.

My pulse whooshes violently in my ears. But it isn't long before the sound fades and everything goes quiet.

Finally. Peace.

Beeping echoes in my ears in time with the pulsing throb in my head. Goose bumps erupt on my skin in the cool air. My throat is sore and my stomach cramping. A pinch of pain in my elbow.

Slowly, I peel my eyes open then slam them shut to avoid the glowing light.

"Anderson," Mom says, voice raspy. "Are you awake?"

I stay quiet for a beat as I prepare for my mother's wrath.

"Sam, get the nurse." Fingers touch my hair. "I think he's coming to."

The nurse? I'm in the hospital?

One blip at a time, memories flood in. The sleeping pills I

stole from the store. Stripping down and taking the entire bottle. The sweating, the cramps, the chills as my body tried to force the toxin out of my system. And then nothing.

How long ago was that? How long did it take for Mom or Dad to break into my room and find their baby boy near death? Too soon, obviously.

"Anderson, can you hear me?"

I want to ignore her. Pretend she doesn't exist. But then footsteps slap the floor. Dad speaks with someone other than Mom and I know I won't be able to shut them out much longer.

"Anderson," a new, deeper voice calls out. "My name is Jerome." Warm fingers wrap around my hand. "If you hear my voice, squeeze my hand."

Against every instinct, the muscles in my hand contract.

"Good. That's good, Anderson." He releases my hand. More footsteps echo in the room, a scratching sound mingling with the heart monitor beeps. A moment later, his hand takes mine again. "I've darkened the room. When you're ready, open your eyes."

Slowly, I peel my eyes open, blinking against the dryness a few times. I survey the room, Mom and Dad on my left, a man in dark scrubs on my right.

"You gave us quite the scare, Anderson." He gives my hand a squeeze then releases it as he checks an IV bag hanging near the bed. He picks up a cup with a straw and brings it to my lips. "Small sips. I'm sure your throat feels raw."

I do as he says and take a few small sips before releasing the straw.

Is my throat sore from vomiting? Is that why my stomach continues to twist every other minute?

"You have questions," Jerome says, as if hearing my

thoughts. "I'll page the doctor and we'll answer everything. Until then, rest. You've been through a lot." He sets the cup on a tray table next to the bed. "Be back in a moment." Then he disappears from the room.

I lift my hand, wanting another sip of water, but my arm doesn't move. Glancing down the bed, my eyes land on a thick leather band circling my wrist. My eyes shift to the opposite wrist to see another cuff pinning me to the bed. I yank against the leather over and over. Thrash in place and discover my ankles and waist are also restrained.

"What the fuck," I scream as I jerk harder.

"Anderson," Dad says, sadness thick in his voice. "They have to, son." I meet his red-rimmed eyes as I grit my teeth. "In your... condition"—he swallows, a tear rolling down his cheek—"they have to restrain you."

"This is bullshit," I mutter as the man from a moment ago walks in with a woman in a white coat.

"Hello, Anderson," the woman says, a tablet in her hand. "I'm Dr. Wexford. Do you know why you're here?"

With a shake of my head, I roll my eyes. "I'm not a fucking idiot."

"Anderson," Mom admonishes.

Dr. Wexford holds up a hand to silence her. "It's fine, Mrs. Everett." She sets the tablet down on the rolling table. "Anderson, I know it's a stupid question, but I have to ask."

I study the small dots in the ceiling tiles, clench my jaw and rock it side to side. "Yeah, doc, I know why I'm here." I shift my head on the pillow and meet her soft, warm gaze. Inhaling deeply, I swallow. "Because I want to die. Something else I obviously can't do right."

Out of nowhere, tears spill down my cheeks. My arm jerks as I try to bring a hand to my face to wipe them away. *Dammit.*

"It's been a long twenty-nine hours, Anderson." She rests a hand on my shoulder. "But I promise it will get better from here."

I don't see how that is possible, not when nothing has changed. Not when *she* is gone.

A bolt of fear strikes at the thought of Helena. Does she know I'm here? Does Ales?

I face my parents. "Does anyone know I'm here?"

Mom stares at me, brows tugging together. "What?"

I want to scream. I want to slap some damn sense into this woman. How fucking stupid can she be? But before I get a word out, Dad pipes up.

"No, son. We were waiting for you to wake up before calling your sister."

Relief washes over me, a weight lifting from my chest. "Don't call her."

Now it's Dad's turn to look confused. "Of course, we're letting her know. You're her family."

I growl as the heart monitor beeps louder, faster. "No," I bark out, my throat screaming at me in response. "I don't want her to know. I don't want anyone to know."

"Mr. and Mrs. Everett, Anderson needs to rest. I advise you to go home, have a shower, a hot meal, and a good night's rest."

Thank goodness. Someone else is finally on my side.

"And if Anderson would prefer to keep what happened between the people in this room, that is a choice we should all respect."

Mom looks at the doctor as if she is a bug to step on, but she keeps her irritation to herself. Dad, on the other hand, takes the doctor's orders more to heart. He stares down at me in the bed and gives a nod.

"C'mon, Joan. Let's go home. Anderson is in good hands." He leans over the bed and presses a kiss to my forehead. "Love you, son," he chokes out. "Glad you're okay."

Okay isn't the word I'd use.

Mom kisses my cheek before taking Dad's hand. "We'll be back in the morning," she promises. Then she and Dad exit the room, Dr. Wexford behind them.

Jerome picks up the tablet at the foot of the bed and taps on the screen as he checks numbers on the monitor.

"Can I ask a favor?"

He looks up from the screen and meets my gaze. "Of course, Anderson."

I swallow past the building lump in my throat. "Is it possible to not have them here?" I nod toward the door. "It's better if they're not."

A sad smile tugs at the corners of his mouth. "We can ask Dr. Wexford."

"Thank you."

I close my eyes and let everything that has happened hit me all at once. The backs of my eyes sting, emotion clogging my throat as I choke on tears. Pain ripples through my chest, widening the void in my heart. For a blip in time, I experienced peace. Stillness. A world without worry or shame or expectations.

For a moment, I was free.

A hand rests on my shoulder and my eyes jerk open. With a tilt of her head and a soft purse of her lips, Dr. Wexford nods in silent permission. Gifting me the chance to release every shard and splinter piercing my insides. In this place, I can expose my scars and perceptions without consequence.

"We've got you, Anderson." Her thumb strokes my shoulder once. "Let it all go. We'll catch you."

And for the first time, I shed every ounce of hurt. Discharge every wound darkening my heart. I rip myself wide open.

PRESENT

CHAPTER 38

HELENA

He's here. He's home.

After years of not seeing him, I wondered if this day would come. When I hadn't heard from Anderson for months that stretched into years, I assumed he had forgotten me and moved on. And when I'd come home during summer break from college and he was nowhere in sight, the true loss of him was a knife to the heart.

Almost five years ago, I returned to Lake Lavender. Fresh from college, I was ready to conquer the world. The clothing shop I'd briefly worked at in high school became my second home. It took a few months of rigorous studies for me to decide on a major in college. Washington State didn't offer a program specifically geared toward fashion, so I opted to major in business management and minor in marketing. Regardless of my future, both would help.

Weeks before returning home, I called and got my old job back at In Stitches. Though I wanted more than a standard retail position, I had to start somewhere. Little did I know resuming my old job would turn into the best opportunity

A year of working side by side with the owner of In Stitches gifted me the first chance to take over the store. Living at home with my parents, I stashed most of my paycheck every two weeks. Mom and Dad refused to let me pay rent. All they wanted was dinner together three times a week, basic cleanliness, and respecting the house rules. The deal was too great to pass up.

Gayle, the owner of In Stitches, pulled me aside a week before the shop officially went on the market. Sadness creased the corners of her mouth and eyes as she told me the news, as she told me I might not have a job with the new owner.

I'd gone home with the news and let it sink in overnight. The next day, I chatted with Mags and Lessa. After hours of conversation with them, ideas started brewing. Then I spoke with Mom and Dad. Told them I had a wild idea but didn't know if it was possible. Still young, I didn't have the financial means or credit history to buy a business on my own.

And two days before In Stitches officially went on the market, a solid plan formed.

Lessa had recently opened Java and Teas Me, the town's most beloved coffee shop. Though business was slow, she was in good standing. Mags offered part of her inheritance from when Mrs. Bishop passed. I fought her tooth and nail but gave up when she said her mother would have wanted to help. With a solid financial base, my parents said they would help me get the bank loan by cosigning.

Buying the shop fell into place easily. Joy hummed in my veins the day the Always Classic Boutique sign replaced the In Stitches placard. All my hard work had paid off and I officially owned the cutest women's boutique in Lake Lavender.

But life still felt lacking, and I knew the exact reason.

Anderson Everett.

My first love. The boy I never forgot, regardless of how many dates I went on or men I kissed. The boy I should have fought harder to keep.

Not a day went by where I didn't think of him once. Our love is something people wish for. But we'd been young. We'd had obligations and extenuating circumstances. He'd broken me as much as I'd broken him.

Then he disappeared. Without a word, without any form of goodbye, Anderson vanished.

After the way we'd left things and several years passing without any communication, I assumed he had moved on. Moved on from Lake Lavender and me. I learned to live in a world where I didn't see or speak with him. By no means have I found real joy in my life, but I had to keep moving forward.

And just as I settled into the new shape of my life, he returned. The second my eyes met his, my heart seized in my chest. I wanted to rub my eyes. Double-check that I wasn't seeing things. That this is real. That *he* is real.

He's here. He's home.

"I won't take up any more of your time," he says, his thumb stroking the ring on my finger. *His ring.* "But sometime soon, I'd like to catch up." Another tear cascades down his cheek. "If that's okay with you."

The corner of my mouth tugs up in a half smile. "I'd love that, Ander." Reluctantly, I drop his hand, take out my phone, unlock it and open my contact list. I tap his name and hand him my phone. "Will you update your number? I'll text later after I check the shift schedule."

Seconds pass and he simply stares down at my phone. The screen dims and he taps it awake. Without changing a thing, he hands me back my phone.

"Please don't be mad," he says then winces. "After you

left, I wasn't in a good place." He levels me with glassy red eyes, his Adam's apple bobbing with a hard swallow. "The doctors suggested I block all forms of communication while I healed."

What is he talking about?

"Heal from what?"

Pain lances his expression. "When the time is right, I promise to tell you." He pulls his phone from his pocket and taps the screen several times. Then he stows it back in his pocket. "Text or call whenever. I'm staying with Ales until I figure out something else." He takes a step back, a sad smile on his lips. "Talk soon."

Like a tornado, he's gone as quickly as he arrived. I stand on the sidewalk, stunned, as residents and tourists stroll past. The din of laughter and conversation and passing cars on the street filter back in. But I don't move. Don't look away from the man slowly disappearing from view as he walks farther down the road.

He's here. He wants to talk.

After Lessa took a call at a recent weekly dinner, I knew he'd returned to town. But days passed since that Friday night without a word—from him or Lessa—and I assumed he stopped by but decided not to stay.

Our past is far from simple. He isn't just some guy I loved and lost. Anderson is the one that got away. We both had a hand in our downfall, but I blame myself more than him. As we fell deeper in love, my attention shifted to focus solely on him. And in that move, all the other pieces of my life crumbled, suffered. I neglected my schoolwork, my family, my other friends. When it came back to slap me in the face, it hit him just as hard. Maybe harder.

I did my damnedest to repair what I'd broken, but we were

never whole again. And watching him wither away during my senior year... the images still haunt my dreams.

"But he's back," I whisper to myself, clasping my hands and rubbing the ring he gave me as he vanishes from sight. "And maybe this is our second chance." *Or third.*

I wander back into the store and apologize to the customers waiting with an armful of clothes near the fitting rooms. Fumbling for the keys in my pocket, I give them my best customer service smile.

"Sorry about that, ladies. An old friend surprised me and I stepped out to say hi."

They shuffle into the rooms and wave off my apology. While they try on clothes, I dart to the office in the back. My hours are the same every week, but I double-check that one of my two employees hasn't asked for time off. After a quick glance at the schedule, I exit the back and straighten clothes on a nearby display table as I wait for the women to leave the fitting rooms.

"This dress is to die for," the brunette says as she steps out, holding up one of the new floral dresses I got in last week. "So happy I stopped in today."

I take the stack of clothes from her hands when she approaches the checkout counter. "Isn't it perfect?" My cheeks tighten as I smile brighter. "When the designer emailed pictures, I immediately told her I wanted it for the shop."

The red-haired woman sidles up to her friend with her own stack of clothes and a handbag. "You've really done incredible things with this shop..."

"Helena," I offer.

She nods and smiles, her eyes roaming the store. "Gayle was wonderful, but you have a keen eye. Every time I set foot in here, I want half the shop in my closet."

I bag the brunette's purchases as she taps her card on the payment reader. "I truly appreciate the business, ladies."

"I'm Catherine," the brunette offers. "And this beauty is Sherry-Ann."

The other woman smiles.

"It's wonderful to meet you both. If there's anything you'd like to see in the store, let me know. I work with a few designers whose style reflects my own, but I'm always open to new ideas."

After I tally Sherry-Ann's order, she pays and points a finger my way. "I'll think on that and get back to you."

They turn and head for the door, large brown bags swinging from their arms with my store logo on them. One last "see you soon" before I am once again alone.

I take out my phone, unlock it, and open the chat between me, Lessa, and Mags. My fingers hover over the screen as I lose focus.

What are you doing, idiot? You can't just text Lessa and Mags to ask for advice on Anderson.

I shake my head and exit the chat, but not the messaging app. Instead, I gather every ounce of courage and tap the icon to start a new text.

My heart pounds viciously in my chest as I stare at the blank screen. I'd long since deleted the unanswered texts I sent Anderson. Months turned into years and when I hadn't heard a peep from him, I assumed he no longer had the same number. So I stopped trying but never deleted his contact.

I hit the plus sign and scroll my contacts until I land on his name. And then my fingers hover over the keys again. Unsure what to say, I type out a generic message.

Hey, it's Helena.

Then I tap the delete key and start again.

Hey Anderson, it's Helena.

Why the hell is this so difficult? This is Anderson, not some random stranger hookup from a dating app. I smash the delete key and huff at the screen. Closing my eyes, I drag in a deep breath, hold it to the count of three, and exhale slowly. My fingers fly across the screen. Short, sweet, and to the point. Before I stop myself, I hit send.

HELENA

> I work 9-6 Tuesday through Friday and 9-3 on Saturday.

My eyes lock on the screen as I wait for any indication he's seen it or is responding. The screen dims and I tap it awake. I nibble on the corner of my bottom lip, occasionally peeking up to see if anyone is lingering outside the shop.

The *delivered* beneath my blue bubble changes to *read* and my pulse kicks up. How does something as simple as him reading my message spike my pulse? God, my reaction is so juvenile and virginal. Sweaty palms, ragged breaths, that swirling energy beneath my diaphragm.

When did I last feel this *buzz*? Anderson and I didn't part on the best of terms, but no matter how hard I tried, I never connected with anyone else. Not like I did with him. I never experienced that delightful hum of anticipation with another person.

Much as I wanted to move on, I had difficulty saying yes to dates two or three with a guy. I tried—truly, I did—but guilt consumed me every time I compared them to Anderson. Their hair and jawline and frame were all wrong. The scent of their cologne missed the mark. How they looked me up and down made me shiver, and not in a good way. And their views on life didn't match mine. Worst of all, the egos. God, I was done with men and their need to prove how extraordinary they were.

At the end of the day, and at no fault of their own, they just weren't who I wanted.

It's difficult to move forward and find *the one* when you can't move past the first or second date.

The first year of college, I kept my head down and nose in textbooks. I wanted to make Mom and Dad proud. By sophomore year, I had relaxed a little. Took a breath. Went out with Lessa to a few parties. And the guys... noticed.

I wanted to want someone else. Wanted to let go of the past. But no guy or distraction had been enough. I gained some great guy friends, but it never evolved past friendship or an awkward, regrettable date.

The summer between junior and senior year of college, I hoped to see Anderson when I came home. Like the previous summers, he'd disappeared. When I asked Lessa about his graduation, she said he opted out of the ceremony, earned his diploma early, and hasn't been seen since.

He left. Lake Lavender, his family, me. And no one knew where he was.

But the way Lessa talked to him on the phone at dinner, the ease and lightheartedness of her words, she had to have been in contact on a regular basis. That stung. A lot.

Now, he's back and he wants to talk.

ANDERSON

Whatever evening works best for you. I have no plans.

Friday is typically dinner with Lessa, Mags, and the guys, but sometimes we swap Friday for Saturday. Much as I'd love a reunion with everyone present, I want time alone with him more. I want to ask questions without hesitation or interruptions. If others join, I'll lose courage or hold back.

HELENA

Saturday? Maybe 6? You choose where.

ANDERSON

Saturday at 6 is perfect. I'll figure out where and let you know.

Weirdly, I want to thumbs up the message, but I resist.

HELENA

See you Saturday.

The gray bubble dances on the screen and I nibble on my bottom lip as I wait for his next message. The bubble disappears, reappears, then vanishes again. I picture him typing and deleting like I did before I sent the first message. Minutes pass before my phone vibrates in my hand and his message fills the screen.

ANDERSON

Was great seeing you today. Missed you, North.

The backs of my eyes sting as my vision blurs. A tear splatters the screen as memories flood in. "Missed you too, Ander. So much."

CHAPTER 39

ANDERSON

Lost in my thoughts, I stroll Main Street and take in the improvements since I left. A lot has changed in the nearly six years I was gone, yet so much remains the same. Updated lampposts with colorful dangling potted flowers. Fresh, vibrant paint on store signs. Tall, robust evergreens shade much of the sidewalk and street parking. Lavender-colored metal benches outside the bakery, ice cream shop, and other food establishments.

The face of the town had a fresh appearance, but many of the townsfolk were very much the same.

Years and distance from Lake Lavender had been good for me. The initial pain I had upon leaving morphed into a dull ache over time. A muted throb beneath my sternum. Then one day, that pain split in two—one part for Helena and the other for my parents. Though I'd been hurt by them all, I'd never heal by lumping them in the same category.

The scars from Helena are not the same as the scars from my parents. But all of them are the result of heartbreak.

Memories rush in as I pass the town diner, a place Helena and I went countless times—just the two of us or with Ales and Mags. I peer through the window and watch the hustle and bustle of servers, bussers, and the elderly owners. My gaze shifts to a booth in the far corner, a family filling the benches, burgers and fries and sodas crowding the table. Once upon a time, that was our booth. The one we sat at if it was open. Not just me and Helena, but anyone in our group.

Seeing other people in a place we once labeled ours is odd, yet refreshing.

After Helena left for Washington State and I broke, life changed in so many ways.

Weeks in the hospital had been the beginning. The therapist I'd been seeing was fired and replaced with another. Mom and Dad policed my every move in fear of what I might do. The door to my bedroom had been removed, the hinge pins hidden away. I literally couldn't make a move, take a breath, eat or drink something without Mom or Dad knowing.

Them smothering me slowly chipped away my soul more. So I focused my energy elsewhere. I busted my ass in school and ignored everyone. When summer break came each year, I spent my days with Dad until I got a job. It wasn't ideal sitting in his truck or watching him work all day, but it was better than triggering what finally tipped the boat and took me down the darkest possible path.

The loss of Helena.

At all costs, I avoided her. Blocked her phone number, email address, and social media profiles. I shut her out per my therapist's instructions. *"Wounds don't heal if you keep picking the scab."* It was a gross metaphor, but one I understood.

Once I had a job, I asked for the maximum allowed hours. I

worked hard and saved every penny. Mom had my boss on my radar too. At least he hadn't been a nag. He'd ask how I was or if I needed anything, but otherwise, let me work. For nearly two years, work became a safe haven of sorts. A place to escape my badgering parents. A place that helped me focus my thoughts on something else.

During sophomore year, with the help of my guidance counselor, I signed up for online classes. Little by little, I earned credits faster. Just before winter break of senior year, the guidance counselor called me in and said I'd earned all the required credits to graduate.

With my diploma secured, I took almost every penny I'd earned, bought a car, packed necessities, and left Lake Lavender with zero regrets.

I learned a lot on the road—about myself and life. More than anything, I found peace. Something I desperately needed. I may not be one-hundred-percent happy with my life, but at least I am free. The shadow that darkens my life, though it never fully disappears, it no longer rules my every thought or action.

My phone rings in my back pocket and I pull it out to see Ales's name flash on the screen. I tap the green phone icon and lift the phone to my ear. "What's up, Ales?"

"Getting off work in a minute. Mags and Geoff decided we should do dinner at their place instead of Black Silk tomorrow. Want to join us?"

Turning away from the diner, I trail down the sidewalk toward her coffee shop. "Uh, I don't know." I wince. "Not really feeling like peopling, Ales."

"It's not peopling, Baby A. The only new people are the guys Geoff works with. Logan's a jokester, but Owen's pretty chill." A door slams and I hear stomping as she huffs into the line. Then the line quiets around her again. "Braydon will be there, too. You guys can talk traveling and hiking and the great outdoors. Plus, free food you don't have to cook."

"I like to cook."

"I know, but you can take a night off."

Less than a block from the coffee shop, I sigh into the line and cave. "Fine. I'll be at the apartment in a minute."

"Yay. See you soon."

The call ends and I stuff my phone back in my pocket. "What did I just sign up for?" I mutter as I cut between the buildings and climb the stairs to her apartment over the coffee shop.

Mags's house is exactly as I remember it. New pictures and art decorate the walls, some of the furniture has been replaced with more modern pieces, but her house is otherwise the same. I inhale deeply and catch a hint of Mr. Bishop's cologne in the air. Though he passed years ago, it's nice to feel like he is still here.

Ales all but plows into Mags, wrapping her in a death grip hug. Mags laughs and squeezes her with equal fervor.

"You act like I didn't see you this morning," Mags says with a shake of her head. She taps Ales's shoulder and scans the room. "Someone rescue me from a love overdose."

"Firecracker," Braydon says as he hooks his finger in the belt loop of her shorts and tugs. "Let the woman breathe."

Mock offense highlights Ales's face as she rolls her eyes. "She could breathe. Don't be so dramatic."

Braydon bites his tongue as he wraps an arm around my sister's shoulders. The room quiets as eyes shift in my direction. Unfamiliar faces stare my way, waiting. I suspect these are the guys Geoff, Mags's boyfriend, works with at the architectural firm. When I left Lake Lavender, there were no architects in town, let alone offices.

"Hey, Anderson," Mags says as she crosses the room with open arms. I pull her in for a gentle hug. "It's been a while." She releases me and inches back. "You look good." A soft smile tugs at the corners of her mouth. "Time away has served you well."

I shove my hands in my pockets and rock back on my heels. "Thanks, Mags. Good seeing you, too. Sorry about your dad."

Her eyes glaze over and she blinks away the threatening tears. "Thank you. Can't believe it's been years. Just have to take it one day at a time."

Mags formally introduces me to Geoff, Logan, and Owen. Though they give off different energy, the friendship they share is obvious. As Ales forewarned, Logan is the exuberant one in the group. Owen is quiet and pensive and seems to only speak up when he has something noteworthy to say. I like Owen. Geoff is an interesting blend of Logan and Owen. Reflective yet outgoing. A hint of melancholy in his eyes, as if a piece of his past shaped who he is today. But the way he looks down at Mags says more than words. She has his whole heart.

I wince at the slight twinge beneath my sternum.

I had that once.

As if my thoughts are a beacon, the front door swings open and Helena walks in.

"Sorry I'm late." Her eyes scan the room and she snaps her mouth shut.

Mags waves her off and steps up to hug her. "You're fine."

Without a word, I wander down the hall and close myself in the bathroom. I flip the light on, drop my hands to the vanity, and stare at my reflection. *Idiot.* Straightening my spine, I slap the heel of my hand to my forehead over and over. "Stupid. Fucking. Idiot."

Of course, Helena would be here. She, Ales, and Mags have been friends for more than twenty years. Why wouldn't she be here?

It took hours of mental hype and convincing to leave Ales's apartment and seek her out. To see the woman she is now. To speak to her and ask for her time. I wanted to find her the moment I rolled into town but knew nothing about her current life. I still know nothing.

She may have shown up to the gathering alone, but that means nothing. She may have agreed to meeting up on Saturday, but that also means nothing. Years of silence stretched between us, and in those years, she could have met someone. A casual fling or serious love. We'd hidden our relationship from everyone. What's to say she isn't doing the same with someone else?

My stomach sours at the idea.

Staring at my reflection, I take a deep breath and recall one of the messages from the self-help app I've used for years. "Assumptions lead to misery and heartache. Assumptions live to steal your joy. Never assume." I repeat the mantra a few more times, turn on the faucet and splash my face with cold water, take one last cleansing breath, then exit the bathroom.

Chatter echoes down the hall, soft music playing in the background as I enter the living room. Everyone crowds around the coffee table, either on the couch, chair, or floor, as they catch up and share stories. I drop to the floor near Braydon, who smiles but doesn't say a word. He and Ales have been together for months, so this group of friends is still new to him too.

At least I'm not alone.

Naturally, Ales has the best stories of the group since she sees the most people in town. She could be her own gossip mill with all she sees and hears. But spreading hearsay for attention isn't my sister's style.

Braydon nudges my arm with his elbow and I turn my attention to him. "We've talked all things Washington travel, but I want to hear about the places you've been outside the state. Let me live vicariously through you."

I chuckle and pull my phone from my back pocket. As I unlock it and open the photos app, warmth grazes my profile. And without shifting my attention across the room, I know Helena is watching me. She may not be staring, but her eyes are on me more often than not.

Years ago, it was the opposite. I sat in the corner or masked in the shadows, my eyes on her when no one was looking. And the moment her eyes met mine, this warmth bloomed beneath my skin. During friendship, I had no idea what it meant when that heat struck. But as we got older and our relationship morphed into something more, an awareness hit.

The fevered skin, sweaty palms, erratic heartbeats, and labored breaths were my body's emotional response. Even before I truly understood the meaning, I was in love with Helena Williams.

And now, as I talk to Braydon about my time in Big Water, Utah, as I thumb through the pictures, I feel each and every one of those emotional responses. I hand my phone to Braydon and let him zoom in on the pictures. While he is distracted, I peek in her direction. My eyes meet hers and pink stains her cheeks as she averts her attention back to Mags.

"These are incredible, man. I envy your ability to get out there and explore." He hands back my phone. "Maybe down the road, I'll convince my dad or brother to expand the company. Create features or side magazines for other destinations." He slaps his leg as his eyes widen. "Or maybe some of those *'If you like this town, you'll love it here'* features." He whips out his phone, opens the notes app, and types out his idea.

"Love the last idea," I tell him. "There are several places less traveled because people don't talk about them. And some of those places would greatly benefit from tourism dollars."

I started travel blogging officially about a year after I hit the road. I'd been posting pics sporadically beforehand, but none of them had traction. Wasn't until I posted about my week in the Grand Canyon that things picked up. Hours after posting, I had thousands of likes and just as many new followers. Within days, offers hit my inbox, one after another. Travel companies asked me to visit specific places, take photos, and write reviews in exchange for hefty paychecks.

Not only did I travel the country at my own pace, but my trips were also funded by tourism companies. I got paid to do what I love.

It was great until it wasn't.

After years on the road and thousands of miles under my belt, something beckoned me home, back to Lake Lavender. I want to believe Helena is the sole reason, but I'd be an idiot to assume it's only her. I left home without looking back. I hit the road, blocked out everyone damaging to my mental health at the time, and took my first true breath.

On the road, I never felt more alive, more myself. For years, I was happy. Well, as happy as I could be. I love the open road.

I love the freedom. But over the past few months, something had been missing.

Maybe that something is her. Helena.

Now that I know myself better, maybe it is time to heal past wounds.

CHAPTER 40

HELENA

Sitting in the same room as Anderson and not interacting with him feels wrong.

I walked through the front door and he bolted for the bathroom. I tried not to let that sting, but it was a hard slap to the face. Our history runs deep, and so do the wounds inflicted. Wounds I hope to heal.

Anderson isn't just some boy I loved. He isn't just a friend I lost touch with because I was too distracted by school and people and life. Anderson is the guy I never let go of. Not fully.

No relationship is perfect—friendship or romantic. What we had doesn't just fade away. There will always be a piece of my heart reserved for Anderson Everett. And seeing him again has that piece expanding with each breath.

"Food's ready," Mags hollers from the kitchen.

Earlier today, Mags sent a text in the group chat between everyone. *Geoff and I can't make dinner tomorrow. Our place tonight?* Out of everyone here, Lessa has the more hectic schedule. We all answered yes before her. I half expected her and

Braydon to decline. But she sent a *we'll be there* with a smiley face emoji. By *we*, I assumed she meant her and Braydon. Not once did I consider Anderson showing up.

I like that he is here. I more than like it.

What I don't like is his keeping his distance. Like us talking or existing in the same space around others is uncomfortable or needs to be a secret. Again. As if we had never been friends once.

Rising from my seat in the living room, I shuffle behind everyone to the kitchen. We file into line, grabbing paper plates to load up with whatever is on the menu. Pulling up the rear, Braydon spins around in front of me and asks about the shop as we wait. He and Lessa haven't been together long, but he slid into our group with ease. We each got to know him while he wrote a story about the town.

Lessa got herself a good guy with Braydon, and I am happy for them.

"Care Bear?" He shifts his attention from me to Lessa. "Come help me, please."

One corner of his mouth kicks up in a half smile. "We'll catch up at the table." He shuffles out of line, sidles up to Lessa, kisses her temple, and whispers in her ear. The blush on her cheeks is impossible to ignore.

Shifting my gaze away from their obvious intimacy, my eyes land on a lean, broad shoulder not far from my face. Following the line of his shoulder, I survey the tanned skin of his neck, a few darkened freckles at his nape, the dark-blond shaggy locks that are shorter in the back than on top, the sharp angle of his profile as he stares at the buffet.

So much of him is physically the same, yet I pick up the small differences with ease. How straight he holds his spine.

How he squares his broad shoulders. His willingness to spark conversation rather than shy away from it.

This new version of Anderson is bolder, stronger—physically and mentally—more comfortable in his own skin.

On an inhale, I discover one of my favorite parts of him remains unchanged. Something I will forever associate with Anderson. His scent hits me—cedar and earth with a hint of fire—and rouses countless memories. Subconscious souvenirs tucked away for safekeeping. Movie nights and roasting marshmallows and hiking in the woods.

I close my eyes and beg my heart to calm down. Tell my lungs to breathe slower, quieter.

It's been years, yet it feels like a lifetime. A lifetime without his words, a lifetime without his hand in mine, a lifetime without the smile he reserved for me only. A lifetime without his heart.

While our time apart seems to have been good for him, I can't say the same.

"Hey." His voice, low and raspy, hit my ears and I open my eyes. Blue eyes dart between my greens as unspoken questions weigh heavy in the air. "You okay?"

Why is this so weird? This is Anderson. The boy I spent more than half my life around. We were never like this. Fidgety fingers and sealed lips. We never fumbled for words. Especially me. Not with him.

I hug the plate to my chest and nod. "Yeah." The fib spills from my lips with ease. Were it anyone else, I'd have said, *"Define okay."*

Just as he could years ago, Anderson sees past the lie. His eyes narrow and I squirm under his scrutiny.

Since when do I feel intimidated by Anderson?

He purses his lips and inches forward, adding a scoop of

pasta salad to his plate. "I'll let that slide for now," he mutters. He looks at me out of the corner of his eye as he adds pulled chicken to his plate. "But not Saturday."

Before I rebut his comment or toss out another lie to cover the last, he steps away, fills his plate, and heads for the table on the patio. Every other breath, I peek out the sliding glass doors as I add more food than I'll eat to my plate. With cutlery and a napkin in hand, I amble toward the patio and scan the table for an open seat.

And, of course, the gods are out to torture me tonight. Because the only open seat is an added chair between Anderson and Logan.

At least Logan won't be offbeat.

As I drop down in the chair, Geoff rises with a brown bottle in hand. "Thanks for accommodating our change in plans this week." His eyes fall on Mags, a soft smile on his lips. "Wanted a weekend away with my girl starting tomorrow."

On the opposite end of the table, Lessa *oohs* over the announcement. "And where is it you plan to whisk my bestie off to?"

Geoff resumes his seat and takes Mags's hand in his. "I booked a weekend at West Beach Resort on Orcas Island."

"Good choice," Anderson says around a bite.

"You've been there, Baby A?"

He looks up from his plate and stares down the table at his sister, incredulity written all over his face. For a split second, I think he is going to give her some smart-ass answer. Of course, he does the opposite.

"Ales, I've been on the road for six years." A subtle smile softens his expression. "Exploring all of Washington was at the top of my list." He drops his gaze to his plate and spears pasta with his fork. "I'd seen it all before you were home from college."

An ache blooms in my chest at the idea of Anderson out on his own, driving from one corner of the state to the other to escape all the hurt here. To escape me... because I am part of that hurt.

The table falls quiet as everyone turns their attention to Anderson. The boy I knew years ago would have shrunk under such treatment. He'd have gotten up from the table and found a nook away from the group. Somewhere dark and undisturbed. The man before me is no longer that boy.

Still reserved, he isn't blurting out the past six years on the road without provocation. But he isn't shy about his time away. He doesn't hide himself.

Though I've missed him, his happiness gifts me some peace.

"I'd love to hear of your travels," Geoff says. "Maybe later you can share your favorite spots on Orcas."

A bright smile highlights Anderson's face and my mouth goes dry. *Damn.*

"After dinner, I'll share some photos."

The table erupts in conversation once more while I sit awestruck. Everyone is deep in discussion, except for me. Social butterfly was never a title I received, but I'd also never been reticent either. I always fit somewhere in the middle.

For some strange reason, seeing Anderson again, existing in the same space as him again, has my life off-kilter. Wobbly. In a good way.

For the first time in years, I am awake. Alive. Able to breathe fully.

All because he is here.

And if I am lucky, maybe this time he will stay.

CHAPTER 41

ANDERSON

When did Helena become the quiet one?

Ales garnered most of the attention when we were younger, but Helena never recoiled during conversations or gatherings. She stood tall next to my sister and Mags, sharing her piece in any given moment. Of the three of them, Mags had been the most reserved.

Seeing her so aloof among friends has me dizzy. Her reticence brings a long list of questions to the surface. Questions I'm not sure I want answers to.

Did she fall madly in love with someone else, only to have her heart broken? Did something happen to her parents? During one of my sporadic check-ins with Ales, she'd mentioned Mr. Bishop passing but nothing about Helena's parents. Has she lost one of them? Both of them? If not them, what has her so withdrawn?

Earlier, outside her store, I hadn't been oblivious to the melancholy highlighting her expression. I hadn't been impervious to her caved posture and fabricated smiles.

My appearance tonight was unexpected, I'm sure, but the moment she walked in the door, I anticipated at least one solid conversation with her before going back to Ales's apartment. Since exiting the bathroom, I've mentally prepared myself for an onslaught of questions, even if generic or forced. Yet, we have exchanged less than twenty words.

I don't get it. What am I missing?

Mags and Geoff rise from their seats and carry dishes to the kitchen. Ales and Braydon get up to help, shuffling inside with plates and serving dishes. Logan's eyes are glued to his phone, his fingers moving rapidly over the screen.

Owen stands, downs the rest of his water, and extends a hand in my direction. "Was nice meeting you, Anderson. Sorry to eat and run, but I have more work to do before crashing. Hope to see you at the next gathering."

With no definitive plans on how long I will be in Lake Lavender, I take his hand and keep my response vague. "Nice meeting you. Don't work too hard."

Eyes still on his phone, Logan scoffs. "Owen is married to work, unlike the rest of us." He peers over his shoulder and lands on Ales at the sink. "Kind of."

In my short time back, I've witnessed the relentless hours Ales puts in at the coffee shop. Before returning home, anytime I called or messaged her, she was working. Since Braydon, she has backed off the number of hours she clocks each week. Not an easy feat for a small business owner. Then the vandalism and fire happened, and time has been this strange thing for her and everyone at the coffee shop. Boards still cover the broken glass on the doors, but the shop is slowly returning to its former glory. One day at a time, her pride and joy is getting back to rights.

Logan bolts up from his seat, a bright, toothy smile on his

face. "Good to meet you, Anderson." He offers his hand and I shake it. "See you next week, Lena." He lifts a hand to his face and salutes us before stepping inside.

Everything goes hazy as his familiarity with Helena sinks in. The way my sister's shortened version of Helena's name rolled off his tongue with ease. Too much ease.

I have no right to be upset, no right to correct him. But neither of those facts stops my blood from boiling. Neither stop my fists from clenching beneath the table or my molars grinding hard enough to crack a tooth.

As if the irritation rolling off me hits her like a wall, she elbows me in the arm. A subtle hint to relax.

One breath after another, I count to ten and calm the displeasure I wear on my sleeve. Deep breathing never wipes away the problem completely, but it does bring me back to center, back to a clearer headspace.

"Don't worry about Logan," she says, twisting in her seat. "It takes a while to get used to him. He's... extra." She chuckles with a shake of her head. "Before Mags met Geoff, Logan tried to pick Lessa up at a bar with some cheesy line." Pressing a finger to her lips, she looks toward the kitchen. "Shh. That's a secret between us girls and Braydon. Lessa says he was three sheets to the wind and doesn't remember. Which is good for the rest of us."

Speechless, I hold her green eyes. Get lost in the serenity only her greens provide. Maybe it's the thick, wing-like kohl highlighting her eyelids or the dusty-rose powder accentuating the space between the kohl and her brow, but I can't look away.

For more than an hour, she barely said a word. She let everyone else start or dominate conversations while she sat back and picked at her food. As if her life is less interesting.

"What changed?" The words spill from my mouth without effort.

Something else I gained while on the road... confidence. It may not be hard as steel or the best armor on the market, but it's strong enough for me to stand my ground. I no longer take shit from anyone, regardless of their title in my life. Family, friend, acquaintance—no one is exempt. I speak my mind, speak the truth, and only hold back if it's not an appropriate time for what I have to say. I spent enough years of my life being talked down to and made to feel less than.

If it—or they—no longer serve me, I say no more and move forward.

A ridge forms between Helena's brows. "What do you mean?"

I lean back in the chair and roll my head in her direction. "Until five minutes ago, you've been on mute. What changed?"

Rolling her lips between her teeth, she shrugs. "I'm kind of the fifth wheel if you haven't noticed." In the periphery, I spot her fingers twisting the ring on her finger.

Does she do that often? Is the ring I gave her all those years ago a touchstone for her?

I don't want to have this conversation now. I don't want to ask about the years we spent apart while my sister helps prep lemon gelato and fresh berries for dessert. Once one question is out, the rest will follow. And we can't have this conversation here. Not when we will be interrupted and bombarded with curious eyes.

"Didn't see it that way. Not with Logan and Owen here."

"Well, sometimes it feels like everyone tries to appease me with an invitation. Mags and Geoff are sappy and occasionally annoying. Lessa and Braydon are fun and flirty and unrestrained at times. Owen only cares about work. It's honestly a miracle he shows up sometimes. Logan is... Logan." She rolls her eyes. "His weekly goal is to find someone new to hook up with. Mostly tourists or infrequent visitors." Her lips flatten in a tight line. "And then there's me. Little ol' Lena."

I open my mouth to ask if she's ever had a date during these weekly dinners, but Ales and Mags walk out with bowls of gelato. Braydon and Geoff follow in their wake with mugs and a pot of coffee. I snap my mouth shut and stash the question for when I see her Saturday.

The night progresses with light chatter. Ales shares next week's repairs at the coffee shop and how thankful she is to live in such a supportive community. Mags talks about the youth center, the expansion they're planning over the next five years after a generous donation, and that she's resuming college to further her degree. Geoff mentions the Lake Lavender beautification project they've been working with the mayor on and his excitement to get started. Braydon has time off from work while he helps Ales get Java and Teas Me back in order.

As for Helena, she doesn't utter a word. Nothing about her store or the next wave of merchandise coming in. Nothing about trips she wants to take or places she wants to visit. Nothing about strange customers or fun events coming up in town.

Not one single thing.

I nudge her arm with my elbow. "Sure you're okay?" I whisper-ask.

Try as she might, Helena Williams cannot lie to me. Not outright. And I know for a fact she is not herself. Not the girl from before. Not the girl I fell in love with.

Her eyes dart around the table, noting the side conversations and attention elsewhere. When her eyes meet mine, I don't miss the glassy sheen. Don't miss the slight wobble of her chin. "No," she whispers, then swallows. "I really missed you." Her words are so soft I almost miss them. "So much."

And with her simple confession, Helena has me wrapped around her finger. Again.

Fuck.

CHAPTER 42

ANDERSON

Sleep hasn't been my friend for years.

While I was on the road, away from the noise and my mother's incessant badgering, I discovered a sense of peace I'd never known. A stillness only found when you step away from all the screens and take time to truly appreciate what life has to offer. With each passing year, I learned something new about myself. Learned what truly mattered. What I should give my energy to.

Over time, I let go of burdens. I let go of the anger and hurt. In its place, I welcomed beauty and joy and hope. I opened myself up to reality, away from the chaos that circles most people and spreads like a virus. And with each step forward, with each weight I released, the problems of my past no longer held me back.

Helena… she is something, *someone*, I never let go. If anything, I tucked her away in my head and heart for safe-keeping.

In the beginning, when I unrolled my sleeping bag and stared up at the stars alone, I only thought of her. Where she was, what she was doing, if she was happy. Every night under the stars, I imagined her next to me, staring up at the heavens and painting lines to connect the constellations.

"I really missed you. So much."

"I missed you too, North," I whisper to the dark ceiling as I beg for sleep.

Closing my eyes, I start a simple meditation practice I learned early on during my years on the road. It doesn't necessarily make me fall asleep, but it helps focus my thoughts and shut out the noise—like my sister giggling across the hall with her boyfriend.

Halfway through the exercise, my limbs grow heavy. My thoughts drift away from the meditation and into the darkness. One focused breath after another brings me closer to sleep. But before I doze off, I think, *please let me dream of her.*

"Exactly what I need," I huff out as I crest a hill on the trail.

Once I drifted off last night, I slept hard. Usually, I wake to sounds throughout the night. Town has more noise than the offbeat trails and pull-offs I park at for the night. So do buildings. It'd been years since I occupied a residence with creaky floorboards, whining pipes, and sectioned spaces.

Each night in Ales's guest bed, I hear every groan the apartment above her shop makes, except for last night.

My head hit the pillow, and after fifteen minutes, I zonked out for a solid seven hours. Not even Ales getting up hours before sunrise stirred me from sleep.

I didn't need psychic abilities to predict Helena would be the reason I woke with a gasp.

Sheets damp and breath ragged, I bolted upright with the heel of my hand thrust to my sternum. The dream had been far from a nightmare. Quite the opposite. Seeing her yesterday, engaging with her for the first time in years, stirred up our history. Some memories I treasured and held close to my heart. While others, I'd rather forget.

It isn't her fault my subconscious went haywire after mingling in her orbit again. But I need to clear my head. Need to remind myself how long it took to move forward after her.

Helena isn't just some woman I dated. She isn't some random acquaintance of the past. Our lives were intertwined long before either of us understood what was happening.

Connections like ours, especially those teetering a fault line, aren't easily made whole.

I reach a lookout point and pause my hike. Unscrewing my canteen, I take a hefty sip of water before replacing the cap. I lean against the wood rail and stare out at the lake below. Rows of the bold-purple lavender line the shore closest to town, the subtle perfume soft in the air where I stand, miles away. A wide path is lined with people as they stroll the fields, while others sit in Adirondack chairs closer to the water and soak up the sun.

I take a deep breath and fill my lungs with crisp, piney air. Closing my eyes, I let my mind wander. Give myself permission to think and feel and react in whatever way comes naturally. Give myself permission to be vulnerable while no one has the chance to muddle my perspective.

"Helena," I whisper, her name drifting with the wind.

And with only her name falling from my lips, a whirlwind spins in my chest. Slow at first as early memories of her, of us, climb to the surface. Her jubilant smile and twinkling laughter. The way she sought me out when I pulled away from the crowd and sat in the shadows. How she was just as much my friend as she was my sister's friend.

Before things escalated between us, she was the faintest light in my dark world.

I sink to the ground, crisscross my legs, plant my elbows on my knees, and drop my head in my hands as deeper, more potent memories swirl to life.

The first time she held my hand and I swore my heart would explode in my chest. We were still only friends at the time, but that small touch was a lifeline. A hint of hope and want.

Every time she chose to spend time with me rather than Ales or Mags... God, for the first time in my life, I felt important. Prioritized. Consequential. And damn, it was addictive.

The first time she wrapped me in her arms and it felt like *more*... Warmth and life and love spilled from her arms and gave me purpose. A reason to wake up every day. Something to look forward to. Helena brought value to my life when all I felt was worthlessness.

My breaths come faster, harsher, as my pulse whooshes in my ears.

Winter break of seventh grade. The first time we kissed. The first time we crossed the friendship line and moved into girlfriend-boyfriend territory. Her face when I gifted her the gold and sapphire ring.

Summer break before eighth grade. Helena in my arms, bare skin pressed to mine as we lost our virginity.

I suck in a sharp breath and hold it. Fist the cotton of my shirt just above my heart. Peel my eyes open and scan my surroundings to make sure no one is nearby to witness my impending panic attack.

Dropping my hands to the earth, I curl my fingers in the

dirt and anchor myself to solid ground. My eyes fall shut again as I exhale and let my senses take over.

Gritty, cool soil. Somewhere solid to stand.

I inhale deeply and hold the crisp air in my lungs.

Pine and oxygen. Something to give me life.

Slowly, I open my eyes and twist to look at the trees.

Tall and sturdy and expanding. Evidence you can have roots and still spread your wings.

I open my canteen, bring it to my lips, and take a long pull.

Abundant and fluid. Proof you can move forward and change with each bend or twist.

Rising to my feet, I take a calming breath and let go of the last of the nervous energy in my chest. Take one last look at the lake below as my heart resumes its normal rhythm. And then I curl my fingers around my backpack straps and walk the trail back to town. Back to the noise. Back to her.

CHAPTER 43

HELENA

The bell over the door jingles as a woman exits the store with a bag on each arm.

Still in the thick of tourist season, inventory flies out of the store faster than I have time to replenish it. No one will hear me complain about having the best sales year since taking ownership of the shop. Every sale is another opportunity to bring in something fresh and trendy. A new piece to garner the attention of not only the townspeople but also those visiting.

The designers I work with never make the same garment twice. I discuss ideas with each of them, homing in on their individual personalities. They sketch up ideas and share them with me days later. I tell them how many I want and then it's production time. Quantities are small, so each piece feels more individualized for customers.

From idea to rack, it takes six weeks to get new items in the store. Fashion is never simple, but staying ahead of the game is the hardest part. Thankfully, I procured the best team of women for my business. I support their small business, and they do the same by sending friends and family my way. It's a win-win.

On the far wall, I straighten tops on wooden hangers and organize any items out of place. I move down the line and make sure everything on the rack looks impeccable and eye-catching. As I adjust a knee-length gray dress on a hanging bust, the bell over the door chimes.

I plaster on my brightest smile and spin around to greet whoever walks in. "Good after—" The welcome catches in my throat as Anderson stands feet from the entrance.

His eyes roam the store at a leisurely pace until our gazes lock. My heart soars with his expression, awe and pride lighting his eyes and smile.

He'd been in the store before, years ago when Gayle owned the shop. Although I kept some things the same—the white shiplap walls and iron pipes used as clothing rods—the store has an entirely new vibe.

Most of what Gayle offered was bold colors. Vibrant reds, royal blues, rich greens, and sunny yellows and oranges. Living closer to the city during college, I frequented countless retail shops for clothing and researched. During those visits, I discovered what I gravitated toward, what caught my eye. I also eavesdropped on others' conversations as they perused stores and wished they could find this or that.

When it came time to make this shop reflect my style, I did it with ease. Whites and creams. Soft palettes—blush and baby peach, sand and beige, cloudy and silver grays. Pale blues and lighter denim. Every now and then, mostly in fall or winter, I add a few darker pieces.

The pride in Anderson's eyes gives me an odd sense of validation I didn't realize I wanted or needed. Others are proud of what I've done with Always Classic—my parents,

Lessa, Mags—but something about earning his approval makes it stick. Makes all the hard work and countless hours sink in.

I don't need his endorsement to find joy in my accomplishments, but I *want* it.

Because Anderson's opinion always weighs heavier.

"Sorry to…" he starts, stepping farther into the shop. "This is"—his eyes roam the store again—"incredible." The corners of his mouth curve up into a heart-stopping smile. "Everything you do is remarkable."

I open my mouth to thank him, but snap my lips shut as confusion filters in. It isn't because Anderson never complimented me or sang my praises years ago. More that he had never been so candid or forthcoming.

"Don't mean to barge in or disrupt your day." Step after step, his hiking boots eat up the space between us in five long strides. "We agreed to tomorrow, but I needed to see you again. Before then."

Clasping my hands together, the fingers of my left hand automatically go to the ring on my right hand, spinning the thin double band. His eyes drop and catch the action, a soft smile tugging at his lips. I unclasp my hands and let them fall to my sides.

"Why?" I ask, unsure I want the answer.

He rolls his lips between his teeth as he turns his head to the side. I study his profile and get lost as I catalog a new image of him. Beard lining his angular jaw, the dark-blond hair is thick and wiry. Light dances over his skin, the gleam creating occasional shadows and highlighting his cheekbone and brow. The slope of his nose looks much the same, but the definition of his philtrum and cupid's bow are nothing like I remember.

For a split second, I imagine closing the distance between us and pressing my lips to his. Feeling the pressure of his lips on mine and running my tongue over them. Tasting him for the first time in…

"You can't say stuff like that," he mumbles as he levels me with his gaze.

Shit. Did I say something while off in lip-lock land?

My palms sweat and I press them to the sides of my thighs, nonchalantly wiping them on my jeans.

With a subtle shake of his head, he continues. "Last night." He licks his lips and I can't help but stare. "You confessing how much you missed me." My eyes dart back to his. "How?"

Thrown off by his question, I mentally stumble backward. *How?* What a redundant question. He has to be joking. "I don't understand." Really, I don't get it. Yesterday, outside the store, I admitted missing him. He questioned it then as well, but also said he missed me too. So how is it odd for me to repeat the sentiment?

He shoves his hands in his pockets and rocks back on his heels, his lips tightening a second before he speaks. "Just felt like there was more to it. Like you repeating it, emphasizing it, hinted at something else."

God, I want to touch him. Reach out, tug his hands from his pockets, hold them with mine, and lace our fingers.

But we aren't those people anymore. My heart is still his, but I don't know if his is still mine.

Realization hits as I stare at him. My stomach cramps and nausea crawls up my throat. I backpedal and second-guess every thought I've had since seeing him again. Now that it's surfaced, I can't shake the thought.

What if Anderson is in love with someone else?

Gut-wrenching as it is, it makes sense. He is happy.

Happier than I have ever seen him. Easy smiles and comfortable socialization. Occasional laughter mixed with a more laidback energy. Strength in the way he carries himself and confidence in his words and tone.

His hands leave his pockets as he takes a step forward. In a blink, they cup my cheeks, his thumbs softly skating my cheekbones. And then he tips my head, lifting my bewildered gaze to his inquisitive eyes.

"What's going through that pretty head of yours?"

Pretty...

Calloused thumbs gently brush my cheeks again and my eyes drift closed. Heat spreads from the point of contact and blooms like a flower seeing the sun for the first time. For three ragged breaths, I bask in the warmth blanketing my skin then meet his waiting stare.

"Talk to me—"

"Are you in love with someone else?" I blurt out before I lose the courage.

His whole body stiffens, the pads of his fingers firmer on my jaw. Eyes tight and narrowed, the muscles in his cheeks flexing. Each reaction is a blow to the chest. A slap to the face.

The longer it takes him to answer, the harder my heart bangs beneath my breastbone. The longer he remains unmoving, the tighter my rib cage constricts around my lungs. A light sheen of sweat blankets my skin, my fingernails digging into my palms as I hold my breath and wait. Wait for something, anything, from him.

As if he feels my impending panic attack, he softens. His warm breath faintly brushes my lips a beat before his thumbs caress my cheeks. The tight lines along his jaw and the corners of his eyes relax.

"Breathe, North." Another stroke of his thumbs as he drops his forehead to mine. "Please breathe."

I gasp, cool air filling my lungs and soothing the burn. But it isn't enough. Not even close. Because he still hasn't answered my question. "Ander..." I choke out his name on a whisper.

"No, Helena." His eyes fall shut. "Never."

Sweet relief replaces dread. The sharp pain in my chest fades as my heart returns to its normal, steady rhythm. My fingers unfurl at my sides as my arms tremble. Without hesitation, I reach for him. Fist the cotton of his shirt in my hands and sigh.

It doesn't escape my attention that he called me by my given name and not the nickname only he uses. As if to make his point more notable. To reinforce the meaning behind those two simple words. To subliminally tell me he will never love anyone else. Not the way he did me.

The tip of his nose trails up the side of mine before he inches back and drops his hands. I immediately miss his touch, his warmth, him.

He peers over his shoulder, eyes on the door and window as people stroll past the store. On a deep inhale, he licks his lips, swallows, then brings his attention back to me. Vulnerability mars his expression, a hint of trepidation in his steel-rimmed blues.

"Now isn't the time to get into heavy topics." He exhales a shaky breath. "Something inside me broke when you left," he confesses. "Things between us had been rocky before you and Ales left for college, but something about watching you drive off... it doesn't get much darker."

"Ander..." I inch closer to him. "I hate how we left things." Reaching for his hand, I sigh when he doesn't shake off my hold. "That last year was chaos and exhilaration and heartache. Sure, not being with you helped with school. But that's it. Everything else was a blur because none of it mattered." I drop my gaze to our hands and lock the visual in my memory before meeting his gaze once more. "The day I left for college, I bit my tongue so many times."

He twists his hand and laces our fingers. "Why?"

I laugh without humor. "College wasn't my dream. I went for my parents. I went because it'd been drilled into my head that college equals a future with more opportunities. While I believe that has merit, I also accept college isn't for everyone. Sure, I acquired an abundance of business knowledge. But everything I needed to know to run this shop"—I wave my free hand toward the open store—"I learned from Gayle. It came easier because I'd been taught record keeping and marketing and general hospitality, but I would've learned those things without college too. Just differently.

"When Lessa and I left for Washington State, I desperately wanted to tell her to turn around. Our goodbye didn't sit well with me. Hell, senior year didn't sit well with me. Every mile marker we passed..." The backs of my eyes sting as I shake my head. "The farther we got, the more it hurt."

Not a day passed where my mind hadn't drifted to Anderson. What he was doing. How he was doing. For hours, I lay awake at night, eyes on the ceiling and out of focus, as I sent a silent request for him to answer one of the countless texts I sent. My pleas went unfulfilled.

When summer rolled around, excitement roared in my veins at seeing him, at the chance to spend lazy days with him. But those dreams went out the window when I returned home and learned Anderson was never around. Mr. Everett mentioned Anderson having a job but wouldn't tell me where he worked. He'd also grumbled that Anderson frequently went off on his own for days at a time.

Each year I didn't see Anderson, the hurt encompassing my heart expanded, grew heavier, had me questioning if he ever loved me the way he claimed. Each year without him, I lost sight of what we had while the memory of him faded.

And then he was gone.

The summer before my senior year at college, I had a plan. Return home, locate Anderson, and say whatever it took to clear the air between us. But I never got the chance. Because during that summer, I learned Anderson graduated high school six months early. And to ring in the new year early, he left Lake Lavender.

His fingers tighten their hold on mine. "Much as I wanted you to come back, it's better you didn't."

"Why?" I ask, the single-word question barely audible.

"Things were bad when you left. Really bad." Glassy blues pin my greens. "But I needed that pain. I needed to experience that level of destruction in order to heal." He licks his lips then swallows. "I'll never be fully healed." He shakes his head. "I'll always have scars here"—he taps his temple then over his heart before gesturing the length of his body—"and here. Only now, I have the wherewithal to heal my wounds before they change from scratches to gashes."

The bell over the door jingles and I blink away the tears rimming my eyes. Sucking in a sharp breath, I avert my attention to the couple that steps inside. "Good afternoon. Thank you for coming in." I force a smile and pray it looks genuine. "Please let me know if you need anything."

The couple smiles and thanks me as they breeze over to the opposite wall and scan the racks.

"I should go," Anderson says. "Text you in the morning with dinner plans?"

Much as I don't want him to leave, he is right. I'm at work and this isn't the place to dredge up our past. I nod.

To my surprise, he leans in and presses his lips to my forehead, keeping them there for one, two, three ragged breaths. He gives my hand a quick squeeze then lets go.

"Tomorrow," he vows as he takes a step back.

"Tomorrow," I say with equal conviction.

CHAPTER 44

ANDERSON

I've never been on a date. Not a real date. Plans and reservations mixed with sweaty palms and questions about clothes and hygiene.

But it seems I still have more firsts to share with Helena.

Staring at my reflection in the bathroom mirror, I brush my hair and pray the few errant hairs will lie down and behave after I exit the room. I swap the hairbrush for a lint brush and roll it over the black button-down Braydon let me borrow. The stiff material makes my skin itch, but I refuse to slum it tonight.

This morning, I messaged Helena and suggested Trixie's Thai House. She replied, *great choice*. The restaurant is small, quaint, and far from fancy. I hadn't been inside for years, but the outside still had the same wood sign with gold lettering.

Change isn't something that often happens in Lake Lavender. Many businesses pass on to the next generation. Occasionally, a new business pops up, like Ales's coffee shop. But some get a new owner and face-lift, like Helena's clothing store. Most importantly, the town likes to maintain the same overall feel. Small, independently owned businesses with welcoming smiles and a reason to stay or visit again.

I considered asking Helena to Black Silk, a classier restaurant that opened while I was away. But after learning from Ales that the whole group went there regularly, I opted for something simpler.

"You look nice, Baby A."

I set down the lint roller and meet her gaze in the mirror. "Thanks, Ales."

"Hot date?"

Cue the awkwardness. Ales isn't completely oblivious to the relationship Helena and I shared before their senior year of high school. But she doesn't know all the intimate details. Ales and Helena may be close, but I doubt Helena was forthcoming with the extent of our relationship. How we went from friends to best friends to lovers. Then everything imploded and blew us in opposite directions.

"Maybe?" I phrase my answer like a question, not wanting to lie to my sister but also not wanting to dive into the gritty details.

She steps into the bathroom, spins me to face her, brushes her hands over my shoulders and down the sleeves rolled up to my elbows. Then she steps back, holding me at arm's length as she surveys my attire.

The corners of her mouth curve up into a warm, soft smile. "You look handsome, little brother." She leans in and presses a kiss to my cheek. "It's nice to see you happy."

Happy. A simple word with such a complex meaning.

"It's a constant work in progress, but I'm trying."

She cups my cheek. "If you need anything, I'm always here. Need to bitch? Lay it on me. Need to scream? I'll drive us to the trail and stand there as you yell at the mountain. If you need to talk about demons, I'll always listen."

God, how long I've wanted someone other than a therapist to listen to my inner turmoil. Not that I plan to immediately spill every dark secret with my sister. Her tears as I share some of my monsters will undoubtedly add a fresh wound next to my scars. But having her in my court, having a safe space, is the best gift.

I swallow past the emotional swell in my throat. "Thanks, Ales." Stepping into her, I haul her to my chest and hug the breath from her lungs. "Means more than you know."

With a cough, she taps my shoulder. "Can't breathe."

I release her on a laugh. "Now you know what your hugs feel like."

She playfully rolls her eyes. "Yeah, yeah." Her fingers fumble with the collar of my shirt. "Go on your date already."

After one last look in the mirror, I exit the bathroom and slip on shoes. Out the door and down the stairs, I take a deep breath and calm the nervous buzz in my chest.

This is what you've always wanted. She *is what you've always wanted.*

In a flowy, full-length cream sundress, Helena crosses Main and weaves between cars before stepping onto the sidewalk. Sleek, short hair out of her face and pinned with a clip on her crown. Her lips are painted a bold red and her eyes are lined with kohl.

Damn, she is breathtaking.

One step after another, she closes the distance between us.

She has yet to notice me outside the restaurant, and I use the time to stare unabashedly. Locals wave, smile or greet her as she passes them, and she returns each gesture or sentiment without hesitation.

Two storefronts down, she spots me in the evening crowd. Her stride stutters for a split second, but I don't miss it. A soft smile tips up the corners of her mouth as she tugs the strap of her purse higher on her shoulder. Each of her steps kicks my pulse into the next gear. When she reaches me, I take a deep breath and beg my heart to settle.

"Hey," I croak out.

"Hey, Ander." She clasps her hands at her waist and fidgets with her ring.

"Shall we?" I open the door to Trixie's and gesture for her to enter.

Stepping inside, the hostess takes my name, grabs menus, and weaves us through the packed tables. We are seated at a booth near the back of the restaurant. Quiet and somewhat private, I slide into the booth across from Helena.

Years ago, you never needed a reservation for any of the restaurants in Lake Lavender. But when I looked up a few online, I noted each recommended reservations from Friday through Sunday, May to October. I love seeing our small town thriving but miss the lesser foot traffic and quieter streets.

Handing us each a menu, the hostess mentions tonight's special then walks off. Before I get to read all the appetizers, a young woman sidles up to the table.

"Hey, Lena. How are you?"

A nervous smile highlights Helena's expression. "Hey, Angelica. Good, thanks. And you?"

The server pulls a pad of paper and pen from her apron, pen poised to write. "Great. Been busy tonight. Half the town must be here. And the number of take-out orders… don't get me started. But you can't go wrong with padding the piggy bank. Am I right?" She shifts her attention to my side of the table. "Hi there, I'm Angelica. What can I get you to drink?"

This woman, not much younger than me, has more energy than I can handle. Her smile is kind and personality warm, but her exuberant extroversion makes me step back mentally.

I swallow and smile, hoping it doesn't look like I'm in pain. "Water, please."

Helena orders Thai iced tea and asks her to give us time to look over the menu. When the server is out of earshot, Helena chuckles. "Intimidating, isn't she?"

I scan the restaurant to make sure she isn't at a nearby table. "Uh, yeah." I grip the menu tighter. "I may not be as reserved as years ago, but when people invade my space, it throws me off."

Being on my own, out in the wild for years, it wasn't often I was near other people. I wasn't completely isolated from humanity, but my interaction with others was minimal. I made friends within the van-life community, but we mostly kept in contact online or through texts. Occasionally, we met up and hiked trails as a collective. But I enjoyed solitude. I enjoyed separating myself from people and connecting with nature.

In the middle of nowhere, I never felt freer. I never felt lighter.

Now, it is time to find the same peace with my past. And hopefully, my future. Which also means I need to coexist with different personalities and crowds.

Angelica returns with drinks, takes our menus after we order, and promises to return soon with the appetizer. Honestly, the kitchen could take an hour to make the food and

I wouldn't care. I am here with Helena, and she is what matters.

"So," she says, sipping her creamy tea. "Tell me about van life."

My eyes widen as I scoff. "Where do I start?" I shrug. "It's liberating and terrifying and adventurous. And as much as I love it, the road gets lonely."

She rolls her lips between her teeth, her eyes on the table a beat before they meet mine. "I get that."

Which part? The freedom and open road or the loneliness?

Loneliness on the road is different than isolation among others. If I am honest, lack of companionship in the thick of people is worse than on your own in the middle of a desert. Being surrounded by people who don't want you eats away at your soul. Rips you apart. Keeps you constantly teetering on the edge of poor decisions.

Beneath the table, I wring the cloth napkin in my lap. Twist it tight enough to sting my palms.

"Helena, I—"

The server deposits the appetizer on the table. I nod with a forced smile and a muffled thanks.

I use the momentary interruption to take a sip of water and mull over how to proceed. Taking a bite of spring roll, I give myself another minute. Helena isn't oblivious to my stalling tactics. Her attention is fully mine as she nibbles on a spring roll and waits for me to continue.

"There are things you don't know, things Ales doesn't know." I draw in the condensation on my glass. "When you left for college, I hit an all-time low. I got swallowed by the darkness." My blues meet her greens across the table, my stomach cramping. "Before I say more, I need you to promise me something."

Setting the spring roll down, she wipes her hands with a napkin and nods. "Sure."

"This is a heavy promise to uphold, but I need your word."

Her forehead wrinkles as her brows pinch together. "I swear, whatever it is."

"Promise not to feel guilty. What I need to tell you, it isn't your fault. You need to know my mind would've steered me down the same path eventually. It's chemical."

Tears rim her lids as she pins me with veiny eyes. "That's a difficult promise to make without details, but I'll try."

Inhaling deeply, I hold the breath in my lungs until they beg for release and fresh oxygen. On an audible exhale, I step outside of my comfort zone and prepare to put my soul on the line.

Scanning the nearby tables, relief washes over me as I note no one's attention is on us. I take one last cleansing breath and swallow past my nervousness. "Not long after you left, I started cutting again."

She sucks in a sharp breath, but I ignore it and trudge forward.

"The momentary euphoria and relief sated me the first week. Then it wasn't enough." That first time I felt nothing when the blade sliced my flesh, I was angry. Pissed off at my body for betraying me. I needed release and my body refused to give me what I was desperate for. "So, I needed a new escape. Something less... *temporary*. For days, my mind was a black hole. Thinking, planning, on the path toward executing."

Across the table, Helena holds her breath. Her chin wobbles as she bites the inside of her lips. And as much as I'd like to skip the grim parts, she needs to hear it all.

In order for us to move forward, in order for us to have any type of future, this needs to be out in the open.

"In the middle of the day, I strolled into Lakeside Grocer and stole a bottle of sleeping pills." I curl my fingers into tight fists under the table, my nails biting the flesh of my palms. The pain a welcome reminder that I am here. I am alive. That this moment in my life, though dark and frightful, does not define who I am. "I swallowed all of them when no one was home." Tears blur my vision as my throat swells with emotion. "All I wanted was to fall asleep and never wake up. All I wanted was freedom from pain, from burdening others, from being undesirable on every level."

Tears paint her cheeks as she chokes out, "Ander…"

"I woke up in the hospital more than a day later. They'd pumped my stomach and restrained me to the bed. For weeks, I sat in a psychiatric ward and talked about my feelings." Those constant sessions didn't change the way I viewed life and the world, but they taught me ways to cope with my biochemistry and the natural thought deviations I experienced.

I lift an arm from my lap and lay it on the table, palm up. Without hesitation, Helena rests her hand in mine, holding on to me with unimaginable strength. And god, it makes me love her more.

"This will always be part of who I am. Only now, I've learned how to coexist with it and still live a happy life. Some days are easy. Some days, I am happy. But other days, I stay in bed and avoid life."

Helena wipes her cheeks with her free hand. She stares down at our joined hands, her chest expanding before she audibly exhales. "Ander, I'm sorry. I-I—"

"No. Please don't apologize. We may have been rocky that last year, but what happened isn't your fault. You had a lot on your plate, too." I lean over the table and bring her hand to my lips, kissing the top. "It's a lot to take in, but I don't want secrets between us. And I wanted to tell you before I let Ales know."

"I..." She sniffles. "I don't know what to say."

My thumb brushes her knuckles. "You don't have to say anything. Part of healing is becoming vulnerable." I lace our fingers. "And I've always been the most vulnerable with you." I drop my gaze to our hands and lose focus. *Damn, I missed this. Her.* "I'd like us to start over again," I confess as I meet her waiting stare.

"Start over?" She tilts her head.

"Friendship."

"Oh." The single syllable is almost inaudible, but I hear her disappointment in those two letters.

The server returns with our meals, confusion scrunching her brow. "Are the spring rolls okay?"

Helena blinks a few times, plasters on a faux smile and looks up at her. "They're fine, Angelica. Just catching up. Thank you."

Relief relaxes her expression. "Okay, good. Let me know if you need anything else." And then she wanders to another table.

I release Helena's hand and finish my spring roll. Silence falls over the table as we dig into our meals. But it isn't long before I break the silence.

"It's important that we start at the bottom again. Believe me, I want more," I admit with a subtle nod. "But it isn't that simple. My therapist says rebuilding relationships is vital. Trust and confidence were two things I lacked years ago. To have healthy future relationships, I need to gain them."

"I trust you, Ander."

Piercing a carrot and piece of chicken, I dunk the forkful in the curry. I shove the bite in my mouth and give myself a moment before responding. Swallowing, I sip my water.

"That means a lot."

She smiles as she brings noodles and broccoli to her lips.

"Don't take this the wrong way, but I need to feel it." I tap a hand over my heart. "After you left and I did what I did, no one trusted me. Time alone was a luxury I no longer had. It was stifling. Suffocating." Parents, teachers, the town gossip mill, everyone tiptoed around poor little Anderson. Every day, I was asked how I felt by dozens of people. I understood why, but after a while, it came across as less than genuine. Early on, I'd tallied how many times I was asked each day. Some days, it was fifteen. Other days, it was thirty-two.

Either way, it was a nuisance and constant reminder.

"I buried myself in school assignments. Set myself up to graduate early. Worked at the same grocery store I stole from. Saved every possible penny and formed a plan." The plan was rocky at best, but it was the only escape I had within my means. "I won't lie, leaving was rough. There were lots of skipped meals and odd jobs that first year. But the longer I was away, the easier it got." After years of parental suppression and a mountain of demons on my shoulders, being on the road let me breathe my first real breath.

"Friendship." The word spills from her lips. She sets her fork down and lays her arm on the table, palm up. I slide my hand in hers and swallow. "Ander, there is nothing I won't do for you."

I lock on to her soft green irises as my thumb brushes the ring on her finger. The small token sends a jolt of energy from my finger to my heart. And in that single zap, I know... I am right where I need to be. With Helena Williams. North. *My North.*

CHAPTER 45
HELENA

My phone dings with an incoming text.

ANDERSON

> Ales and Braydon are driving me crazy.

I snort as I read the message.

Braydon is a great guy, but he and Lessa can't keep their hands to themselves. For two people who weren't into dating or relationships before each other, they give sappy a whole new definition. They aren't shy about public displays. Don't get me wrong, I am happy for my best friend. Thrilled she found someone that makes her whole. Someone she wants to spend time with more often than not. Their lovey eyes and dopey smiles are adorable... and nauseating.

But only because I want something like that too.

HELENA

> Welcome to the club

I pocket my phone and step out of the office in the back of the store. Talking with a customer, Becca smiles when I step into view. I lift my hand and make a drinking motion, then point down the road. I raise my brows, silently asking if she wants a coffee. She gives a subtle nod before directing the customer to the new midriffs we got in yesterday.

Exiting the store, I stroll down the sidewalk and breathe in the light perfume punctuating the air. Mixed with the rich scent of evergreens, lavender blankets the town in a natural balm. More than once, I've joked it's the main reason the residents are so laid back. Though it ends soon, lavender season is a favorite of locals and tourists alike.

Lake Lavender doesn't have an apothecary or skincare shop. The pharmacy or beauty aisle in Lakeside Grocer doesn't count. And because we lack both, I've mulled over adding something to Always Classic. Lavender products made locally for women by women. Scented bags for dresser drawers and closets. Teas and soaps and lotions. Candles and dried flower bundles. The possibilities are endless.

Discussing the idea with Mags and Lessa is on my to-do list. I doubt they'd shut down the idea, but as my business partners, I want their ideas and insight.

My phone buzzes in my pocket and I pull it out as I reach Java and Teas Me.

ANDERSON

Club Lesdon 😄

I snort-laugh as I walk through the restored front door of the coffee shop.

HELENA

Lesdon? I dare you to say that next time we're all together.

ANDERSON

Dare accepted.

"What's so funny?"

I startle and shove my phone in my pocket. "Nothing." I tuck a wayward lock of hair behind my ear as I scan the dining room. "The café looks great. Like nothing happened."

Weeks ago, two guys broke into Java and Teas Me long after closing. They vandalized the walls and broke furniture and appliances. Then, they started a fire in the kitchen. Little did they know, Lessa was in the office off the kitchen. Had she not been in there and heard them break in, the building might have gone up in flames.

It took threats of serious jail time to get the guys to speak up and reveal the person behind all the damages. Someone with a massive ego and a severe sense of entitlement. Needless to say, much of the town was shocked. But they banded together and pitched in to help one of their own.

Small towns... may have their frustrating moments, but at the end of the day, there is more good than bad. And Lake Lavender proved as much when Java and Teas Me had to close its doors for repairs. Not only did they lend time and tools, but they also gave warm hugs and brought food and drinks.

"I'll let that change of subject slide, but I expect answers. Soon."

I roll my eyes. "Okay, *Mom*."

Lessa wraps me in a tight hug and, surprisingly, releases me before I tap out. "Here for drinks?"

"Yes, please." I follow her to the service counter. "My usual matcha and a lemon-iced lavender scone. A Light Weight latte, iced with oat milk, and Walk of Shame sandwich for Becca."

She keys in our drinks and food then cashes it out without making me pay. One of the perks of a business partnership... unlimited caffeine and provisions. I pull a twenty out of my pocket and shove it in the tip jar. Though I don't need to pay, I drop money in the tip jar every trip. It's only right. Not only does it support my friend and our business, but it also keeps her staff happy.

"Food will be out in a few." She spins around and gets to work on the drinks. In no time, she pops two cups in a cardboard carrier and sets my bagged scone in a free slot. Leaning a hip on the counter, she narrows her eyes as she studies my face. "You're different."

I tilt my head and purse my lips. "Thanks?"

She pushes off the counter and tips her head toward the end of the service counter. I grab the cup holder and meet her at the end. Her thin fingers fiddle with the strings of her apron but stop when I drop my gaze to the action.

"Weeks ago, you were mopey and weird."

"What the hell, Lessa?"

She huffs. "That came out wrong." She crosses her arms over her chest. "It's just... you seemed down. Quieter than normal." Unlocking her arms, she shrugs. "And now, you're more yourself."

Alessandra Everett, always a keen observer. Neither she nor Anderson misses much. The one thing she always missed, though, is the relationship between me and her brother.

And now that he is back and we are rebuilding us, I am happier.

"Again, thanks?"

With a roll of her eyes, she leans across the counter and lowers her voice. "Whatever it is, I'm always here to listen."

Much as I'd love to share why I've smiled more in the past few days than I have in the past year, my lips are sealed. The selfish part of me wants more undiluted time with Anderson. If I tell Lessa the reason for my better mood, I will never hear the end of her questions.

Plus, I'd like to break the news when Anderson is in the room. We'd incur her inundation better as a team.

Team. I love that word on my mental tongue.

I shrug a shoulder. "I appreciate that."

The bell between the kitchen and service alley dings as August calls out an order number. Lessa shuffles down the line and grabs the small box with Becca's sandwich. Popping it in a brown bag, she takes my scone from the carrier, sets it in the bag, and folds down the top.

"Still on for Friday?"

Picking up the drink carrier and bag, I step back from the counter. "Of course."

"Maybe we'll hit up On Tap."

"Mmm. Onion rings."

She laughs. "Love you."

I head for the door, twisting to call over my shoulder, "Love you too."

CHAPTER 46

ANDERSON

I want to be more of a people person, but the struggle is real. The crowds, the noise, the constant go-go-go energy—they make me itchy. Everyone is always in your face, asking personal questions and touching you without permission. The endless invasion of personal space and privacy, like it's their right to know or own every piece of your life.

I may have grown up in Lake Lavender, but this small town is not the same place I left.

"Stay," Ales pleads. "At least an hour."

My molars grind as I scan the bar and grill. According to the sign outside, a live band is playing tonight. If you spend ten dollars, you get to stay during the entire set without paying a cover. This is a change I can get behind. Just wish the place wasn't at max capacity.

"Food and one hour," I promise.

As it stands, I have no room to complain. Ales is giving me a free place to stay. Sure, I have my van and can drive to the outskirts of town to sleep, but I missed Ales. Her light-hearted nature and warm, vigorous hugs. Our occasional calls or texts appeased me for years, but as of recently, it wasn't enough.

Plus, I have other relationships to sort out.

Mom and Dad haven't been at the front of my mind in a long time. I chose to block them from my life and move forward without any communication. It took weeks for me to see how much they impacted my mental health. Mom always came across as loving and saying things to *make my life better*. She once called it tough love. A love no one but me received. Dad had never been tough on me, but he'd also never stood up for me when harsh words spilled from her lips. Unbeknownst to him, he enabled Mom to be cruel on the sly.

I don't know if my relationship with my parents is repairable, but I want to give it a chance. Time away might have done us all some good. I want to speak with and see my sister more often. We may be polar opposites, but her love for me has always been the same. Constant.

More than anything, I want to feel wanted. I want to feel loved. And now that I've had time to get to know myself better, I am ready to open up and start fresh.

Leaning into Ales, I ask, "Where's the bathroom?"

She points to a short hallway in the back corner.

"Be right back. If the server comes back, a water, cheeseburger, and fries, please."

She pats my shoulder. "I got you, Baby A."

Sliding off the stool, I weave through the tall tops, shrinking away from flailing arms and dancing bodies. I step inside the bathroom, and thank goodness, it's empty and clean. I teeter back until I hit the wall, the cool tile settling the building panic in my veins. After a few deep breaths, I use the urinal and wash my hands. With one last look in the mirror, I nod at my reflection.

You got this.

I make my way back to the table but stop short two tables away. Sitting on the stool next to mine is Helena. She hasn't seen me yet. With a bright smile on her face, she talks with Ales and Braydon while sipping her drink. For a moment, I remain hidden behind other patrons and watch her.

She looks happy.

But from everything I've witnessed, when friends aren't around, some of her happiness is a mirage.

Sitting back on her stool, she scans the crowd. It takes her seconds to spot me less than fifteen feet away. Her green irises lock on to me as I slowly weave through the tables. She swallows but otherwise doesn't move. Doesn't take her eyes off me as I step closer.

I take the only vacant seat, which is next to her, and nudge her leg with my knee. "Didn't know you'd be here."

She audibly exhales. "I can go."

Without thinking, I rest my hand on her thigh. "No. Please don't." Then I rip my hand away and shove it between my thighs. "Sorry."

"It's fine."

Is it, though?

Touching an arm or hand is one thing. But my hand on her thigh is wholly different. It opens doors I closed years ago. Doors to memories of how soft her skin was and the way she shivered as my fingers ghosted her flesh.

Before I go off on a mental tangent, the server stops at the table and we order enough greasy food to feed twice the people at the table. The bar owner jogs to the small stage and jumps up to the mic.

"Good evening, Lake Lavender. How is everyone?"

A roar echoes in the space and I slap my hands over my ears. *Too much damn noise.*

"Thanks for coming out tonight. Remember the rules. Spend at least ten to avoid the cover charge. And be kind to the staff, they're busting ass tonight."

Another booming roar from the patrons.

"Let's welcome back our favorite Stone Bay rockers, Hailey's Fire."

A deep thud reverberates through the bar as the drummer thumps the bass. Then the simmer of the cymbals hits the air a moment before the lead singer strums his guitar. The song starts off slow and melodic before picking up momentum and gusto.

They're good.

Stone Bay. I visited the small town years ago, but don't remember much other than nearby forestry and mountain trails. Maybe the town deserves a second trip. Maybe there are hidden gems in the businesses, like kick-ass local rock bands.

"So..." Helena says, barely over the music. "About that dare."

I snort and shake my head. Of course, she would remember the goofy blended name I came up with on the fly for Ales and Braydon. Lesdon. It's stupid but funny. And Ales will hate it.

Cocking a brow, I shift my attention to my sister. "Ales," I holler over the music.

Ales stops talking about some older woman in a crocheted dress that came in for a blueberry muffin yesterday, her hair a foot high and unmoving, and twists on her stool. "What's up, Baby A?"

That nickname... I love it but wish she'd retire it already. *Ding, ding, ding.* Light bulb moment.

"I want to strike a deal."

Blue eyes similar to mine narrow. "A deal?"

"Yep."

She shrugs. "Okay. What kind of deal?"

"You stop calling me Baby A—which was cute when we were kids—and I won't use my new name for you two." I gesture to her and Braydon with a finger.

Her eyes drift toward the ceiling in contemplation. "Depends on the name," she says, leveling me with a stare.

I bite the inside of my cheek, doing my damnedest to keep a straight face as the word rolls off my tongue. "Lesdon."

Loud laughter rips from across the table as Logan slaps his hand on the lacquered wood. "That's some funny shit, man." Logan isn't necessarily someone I'd hang out with often, but he is a riot. If someone were my complete opposite, it'd be him.

Ales, on the other hand, doesn't find the name or Logan's commentary funny at all. Her stone-faced expression is a mix of disdain and irritation. "You are *not* calling me or us *Lesdon*," she states firmly. "Which is far more horrible than Baby A."

True, but I am over the childish name. I shrug. "Take it or leave it. Your choice."

The server sidles up to the table with the first round of food. Fryer grease hits my nose and my stomach growls. Until returning to Lake Lavender, fried foods hadn't hit my plate in years. On the road, I ate lean and lighter to not cause stomach issues while hiking deserted paths. Every other birthday, I splurged and ordered takeout from a nearby restaurant. The occasional indulgence had been enough to quell the hankering.

Birthdays.

Ours is a few weeks away, and it has been what feels like a lifetime since we celebrated together. As kids, our parents threw us joint parties. As we got older, the parties fizzled out and were replaced with cookouts and cake.

Will she want to celebrate? Is her birthday a tough day to enjoy too? It always felt like *our* time, *our* month. And not spending close to a decade of birthdays with her... it just feels like any other day.

The last of the orders are deposited on the table, along with bottled condiments. Applause fills the air as one song ends and a new one starts. Everyone at the table dives for the food on their plate while I sit dumbstruck.

"Fine," Ales grumbles, and I snap out of my mental fog. "But what am I supposed to call you now?" she asks, practically whining.

I pluck a fry from my plate, dunk it in mayonnaise, and pop it in my mouth. Swallowing, I give my best *seriously?* look. "My name," I deadpan.

"That's boring," she says with a hint of snobbery.

"Wow, thanks."

"You know that's not what I mean." She rolls her eyes, swiping up a chicken wing and taking a bite. Hand over her mouth, she continues. "The only time I call you Anderson is when I'm talking to someone that doesn't know you or I need to be formal."

The table falls quiet as we eat our respective meals. Bite by bite, I demolish my cheeseburger and fries. At this point, I assume the conversation is done. Which is fine by me. I grab a fresh napkin from the middle of the table and wipe my hands and mouth. Just as I open my mouth to call it a night and head back to the apartment, Ales cuts me off.

"I'll call you Ander. Like Lena does."

Beside me, Helena chokes on her soda. I pat her back a few times, then rub small, slow circles as the coughing settles.

"You okay?"

On another cough, she nods.

I look to my sister. "I'd rather you didn't."

Her eyes narrow then relax. Then her blue eyes shift to her best friend and I stop breathing. She swallows, then returns her gaze to mine. "Yeah. Sure."

Dropping my hand from Helena's back, I push away from the table. "I'm headed out." Pulling out my wallet, I drop a twenty on the table. "Was nice seeing everyone."

And before anyone can ask questions, I bolt for the door. Ready to escape the crowd, the noise, and too much attention aimed in my direction.

Ugh. Is this a mistake? Is returning to a life no longer mine a bad idea? I think it might be.

CHAPTER 47

HELENA

I haven't heard from Anderson since he walked out of On Tap Friday night. I sent him a message yesterday morning, asking if he was okay, but he has yet to respond. My relationship with Anderson may be back at square one, but I still know his tells. I know when he is uncomfortable or restless.

Friday night, with the exception of the joke about Lessa and Braydon, he'd been out of his comfort zone.

And like every time he felt like an outsider when we were younger, I want to erase his unease. Want to bring him into the fold with open arms. Show him he is wanted and loved.

But how well do I know adult Anderson? Not well at all, I'm ashamed to admit. Hopefully, he will give me the opportunity to change that.

"What do you think, Smoky?" I pet the gray tabby currently curled in my lap. "Will I get a chance?"

Her closed eyes crack the slightest bit as she purrs louder. Curling into a tighter ball, she drapes her tail over her eyes, a silent message for me to let her sleep.

"Fine," I whisper. Tugging the throw blanket off the back of the couch, I create a soft, warm nest. Gently, I move Smoky to the nest and rise from the couch. "You hang out here. Guard the fort. I'm going for lunch." I check the time and note it's not eleven yet. "Or brunch."

Smoky digs at the blanket a few times before sitting down and licking her fur. I scratch her head and get a scratchy meow in return.

I pad down the short hall and head for the closet when I step inside my room. Tugging a cream off-the-shoulder top from its hanger, I fetch a pair of black denim jeans. I ditch my camisole and pajama shorts for the outfit, then go about brushing my hair and teeth. After adding eyeliner and a swipe of lip gloss, I slip on cream flats, shoulder my purse, and give Smoky one last scratch.

"Later, pretty girl."

Locking up, I jog down the stairs from the apartment and round the building for the sidewalk. One of the best parts of renting or owning the spaces on Main, we have the choice to also have the second floor. Most businesses own the space above their store, but some opt to sell or rent out the apartment.

Like Lessa, I live above my business. Not only do I save money, but I can be in the shop in seconds.

The two bedroom, two bathroom is more than plenty for me and Smoky. Before Gayle sold me the shop, the space sat empty for years. The previous renters lived there for more than a decade and upgraded much of the space. Aside from adding a laundry room, they'd torn down the walls between the kitchen, dining, and living rooms. The open floor plan made the smaller space feel large and welcoming. With a few tweaks with walls, they'd also expanded the bedrooms and bathrooms.

For eight hundred fifty square feet, my apartment is cozy and more spacious than imaginable.

As I walk toward Java and Teas Me, several residents greet me with a wave or smile and "good morning." I return the sentiment in kind. One of my favorite parts of living here is how considerate everyone is. Like all cities or towns, there are grumps and complainers. But most of them keep to themselves or huddle together to whine. We happy folks do our best to avoid them.

I tug open the door of Java and Teas Me and inhale the scent of heaven. Mandi greets me with a jovial, "Welcome to Java and Teas Me." When I don't see Lessa behind the service counter, I scan the dining room. Not spotting her, I assume she's either in the back or, by some miracle chance, took the day off.

I step up to the counter. "Morning, Mandi. Been busy today?"

She blows out a breath, the wisps of hair on her face floating up, then falling back in place. "Yeah. We're almost out of scones and muffins." She straightens the stack of numbered table tents. "Lessa ran down to Sweet Spot to see if we can get more."

No days off for Alessandra Everett.

"Wow." I tip my head toward the packed tip jar on the counter. "At least it's a good tip day."

"Best perk of the season." Smiling, she rests her hands on top of the ordering kiosk. "What can I get you?"

"Large iced matcha latte with oat milk, and add vanilla." I scan the menu board overhead. "And a slice of the vegan sausage and cheese quiche."

Mandi keys in my order. "Eating here or taking it to go?"

It's been a while since I've occupied the quirky dining room. "Here, please."

Grabbing a table tent, she keys the number in with my order then hands it over. "Quiche should be out shortly. Let me get your drink."

I shove cash in the tip jar and move down the line and wait for my drink. With another scan of the dining room, I opt to sit out on the patio. The day is too nice to be inside.

Drink in hand, I weave through the tables and step out onto the semi-enclosed patio. I sit at a table for two near the rail, sag into my seat, and sip my latte as I wait for the rest of my order.

People bustle on the sidewalks on either side of Main. Children point at the candy and ice cream shops. A handful of people stand in front of For the Love of Paws, hands cupped to the glass as they watch puppies play not far from the window. Others stand near the small cart outside Rosie's Bouquet and ponder which flowers to purchase.

As a kid, the warmer months always brought residents from sister towns and tourists from far away. The influx of traffic and people in town was nice. New faces and possible friends. But in the past three years, the number of visitors has increased quite a bit and I have mixed feelings about the change.

More visitors means more money for the stores and town, which is wonderful. But in the same breath, it brings in unsavory people.

Crime had always been low in Lake Lavender. Unfortunately, that statistic is no longer true. During the last town meeting, the mayor prattled off the higher crime numbers. Figures that did not include the vandalism and fire at Java and

Teas Me. The only thing the mayor and sheriff offered... stay vigilant and report anything suspicious.

"Here you are, Lena." Mandi startles me from my introspection.

My eyes shift from the plate to Mandi. "Thank you."

"Welcome. Nice seeing you."

"You too."

I stab the quiche and moan as the bite hits my tongue. August and Sharon are miracle workers in the kitchen. Everything they create is pure bliss. Though I'm not a full plant-based eater, I incorporate the foods into my diet. People that skip vegan-labeled foods because they think it'll be gross are missing out. Sure, it tastes different than what they're used to, but it's still damn good. Especially if made here.

Just as I moan around another bite, Anderson drops in the chair across the table and sets a bottled water on the table. My eyes widen as I stop chewing.

"Hey, North." A smirk graces his lips. "I take it the quiche is good."

Lifting a hand to cover my mouth, I chew faster than humanly possible, swallow, then sip my latte. "Hey." I wipe my mouth with the napkin. "Uh, yeah. It's good."

He chuckles. "Had it the other day. August is a kitchen genius."

Much as I love any conversation with Anderson, this one feels weird. Generic. Something to fill time. And something so far from who we are.

"He is." I cut off another bite of quiche and load my fork. "What's up?" I shove the bite in my mouth.

His blue irises darken as he regards me for a moment. Then his gaze shifts down the street and he loses focus. And while he ponders over what to say, I put myself in his shoes.

Far as I know, this is the first time Anderson has set foot in Lake Lavender since he left mid–senior year. And in the almost six years since he got in a car and watched the town disappear in his rearview mirror, so much is different.

Though most of the people I see daily are the same, several new faces have relocated here from Seattle and Tacoma in search of less commotion. Until a year ago, the town had no new housing developments. Now, we have three additional subdivisions housing anywhere from ten to thirty homes. Some may say that it is small, but for us, it's pretty big.

"Thought coming back was a good idea." He blinks a few times before his blues meet my greens. "Now, I'm not so sure."

I set my fork down and push my plate aside. Lean closer to the table and sip my drink. Swallow past the twinge forming in my chest. "Why?"

He huffs out a breath. "I had this grand idea." Mirroring my position, he draws invisible images on the table. "Come home and fix everything. Feel less lonely." The last part comes out just above a whisper.

Loneliness... what a fickle creature. Some days, loneliness is this empty sadness just under the surface. Sometimes it feels closer to homesickness. An ache for something you no longer have. On the worst days, loneliness feels like no one will truly understand or love you. On the worst days, you feel worthless. I've felt the last one more than I care to admit.

Wasn't until Anderson and I had a falling-out that I experienced loneliness for the first time. College kept me busy enough, but every night when my head hit the pillow, loneliness blanketed my soul and robbed me of sleep. Since returning from college, loneliness and I have been on a first-name basis.

The only glimmer of hope to shine a light on my loneliness

came two and a half months ago when Lessa's phone rang in the restaurant and Anderson was on the other end.

I can live without Anderson Everett in my life. I have for the past nine-ish years. But I don't *want* to live without him. Now I have a second chance with him, whether friendship or something greater, and I don't plan to waste it.

"Not sure what it is you want to fix, but are you the only person who needs to do the fixing?"

His brows furrow before he sits back in his chair and drops his hands to his lap. A lightness fills his expression as he scoffs. "My therapist would say no. He'd remind me that issues concerning more than one person means all parties are equally at fault."

I purse my lips and nod. "Seems legit."

He kicks a foot out beneath the table, his leg leaning against my calf. "He'd like you."

"Not sure if that's a compliment," I say with a laugh. I pick up my fork and poke at the crust bits on the plate. "Seriously, I have just as much work to do, if not more, when it comes to us."

Grabbing his water bottle, he picks at the damp label. "Highly doubt that."

Far back as I recall, I have loved Anderson. My love for him was different early on—a sibling or friend love. Innocent. But as the years passed and I embraced what I felt, my love for Anderson bloomed. I'd fallen for him, truly fallen, at fifteen. That love was sealed at sixteen, then broken, although still present, at seventeen.

To this day, I still love him. I will never not love him.

"Ander, I loved you." His eyes fly up and latch on to mine. "I love you," I confess, a breath above a whisper. I look over his shoulder and lose focus. Swallow and close my eyes. "And

I admit I didn't put in enough effort when things got hard for us. Nowhere near enough. I should've done more. I should've fought harder."

At the time, I didn't know how to balance school and Ander and keeping my parents happy. My immature mind said to eliminate the one that didn't coincide with the other two. It'd been a foolish move I regretted daily. Something I will work tirelessly to make right.

"I should've tried harder too. But harping over what we should've done won't change the past. Nothing will. What matters now is how we navigate the future."

A smile plumps my cheeks. "I've missed your wisdom, Anderson Everett." I sip the last of my latte. "But not as much as I've missed you."

Soft blue eyes hold my greens as he soaks up my words. "We should do something for our birthdays this month."

"I'd love that. Anything in mind?"

He sits up, untwists the cap on his water, and takes a long pull before securing the cap again. "Not yet. I'll think on it." His lips pucker and bounce side to side. "Are you able to take time off from work?"

Aside from my normal days off, I haven't taken vacation time in… I've not taken scheduled time off since owning the shop. *Wow.* My self-care needs some serious love.

"I'd have to speak with my employees, Lessa and Mags, but I'm sure it's doable."

"Ales and Mags?"

Why can't I go back a decade and change all the stupid shit that happened? Maybe then we wouldn't be here. A point where we don't know much about each other. Anderson is no stranger, but I don't know the man across the table. Not the way I want to know him.

"We're all partners of Java and Teas Me and Always Classic. If Mags owns a business one day, we'll be partners in it too."

"Ah."

"Anytime one of us needs help or has a staff shortage, we ask."

Requiring help is rare, but the need arises once in a while. Maybe once or twice a year. Something as simple as pulling on an apron and filling drink orders or straightening clothing racks and cashing out customers. Pitching in a few hours to support one of our businesses and alleviate unnecessary stress.

"You check schedules and I'll come up with ideas. Sound good?"

I push back on my chair, rise, and shoulder my purse. "Perfect."

He stands and grabs my plate, taking it to the tub near the trash bin. Drinking the last of his water, he deposits the bottle in the recycling bin. He spins around and steps into me, taking my hands in his. His gaze falls to where his thumb strokes my ring, the corner of his mouth twitching.

"You're the best part, you know."

My brows tug together. "Best part?"

Slowly, he levels me with his stare. The steel-blue rim of his irises is darker, bolder, certain. His tongue darts out and wets his lips, my eyes following the action. He swallows with a nod.

"Returning home. You're the best part." His thumb brushes my ring again. "The main reason I'm here." He leans in, the scruff of his beard scratchy on my cheek, his breath warm on my ear. "I love you too, North." Inching back, he drops my hands. "Always."

CHAPTER 48

ANDERSON

This is a bad idea. What the hell am I thinking?

It should be no surprise that being in Helena's presence again has me making irrational decisions. I told her I wanted to start over. Back to square one as friends. Get to know each other again.

And here I am, scrolling through my phone, looking at nearby getaways. Places to take her. Alone.

A very more-than-friends activity.

Yet, I don't stop myself. Don't stop the wayward path my thoughts have taken. Don't stop pressing forward or striving to make up for lost time.

"Bad fucking idea," I mutter as I continue my online search.

Familiar with most of the trails and camping spots in the state, I filter them by terrain, amenities, and highest-rated views. Not sure of the last time Helena went camping or hiked the woods, but with running her own business, I assume she is out of practice. Her current version of roughing it probably consists of losing power during a snowstorm and having to light a fire by herself. Pompous of me to think such things, especially with her dad being a ranger, but she looks softer than the girl I knew.

I star a few favorites to save for later review, swipe away the app, lock my phone, and shove it in my pocket. Rising from the bed, I wander to the kitchen in search of lunch.

"Hey, man," Braydon greets from the couch as I enter the main living space. "Didn't realize you were here."

"Afternoon." I shuffle toward the kitchen, open the fridge, and take out fixings for a sandwich. "Hungry?"

Eyes on his computer, he nods. "I could eat. What's on the menu?"

Unstacking the deli packages, I spread them across the counter. "Roasted chicken, honey ham, some kind of meat alternative, cheese."

From his spot on the couch, Braydon chuckles. "Yeah, we're experimenting with more meatless options. Some are… undesirable. Others are surprisingly good."

Ales offers a variety of foods in the coffee shop, wanting to accommodate anyone walking through the door. Makes me happy she tries the foods she puts on her menu too. Such a smart businesswoman.

Plant-based options aren't a complete turnoff. On the road, I tried to keep minimal perishables on hand. I have a fridge in my van, but it doesn't hold much. I reserve the space for necessities. Meat and dairy haven't always been essential. Being on the road taught me how to make the most of food. How to get requisite nutrition with a mix of fruit, vegetables, nuts, and grains. Occasionally, I splurged on jerky, but the salt deterred me more often than not.

Dehydration mixed with hiking ten miles does no one any good.

"Whatever is running low, I'll take the last of it. Mustard and cheese, please."

"Sure thing."

I go about making sandwiches for us, cutting them down the middle and plating them with chips. After cleaning the counter, I carry the plates to the living room and park next to him on the couch.

"Thanks," he says, setting his laptop aside and taking the plate. "Appreciate it."

"No problem." I tip my head toward his laptop. "Working?"

He finishes the bite in his mouth, washing it down with water. "Yeah. Well, trying to." He pops a chip in his mouth and exhales audibly. "After everything that happened with the shop, the vandalism and fire, I told my dad I wanted to try working remotely."

"Is he not okay with it?" I bite into my own sandwich.

Braydon turns to meet my gaze, a wrinkle between his brows. "He's more on board with it than I expected."

"But?"

Without a doubt, Braydon loves being here with Ales. They are sickly adorable. All hands and lips and public displays whenever possible. But I sense a struggle within him. One he won't share with Ales.

"Dad told me to take time off to help JTM get back to rights. Now that most of it is done, I'm bored."

If anyone understands this feeling, it is definitely me. Being on the road is exhilarating. One day to the next, you never know what will happen. Who you will meet. What surprises you will experience on each adventure. Seeing as Braydon traveled the majority of the time for his job, and now he isn't, I understand the itchy need to get up and go.

"I haven't hung out with my sister much in years, but if she's anything like I remember, she won't hold you back. Her dream is the coffee shop. It always has been. But her dream doesn't have to be yours. And she'd be upset with herself if she thought you gave up everything for her."

Ales loves Braydon. I see it in every smile and hug and kiss they share. But she will beat herself up if she thinks he is unhappy here. She will push him away to let him have the life she thinks he wants. I may have been gone for years, but I still know my sister. She'd sacrifice her happiness for others. She'd let him go, even if it hurt, so he doesn't feel anchored to an undesirable life.

"Honestly, I'm good with working remotely for Dad, but would like to find a job at the local paper." He sets his plate on the table, then rests his elbows on his knees. "I love traveling, but I no longer want to do it alone. Unless it's a day trip, it holds no interest." He tilts his head to meet my eyes. "Know what I mean?"

Did I ever.

I love living on the road. The fresh air. The freedom to be myself at every turn. No one whispering in my ear, telling me every way I've fucked up. If I wake up and don't want to leave bed all day, I don't. On the road, I answer only to myself. It's on the road that I learned how to listen to my body and heart. I learned how to respect my own desires and not fear what others thought of them.

Living in the van is the most incredible form of liberation.

Then one day, I missed home. Not necessarily the town or house I grew up in. Home has never been a specific location. Helena... has always been my home. My light. My peace.

And damn, I missed her. Knowing she missed me just as much... *fuck*, it is pain and relief and scary as hell.

"Yeah. I get it." I pause for a moment, contemplating my next words. *Fuck it.* "Which is why I plan on asking Helena to go vanning with me for a week."

"Helena?" He sits straighter, his gaze scrutinizing every line on my face. "I didn't realize you two—"

"Please don't say anything." I shove a chip in my mouth. "Ales doesn't know everything. It was a long time ago." On an audible exhale, I swallow past the fear bubbling in my chest. "I came back for her. To fix things. To find our way back to…" I shrug. "I don't know. Something like before, I guess."

He holds up both hands in surrender. "Promise not to say anything, but don't keep it from her long." Soft laughter leaves his lips. "Your sister is my weakness, and I won't keep secrets from her."

Braydon really is a good guy. Though neither he nor Ales were interested in a serious relationship, they had an undeniable connection. He couldn't stay away and she was tired of fighting her feelings. It hadn't been easy for her to confess, but I'm happy she did. His love for her makes her glow.

"Thanks." I pop another chip in my mouth. "Hoping time alone changes things. That we find us again." I pick at an invisible piece of lint on my jeans and drop my gaze. "There're some other things I need to talk with Ales about. Not yet. Soon, though."

"Sounds serious."

I purse my lips and nod. "You have no idea."

He rests a hand on my shoulder. "We haven't known each other long, but if you ever need a friend…"

"Appreciate it." I straighten and point to his plate. "Done?"

With a nod, he hands me the plate. I take them to the kitchen, scrub them clean and set them in the rack. Wander back down the hall without a word, go into the guest room, and plop down on the mattress. I stare at the ceiling and get lost in my thoughts.

First, fix things with Helena. Then, sit down with Ales and spill every dark secret.

It's the latter thought that twists my gut. Of all people, Ales always supported and loved me. Shame washes over me at the fact I haven't been completely forthcoming. I hope exposing the truth doesn't hurt her. It will hurt I didn't tell her sooner, but I needed my own time to heal. Hopefully, she understands. Because damn, I can't lose her. She's all I have left, at least for now.

CHAPTER 49

HELENA

I'm sorry, what? *A week? He wants to go away for a week?*

"What would we do for a week?"

The question sounds stupid the second it leaves my lips. Like I've never spent a week away from town. Unfortunately, the last time I went on a real vacation was years ago. Owning a business, especially in the early years, makes it difficult to get away.

Business has been good, more than good, and I am beyond grateful.

After reviewing the schedule and speaking with Becca and Charise, they were more than willing to take on extra shifts to gift me time off. They also want every detail of my trip when I return.

When Anderson mentioned the idea, I figured two or three days tops. Boy, had I been wrong.

I twist the ring on my right hand as nervous energy swirls beneath my diaphragm.

Being away from the store for a week has me a little on

edge, but it isn't the root cause of this nervous buzz. The store will be fine, of that I am sure. Becca and Charise can run the store with their eyes closed.

No, it's the time alone with Anderson that has me highly strung. Minutes and hours and days of uninterrupted time together. Perspiration dampens my skin as my hands start to tremble. My hands fall to my sides as I curl my fingers tight. Seconds later, I relax my hands and wipe my sweaty palms on the sides of my thighs.

Am I ready for a week alone with Anderson? Just me, him, and the wilderness. I don't hate the idea.

He chuckles. "Whatever you want." Stepping into me, he reaches for my hand and brushes his thumb over my ring. *His ring.* "I've checked out campgrounds nearby. Trails and spots you might not have seen. We can spend time hiking, but I'm also cool with chilling in the van and catching up."

Catching up with Anderson. It sounds dangerous and delicious. Much as I'd love to curl into his side for an entire week and hear about every part of his life I missed, being constantly close to him may be a hazard to my health. And his.

"I have a cat," I blurt out.

His brows shoot up. "Okay."

"I can't leave her for a week."

He shrugs. "Bring her with us."

God, he makes it sound so easy. *Pack a bag and bring your cat for a week on the road.*

What if she's scared of car rides? Cats in cars are different than dogs. My baby is barely a year old and has only known the four main walls of my apartment for ten of those months. Will nature freak her out? Will she run off? What if I lose her?

No.

"It's not that easy."

"Why?"

What does he mean? Maybe because he hasn't had a pet, he doesn't understand. "Aside from the trip home, Smoky has never been outside the apartment. Being in a car might scare her."

"Might." He shrugs again. "Or maybe she'll be fine." He reaches for the back of his neck and rubs his muscles. "If you want, I'll go to the sporting goods store outside of town. They probably have travel packs for small pets."

My entire face scrunches to the middle, tight with confusion. "Travel packs?"

A smile kicks up the corner of his mouth. "Yeah. Another hiker I met on the road had one. Basically, it's a clear, hardshell backpack with holes for ventilation. A cat or small dog can sit or lie in it while you hike."

Damn, he is determined for us to go on this trip. Not that I *don't* want to go. More like I'm scared. It's one thing to see him here, on home turf, where I can easily walk away if things go south. But on the road, if I upset him or vice versa, we are stuck together until we resolve things or return to town.

I may have known everything about Anderson years ago, but I can't say the same anymore. That fact twists the guilt knife embedded in my heart. The same piercing blade that took up residence months before college.

Exhaling a tired breath, I clasp my hands again and twist the double gold band. I clench my teeth then relax my jaw. Stare out the front window of the shop and let my eyes lose focus.

Now or never. Better to see if we're fixable now rather than to drag it out.

"Okay. Fine." I suck in a sharp breath and slowly exhale. "Tell me the days and I'll get things squared away here."

A victorious smile lights his expression and I stop breathing. *Wow.* In a blink, heat spreads from the center of my chest to the tips of my fingers and toes. My heart pounds viciously against my rib cage, begging to get closer. To get a heftier dose of his addictive smile.

The bell over the door jingles and Becca walks in with a Java and Teas Me cup in hand. "Hey, Lena." She waves.

I lift a hand and wave back. "Afternoon. Becca, this is Anderson, my—" My what? Friend? Best friend? Former boyfriend?

Ugh.

Anderson offers his hand as Becca approaches. "Anderson." He peeks at me from the corner of his eye. "Childhood best friend."

She shakes his hand, and my eyes drop to their clasped hands. Cordial as it is, heat sears my veins at their contact. I have zero room to be jealous, especially over an introduction, but here I am, fuming.

"Oh. Hi. It's nice to meet you." She releases his hand and tucks some hair behind her ear before straightening her spine and pushing out her chest.

Damn it.

"Becca." She blinks, then gives me her attention. "Anderson is the one I'll be out of town with." Marking territory or feeling green is not my style, but the way she is eyeing him, best I nip this in the bud early.

As if he senses the irritation radiating off me, Anderson inches closer to my side and laces my fingers with his. Becca's eyes drop long enough to notice the simple gesture, her cheeks flushing as she looks up.

"Cool." She swallows. "Was nice meeting you, Anderson." Jabbing a thumb over her shoulder, she says, "Time to work." She spins on her heel and walks over to the register, tapping the screen to clock in.

Anderson gives my hand a gentle squeeze and I twist to meet his stare.

"That was cute."

My brows twitch. "What? Becca?"

The corner of his mouth lifts into a subtle half smile. He shakes his head, eyes never leaving mine. "No."

It would hurt but not surprise me if Anderson is attracted to Becca. With long, wavy blonde hair and a figure most men drool over, it's impossible to not find her beautiful. Without effort, she can have any guy in Lake Lavender.

Except Anderson.

"Then what?"

Lifting his free hand, the rough pads of his fingers graze the line of my jaw. He grabs a lock of my hair and holds the strands prisoner, rubbing them between his fingers.

"I like that you're jealous."

"I am not—"

"Yeah. You are." His hand falls away and takes my other as he steps impossibly closer. "And it's okay to admit it. I'd rage if another man so much as touched you."

Well, damn.

He leans in, rests his cheek on mine, and breathes me in. My eyes fall shut, my pulse wild and loud in my ears.

"I'll text the dates after I stop at the store." He kisses the angle of my jaw near my ear. "Love you, North."

I tighten my hold on him. "Love you, Ander."

And before I can make sense of my dizzying thoughts, he pulls away, turns around, and walks out the door.

A week alone with Anderson may be the best or worst idea I've agreed to. Either way, after this trip, all doubts and questions will be answered.

CHAPTER 50

ANDERSON

Perishables aren't something I typically have often on the road, but since I won't be the only one in the van for a week, I purchased atypical items. Small comforts for Helena.

I stock the van's chest fridge with chicken, block cheese, eggs, fruit, and vegetables. Then move to the cabinets I use as a pantry, loading them with bread, nonperishable produce, nuts, cashew butter, dried fruits, individual nondairy milk cartons, rice, beans, coffee, tea, and water. While shopping, I also made a point to buy s'mores supplies.

The van has four overhead compartments and five base cabinets, plus shelves beneath the platform bed for storage. Two of the overheads hold dishware—two each of plates, bowls, cups, mugs, and four-piece sets of cutlery—and cooking dishes—a frying pan, two small pots, a cutting mat, kettle, and cooking utensils. The other two overheads hold staples for outdoor life—matches, lantern, toilet paper, first aid kit, sunscreen, and repellent. Two of the five base cabinets are pantry space, one for sanitation supplies, one for linens, and the largest for clothes. Typically, the space beneath the bed houses a collapsible chair, books, notebooks, and excess staples.

With this trip, unlike my usual days on the road, most of the space beneath the bed is empty. The additional space allows more room for Helena's clothing, necessities for her cat, and extra play or hiding space for Smoky.

"You are coming back. Right?" Ales asks, arms crossed over her chest as she watches my every move.

I peer over my shoulder and contemplate how much to tell her. Though I have yet to reveal every piece of my past to her, I won't lie if she asks outright. Some things just need to be eased into with her.

"Yes." I shove clothes into the cabinet then close the door. Stepping out of the van, I plant my hands on my hips and look to the side. "Kind of have to."

Her forehead wrinkles. "Not that I'm not happy to hear those words." The lines deepen. "But why?"

I lift a hand to the back of my neck and rub the suddenly tense muscles. "I'm not going alone."

This gets her attention. Her brows shoot for her hairline. "Back for a couple months and already found a lady friend? Ooh la la, Baby…" She pauses. "Just A. Sorry."

A sad smile tugs at the corners of my mouth as I step closer and pull her in for a hug. "No need to apologize. It's been your nickname for me for twenty-three, almost twenty-four years. But I do appreciate you trying."

Her arms band around my middle as she rests her head on my shoulder. There are few things I miss about home, but my sister and her enthusiastic hugs are definitely on the list. Nothing compares to a hug from Alessandra Everett.

"Don't think you've evaded answering me, little brother."

Releasing her hold, she pulls back so we are eye to eye. "Who's the road-trip buddy?" Firm hands land on my biceps. "And what about your birthday?"

Helena's birthday is in a few days, and mine in two weeks. Though we will be back days before mine, I hope Ales doesn't wring my neck for stealing Helena away during hers.

"I'll be back before my birthday." *Tap, tap, tap.* My fingers drum over my thigh. "But..."

Twin blue irises level me with a hard stare. "But what, Anderson?"

I bite the inside of my cheek until the faint taste of salty iron hits my tongue. "But Helena won't be home for hers."

Time stands still for a moment as what I just said registers in Ales's mind. The moment understanding hits, her eyes widen. A small *oh* on her lips. Her grip on my biceps loosens as she nods and nods and nods. It's no secret Helena and I were close years ago, but in this moment, my sister is figuring out exactly how close.

I have zero expectations for this trip except for getting to know who Helena is now. Would I like to hold her in my arms? Would I love to kiss her? Without a doubt, yes. Do I anticipate either happening over the next week? Not at all. Sleeping in the same bed is the closest we will be physically and I am good with that.

Dropping her hands to mine, Ales looks at me, *really looks*, for the first time since I've returned. A rare softness takes over her expression. "You have a good heart, A. So long as you're happy, that's all that matters."

I don't need Ales's approval when it comes to who I love. Love isn't a debatable emotion family or friends get a say in. Love is personal. Distinct. Indisputable. Love is honest and humbling as well as tragic and destructive. It's the one emotion to deliver the highest of highs and lowest of lows, both of which I experienced with Helena. I may not need my sister's consent for who I love, but I more than appreciate having her on my side.

"Right back at ya." I pull her in for another quick hug. "Better get going." The trip out of town isn't long, but I do want us situated and comfortable hours before nightfall. And I suspect the cat will need more adjusting than Helena.

"Be safe." She ruffles my hair. "And bring my friend back in one piece. It's been a while since we've been outdoorsy." Ales's whimsical laughter filters through the air.

Sliding the side door closed, I round the front of the van for the driver's side door. "Noted. Love you, Ales."

Stepping back to lean against the stair rails leading to her apartment, she lifts a hand to wave. "Love you more."

Throwing the gear in reverse, I back out of the space then aim my tires up the alleyway. With Ales in my rearview, I focus on moving forward. Toward the one person that brought me back to Lake Lavender. Toward my North.

CHAPTER 51

HELENA

To my complete surprise, Smoky enjoys car rides. Within fifteen minutes, she leaped from my lap and began investigating every nook and cranny of the van. Now, she is a curled ball of fluff sleeping on one of the bed pillows.

As for me, I am borderline nauseous every time Anderson takes his eyes off the road to look at me for three hour-long seconds. It's not *him* that has me twisted in knots. It's my damn mind working overtime.

What the hell was I thinking saying yes to this trip?

A half dozen times, Anderson has assured me this week-long rendezvous is nothing more than casual. Just two friends getting reacquainted after years apart.

Thing is, the last time Anderson and I existed in the same bubble, we were more than friends. The term ex didn't sit well with me during senior year, so I never regarded Anderson in that light. But hindsight is a slap to the face and I see reality for what it is now.

Our transition was gradual from friends to best friends to

lovers. What we had, the love we shared, took years to build. It was unhurried and irresistible. Unequivocal and magnificent. We fell into one another, handed over our hearts, and forgot about the world.

Then, the world came knocking with iron fists. We'd been torn apart. And while he fought to keep us together, in some way, in any way, I thickened the wedge between us.

By the time I stepped up to right my wrongs, it'd been too late.

Now, by some chance miracle, I have an opportunity to correct my mistakes. In my heart, I know Anderson has no romantic expectations for this week. Neither do I. But before we drive back to town, I do want to clear the air. Tell him where my head and heart are in regard to him.

My gaze falls to my lap as I press my thumb and middle finger to either side of the ring on my finger. Back and forth, I twist the ring. Without looking up, I *feel* his eyes on me, heating my skin. I absorb that heat and take a deep breath.

My phone buzzes in my back pocket, and without looking, I know it is one of my parents. Dad messaged me in our family group chat last night, asking what I wanted to do for my birthday. Since it was late, I pushed off answering until this morning. My reply had been simple.

HELENA

I'll be out of town until Saturday. Let's do something when I'm back.

Guilt gnaws at me for not going into further detail. Every time my phone buzzes, the guilt grows a little thicker in my veins.

But I need this time away. I need this time with Anderson. And he needs it too.

One week. It will either break us further or heal our scars. I pray for the latter.

More than two hundred miles and a quick stop for deli sandwiches later, Anderson steers the van into North Cascades National Park. Lush, skyscraper-tall evergreens and dense grasses line either side of the highway. Snow-capped indigo mountains fill the foreground. Fluffy white clouds dot the powder-blue sky.

Rolling down the window, goose bumps dance over my skin. I inhale the brisk, piney air and sag deeper into the seat. Extending my arm out the window, I weave my fingers through the wind. Let my mind wander as I truly forgo every stressor and responsibility I deal with in day-to-day life.

For the first time in nearly six years, vacation and relaxation are priority number one.

"God, I miss this."

His stare warms my profile, much longer than the previous one during our drive. And the second his eyes are back on the road, I miss the heat of his attention. "Nothing beats days in the middle of nowhere."

"Getting lost on purpose." I smile.

He pats the cargo pocket on the side of his shorts. "Good thing I have my trusty compass."

Instantly, my eyes are on him. Watching every twitch of his facial muscles. His own reaction to what he said.

Compass. As in *my* compass? The compass *I* gave him when we were kids? After all this time, he still has the personally engraved gold compass?

"When you're lost," I mumble, voice catching on the wind.

He reaches across and brushes his knuckles from my shoulder to my elbow. Fire sparks beneath his touch and my breaths come in jagged bursts. My heart beating a new, wobbly rhythm.

Years. It has been years since I felt this unhinged, this exhilarated, this entranced by someone.

Most guys at college were either immature or nose deep in their studies. There weren't many guys in the middle, but they did exist. I'd said yes to my share of them when they asked me to dinner or a movie. Not a single one lasted after date two or three and the inevitable kiss good night. Prior to college, Anderson hadn't been the only guy I kissed. But kissing another man after him... felt wrong.

Since college, any guy that came knocking, I politely declined anything beyond friendship. Years of artificial smiles and going against my instincts came to a screeching halt. It didn't stop Lessa from giving me a nudge from time to time. When she did, I rejected each night out with an irrefutable excuse.

Years have passed with no genuine romantic connection. My last undeniable bond had been with Anderson.

"Find true North," he finishes.

Time away has been on my to-do list for far longer than I care to admit. As is making things right with Anderson. This trip checks one off the list. If I play my cards right, if I don't get swept up in the sights and sounds and *him*, I may be able to check off the other too.

Anderson isn't just some task to be accomplished. He will always be so much more. And by the end of the week, he will sit comfortably in the friend category... or something I refuse to think.

Not only is Smoky a fan of car rides, she also seems quite at home with her new harness and leash. As if she was always meant to be a camping or hiking companion.

Who knew? Certainly not me.

Smoky sits near a large rock and watches on as Anderson builds a fire and I riffle through the cabinets in search of what to make for dinner. With the side and back doors ajar, a light breeze passes through the van. A retractable canopy extends over the sliding door, the awning creating a covered porch between the van and firepit. Two collapsible camping chairs are parked on the makeshift lanai facing the pit.

I opt for chicken with potatoes and carrots, wanting to cook the perishables first. Rummaging through the cabinets, I locate a knife and silicone mat then get to work cutting the vegetables. It's been far too long since my last outdoor excursion, but all the skills Dad taught me about campfire cooking come back the moment I slice into the first carrot.

"Cooking over a campfire is different from the stove, Bug. The temperature isn't as easily controlled. You have to be ready for anything. Cut the food small enough to cook quickly, but not too small."

Distracted with my task, I startle when Anderson steps up behind me and peeks over my shoulder. The knife stills in my hand, his body inches from mine as he wordlessly hovers. Then his hands are on my hips and I forget how to breathe. How to blink. How to do anything other than stand there and wait.

"We can cook in here or over the fire." His grip on my curves tightens. "Whichever you want."

If I had any idea of what I wanted right now, I sure as hell wouldn't be standing here mute and frozen. Anderson means cooking, but my brain automatically goes into this spiral, searching for hidden messages in his words. Because his hands are still on my hips. His breath continues to dance over the skin just beneath my ear. And his proximity lights every molecule in me on fire.

My eyes fall shut as I attempt to contain the inferno beneath my sternum. As I try not to think of how close his lips are to my skin. How I want his lips *on* my skin. On my lips. How I want his taste on my tongue.

For crying out loud.

One. Don't jump to conclusions. His hands on you don't equal more than friends.

Two. Quit overthinking every single word or action. He may still love me, but until he indicates otherwise, our love isn't like before.

Three. Calm the hell down. He comes in talking about food, and all you think about is shoving your tongue down his throat.

Get. A. Grip.

Opening my eyes, I inhale deeply and nod. "Over the fire would be nice." I twist to meet his gaze, the tip of my nose brushing his. Swallowing, I continue. "Been a long time."

For more things than I care to admit.

The corner of his mouth twitches before he runs the tip of his nose along the side of mine. Mere inches separate our mouths as his breath ghosts my lips. My synapses rapid firing as we stand frozen.

Will he kiss me?

As quickly as the question enters my thoughts, he releases my hips and steps back.

"I'll get the grate." He exits the side of the van and rounds the back, riffling through the storage beneath the bed. "And don't worry about the chicken. I already cleaned and cut it." Then he is next to the fire, setting up the grate and talking to a mesmerized Smoky as she eyes the fire.

I'm equally spellbound, but it has nothing to do with the fire.

If I owned a diary, today's entry would read…

> Dear Diary,
> It's day one of my trip with Anderson. Three hours after parking in the North Cascades, I wanted to kiss him. I want more than friendship already. But we're starting over and friends don't kiss. Not the way I want to kiss him. Ugh. Being in the friend zone sucks. Diary, this is going to be a long week. Wish me luck.
> Love,
> H

CHAPTER 52

ANDERSON

Every morning this week, I've woken to Helena in my arms and Smoky curled up near my head on the pillow. During the first hour of each day, I bask in her warmth, her light, the feeling of her in my arms. Such a small act, but damn, does it hold tremendous power.

Beside my head, Smoky stirs, stretching her little limbs and curling her nails in my hair. Purring filters through the van as she scoots closer and kneads my scalp. Thankfully, Helena trims her nails often enough the action feels more like a massage than acupuncture.

I have never owned a pet, but if I did, I'd want one like Smoky. Adorable as hell, road trip ready, and curious.

On a couple of our longer hikes, she happily sat in the travel backpack. Eyes constantly on the move, she refused to miss a single bit of our excursions. On the shorter trails, she walked beside us, little nose smelling the earth and plants as often as possible.

Lifting a hand over my head, I give her a scratch behind the ears. "Last day, little one," I whisper. She twists her head and gives me all the places she wants scratched. I pull my hand away and she nudges my head, something I've learned is her way of asking for more. "Greedy."

Helena stirs at my side, her arm around my waist tightening a beat before her hand trails up my chest. Her head nestled in the crook of my neck, inches closer, nuzzling.

Fuck, I am going to miss this.

It took twenty-four hours for Helena to let down her guard. Though this is the most physically intimate we've been during the trip, the emotional intimacy has been off the charts. I can't not be close to her.

When we leave the park today, I refuse to let things go back to the way they were. I refuse to not be close to her.

"Don't wanna," she mumbles against my skin.

I tighten my arm banded around her middle and hug her closer. Without hesitation, I press my lips to her crown. "Me either," I reply, unsure if she means getting up or leaving this afternoon. Regardless, my answer is the same.

Smoky crawls across the pillow and nudges Helena, her scratchy meow saying either "me too" or "feed me." Not sure which.

Helena inches away from my side and pushes up on her elbow. Giving Smoky a thorough head scratching, she sits up and stretches her arms. And like every other morning, Smoky plods across the bed and rubs against Helena, purring and mewling.

"I'm getting up, little one." Helena twists and hops off the bed, Smoky following her. Adding a scoop of food to her bowl, she pours a small amount of water on top, then sets the bowl down near the passenger seat.

As for me, I remain frozen beneath the covers, my eyes on Helena.

Damn, I really missed her. Missed us.

This week has been beyond great, yet nowhere near enough. The old photo of us stashed in the glove box is no longer enough. I want more. I *need* more.

More easy mornings in each other's arms. Her sweet floral and amber scent in the air and on my skin. Soft words and gentle caresses as we linger in the same space. Breakfasts in bed and dinners on the couch with our favorite movies or shows on the television. Walks in the park or lakeside near the lavender fields. Trips on days off and vacations out of town. Laughter and love and making new memories. Birthdays in the woods with roasted marshmallows and s'mores instead of cake. Sunrise hikes and sunset cuddles. Nights side by side as we look up at the stars.

I want more, but know I need to not rush this. Rush us. The last time I wanted the next step with Helena, we took it. For a short time, our relationship felt indestructible. Unfortunately, the foundation beneath us had been molded by others. And when it shook hard enough, our world was flipped upside down.

Before we take that step again, I want reassurance. I returned to Lake Lavender to right my wrongs and mend old wounds. Over the past week, my Helena-shaped scars have become distant memories. They are no longer painful, angry reminders of the worst time in my life. Now, they are a symbol of the trials I survived.

With those wounds healed, it is time to work on the others.

While she steps out to find the perfect bush, I slip out of bed and tug on shorts. I fill the kettle with water, light one of the burners, and go about prepping for breakfast. Fetching the last two eggs from the fridge and oats from the cabinet, I retrieve cookware from the overhead compartment next. By the time Helena returns, I have oatmeal with diced apples on the stove and am whipping the eggs with cheese.

I point to the mug on the table between the driver and passenger seat. "Green tea. Should be steeped enough."

A faint blush colors her cheeks. "Thank you." After giving Smoky another head scratch, she sits down, hikes a leg up in the chair, and cradles her tea in both hands.

After a quick trip to relieve myself, I serve up breakfast and join Helena at the table. We sit in comfortable silence, Smoky weaving between our legs and hopeful for scraps. When our dishes are empty, Helena takes them to the sink and cleans up. I sip the last of my coffee and simply watch her in my space.

Since the day I hit the road all those years ago, I've loved van life. Well, initially, it was car life, but I still loved it. The peace and freedom and solitude. The ability to live life on my own terms. My vehicle registration may have said I lived in Lake Lavender, but the open road had been my home.

Now, I love everything about the open road except the solitude.

The first eighteen years of my life, I existed under my mother's thumb. It took almost six years to want to mend things with her. To explain why I acted how I did years ago. My lack of respect for her and partial respect for my father. Why I evaded the crowds during parties or gatherings. The days I spent locked in my room, the cutting, the pills.

It took deeper explanations from therapists to understand my brain chemistry and why it flips on occasion. But it didn't take much clarification for me to understand that toxic people, whether a loved one or stranger, should be let go. I simply had to bide my time. Wait until my eighteenth birthday and the guidance counselor's written letter saying I'd officially graduated high school.

I left Lake Lavender in my rearview mirror before my diploma hit the mailbox.

After years of healing and rediscovery, I want to mend the past and move forward with my life. And if repairing the remaining scars leads to never speaking with my parents again, so be it. In time, I will forgive them on my own.

Shaking away the path of my thoughts, I watch Helena wipe dry the last of the dishes and stow them in the cabinet. She spins to face me, tossing the towel over her shoulder and resting her hip on the counter.

"What's the plan for today?" She checks her watch. "We have three to four hours before we hit the road."

Rising from the chair, I drain the last of my coffee from my mug and set it in the sink. I inch past the table and step into Helena's space. Band my arms around her middle and hug her to my chest. Breathe her in a moment before resting my cheek on her crown.

This. This is all I need.

"Anything you'd like to see? Here or on the way back?"

Cheek pressed to my bare shoulder, one of her arms unwinds from our embrace as her fingers go to my tattoo. She discovered it our first night here when I stripped my shirt off before bed. A compass on the inside of my bicep, covering dozens upon dozens of small thin scars. The only direction inked on my skin… North. *Her.*

Helena Williams will always be my true North. The one star in an inky-black sky. To lead me in the right direction. To ease my anxiety. To brighten the darkness. Even apart, she was still with me. Even when it hurt, she still guided me.

"Don't want to leave," she says, fingers gently caressing the black ink. "But maybe let's do some sightseeing on the way back. Stop somewhere for lunch. Drag out our return."

I crush her to my chest, close my eyes, and kiss her hair. "Sounds like the perfect plan."

Slowly, silently, we clean up. Put everything exactly as it was before we arrived. In less than an hour, I drive us away from the sliver of paradise we called ours for the past week. I guide us out of the park and south toward Lake Lavender.

And as I peek at her from the corner of my eye, I vow to drag this four hour drive out to six or more. Because I am not ready for the week to end. Not yet.

CHAPTER 53

HELENA

L ife is equal parts bliss and torture. Our happiness occasionally defined and judged by those not in our shoes.

Three days have come and gone since Anderson and I passed the Lake Lavender welcome sign. And during those three days, countless eyes have been on us. Watching our every move as we eat dinner at the cantina. Whispering as we pass on the sidewalk, hand in hand. Passing gossip from one townie to another faster than an STD.

Since early childhood, I've loved living in Lake Lavender. I love the tight-knit community and helping hands. Love the camaraderie and sense of security in knowing so many faces, names, and people. Love the slow and simple life within the town's borders not found in big cities.

But as the eyes and ears and mouths turn their attention toward me and Anderson, I lose an ounce of that familiar comfort each day. They stare and listen and blather as if we aren't real people with actual feelings. They talk about our lives as if what we do is their business, as if their exploitation shouldn't be bothersome.

The disgust I feel is unsettling. Gossip has my love for this town diminishing while my distrust flares to life.

I hate it.

My phone buzzes in my pocket, snapping me out of my scrutinous stare out the store's front window. Inhaling a cleansing breath, I shake away the negative thoughts and pull my phone from my pocket.

"Never let them knock you down. Never let them steal your joy," I mutter. Life is too short to let someone else rule your happiness. Life is too short to waste time, always trying to please others. "You can't please everyone."

Unlocking my phone, I tap on the text notification from Lessa to the group.

> **LESSA**
>
> Is everyone cool with switching Friday night dinner to Saturday? We have birthdays to celebrate.

I roll my eyes at the screen. A party to celebrate me and Anderson. *Ugh.* Please let it only be just the group. The last thing I want is half the town tossing fake smiles at me like confetti to get juicy gossip.

My phone buzzes in my hand as message after message fills the screen.

> **LOGAN**
>
> Absolutely. Let's fucking party 🕺
>
> **MAGS**
>
> When was the last time we did something big for one of our birthdays? I say yes.

GEOFF

I'm with Mags

BRAYDON

I go where you go, firecracker 🔥

My fingers hover over the keys as I fight every instinct to not say something unkind. Yes, the party will be for me, but it will also be for Anderson. Her message said *birthdays*. I don't foresee Anderson turning her down. It's his sister, and they haven't spent a birthday together in almost a decade. But is he comfortable with a party? His answer is equally as important as my answer.

Another buzz and I blink down at the screen.

ANDERSON

If it's small, you have my blessing.

Good. He and I are on the same wavelength.

I type out a quick response and tap send.

HELENA

Just the Friday night dinner crew. Please.

It shouldn't have to be said, but I hope the hint comes across in my message. *No parents or other townies.*

LESSA

Yay! Was thinking we could use JTM. Music, food, drinks. Still ironing out details.

LESSA

Is it alright if August and Sharon are there? Was thinking maybe they could cook and then stay as a thank you.

I love August. He reminds me of those ginormous stuffed

bears at Costco during the holiday season. Warm and cuddly and huge in every sense of the word. When I think of August and Sharon, I think of my chosen family. Having them join us feels right.

HELENA

Yes from me for August and Sharon.

ANDERSON

All good

Lessa is undoubtedly squealing with delight. I picture her parked in the chair behind her desk at the coffee shop, fingers flying over the screen as August enters her office to ask if everything is alright. Her screech of excitement probably scaring the patrons as they are sipping drinks or devouring tasty morsels.

SOS. Someone, please save us.

LESSA

I'll text everyone tomorrow with an update. xo

The bell over the door jingles. I lock my phone and shove it in my pocket as I greet three unfamiliar faces. "Good afternoon. Welcome. Have you shopped Always Classic before?" My phone buzzes in my pocket, but I ignore it.

A curvy woman with beautiful brown skin and curls I would kill for meets my stare and smiles. "This is our first time." She glances to the women at her side. "We're in town for the National Lavendula League annual convention. Thought we'd browse on one of our free days."

In the past year, our small town has grown in popularity. The centennial festival last October attracted people within a hundred-mile radius. Or so I've been told. But it was Braydon's story in Washington's Hidden Gems magazine that really brought in so many new faces. Most stay for a long weekend or weeklong summer vacation.

Tourism this year has been phenomenal. The small bell on my door has jingled more this season than any previous year. And thanks to the influx of traffic and sales, I've been able to add more inventory I love.

"Nice to have you all here." A smile stretches my cheeks. "Are you staying at the B&B?"

An older, taller, stockier woman with tan skin and black hair hikes a purse strap up her shoulder. "We are. The place is massive for a bed-and-breakfast."

I clasp my hands at my waist, twisting the ring on my finger. "It's grown over the years. When I was little, it was half the size. My parents say it started off as a four-bedroom home before their time." Freeing my hands, I wave an arm around the store. "I won't bore you with the town's history. Have a look around and let me know if you have questions or need assistance."

After a smile and "thank you," the women weave through the tables and racks, browsing leisurely.

I wade toward the rear of the store and step behind the checkout counter. I pull out my phone and unlock it, tapping on a new text from Anderson.

ANDERSON

Dinner tonight?

After a quick glance up, I type out a reply.

HELENA

Yes. My place? Dinner and a movie?

I bite the inside corner of my lip as my eyes dart from the

screen to the customers. Up and down, over and over, I get a little dizzy.

Last night, I had to pass on dinner with Anderson. A birthday celebration was in order with my parents. Dinner at J's Sushi, followed by ice cream at All Scooped Up. With a full belly of tempura, sushi, udon, and ice cream, I waddled up the stairs to my apartment later than most weeknights.

After a quick shower, I'd slipped on pajamas, crawled under the covers, and passed out. When I woke this morning, I had a text notification from Anderson. I'd worried my bottom lip for minutes before opening it. We were rekindling our relationship—slowly, steadily—and I didn't want to upset him.

Last night was our first night apart in ten days. To be honest, I didn't know how he'd take it. My worry had been pointless. His text this morning read, *I missed you.* Those three words kept a smile on my face today.

ANDERSON

Cook or takeout?

I survey the store. Clothes draped over their arms, the ladies moved to the opposite side of the store, riffling through racks on the wall. My window to chat was shortening.

HELENA

Cook. Something we can make together.

The little gray bubble dances on the screen.

ANDERSON

I'll pick up groceries. What time?

HELENA

5:30

ANDERSON

Love you.

HELENA

Love you too.

Just as I send the message, the bell over the door jingles. A man and woman step inside, her eyes filling with delight as his fill with dread. Stuffing my phone in my pocket, I greet them with a bright smile.

For the first time in years, my smile doesn't feel forced and fake. For the first time in years, my smile is a reflection of how I feel. Happy.

CHAPTER 54

ANDERSON

I snatch the grocery tote, exit the van, and climb the stairs to Helena's apartment. It feels so routine and normal to scale these stairs. To twist the door handle and push inside. To find her in leggings and an oversized off-the-shoulder shirt with a smile on her face. A smile for me.

We have spent every available moment together since returning from our trip. She cooked dinner the first night back. I cooked on night two. Night three was takeout. Last night, she'd been with her parents.

Each time I walk through her door, my breaths come easier. Any time I enter her bubble, I am home.

Smoky prances from the living room to greet me as I close the door. "Hey, little lady. How's my favorite girl?"

"Hey," Helena calls from the kitchen, hand on her hip. But her expression is playful. Teasing.

"Sorry, North." I scratch Smoky's head. "My favorite *furry* girl."

She shuffles across the room, fuzzy socks on her feet and a

glass of wine in her hand. "That's better." She winks. "How was your day?"

I toe off my sneakers and pad toward the kitchen, setting the bag on the counter. "Good. Helped Ales in the coffee shop. A little paperwork and heavy lifting when the deliveries came in. What about yours?"

She sips her wine as I unload the bag. "Tourist season is tapering off, but I still had several visitors come in."

I lean into her and press my lips to her hair. "That's great." Shuffling around the ingredients, I twist to face her. "Thought it'd be fun to do breakfast for dinner."

After a hefty gulp of her wine, she sets down the glass and rubs her hands together. "Where do you want me?"

Keep your head out of the gutter, Anderson. She's talking about cooking.

I swallow and hand her the baking mix. "You're in charge of pancakes."

Over the next twenty-ish minutes, I do my damnedest not to stare at her. The way her tongue darts out, trapped between her teeth as she stirs the batter. The way she cocks her hip as she waits to flip the pancakes. Or the way she sucks the funnel on the whipped cream can.

I do my damnedest, but I fail.

A bang fills the room and I startle awake. The fog of sleep fades enough for me to recognize the sound came from the television. Relaxing my muscles, I melt back into the couch. It takes ten groggy seconds for me to realize Helena is asleep on my chest. That we fell asleep on the couch. And as much as I want to stay exactly like this, both of us will be cranky in the morning if we wake with sore muscles.

Reaching for the remote, I turn off the television. Slowly, I sit up and twist to a seated position, shifting Helena as I go. I rise from the couch with her in my arms and pad down the hall to her bedroom. It takes some awkward finagling, but I pull back the covers and gently lay her down.

Not a second after I pull the covers to her chin, her hand wraps around my wrist. "Stay," she whispers.

It's late, after midnight. Ales will wring my neck if I disturb her beauty sleep, especially on a weeknight. "Are you sure?"

Every night of our trip, Helena slept close or in my arms. And every night since our return, my sleep has been shit because we were in separate beds, in separate spaces, blocks apart. The idea of slipping between her sheets, wrapping her in my arms, and drifting off with her has me exhilarated and terrified.

"Yes." She whips the covers back and inches across the mattress, giving me room.

Shoving aside any doubts, I tug my shirt over my head, unbutton my jeans and slide them down, then crawl in the bed. Blanket pulled up, I wrap an arm around her waist and haul her closer. Mold every dip and curve of her body to mine. As I breathe in her sweet floral and amber scent, my eyes drift shut and I relax into her embrace.

Without thinking, I dip down and kiss the sensitive skin beneath her ear. She doesn't react and I assume she fell back asleep. Until her fingers on my arm draw slow, lazy circles and her hips shift slightly. I press my lips to her skin again but make no move to pull away. For a moment, I relish in her warmth and the pounding of her pulse beneath my lips. Instinct takes over as my tongue darts out and tastes her skin.

So much sweeter than I remember.

Then she is twisting in my arms. Her hand trails up my bare chest, over my shoulder, and up the back of my neck into my hair. Her fingers curl in my strands a breath before her lips crash down on mine.

Fire floods my veins as I kiss her back. My skin buzzes as she inches closer, our bodies flush from shoulder to hips. With each kiss of her lips, my breathing becomes more jagged. Stilted. My heart bangs against my rib cage, begging for this moment to never end.

My tongue darts out and licks the seam of her lips. She gasps and opens up for me. Invites me in with a swipe of her tongue. And damn, nothing has tasted so divine or felt this euphoric. Our tongues tangle and I taste her for the first time in far too long.

Fingers knead and grope and caress. Arms tighten their hold. Lips kiss as teeth nip and tongues taste.

And it takes every ounce of strength to resist doing more. To peel her clothes off and shape my body to hers without barriers. To taste more than her mouth. Her skin and lips and tongue taste better than I remember. A little salty with a hint of sweetness.

Is the saltiness of her arousal beyond sublime? I never went down on Helena when we were younger. Immaturity plus our combined lack of knowledge of physical intimacy—and our short-lived relationship after sex entered the equation—left us in the dark when it came to oral pleasure. But god, how I ache to dip my tongue between her thighs now.

I have no expectation of tonight being more than this— wild kisses and light petting—but my body begs for more, craves more. Much as I wanted to take things slow, I won't be able to deny this hunger for long. The more time we spend together, the harder it is to refuse Helena or myself what we both want. If she begs, I will cave.

The hand not in my hair strokes over the bulge in my briefs and my grip on her tightens. A moan spills from me into her. My eyes roll back in my head as her fingers curl around my length.

Goddamn.

Her hands on me feel incredible. Up and down, she strokes my hard length through my briefs. Rocks her hips in time with her strokes.

Fuck.

If I don't stop her now, I'll not only break the waiting rule, but I'll also make a mess. My mind says stop while my body begs for this moment to never end. And because I want more than sex with Helena, I listen to my big head.

Reaching between us, I lay a hand over hers and freeze. I count to three, suck her bottom lip between mine, and then break the kiss. "We should stop," I whisper against her lips.

She leans in, presses her lips to mine, and tries to deepen the kiss. But I keep my lips sealed. Inching back, her eyes search out mine in the darkness. She pulls her hand between my legs away as a deep crease forms between her brows. "Did I do something wrong?" Her voice cracks at the end.

I haul her to my chest and wrap her in a ferocious hug. "God, no. Quite the opposite." Loosening my hold on her, I kiss her hair. Bring a hand to her cheek, tip her head back, and level her with my stare. See a hint of glassiness in her eyes as I stroke her cheek with my thumb. "Believe me, I want more." I drop my lips to hers in a chaste kiss. "So much more. But not tonight." I kiss her forehead. "I want to wait. Want to do things right."

She leans into my touch. Twists and kisses my palm. And with a slow nod, she whispers a barely audible, "Okay."

Dropping my forehead to hers, my eyes fall shut. The tip of my nose caresses the bridge of hers. "I love you, North. Always." I suck in a sharp breath. "You were my first. I want you to also be my last."

Wetness hits my hand. "Ander," she chokes out. "Love you too. Always." She kisses my palm again. "I want that too. To be your last, and for you to be mine."

CHAPTER 55

HELENA

Shiny and bright. That's all I think as I survey the room around us. Bless my best friend for wanting to celebrate me and Anderson, but this is a bit over the top.

The Friday night dinner crew is present, plus the addition of August and Sharon. Ten of us total and, for whatever inexplicable reason, Lessa decorated the Java and Teas Me dining room for a party of fifty.

"Uh." My eyes scan every inch of the room. Take in the big shiny letters that spell out *Happy Birthday* beneath the menu board. Sheets of shiny thin strips hang throughout the dining area like disco-era curtains. Several tables are shoved together, a sheet cake in the middle with four number candles to make twenty-four and twenty-seven. Party hats and kazoos and sashes that read *Birthday Girl* and *Birthday Boy*. "This is…"

Beside me, Anderson snickers. "A bit much." He hugs my hand with his. "If I'm honest, I feel light-headed." He rubs his temple. "Dizzy, for sure."

Lessa playfully slaps his arm. "Shush, you." She folds her arms over her chest. "No birthday parties for years… I have every right to do whatever I want. And dammit, we're celebrating." Her hands shift to her hips. "So, put on a party hat, prepare for a ton of delicious finger foods, a mountain of cake, and horrible party games."

Anderson throws his head back and laughs. His joy is breathtaking. I watch him a second, then join in on the laughter.

Damn, that feels good.

"Only because you're my sister." Anderson nudges her arm with his elbow before his expression grows serious. "But next year and every year after"—he waves a finger around the room—"we aren't doing this."

She rolls her eyes. "Fine," she huffs out in faux annoyance. "Whatever you say."

Pop music pipes through the overhead speakers that typically play coffeehouse acoustic. Several conversations spark, the light chatter foreground to the music. Fried batter and a hint of spice float through the air, my stomach growling and mouth salivating for whatever August and Sharon have in the kitchen.

Anderson leans into my side, his lips at my ear and breath warm on my skin. "Is it just me, or does this feel reminiscent of our joint parties before puberty?"

I elbow his side. "Ander," I admonish under my breath, then chuckle.

"What? You know I'm right."

My eyes scan the room again. Bright colors highlight much of the space, which is so not us. Two sets of party plates sit neatly stacked on a table—one with hot pink fading into purple with a mermaid silhouette, the other with colorful dinosaurs on a white background. Matching napkins are next to the plates, of course. Mylar birthday balloons are tied to our respective chairs while latex balloons in every color decorate most of the room. Bottles of bubbles at each place setting while paper confetti litters the entire table.

And the games... my goodness. Pin the tail on the donkey and limbo. Jenga and bobbing for apples. Donuts tied to strings and dangling from a rigged pole above. But it's the piñata that really grabs my attention.

"Yeah. I guess so." Eyes wide, I spin and look up at him. "Let's pray she and Braydon don't have kids. At least, not anytime soon."

Snorting laughter rips from his nose and throat. "Thankfully, she's nowhere near ready for that step."

Minutes later, August and Sharon join the crew with platters of food. Warm spinach and artichoke dip with fresh bread. Caprese skewers and crostini topped with sliced sausage, smoked salmon, and something creamy. Bite-size burgers and tacos. A Mezze platter packed with hummus, baba ghanoush, falafel bites, olives, cucumber slices, grape tomatoes, red and green grapes, cheeses, cut pita, toast points, and tzatziki.

"Wow," I whisper as I take my seat. If we have food like this at every birthday party, it more than makes up for the childish themes.

Everyone pulls out a chair and takes a seat. Plates get circulated and drinks get poured as we ease into conversation once more. Stories of the past get shared alongside stories from our time apart. Everything in the moment feels carefree. Perfect. Normal.

Beneath the table, Anderson rests his hand on my thigh. He carries on a conversation with Braydon about whale watching on Orcas Island. As for me, I do my best not to stutter while talking shop with Mags and Lessa. Perspiration licks my skin, but not enough to be visible through my clothes. *Thank goodness.*

As if he senses my jitters, Anderson's thumb slowly strokes my denim-clad thigh. Slow and steady and an instant balm to my frazzled nerves.

"So," Lessa says. "How was the week off?"

"Ales," Anderson chides. "Not now."

She spears an olive and pops it into her mouth. "What?" she mumbles around the bite, then swallows. "It's new. A little expected, but still new."

I lay my hand over his, silently telling him I am here for him as he is for me. Then I turn my gaze to Lessa. "Not here." My eyes widen in a wordless plea. "Later. With fewer people."

Anderson flips his hand over and laces my fingers with his. "After the party"—he purses then relaxes his lips—"maybe we should talk." His grip tightens and I know he wants to talk about more than our relationship. "Upstairs. The four of us."

A ridge settles between Lessa's brows as her forehead wrinkles in concern. With a subtle nod, she swallows. "Yeah. Okay. We'll talk."

Anderson opens his mouth to say something, but his entire body locks up. He squeezes my hand with such intensity it's borderline painful. The muscles in his jaw tense up and his expression grows cold. I sandwich his hand between both of mine and try to ease whatever has him suddenly on edge. But he doesn't relax.

I glance up, but his gaze is elsewhere. Locked in place, he stares past everyone at the table and out the front window of the coffee shop. I follow his line of sight and suck in a sharp breath when I see what has his attention.

On the other side of the glass, Mr. and Mrs. Everett stand idle on the sidewalk. He appears to nudge her to move forward, but she isn't having it. No, Mrs. Everett's eyes are on her son. After not seeing him for six years, she should have joyful tears in her eyes. Or perhaps woeful tears. She should want to storm through the door and wrap her arms around him and never let go. She should be apologizing profusely for all the hurt she caused over the years and begging for his forgiveness. Implore him to let her make things right.

But there isn't an ounce of sadness or relief in her expression. Not a hint of remorse for the pain she inflicted on her baby. Instead, angry lines mar her face. Bitterness curls her upper lip. And her posture screams fury as Mr. Everett continues to try to pull her away.

I shiver as I watch their exchange. Her icy glare on him chilling me to the bone.

And I am done. Done with whatever subconscious issue she has with Anderson. Done with her bullshit.

I will not allow this woman to wipe away all the progress Anderson made in his life. I will not *let* her tear him down to make herself feel better.

Leaning into Anderson's side, I hover next to his ear. "She no longer dictates your life. Do not let her steal your joy. Don't give her any power." I squeeze his hand between mine. "Look at me, please." I inch back and he slowly twists to meet my gaze. "I love you. Unconditionally."

His grip loosens slightly. "Love you, too."

I lift a hand to his face and cup his cheek. "Only you decide how you want your life to be. No one else. Not me, not Lessa, and certainly not your parents." My thumb strokes the apple of his cheek. "You are your own person and what you want for your life is what matters most."

He closes the space between us, kisses me chastely, then rests his forehead on mine. "Thank you," he whispers.

I open my mouth to tell him I will always have his back, but Lessa cuts me off.

"What the hell just happened?" Her tone is sharp and a touch frightening.

Reluctantly, we pull apart and Anderson levels Lessa with a harsh stare. Then he juts his chin toward the window, where their mother looks more fired up than before.

"Goddammit," she mutters.

A screech fills the air as wood scrapes wood, Lessa shoving her chair back. In a blink, she is up and stomping toward the front door. Twisting the dead bolt, she steps outside and up to their parents. Finger-pointing and heated exchanges happen for all to see. Minutes pass without hearing a word of what's happening outside, but it's easy enough to see Lessa keeps telling them to leave.

Several minutes pass before Lessa steps inside and locks the door. Cheeks red, she immediately lowers the blinds across the face of the store. She returns to her chair, drops her head in her hands, and sighs. Braydon kisses her crown and rubs a hand up and down her spine.

"Tonight," she says as she straightens her spine and levels Anderson with her gaze. "I need to know tonight."

Swallowing, Anderson gives her a nod. "Tonight," he agrees.

I rest my head on his shoulder and reinforce my grip on his hand. Tell him without words that I will be at his side. That he can lean on me. That I will hand over every ounce of strength he needs to get through this.

I am here and I love you. Always.

CHAPTER 56

ANDERSON

"I'm sorry. What?" Ales asks, her voice shaky and laced in disbelief.

"Please don't make me repeat it," I beg. "It hurt enough the first time."

After the parental sighting, the mood of the party plummeted fast. We skipped all the silly games but did blow out candles and eat cake. August and Sharon volunteered to clean up, and Ales promised them a bonus for the work. Goodbyes and hugs were exchanged moments before we exited the back and trudged up the stairs.

In the living room, with Helena at my side, I spilled my secrets to Ales. Shared every vulnerable detail of my past she hadn't been aware of. The cutting, the pills, my time in the hospital… and my relationship with Helena.

More than anything, I thought my secret love affair with her best friend would bother her most. She barely blinked when those words spilled from my lips.

Devastation lines her face. Tears well up in her blue eyes.

Braydon wraps a blanket around her shoulders and hauls her into his side. He kisses her temple and whispers words only for her. She blinks, then nods, tears trailing down her cheeks.

Securing the blanket around her frame, she pins me with her sad eyes. "You could've talked to me. Trusted me with your secrets. I would've listened. Would've done something. I *will* listen. You know that, right?" A hand slips out of the blanket and wipes her now tearstained cheeks.

A sad smile curves my lips. "I know that now." I rub the back of my neck. "Back then, I didn't want to be a burden. You were so happy and I didn't want to drag you down with me. My immature and bleak mind didn't want to drag you into the dark too."

Helena combs her fingers through my hair, her nails lightly scratching my scalp. I lean into her touch, her comfort. Allow it to soothe the reopened wounds. Let her love assuage the scars of my past.

Ales shifts her gaze to Helena. "Since you're not freaking out, you obviously knew."

She drops her hand to my waist and fists the cotton near my hip before resting her head on my shoulder. "Not long," she answers. "Around the beginning of August." She twists to look up at my profile. "Believe me, I was shocked." Her fingers curl more in my shirt. "And hurt," she chokes out. "But we want to live in the present and take steps toward the future, not exist in the past."

Damn, I fucking love her.

Ales always stood up for me when we were younger. Went to battle for me when I'd been content ignoring the issue. But it was Helena that gave me real strength. It was Helena that showed me real love. And it will always be Helena I am most vulnerable with.

I love my sister, but that love is microscopic when compared to how I feel about Helena. Ales and I will always have this easy familial connection. But my bond with Helena is fierce. A force to be reckoned with. An intoxicating and addictive and undeniable passion.

We agreed to take things slow. To ease back into us. But with each passing day, the buzz in my veins begs me to move faster. To hold her closer. Secure her hand in mine and never let go. After all the ups and downs, she is still my best friend. The first person I think of in the morning. The last person I think of before falling asleep. And based on our incessant need to spend every free moment together, the lover part of our relationship will reignite sooner rather than later.

Much as I wanted to wait, to take things slow, I don't want to waste time. Who knows what tomorrow will bring. We've already lost enough in our time apart. I refuse to lose more.

I twist and drop my lips to hers. Press a sweet kiss on her mouth. "Love you, North."

Her lips tip up at the corners. "Love you, Ander."

"Alright, you two."

We break our stare and look at Ales.

"Getting a little nauseous over here."

I grab the closest pillow and chuck it in her direction. "Shut up." I chuckle. "At least we aren't face fucking like the two of you." I wag a finger between her and Braydon. "No one will complain if you tone down the PDA."

She tosses the pillow back and hits my head. "Not my fault." Unashamed, she shrugs. "Chemistry. It is what it is."

I could argue with my sister. Tell her Helena and I have more chemistry than the two of them. Debate it with years of angst and secret touches and discreet physical affection. But I won't. Last thing I want to hear is what she and Braydon do behind closed doors. And I sure as hell am not sharing what Helena and I have done. Hard pass.

"Serious talk," she says, loosening her hold on the blanket around her shoulders. "Do you want to try to fix things with Mom and Dad? No pressure. It's your call." She leans into Braydon. "I want to be on the same page as you. I don't want to say or do something opposite of what you want. Not after everything you just shared."

Dropping my gaze to my lap, I fiddle with the fringe on the pillow. Ponder over where to go from here.

When I initially decided to return to Lake Lavender, it was for two reasons. Rekindle my relationship with Helena or let her go. Repair the strain on my relationship with my parents or let them go. Ideally, I want to have happy, healthy relationships with everyone. But the world doesn't always work in ideals.

Months ago, I rolled into town with a twinge in my gut.

Mending the past with Helena and navigating our way toward the future was second nature. Through thick and thin, our connection always existed. Like any couple, we suffered struggles and roadblocks. Unfortunately, I battled those darker moments with a warped mind. But we were young. Naive. Optimistic for things we didn't quite understand during that stage of our life.

Now, we have experience and heartbreak and reason under our belts. We talk and share everything on our minds. More than that, we support and fight for each other. I am her strength as much as she is mine.

Stitching up and rebuilding my relationship with my parents... isn't so cut and dry.

I don't know what it is my mother dislikes about me, but I do know it isn't my place to fix it. If she wants me in her life, she needs to work on herself. She needs to see a therapist like I did. She needs to open up and give a voice to whatever causes her to cast me aside, to look at me with such disdain.

After the stare-down tonight, after witnessing her rage, I refuse to sabotage my mental health for her. Until she seeks help and shows signs of improvement, I have no desire to be anywhere near her.

As for Dad... if he chooses to continually pacify her behavior, I will let him go too. I won't listen to his pleas to placate her actions and words. I won't stand next to a spineless man because he wants his wife to feel like a queen when she is anything but.

I don't want to let either of them go, not fully, but am mentally prepared to do so.

Inhaling deeply, I lock on to blue irises. "I want to try, but don't know if I'm ready."

With a gentle nod and soft smile on her lips, Ales says, "Say the word. I'm here whenever you need." She extends her hand and I take it.

"Thanks, Ales. Love you."

"Love you more, A."

CHAPTER 57

HELENA

Weeks have come and gone without bumping into Anderson's parents. The stress of seeing them, of sharing secrets with Lessa, has vanished.

And over the past month, Anderson and I have settled into a new way of life. A new love.

Unofficially, Anderson has moved into my apartment. One day bled into the next, and less than two weeks after the party, he crawled into my bed each night, held me in his arms, and never left. Lazy Sundays and movie nights on the couch. Grocery shopping and cooking meals together. His jacket on a hook near the door and shoes in the basket beneath it. His toothbrush in the holder on the bathroom vanity and shampoo on the ledge in the shower. His laundry in the basket with mine. And his van parked next to my car out back.

All of it is so normal. Natural. Us.

The only part we haven't eased into yet… Sex. There is no shortage of desire. No lack of passion. I feel his want in every soul-consuming kiss. Feel his need every time he gropes my breasts or fists my hips. Hear how much he craves me with each growl as he grinds his underwear-covered cock over my pajama-clad center.

I won't push Anderson to take a step he isn't ready for. Doesn't mean I won't show him what he is missing.

Anderson left late this morning to help Lessa at the coffee shop. Since the whole fiasco with Myrtle Payne and all the havoc she caused, Anderson spends more time with Lessa during the week. Mostly cleaning and restocking in the back, then the front when the door locks for the day.

He works to pass the time and catch up with his sister. When she insisted on adding him to the payroll, he refused to accept payment. She is his family and he wants to help. He earned a hefty wage on the road and doesn't need the income. He would prefer the money go back into her business than his pocket. Still, she wants to pay him.

So he accepts the money. Then he turns around and secretly adds twenties to the tip jar once or twice a shift. I sit back, laugh, and let them duke it out.

Earlier, I messaged Lessa and asked if she would keep Anderson at the coffee shop until at least four. I have plans for tonight and need to set up first. She sent a thumbs-up and wished me luck.

Tote bag slung over my shoulder, I unlock the apartment door and zip inside. After toeing off my shoes and giving Smoky a quick head scratch, I dash to the kitchen and unload the bag—takeout from Black Silk and sweets from Harvey's Handmade Candies.

Smoky weaves between my legs, mewling as she turns around and makes a figure eight.

"I'll get you a treat soon. Just let Mama finish up."

Portioning the main entrée onto two plates, I set them on a sheet pan, turn the oven to *keep warm*, and set them inside. The sweets from Harvey's and the side salad for our dinner go in the fridge.

"Alright, lil' Smoky." I open the cabinet where I store her food and crack open the treat jar, grabbing a couple. "Always my good girl." I set them on the floor and give her a full-body scratch.

She gobbles them down, looks to me for more, then head-butts my leg. I chuckle at her antics.

"Mama has to change clothes." I give her one last scratch then shuffle toward the bedroom.

I strip down, tossing the denim and long-sleeve cropped sweater in the dirty pile, and grab what I know will drive Anderson crazy. Oddly enough, my comfy clothes are his favorite. I step into forest-green leggings and an off-the-shoulder cream top that hits the top of my thighs.

As I head for the hall, the front door opens and Smoky meows.

He's home.

I take a deep breath and slowly make my way out to the open living space. Squatted with his head down, his fingers in Smoky's fur, he doesn't see me right away. And for a beat, I soak in the sight of him. In my space, in my home, in my life.

Getting this second chance with him... damn, I am a lucky woman.

"What smells good?" he asks just before his blues meet my greens. He hisses, straightens to his full height, and pads across the room until his breath hits my lips. "You give me strength, but damn, you make me weak." Then his lips crash down on mine in a dizzying kiss. And before my mind catches up with my body, his hands are on my hips. Kneading. Massaging. Pulling me impossibly closer.

I love Anderson's soft side. Love his sweet kisses and

tender touches. But there is a new side to him I love more. The severely passionate side. The *I need my mouth and hands on you now* side. A side he didn't have when we were younger. A side that has me eager and hungry and desperate for all of him.

He breaks the kiss and drops his forehead to mine as we catch our breaths. His hands continue to knead my hips as he drops one peck, then another on my lips. "Is there a special occasion I forgot?"

"Uh, no."

Straightening his spine, his hands release my hips and come to my face, cupping my cheeks. He drops another chaste kiss to my lips. "Well, something smells divine." His lips move to the exposed skin of my shoulder. "And this shirt... you know how much I like it, don't you?" Bolder, darker blue irises slam into my greens as his fingertips dance over my collarbone.

I shrug and try to appear unaffected. Shift my gaze to anywhere but at him as I push out my lips. "Maybe."

"Grr." He takes a step back, toes off his shoes, and tosses them in the basket. "Come on, Smoky. Dad needs to change." He pads down the hall, Smoky on his heels.

Dad?

Swoon.

While Anderson changes into something more comfortable, I remove dinner from the oven. Take the hot plates to the two-seater dining table off the kitchen, followed by the salad. Fetch wineglasses from the cabinet and pour chardonnay halfway in each before placing them on the table. Shuffling back to the kitchen, I grab napkins, cutlery, and the lighter I keep in the kitchen.

As I light a double-wick candle at the heart of the table, warm arms band around my middle. Swathe me with heat and hunger and love. My eyes fall shut as his lips kiss up the curve of my shoulder to beneath my ear. The pace slow and torturous yet addictive.

Desperate for more, I tilt my head. Expose more of my neck to him. My heart soars beneath my breastbone as he kisses and licks and nips my sensitive skin. He undoubtedly feels the *th-thump, thump, thump* of my racing pulse beneath his lips.

Inching higher, he sucks the lobe of my ear between his lips and I gasp. One of his hands drifts up, cupping my shoulder, while the other slips down and hooks on my hip, pinning my back to his front. And there is no mistaking the bulge beneath his sweats pressing my lower back.

Dear god.

My head swirls. Lust clouds every logical thought I possess. All sense of rationale leaves my body as I get lost in all things Anderson Everett. His hands on my body equally tender and rough. His woodsy scent in the air I breathe. The soft growl escaping his lips and vibrating my sensitive skin.

And damn, it feels divine. Him. This. Us.

Sublime.

I squeeze my thighs together, praying for an ounce of friction. A dose of relief from the ache between my legs. A hint of respite. I open my mouth, ready to say, *"Screw dinner."*

But I don't get the opportunity.

"Let's eat," he declares, giving my ear one last nip before he steps back. He moves to his side of the table, pulls out the chair, and sits down as if he hadn't spent the last few minutes deliciously torturing me.

No way he isn't affected. No. Way.

Mentally growling, I take a seat across from him. Here I am, pulling out all the stops to seduce Anderson, and he flips the script. *Damn it.*

Reaching for my wine, I bring the glass to my lips and study the man opposite me. He unfolds the cloth napkin, lays it in his lap, and surveys the meal on his plate. His lips tip up in a slow smile as he picks up his fork. Lines bracket his eyes as his smile widens, brightens. He doesn't look up from his plate, but he sees me in his periphery, watching him.

He likes my eyes on him. I like my eyes on him too.

I cast aside any preconceived ideas of seducing him at the dinner table. Instead, I settle into the moment. Pick up my fork, twirl it in the creamy pasta, spear a shrimp, then sigh as the bite hits my tongue.

After the first bite, I ask Anderson about his day at the coffee shop. He tells me how great it feels to have purpose, something he was concerned about before returning. We share the day's events over dinner like a normal couple, like long-time lovers. And with ease, one subject blends into another. As if we have done this our entire lives. As if we are meant to keep doing this.

I love the warm buzz in my chest at the idea of forever with Anderson.

When our plates empty, we take them to the kitchen and clean up. He washes and I dry. We ebb and flow, moving fluidly around each other without a word. As if he's predicting my every move and I his.

"Movie?" he asks as I put the silverware in the drawer.

"Yes, please." I hang the towel on the oven handle and go to the fridge. "I'll get dessert."

He reaches for my hand, hooks a finger with mine, and gives a slight tug. "Don't be long." Then he lets go and walks toward the couch. Smoky mewls at his feet and he scoops her up, tucking her into his side. "Gotta help Dad pick a good movie." He kisses her furry head.

My heart melts again at his referring to himself as her dad.

I grab the box of sweets from the fridge and tear off a few paper towels before joining Anderson and Smoky on the couch. He chooses a movie that looks nothing like what he'd watch—a Hallmark-esque romance—and I narrow my eyes at him.

"Closet romantic?" I tease, biting the inside of my cheek.

The most serious expression dons his face as he gives me his attention. "With you, always."

I swallow down the swelling lump in my throat. Lick my lips and tuck them between my teeth. Warm, calloused fingers dance along my jaw, his thumb stroking the seam of my lips. I release my hold on them and gasp at his touch.

Inch by painstaking inch, he closes the space between us and presses a kiss to my lips. My eyes flutter closed at the soft brush of his lips. A ghost of a caress, powerful in its own right. A buzz ignites where our lips touch. Tingles erupt beneath my skin, goose bumps dancing over my flesh. And the moment I part my lips to deepen the kiss, it ends.

My eyes fly open and meet his hungry gaze. *Why?* on the tip of my tongue. But before I get the chance to ask, he kisses the tip of my nose and settles into the couch.

"What's for dessert?"

"*You,*" I want to say, but don't. Instead, I flip the lid open on the box and offer him a look inside. "Chocolate-covered fruit."

He plucks a chocolate-covered strawberry from the box, takes a bite, and moans at the taste.

Maybe I should have given this idea more thought because, *damn.* The plan wasn't to torture myself. But with every move I make, he counters it in a way I didn't consider. Every touch, every taste, every hungry glance, every time he pulls away... it is exquisite agony.

Pressing play on the remote, he yanks the throw blanket off the back of the couch and tosses it over our legs. I bite a choco-late-covered pineapple slice as I lean into Anderson's side. Rest my head on his shoulder as the movie plays on the screen. Then, I call on some higher power to give me strength.

Strength to get through this movie. Strength to ask for what I want when the credits roll up the screen. And strength to strip his clothes off as we trip down the hall toward the bedroom, lips locked and bodies eager for more than sleep.

CHAPTER 58
ANDERSON

Since walking through the front door tonight, Helena has thrown one hint after another. Hints that she is ready for us to take the next step. That she wants more. It's driven me mad with need.

But I've also enjoyed torturing her at every turn. Dragging out the night and delivering sweet affliction.

My lips and tongue and teeth on her skin. My hands on her cheeks, in her hair, on her curves. Her jagged breaths, her warm skin on mine, her quiet whimpers as she wordlessly begs for more.

Oblivious, I am not. The more upscale dinner, the wine, those damn leggings paired with that relaxed top exposing her neck and skin... If that top was the only one she owned, I'd die a happy man.

When I bent and kissed her near the table, my lips on her skin lit a fire in my groin. Going against instinct, I fought the urge to skip dinner. I fought the urge to strip her bare, set her on the kitchen counter, and feast on her instead.

She planned a nice evening, and as much as I wanted to

skip it all, as much as I wanted to drag her to the bedroom, I refused to ruin it.

For weeks, I've toed the line with my feelings, with my desires. I want the next step. I want to start my future with her. But in the same breath, I want to take my time. Savor the small moments. Create new memories with her. Memories like a romantic dinner, movie, and dessert with the woman I love.

Sex is powerful. Carnal. Natural. It connects people in an unparalleled way. Bonds them for life. And it can be the turning point in any relationship.

But love, devotion, undiluted passion between lovers... nothing is more heady. Euphoric. Enthralling. It not only fuses them for life, but it also changes how they see the world. Every experience means more because they have each other.

It's been far too long since my bare body molded to hers. Since I sank into the cradle of her hips and bracketed her head with my arms. Since I rocked my hips and pushed inside her, her back bowing off the mattress as her lips parted on a gasp. It's been far too long, but I never forgot a single moment we spent together.

Desperate as I am to experience physical intimacy with her again, the idea of taking that step and losing her has me resistant. Desperate as I am to have more of her, to keep her forever, I need more. I need her actions *and* words. I need promises to spill from her lips and take root in my marrow. Need reassurance that she won't break me. Never again.

Simple as it sounds, what I need is layered with so much complexity.

The end credits scroll up on the screen. I stretch for the remote and turn off the television, blanketing us in darkness. Neither of us moves as our jagged breaths fill the silence. My heart rattles my rib cage—*pound, pound, pounding* against its prison walls.

And then her knuckles graze the top of my hand, like silent permission to speak, to move, to leave this couch and escape to the bedroom.

"Ander..." My name rolls off her tongue, so soft, so sweet. A litany. A plea. An invitation.

Still curled in the blanket, I slide Smoky off my lap. I turn over my hand beneath Helena's, lace our fingers, and rise from the couch. Anxiety twists my stomach as I guide us through the apartment toward the bedroom, toward her bed, toward the next step.

Audible breaths bounce off the walls as we enter the room. A current charging the air, the buzz licking my skin and making me hyperaware. Of her, of us, of what comes next. Every hiccup or catch of her breath, every twitch of her fingers in my grip, every shuffled or stumbled step forward, I pick up all of it.

And damn, I love that this moment, this next step, is just as significant for her as it is for me.

I bump the foot of the bed and twist us so we face each other. Take her other hand in mine and step into her. Kiss her crown, her forehead, one temple, followed by the other. With each press of my lips, with each kiss that brings me closer to her lips, her chest rises and falls faster. And when our lips finally meet, she melts under the contact.

Untangling our fingers, I clasp her hips and give a gentle squeeze. I lick the seam of her lips and tangle my tongue with hers when she lets me in. My fingers dance up the sides of her body, grazing the edges of her breasts, skimming the ridges of her collarbones, caressing the length of her neck. She lets out a soft whimper and reaches for my shirt.

Framing her face in my hands, I tilt her head and deepen the kiss. Swallow the moan that spills from her lips and lands on my tongue. Inch impossibly closer as the amorous kiss morphs into something headier. Potent. Explosive.

I tear my lips from hers. "Tell me you want this."

Hot, staggered breaths paint my lips. "I want this."

Reaching for the hem of her shirt, I drag it up her body and peel it off. "Tell me you want *me*."

She fists the cotton of my shirt and hauls it up and over my head. "I want you," she breathes out. "I *need* you."

The back of my fingers skim the exposed skin of her belly a beat before my arms circle her waist. I trail my fingers up her spine and pause when I reach the hooks of her bra. "Tell me you want me, this, us. Forever," I whisper.

Knuckles graze my abdomen, igniting fire under my skin. She flattens her palms and rests one on my pec, the other over my brutally beating heart. The room quiets, the eerie, lengthy silence a slow knife to the heart. Hour-long seconds pass as she doesn't utter a word. I start to hyperventilate. My mind swirling with darkness. My ribs crushing my lungs as fear cripples me from the inside.

Not again. A shiver rolls up my spine, and I shudder beneath her touch. *No, no, no. Not like before. I won't survive. Not again.*

I push up on my toes, ready to take a step back and erect my walls. Prepare to protect my heart.

But my feet never move.

Her hand over my heart shifts to the side. Leaning in, she presses her lips to the skin over my heart and doesn't move. The kiss is simple, tender, a caress of the lips. But *damn*, it means every-fucking-thing.

She straightens her spine, drags her hands up my chest, my

neck, her nails scratching the wiry hair of my beard before she cups my cheeks.

"Anderson Gregory Everett, I have never wanted anything more." She presses a chaste kiss to my lips. "I *want* you." Warm lips kiss the corner of my mouth. "I *want* this." She kisses the opposite corner. "I want *us*." Another kiss, dead center. "And more than anything, I *want* forever with you. Only you. Always you."

I crash my lips to hers as my fingers unlatch her bra. She shimmies the cotton down her arms, tosses it aside, snakes her arms around my waist, and squashes her breasts to my chest.

Fuck. I skim the length of her spine with rough fingers, clutching the back of her neck and pinning her in place.

A whimper falls from her lips, the sweet sound a direct line to my aching cock. I spin us and ease her onto the bed. Hook my hands under her arms and slide her up until she hits the pillows. My fingers drag down the sides of her rib cage, over the dip of her waist, and stop at the waistband of her leggings.

"Please, Ander," she begs, voice raspy.

With a curl of my fingers, I clasp the band of her leggings and panties, tugging them down, down, down until they hit the floor. Hooking my thumbs in my sweats, I shove them down my legs and kick them aside. I lift a leg, press my knee to the mattress, then pause.

Reality hits and I am dizzy. My arms shake and legs wobble as the moment rocks me with uncontrollable force.

I'm here. With. Helena. I suck in a sharp breath. *She loves me. She wants me.* My limbs quake harder, almost violently. *She wants forever.*

Arms and legs band around my body and hug me with indisputable ferocity. She rests her cheek on my chest at the base of my sternum, her lips ghosting my skin. I wrap her in my arms and pin her to my frame. Whisper apologies with every other breath. Absorb her soft *I love you*s in between.

And when the tremors fade, she loosens her hold. Sweeping her legs under her butt, she pushes up onto her knees and frames my face in her hands.

"I love you, Ander." She kisses my lips and inches back on the mattress.

My knee hits the bed and I move toward her. "Love you, North."

Her hands slide down the sides of my neck and spread across my shoulders. "So much." She leans forward and kisses the hollow of my throat.

My eyes roll back and I reach for her hips. "So fucking much." The words staccato on my tongue.

Slowly, she shifts to her back and brings me down over her. Supple fingers trail down either side of my spine, splaying as they reach the swell of my ass. Delicate hands grip my glutes, kneading the muscles as she rocks her hips.

Bracketing her face with my forearms, I sweep a finger across her forehead and brush the hair from her face. Lips a breath from hers, I hold her greens with my blues in the dark.

"I crave you, Helena." I drop my lips to hers and kiss her with slow hunger. "Your words. Your touch." My lips trail the line of her jaw and drift down the column of her throat. "Your lips. Your taste." I pepper kisses on the swell of her breast until my lips graze her pert nipple. "Your love. Your heart."

My tongue darts out and circles her nipple. A gasp leaves her lips as she bows off the bed and thrusts her breast deeper into my mouth. I palm her other breast, massaging the swell of her flesh before taking her nipple between my thumb and forefinger, pinching.

A hiss fills the air, her fingers clawing their way up my

back and fisting my hair. "Please," she begs. For what, I'm not sure.

My mouth kisses a path to her other breast, gifting it equal attention. A whimper echoes in the room as her nipple pops from my lips. But it is soon replaced with ragged breaths as I kiss my way down her belly, past her navel, to the thin tuft of hair at the junction of her thighs.

Another first. One I won't disclose unless she asks.

Aside from Helena, I've only been with one other person.

Two years on the road, I'd had a rough night and just needed a connection. Something to make me a little less lonely. The sex had been meaningless. A random traveler. I didn't ask her name or give mine. We'd met at a campground, several other vans parking there for the night. After a few too many drinks, I propositioned her. It was quick and empty. Disgust washed over me the moment I touched her. And the entire time, I refused to look at her face.

When she'd stepped into her van for the night, I jogged away from camp and vomited in the bushes.

Touching another woman felt inappropriate. Wrong in every way. Even when we were no longer beholden to each other, being with someone else made me ill.

Since that night, I have never sought attention or affection from another. And I never will. Helena is who I want. Who I will always want.

I drag the tip of my nose through her curls and inhale her musky scent. My mouth waters and cock hardens to borderline painful. Eager to taste her, my tongue darts out between my lips and licks up her center. Her salty tang dances over my taste buds and unlocks something primal in my bones. A feral growl vibrates my chest as I hook her thighs over my shoulders, bury my face deeper between her legs, and devour her with newfound hunger. I palm her breasts. Tweak her nipples. Drive her wild with my tongue and hands.

Soft moans spill from her lips as her fingers curl in my hair. She grinds her pussy against my mouth, the occasional "oh god" and "yes" slipping from her lips. One of my hands kneads its way down the curves of her torso, massages her fleshy hip, strokes the inside of her thigh. I flick her clit with my tongue once, twice, then dip a finger inside her.

So warm. So fucking tight.

My cock twitches as I pump my finger inside of her. I add another finger and her cries intensify. Grow louder, faster. The grind of her hips turns aggressive. Her body tightening around my fingers as I hit a spot deep inside her.

And then her hand in my hair yanks the strands. Hard. A tremor ripples through her body as her orgasm drips down my fingers to my hand. As she comes down from the high, I withdraw my fingers, bring them to my mouth, and suck the taste of her off.

My eyes roll back. "Need to be inside you," I say on a growl.

"Yes." The three-letter word breathy on her lips.

I crawl up her body. Kiss her hard. Let her taste herself on my tongue. "Condom," I mutter, realizing I don't have any.

"Bedside drawer."

I inch back and stare down at her as my brows knit together.

Her hand comes to my cheek. "Bought them today." She lifts off the bed and kisses my lips. "The box is still sealed."

I have no right to be upset over Helena finding comfort in someone else while I was gone. She didn't know where I was. Didn't know if I would return. Intentionally, I'd left her in the dark. And with that sequence of actions, she was entitled to move on.

But knowing she needed to buy condoms is a relief and sexy as hell.

Yanking the drawer open, I locate the box, tear at the cellophane, all but rip the box in two, then tear a condom free from the strip. We chuckle as I fumble with the wrapper but grow serious as I roll the latex down my shaft. As I settle between her legs. As I lace our fingers together and slide them up the bed, under the pillows.

"I love you, North." I drop my lips to hers. Kiss her with every ounce of love in my veins.

Her legs wrap around my hips and lock at the ankles. "Love you, Ander."

I line up the head of my cock with her entrance and gently rock my hips forward. Our gasps mingle in the air as I fill her, but not to the hilt. I pull out to the base of my crown, then ease in again, deeper this time. Her grip on my hands tightens.

Every muscle in my body locks. "Did I hurt you?"

She shakes her head but doesn't utter a word.

I drop a tender kiss to her lips. "Talk to me. We can stop."

Her head shakes faster. "No." She licks her lips. "It's just…"

I wait for her to continue. Wait for her to tell me what initiated her death grip on my hands. When a minute passes, I release one of her hands and cup her cheek. "What?" I press my lips to her forehead. "You can tell me."

She lays her hand over mine on her cheek. Turns her face into my palm and kisses the heart. "It's been a long time." Emotion clogs her voice.

Desperate to see her face, I pull out, reach for the bedside table, and turn on the light. Soft light filters through the room, both of us squinting. Once my eyes adjust, they lock on hers. Tears well up in her eyes as I try to puzzle out what has her so upset.

Did someone hurt her? Assault her?

Rage boils my blood at the thought of someone doing atrocious things to her.

Softly, her thumb strokes my cheek. "Whatever you're thinking, please stop."

I take a deep breath and shove aside the errant thoughts. "Then please tell me what has you ready to cry. Because my mind is running rampant."

Bringing her other hand to my face, she levels me with her gaze. Soft greens stare back at me as she swallows. "When I say it's been a long time, what I mean is"—she licks her lips and swallows again—"I haven't been with anyone."

My brows knit together and she brushes a finger over the ridge, making it relax.

"I haven't been with anyone since you."

Shock widens my eyes. "No one?"

She shakes her head. "I tried dating, but it never felt right. Not when I compared everyone to you."

This odd mix of surprise and relief swirls in my chest. Every muscle in my body sighs. "I know the feeling." Not that I will expand on that now. Not while we are skin to skin.

"Sorry if I ruined the moment."

"Never apologize for how you feel." I press my lips to hers. "You didn't ruin anything. But if you want to stop—"

"No," she cuts me off. Her legs circle my hips again. "I want this. God, do I want this." Her fingers comb through my hair. "Maybe we just go slow this time."

I stroke her cheek with my thumb. "Slow," I echo with a nod. "Should probably get a new condom."

After a quick condom swap, I ease down and settle into the cradle of her hips. Kiss the tip of her nose and stroke my thumb over her cheek. Then, ever so slowly, I rock inside of her. We make love with the light on, our eyes locked and fingers laced. Whispered *I love you*s float in the air. And when her breathing picks up, I move faster. Climb the peak to my orgasm right beside her.

Her body grips my cock as she detonates around me. I memorize every second of this moment. Her euphoric expression and slack jaw. The red splotches on her chest, neck, and cheeks. The soft whimper on her lips. How her eyes seek mine the second they open.

I crash my mouth to hers, rock my hips again, and fall into the abyss with her. Where I belong.

CHAPTER 59

HELENA

A shiver rolls up my spine as a gust of wind whips my hair across my face. Anderson hugs me to his side as we stroll down Main Street toward Black Silk. Rubbing a hand up and down my arm, he presses a kiss to my crown.

"Want my jacket?"

Already in my own jacket, gloves, and scarf, I shake my head. If I say yes, his flannel will be his only source of warmth. "We're almost there. And you need your jacket more than I do."

Two blocks from the restaurant, he drops his arm from my shoulders, unzips his coat, opens the front, tugs me back to him, and wraps the fleece-lined jacket around my frame. He kisses my temple and snuggles me close. "Let me at least share it with you."

Clasping his hand with mine, I don't fight his hold. If anything, I strengthen it around my frame. Sink into his warmth and comfort. Bask in this new version of our relationship.

Anderson and I have known each other as far back as memories imprint our minds. We have always been connected. We always will be. From friends to best friends to lovers to...

I shake off thoughts of the darker years but don't forget them. Those years shape so much of who we are now. Though we agree to take things slow, rebuild our friendship and see where it takes us, it doesn't take us long to fall into each other again. To slip into the easy comfort of being together. Lazy days on the couch, wrapped up in each other. Strolls down Main, my hand in his. Nights next to a roaring fire, snuggled in a blanket as we whisper words of love and forever.

It took years apart, years of heartache and misery, for him to heal and for me to recognize how important he is to my happiness.

Anderson is my person. The one person I *need* in my life. To breathe, to think, to love. He stitches my broken pieces together. Makes me complete in ways no one else can.

Our past is rocky and scarred by tragedy. But our future is wide open and brimming with promise.

I snake my arm around his waist beneath the coat, fist the cotton of his flannel, and press my lips to the line of his jaw. "Love you, Ander."

His steps falter and I look up at him. A hand comes to my cheek as he hovers a breath above my lips. Calloused skin smooths over the apple of my cheek. "Love you, North." He eliminates the last bit of space between us and presses a tender kiss to my lips.

An audible gasp nearby has him breaking the kiss. As I blink out the haze his kisses put me in, I spot Mrs. Everett feet away on the sidewalk, a fiery expression on her face. Her husband stands at her side, tugging at her arm in a silent plea to walk away. But her feet are glued in place, fingers curled into fists at her sides as she all but breathes fire.

Anderson turns to stone. His arm around me crushes me to him. Frustration and exasperation roll off Anderson and cloud the space around us and his parents. On every inhale, I fight the urge to open my mouth and tell her off. I want to yell and scream and announce to the world how volatile this woman is. How she, from the day he took his first breath, tore this man down. How she made him feel inadequate and unworthy of love or a beautiful life.

But I clamp my jaw shut and let my anger brew in silence.

This is not my battle to fight. Irrefutably, I will stand with Anderson and support his choices when it comes to his parents. Their past is layered with so much pain and it isn't my place to decide what their future looks like. Never will I steal his choices from him. Never will I suppress him. I will never be her.

I'd much rather lift him up. Remind him how much I love him. How important he is in my life. How I support his decisions and will be his rock when he needs strength. Tell him every day that my life wouldn't be worth it without him. Until my last breath, I will be his light.

"You have *got* to be kidding me," Mrs. Everett chastises, eyes on Anderson, her cheeks a deep shade of red. "I must be hallucinating."

"Joan." Mr. Everett gives her arm another tug. "Let's go."

She looks to her husband and he blanches under her scrutiny. Then her gaze darts back to us as she steps closer. "It's bad enough you aren't doing anything worthwhile with your life, Anderson." Her upper lip curls. "But this," she snaps, loud enough to cause passersby to slow their stride or pause altogether. "This has to be a joke."

A chill rolls through my limbs that has nothing to do with the cooler fall temperature. Uneasiness twists my gut. I take muted, deep breaths and tell my body to relax. Vomiting on the sidewalk in front of strangers and his parents will cause more harm than relief.

On the second inhale, the stiffness in Anderson's frame loosens a fraction. His initial shock fades enough to reinforce his confidence and find his voice. I fist his shirt and stand united with him.

"The only joke on this sidewalk, *Joan*"—disdain drips from his tongue as he uses her given name rather than Mom—"is the woman scolding her adult child after not seeing him in six years." He blinks away from her and meets my gaze. A soft stroke of his thumb on my arm eases any residual anxiety. The corners of his lips tip up slightly before he mouths, *I love you.* Then his attention is back on her and his armor is back in place. "As for what I do with my life... You lost the privilege of knowing long ago."

She steps into us and Anderson draws us back, keeping distance between us. In my periphery, a small crowd waits in the wings. Many of them townsfolk that know the Everett and Williams families. But the occasional unfamiliar face appears in the throng, examining the situation with curiosity or alarm in their eyes.

This is bad.

"You are *my* son—"

"No." Anderson drops his arm around me and advances on her. "You don't get to pull the parent card when it's convenient." He inches forward and I grip the back of his coat, unsure if I'm trying to anchor him or prevent him from getting closer. "You're unbelievable." Tipping his head back, eyes on the starry sky, he laughs without humor. Then he levels her icy stare with his fiery gaze. "Two." He holds up two fingers for emphasis. "There are two key reasons I came back." He pauses, peeks over his shoulder and winks. "Helena is the first." He squares his shoulders, hardens his jaw, then turns his attention back to his parents. "She will always be first."

"That girl *broke* you," she interjects, stabbing a finger in my direction.

"No," Anderson barks out. "She healed me. When I needed love, she gave it to me unconditionally. What happened between us before"—he shakes his head—"we were young and naive. I had my demons and she had hers. She didn't break me, *Joan*. You broke me."

"I did no—"

"I'm not done speaking," Anderson interrupts, loud enough to be heard a block away. "I came back to mend things with us too." He gestures between himself and his parents. "But you're so caught up in yourself, you're so blinded by your disgust for the son you never wanted, there's no way to repair us. I left this town to escape *you*. I've healed. I've grown up and moved forward." He steps back, laces my fingers with his, and shakes his head. "Seems you never will."

Anderson steps to the side and guides us through the onlookers. Behind us, she shouts through the thinning crowd, but I don't make out what she says.

The mellow, loving bubble around us ten minutes ago has fizzled into the atmosphere. Rage and exhaustion have taken its place as we march down the sidewalk toward the restaurant. Eager as I am to calm the brewing storm in Anderson's body, I keep to myself. Again, this is not my battle. No, the fundamental structure of this conflict comes from the woman still screaming on the sidewalk. The woman that claims to love her son but delivers only grief and resentment and revulsion.

When we finally make it to the table, Lessa notices Anderson's icy disposition. I subtly shake my head and she acknowledges it with a minor, quick dip of her chin.

Dinner goes by painfully slow, and with each passing minute, I *feel* Anderson retreating into himself. He hasn't said a word. Hasn't smiled or laughed at any of the stupid shit Logan rambles on about. He picks at his food and clenches the muscles of his jaw.

And when it's time to leave the restaurant, he opts to go to Lessa's apartment after walking me to mine.

He needs time to digest and dispose of what happened tonight. I just wish he'd let me be there as he does.

CHAPTER 60

ANDERSON

I can't fucking breathe.

For the first time in years, fury owns my every breath. Why the hell did I want to fix things with her? Why the hell did I think it was actually possible?

Time apart may have scarred over the wounds my mother inflicted on me, but one ten-minute interaction with her and the scar tissue is slowly tearing at the seams.

"Fuck." I kick the foot of Ales's guest bed. *"Fuck, fuck, fuck."*

Cherry on top of the chaos sundae… I shut down on Helena. When dinner ended hours ago, I walked her home. Outside her front door, I told her it'd be best if I stayed with Ales tonight. I didn't miss the hurt in her eyes, but she nodded and kissed my cheek before ducking her chin and whispering good night.

Instead of letting her light guide me from the dark path my mind walked down, I pushed her away. And I'm more pissed about that than everything else.

The front door opens, Braydon shushing Ales as she giggles. Not like she'd actually wake anyone. They don't know

I'm here and the exterior walls are brick over cinder block. The neighboring tenants would only hear something if it was cranked to deafening levels.

I whip open the bedroom door and pad down the hall to the living room. Ales spots me first, slapping a hand over her mouth in an attempt to mask her drunken laughter.

"Sorry, A." She snort-laughs. "Didn't know you were here."

"It's fine." I go to the fridge and grab a water. "Can we talk? Or are you too drunk?"

Immediately, she stops laughing. Solemnity blanks her face as her eyes roam every inch of mine. "What's wrong?"

I plaster on a fake smile, untwist the cap on the water, and take a long pull from the bottle. "Bumped into Joan and Samuel on the way to dinner."

At this point, it makes my skin crawl to call them Mom and Dad. For me, they don't deserve the title. True parents don't degrade their children. True parents don't make their children feel less than. All Joan Everett has done for me is remind me how much she never wanted a son. She never confessed it outright, but I am no fool. As for Samuel Everett, the few times he stood up for me, she shoved him back down with a menacing glare.

I'd like to think my sperm donor still has the chance to grow a backbone, but his reaction tonight tells me otherwise. Like always, he coddles her. Acts like he's trying to defuse the situation but doesn't possess the strength to do so.

And I refuse to open my arms to a man that can't stand up for himself. If he isn't strong enough to love and sustain his own life, how the hell will he do it for anyone else?

Ales takes my hand and hauls me toward the couch. "Do you want Braydon to leave the room?"

I shake my head. "No. He should stay." I meet his gaze as he sits on the other side of Ales. "Secrets do no one any good."

"Okay." She sandwiches my hand between hers. "Talk to me."

Over the next hour, I tell her about the encounter with our parents. Every ugly word from our mother's mouth, every cowardly move our father made—or rather, didn't make—and each fuse it lit inside my veins the longer I stood there. I spill the pain of my reopened wounds. How one interaction with her enraged me and sliced me open simultaneously.

Tears blur my vision as I confess that repairing the relationship with my parents may be a lost cause. As much as I'd love to meet in the middle and start fresh with our parents, I fear it may not be possible. If Joan Everett isn't willing to let go of the past and make peace in order to move forward, we are at a stalemate.

I won't compromise my integrity, disregard the years of therapy I endured, or cast aside the work I put in to reach this healthy point in my life to appease a woman who won't extend an ounce of effort. If she wants to be a part of my life, if she is willing to work toward a happier future, I will forgive the hurt she inflicted in the past. I will let it all go if she is as willing to wipe the slate clean as I am.

If not... I refuse to let her rob me of a wondrous and passionate future. Whether it be in Lake Lavender or on the road or both. Because, damn it, I deserve happiness.

Ales drops my hand and scoots across the couch until she is in my lap. Her arms wrap around my middle and crush my rib cage. A groan rumbles in my throat, but she doesn't ease up. If anything, she hugs me harder. Lends me her strength. Pours every ounce of love into the firm embrace.

"Love you, A." She loosens her hold and twists to kiss my

temple. "Whatever you need, I'm here." She inches back enough to pin me with a somber stare. "Always."

My lips meet her forehead. "Thank you."

"Is Lena okay?" She scoots off my lap and resumes her spot on the couch. Braydon grabs her hips, hauls her into his lap, and bands his arms around her waist. "She doesn't do well with confrontation."

So wrapped up in my thoughts and anger I shut out the one person I shouldn't have tonight. Knowing her, she is probably on the couch, in the dark, crying because I went into protection mode.

Fuck, fuck, fuck.

"I was an idiot, Ales." I cover my face with my hands, audibly exhale, and drag them through my unruly hair. "I freaked out tonight, went into crisis mode, and abandoned her on her doorstep."

Jackass. I am a goddamn jackass.

Yes, I have to sort through all this shit in my head. But deserting her when we've worked so damn hard to get to this better place, that screwup is on me. And I need to do damage control. Now.

"It was a shoddy move, but she'll forgive it." A soft smile grazes her lips. "She loves you and respects your need for space."

True as that may be, I should have said something. Told her I needed room to breathe and think and evacuate the fury. In her compact apartment, she would have moved to another room while I exercised the aggression from my system. Then she would have filled the gaps with her love and light and spirit.

I bolt up from the couch and yank my phone from my pocket. Then I meet my sister's blues and gift her a half smile.

"Thanks, Ales." I flip the phone over in my hand again and again. "For everything."

The corners of her eyes soften. "You never have to ask. Love you, A."

I pad over to the bench near the door, slip on my shoes and jacket, then give my sister and her boyfriend a wave. "Love you, too."

And then I'm out the door, jogging down the stairs and racing down the road. Toward my heart. Toward my future. Toward my North.

CHAPTER 61

HELENA

Heat from the fireplace licks my skin, but the warmth doesn't seep in. It doesn't reach the chill deep in my bones. A tremor I've felt since the moment Anderson left tonight.

My phone buzzes with an incoming message. Seeing as it's past one in the morning and my do not disturb is on, whoever it is must be on my favorites list. Probably Lessa checking on me since Anderson is at her place.

With a groan, I reach for the phone on the coffee table, tap the screen, and see the notification. But it isn't from Lessa. No, it's from Anderson.

ANDERSON

Still up?

I stare at the screen a moment and contemplate whether or not I should respond. I get that he needed to clear his head, but leaving me like he did... what if he does that every time we have a run-in with his parents? What if he does that every time something stirs up bad memories?

I love him and would do anything to prove my love, but I am not alright with him jumping ship every time the sea gets rocky. That is not how couples handle unpleasant or horrendous situations. We jump in feet first, hand in hand, and kick until we both surface.

HELENA

Yes.

Before I take my next breath, a soft knock echoes through the living room.

He's here?

Finagling the blanket around my shoulders, I pick up Smoky from my lap and hold her to my chest as I shuffle in my fuzzy socks toward the door, pushing up on my toes and peeking out the peephole to see if it *is* Anderson or some random vagrant on my doorstep.

His dark-blond hair may be wind whipped, shadows may block half his profile, but I'd recognize this man anywhere. Anderson will never be *some* guy. After almost a decade apart, the minute I saw him outside my store, I knew it was him. It isn't about looks or scars or mannerisms. No, it's so much more.

My soul vibrates when he is near. Stirs to life. Breathes deeper and sighs with relief. Because my soul calls out to his, just as his calls out to mine.

I unbolt the lock, twist the doorknob, and crack open the door. Smoky mewls at the sight of him. *Traitor.*

"Sorry for my behavior earlier." He rubs the back of his neck as he screws up his lips in a remorseful smile. "May I come in?"

Frozen in the doorway, I remain tight lipped. I don't want him to suffer or think I don't care. But he should know this is not okay. He can't bolt every time things get heavy. He can't cast me aside every time he needs space to think. He can't run away, expecting me to wait for his return, whenever that may be. His actions have consequences. And tonight, his actions hurt.

Without a word, I open the door wider and step aside. He steps past me, shucks his jacket and toes off his shoes as I close the door, then hauls me to his chest. Smoky cries between us. Anderson relaxes his hold enough to let her hop down, then he hugs the air from my lungs.

"I fucked up," he mumbles with his lips on my hair. "I fucked up bad and I'm so damn sorry."

Wiggling my arms free, I step back, open my arms, wrap us both in the blanket, and breathe him in. Though his clothes are chilled from the crisp air outside, the warmth I sought from the fire finally hits my bones while in his arms.

Anderson made an impulsive decision in a moment of distress. An instinctual action I have no right to fault him for. He chose flight over fight, something he has done most of his life.

But if he wants to make changes, if he wants to come home, he needs to take a stand. He needs to choose to fight. And *I* need to remind him I will always fight alongside him.

I choose him. I will always choose him. Even when it hurts.

"Let's sit," I whisper, my cheek on his chest.

We break apart, but his arm around me remains as we stagger toward the couch. I steer us left as we round the arm of the couch, but he keeps us walking forward, guiding us to the rug in front of the fire.

Lowering to the floor, he pats the ground next to him. "Please."

I drop down beside him and wrap us in the blanket again.

Smoky pads across the floor, brushing against Anderson's leg, then curls in a tight ball between us. Nose tucked under her tail, she purrs as she drifts off.

Beneath the blanket, Anderson takes my hand in his and laces our fingers. The calloused pad of his thumb rubs my hand in slow, gentle strokes while his eyes lose focus staring at the flickering flames in the fireplace.

What happened tonight was hard on him, but it was no picnic for me either.

There is a reason I haven't kept in touch with or celebrated special occasions with the Everett parents. Not long after returning from college, Mrs. Everett made it evident she was not my biggest fan. She never gave a clear indication of why, but I knew she blamed me for Anderson leaving. I may have been one of the reasons Anderson drove away from Lake Lavender, but she is the epicenter of his pain.

And tonight, she took a knife to every old wound and made it fresh.

Anderson returned with the hope of healing fully—well, as fully as someone can from such an injury—but this run-in with his parents may have thrown that plan in the dumpster.

"I shouldn't have walked away earlier," he mutters, dropping his chin to his chest, his eyes now on Smoky. With his free hand, he pets her gray fur. Finds an ounce of solace in her sweet companionship. "It was immature." The muscle in his jaw tics. "A juvenile reflex I can't seem to shake." He levels his gaze with the fire. Deep creases form at the corners of his eyes as his brows scrunch together. "I hate it," he whispers, barely loud enough to hear.

We go quiet a moment as I let his words sink in. With Anderson, I don't react immediately. Not with delicate situations. A quick reaction may lead to miscommunication or misinterpretation. I don't tiptoe around what I say to him—I will always be honest with Anderson—but in moments such as these, hasty responses often cause more harm than good.

"I get why you walked off." My fingers tighten around his. "You needed space and time to think."

Dancing flames reflect in his blues as our gazes lock. "I did." He swallows. "But I went about it wrong."

A soft smile barely lifts the corners of my mouth. "You did." Leaning forward, I press a chaste kiss to his lips. "You wanted to approach them when you were ready. You wanted to set the time and place and be in control of the situation. Tonight, you were robbed of all that." I lift a hand to his face, cup his cheek, and lightly scrape my nails through his beard. His eyes fall shut as he leans into my touch. "I love that you were able to heal on your own, away from the source of pain."

My heart spasms in my chest as my stomach twists at those words, but I bite the inside of my cheek. The pain I endured during his absence is incomparable to the hurt I caused him or that he went through with his parents.

"More than anything, you needed the time to yourself," I say, voice raspy. "Not just to heal, but to discover who you are without the influence of others." I nod, more to myself than him. "On the road, you processed hard situations without other people." Lifting our joined hands, I twist them and kiss the inside of his wrist. "Your initial response is to deal with it all on your own. If you still need that, just say the word. Wander the streets. Go for a drive. Kidnap Smoky and spend a few hours in the spare bedroom with her. Whatever you need to clear your head. And if you're open to the idea, I'd love to be there for you. However that looks."

In an unexpected move, Anderson hauls me into his lap. Smoky cries out then scurries off, indignation on her furry face. Anderson mutters an apology, but the words vanish seconds later. He frames my face with his hands, brushes his thumbs over my cheeks once, twice, then his lips are on mine.

The kiss is soft at first. A gentle brush of the lips again and again. Then he tilts my head in his hands. Licks the seam of my lips. Silently asks—no, *begs*—for more. Without breaking the kiss, I shift to straddle his lap. Hook my legs around his hips. Fist his shirt and drag him impossibly closer. Stroke my tongue over his and deepen the kiss.

Strong arms band around my middle and crush me to his chest. A moan spills from his lips and I swallow it eagerly. He flips me on my back and settles in the cradle of my hips, the bulge beneath his zipper pressed between my thighs. Hungry lips kiss my chin, the line of my jaw, the sensitive skin beneath my ear.

Then his lips are gone.

Mayan-blue irises meet my jade greens. His fingers toy with the wayward strands of my hair as he brushes the tip of my nose with his. "Damn, I love you," he whispers, his breath warm on my lips. Soft lips meet mine in a kiss that ends far too soon. "I love how imperfect we are." *Kiss.* "I love how the world wobbles less with you in my arms." *Kiss.* "Most of all, I love the way you love me." When his lips meet mine, the kiss is far from innocent.

Lips and tongues taste mouths and skin. I arch my back, a moan escaping my lips as he licks down my neck and nips the curve where my neck and shoulder meet. Clawing at the hem of his shirt, I tug it up and over his head. Deft fingers unbutton my pajama top then snake beneath me to lift me enough to wiggle free from the material.

My fingers find his hair as he trails kisses down my breastbone. Gentle, followed by greedy laps of his tongue. His lips dance over my skin to my breast, tasting and nibbling while his hands knead my flesh. Hungry. Desperate. I gasp when his tongue darts out and licks my areola a breath before he bites my nipple, the sting and adrenaline shoot between my thighs. My back bows off the floor as he licks and nips his way to my other breast.

"Ander…" I pant out his name.

He crawls back up my body and crushes my lips with his as he unbuttons his pants. Hooking my thumbs in his waistband, I shove them and his underwear down his ass, then his thighs, before kicking them aside. On the next breath, he flips me so I'm above him. His fingers thrust my pajama bottoms and panties down my legs to join his on the floor.

Straddling his hips, I lower myself until we're skin to skin. I run my fingers through his hair. Drop my lips to his. Show him how much I love him without words. His arms band around my middle as he hums. I suck his bottom lip between mine. Nip the plump flesh and smile when he growls.

Palms on his pecs, I sit up and roll my hips back, coating his erection with my arousal. His hands find my hips, gripping them hard as he sits up. I wrap my legs around his waist. Snake my arms around his neck.

On the next rock of my hips, his tip bumps my entrance. I pause, lay my forehead on his, and inhale a shaky breath. Brushing the bridge of his nose with the tip of mine, I lock on to his addictive blue eyes. "I love you, Ander." Then, as I lower myself on him, I drop my mouth to his.

A guttural moan rumbles from his lips as his hold on me tightens. "Love you, North." A hand trails down my spine, resting on my tailbone and encouraging me to move.

In the light of the fire, we shed the last of our fears. Expose our hearts fully to each other. Vow to always love and support the other. And as the sun gradually lights the dark sky, we fall into a blissful sleep beneath the blanket next to the fire.

CHAPTER 62

ANDERSON

"Not happening," I snap, my molars grinding. "Sorry."

Ales gifts me a sympathetic smile. "No need to apologize. Figured that'd be your answer, but I had to ask."

A little more than a week has passed since Joan did her damnedest to belittle me on Main Street. She gave no fucks that dozens of people stopped to watch the spectacle. If anything, it probably gave her some sick sense of joy. Now she has the audacity to act as if it never happened, like our relationship is all smiles and laughter and warm hugs. There are more than screws loose in that woman's head.

"I want closure with her, but on my terms."

Attending Thanksgiving at my childhood home sounds more like a catastrophe waiting in the wings versus the right time to talk and find a peaceful middle ground with my procreators. What I need to say to them, especially her, shouldn't be said in a group setting. Our rift isn't a secret, but that doesn't mean I want to air out my past with a crowd in the room. Her display on the sidewalk is a clear message she doesn't care who hears what.

So long as it garners her attention, Joan Everett doesn't give a damn what people think of her. Holidays with "family" and friends are an open invitation for her to fill her holier-than-thou well.

"You need to do something meaningful with your life, Anderson. Oh, pass the potatoes."

No thanks.

Ales slips on a pair of oven mitts, picks up the corn bread casserole, and carries it to the table. "When you're ready, let me know. I'll be right there with you." Setting it in the middle, she peels off the mitts and tosses them on the kitchen counter. "Until then, it's Friendsgiving time."

"This, I can do." Pulling out a chair and sitting next to Helena, she meets my gaze.

"Everything okay?"

I rest my hand on her thigh and rub small circles with my thumb. "Yeah. Joan asked Ales to ask us to Thanksgiving. I said no." I shrug. "Just need a little longer."

Her hand covers mine beneath the table. "Take as long as you need." She leans in and kisses the angle of my jaw. "Thanksgiving can be just the two of us. Or, if you'd like, we can join my parents." Dainty fingers wrap around my hand and squeeze. "I'm good with whatever."

"Talk about it later?"

"Good with me," she says, giving me a quick kiss. "Now, let's eat before it gets cold."

We elected to stay home on Thanksgiving, just the two of us and Smoky, for our first major holiday as a serious couple. And if future holidays promise to be equally good, I have no qualms about staying in for them all.

Hours spent in the kitchen, we mixed and cooked and flung ingredients at each other. Dinner was enjoyed on the couch, followed by snuggles and movie time. Then, as day turned to night, snuggles shifted from innocent and sweet to hungry and heated.

Yep. I am one-hundred-percent good with every holiday in the apartment, just me and her and our furry little girl.

Across the table, Helena pops the last bite of egg in her mouth. After a swig of tea to wash it down, she knocks me breathless with a smile. "We should get a tree today."

It takes me a second to piece together she means Christmas tree. The last time I gave a damn about Christmas was months before everything went to shit for us. Once Ales went to college, holidays were more about what my mother wanted and less about family.

Now, everything is different. Now, Helena and I have a second chance to create a beautiful life together. To create new traditions. However we want.

"I'd love to. Though my tree-picking skills are rusty."

She takes her plate to the kitchen, rinses it, and sets it in the dishwasher. I finish the last of my breakfast and clean up while she heads for the bedroom. With the kitchen counter wiped down and the dishwasher running, I amble toward the bedroom, peeling my shirt over my head as I go. The shower in the en suite bathroom is running as I enter the room. I strip the last of my clothes away and join her under the hot spray.

Before she soaps up the loofah, I pin her to the tile and make her moan. Shower sex is new and awkward and definitely not as easy as movies make it seem. That just means we need more practice, which I won't complain about.

After we wash up and towel off, Helena dries her hair and we dress for the bitter chill that swept through town last night. Lake Lavender doesn't see snow like the eastern part of the state, but it isn't uncommon to get a few inches every now and again.

"Should we take the van?" I ask.

She wraps a scarf around her neck then shoulders her purse. "Probably a good idea." Her car would support the tree fine, but I'd hate to get sap on the paint.

Slipping on my boots, I scratch Smoky's head. "Be good while we're gone. Mommy and Daddy are getting you a tree to climb." I pocket my wallet and phone, keeping my keys out.

Helena laughs. "I've only had a mini tree since I adopted her. This should be fun."

"I'll go warm up the van." I kiss her forehead, step out and jog down the stairs.

Cold stings my cheeks as I hit the bottom step and the wind whips. I unlock the van and crank the ignition. While the engine warms, I think back to the last time I experienced cold like this.

The past few winters, I drove farther south and explored the Carolinas and southeast. Sure, temperatures cooled off there, but it was nothing like home. Winter in the Southeast was similar to fall in the Northwest. Much as I enjoyed the mild winters, I missed the wonder and change that came with the seasons.

The temperature light flicks off once the engine is warm. I turn on the heat, jump out of the van, and dash up the stairs for Helena. After one last head scratch for Smoky, we leave the apartment.

"Do we need decorations for the tree?" I ask, remembering her earlier comment about not having a larger tree for some time.

"I have some, but maybe we should get more."

"On it."

Since we have to drive out of town to the tree farm, I steer us toward the closest Target. We spend way too much time in the holiday section of the store and load the cart with way more than anticipated. But if it makes Helena happy, I am happy.

Before we leave the store, Helena orders hot cocoa and a baked good from Starbucks. Then she makes me swear not to tell Ales. I don't argue because Ales would have both our necks if she found out.

Once everything is loaded in the van, I steer us toward the tree farm. Located a few miles outside Lake Lavender, the tree farm sits on five expansive acres. As a young child, I loved coming out here with just Dad. It was one of a few family activities without Mom. A happy memory. We'd walk the rows for hours before finding the perfect tree. I got to pick the tree and he'd cut it.

This first Christmas with Helena, where it is just her and me and lil' Smoky, I want us to choose together. A tree we both love.

Flipping on the blinker, I guide us down a long gravel drive, passing under a sign with *Emberly's Evergreens* carved into and painted on cedar. Weaving through the rows, I back the van into a spot at the far end of the lot and cut the engine.

Helena hops out, hot cocoa in hand, and meets me at the back of the van. I take her free hand in mine and guide us toward the entrance between two log cabins—the smaller is an office for the business, while the grandiose cabin is the farm's family home. The attendant hands us a numbered tag and tells us to holler when we find the tree we want. We have the option to cut it ourselves or ask an employee to help. Since I'm a bit rusty at cutting down trees, the assistance is much appreciated.

In no rush, Helena and I stroll the first row of trees. I inhale the crisp, piney air and momentarily close my eyes as it relaxes my muscles. Birds chirp and animals scuttle in the browning grass. Helena's thumb slowly strokes the length of mine, providing a sense of calm no one but she gives.

Opening my eyes, I peer at her out of the corner of my eye. Cheeks rosy from the cold. A soft smile etched on her glossy pink lips. Try as I might, I can't tear my eyes away from her. Her hair is slightly longer than when I first returned to town. *Will she grow it longer again?* Today, she has it hidden beneath a cream-colored, knitted beanie, the ends of her hair peeking out and curling just beneath her jaw. My fingers twitch, eager to reach up and toy with the strands. My lips tingle, eager to kiss her in the middle of the tree farm.

A faint whooshing echoes in my ears, my pulse picking up the more I think of her lips. Impulse takes over and I stop walking.

She jerks slightly then spins around, her addictive smile on her perfect lips. "See one you like?"

Honestly, I haven't looked at a single tree since we've been here. Not really. So I shake my head.

A deep wrinkle forms between her brows. "Everything okay?"

I step into her, wrap an arm around her waist, and hold her close. "Perfect." Then my mouth is on hers, the kiss sweet enough for public but a hint spicier with no one nearby. I lick the seam of her lips, eager for a deeper taste when I hear someone approach.

Breaking the kiss, I rest my forehead on hers. I open my mouth to say *I love you* but get cut off.

"Really, Anderson?" The shrill sound of Joan's voice floats around me and steals every molecule of joy. "Making out at the Christmas tree farm. Like you're a damn child."

Helena's eyes widen as mine vibrate. She tightens her hold on my hand, anchoring me to her as I straighten my spine. Right now, I am so incredibly thankful she is here. Without her, my next move would be much worse. Volatile. Explosive.

"Ah!" I scream far too loud, and the sound bounces as it travels. "Will you stop!"

Her lip curls up into the sneer I've seen more times than I care to admit. She plants a hand on a hip and points at my chest with the other hand. "Don't you dare speak to me in that tone. I am your mother. Show some respect."

I laugh, and not just a little. Head tipping back, I clutch my chest then cover my mouth as laughter pours out. The chortle humorless and empty. As my laughter dies, I level her with my gaze.

"Respect? You want my respect?" I snort with a shake of my head. Lifting a hand, I gesture between us. "It's a two-way street. Respect is earned, not assumed because of who you are."

Fire lights her eyes. The fact that I don't bow or crumple at her authority has her livid. Her nostrils flare, her shoulders square, and she puffs out her chest like some small woodland creature forcing itself to appear bigger, badder, better. Her goal is to scare or intimidate or suppress my strength, my courage, my ability to be more than she wants me to be.

And it makes me sad… for her.

What kind of person is comforted by others' misery? What drives someone to constantly tear another person down to build themselves up?

When I decided to return to Lake Lavender, it was to repair two relationships. Neither would be simple, but I wanted to put in the effort. In the end, I wanted to be able to say I gave my all.

But my bones ache more and more with each attempt with my parents. The fact is that my mother won't give me room to breathe, time to sort out how I want to approach mending things with her and my father, the ability to think clearly without her barking unkind words...

I can't do it anymore.

Every ounce of energy I stored away to restore our relationship is officially spent. If all she wants to do for the rest of her life is belittle me, she will have to do it from afar. Most of my life, this woman made me feel worthless and unloved. She mocked all my successes. Attacked everything that brought me an ounce of happiness. And she did it all with a smile on her face.

And I'm just done. With trying to fix something I didn't break. With trying to love someone who will never love me for who I am. I am done with her.

"All that I've done for you—"

I hold up a hand. "Goodbye, Joan." My eyes shift to my father, a tall man that shrinks next to his wife. "Goodbye, Samuel. Have a nice life."

With Helena's hand in mine, I give them my back and weave between the rows of trees. It isn't until we are halfway across the lot that I stop, bend at the hips and plant my hands on my thighs, and take in a lungful of air. Let the gravity of what just happened truly sink in. Let the truth root itself in my head and heart.

I took the upper hand. Stood up for myself and what I wanted. Put my foot down and said *no more*. Then, I walked away. For the first time in my life, I gave myself permission to be free. Not in theory but reality. And damn, I have never felt lighter.

A hand strokes the length of my spine as I slowly straighten to my full height. I turn to look at Helena, worry creasing her brow.

"We can pick a tree on a different day if you want."

That she will drop anything for me is a shot of serotonin to the heart. I don't know what I did to earn the love of Helena Williams, but I vow to spend the rest of my life doing whatever it takes to keep her.

"No." I close the space between us, wrap her in my arms, and kiss the worry lines on her face. "I've said my piece and it's done." My forehead drops to rest on hers. "We'll handle whatever happens next together." I kiss her lips, the tip of her nose, the line of her jaw, the sensitive skin beneath her ear before nuzzling her neck and inhaling deeply. "For now, I want to find the perfect tree with my girlfriend, take it home, and watch our cat climb the trunk."

Light laughter shakes her chest as she hugs me harder. "Smoky will never leave the tree alone. You know this, right?"

I lean back and look her in the eye. "Consider me on permanent tree-watching duty."

The words dance between us, the slight implication of us officially living together dangling in the air. I would never force anything on Helena, but I won't take back my words. Most of my life, I skirted around the truth to make others feel better. I relinquished my happiness for them.

No more.

I am done holding back.

It may be too soon to consider living together, but it feels as if this has been a long time coming. This version of our relationship is new, blooming, but I have known Helena all my life. I know her heart, her soul, her endless ability to love. And waking up with her each morning, wrapping her in my arms every day, kissing her and whispering I love you often... there is nothing I want more.

Pushing up on her toes, her lips hover a breath from mine. "The job is yours." And then she kisses me as if no one is watching.

CHAPTER 63
HELENA

It's thirty-five degrees outside and I am sweating. *Sweating.* Someone toss me a life preserver.

Anderson parks the car outside Mags and Geoff's place but doesn't cut the engine. He rests his hand on my thigh, his thumb drawing faint circles on the denim. "You've been exceptionally quiet. Everything okay?"

Is everything okay? What a loaded question. If only I knew the proper response.

Swallowing, I swivel to meet his gaze. "Yeah." I nod for emphasis. "Fine."

Anderson is no fool. As easily as I sense his mood shifts, he picks up on mine. And right now, I am borderline panicking.

Deep breaths, Helena. Slow and steady.

Leaning across the console, Anderson kisses me breathless. In one simple move, he erases the bulk of my nerves. "Love you, North."

Bringing a hand to his cheek, I run my fingers through the longer hair lining his jaw. Beards have never been my thing.

but Anderson makes me look at them in a whole new light. Rugged and irresistible. Virile and delectable.

And now, my heart is racing for an entirely different reason.

"Love you, Ander." I drop my lips to his and chase the buzz coursing in my veins. The high only Anderson makes me feel.

Breaking the kiss, he chuckles. "Should probably get inside. Ales will maim us if we don't show." He kisses my cheek. "Or worse, if she catches us in the car with fogged windows."

Heat hits my cheeks. The last thing either of us needs is Lessa embarrassing us in front of everyone.

I unbuckle my seat belt. "Let's go," I say, reaching for the bag on the floorboard with our potluck dish.

Anderson laughs harder as he cuts the engine and opens his door. He waits for me at the front of the car, lacing our fingers as we walk toward the front door. "Bring on the holiday cheer," he teases, waving a hand at the massive display of lights on the house.

Holiday decorations and the change in season get me all up in my feels. The twinkling lights and shiny ornaments. The endless cheer and snowy landscapes. Merry music and the air thick with pine. Marshmallows and chocolate and special recipes set aside for this time of year. I love it all. So long as someone else does all the arduous work.

Not that I am lazy or incapable. More like I want to skip to the good part.

Much as I love holiday decorations, I am thankful our cozy little apartment doesn't have enough room for extensive trimmings or space to store during the rest of the year. As is, Smoky has knocked down the tree half a dozen times and pooped tinsel daily. Next year, things will be different.

"I love that she and Geoff decorate the house." I lean into Anderson. "After her dad's stroke, things weren't the same. Mags rarely left the house. Holidays were just another day."

Memories of an underweight Mags with dark circles under her eyes flash in my mind. In such a short time, she'd lost so much. Her two favorite people disappeared from her life far too early. Lessa and I did everything within our power to lift her up, and Mags was grateful. But she still wanted what we were unable to give her—Maria and Jacob Bishop.

"Until coming back, holidays held no value for me either." We pause at the front door and Anderson twists me to face him. "Not much in life means anything without you, North."

Tears sting the back of my eyes as emotion swells my throat. "You make everything matter, Ander." I step into him, push up on my toes, and kiss him. "Everything," I whisper.

Anderson opens his mouth to say something but is cut off as the front door whips open.

Hands on her hips, Lessa cocks a brow and smirks. "Making out on the porch?" She waggles her brows.

Anderson rolls his eyes and chuckles. "Maybe. What's it to you?"

"Just want it out of your system before you come in. No swapping spit on the couch."

My face twists up in what I'm sure is an unpleasant expression. "Ew, Lessa." I shake my head. "Ander and I are adult enough to show restraint. Unlike the rest of you."

She waves off my comment. "Get inside. It's freezing out."

Hugs and hellos are exchanged as we weave our way through the crowd. The usual crew is here—Mags and Geoff, Lessa and Braydon, Logan and Owen. But there're a few other faces here tonight. August, Sharon, Willow, and Mandi from the coffee shop are huddled near the hors d'oeuvres.

Becca and Charise from the shop are parked on the couch with a very smiley Logan trying to charm them both. *Save us all.* And last, but certainly not least, Beatrice from Statice. That woman is like another mother to Mags and an incredible mentor.

Our group may have grown over the years, but at its core, it is still the same. True and selfless and unending. Through and through, these people are my family. And I am honored to know them all.

I deposit the bag on the counter and take out the salmon spread and crostini. Anderson gets us drinks while I set out our dish. Drinks in hand, we load plates with a little bit of everything, then find seats in the living room.

Jolly music plays in the background as conversations take center stage, the occasional laugh echoing in the room. Every single person has a smile plastered on their face, even me.

Even though I am on the cusp of puking.

Geoff adds another log to the fireplace and I wish he wouldn't have. A fresh round of perspiration licks my skin and I pray I don't look as sweaty as I feel. Across the room, Lessa meets my gaze and cocks a brow. A silent question in her stare. I return her stare and add a brief, flat smile.

She sets her plate down, then clinks her fork to her glass.

Yep, I'm going to throw up.

"Happy holidays, everyone." She clinks the glass again and conversations quiet. "Just wanted to take a moment to say thank you. This year has been a whirlwind and I couldn't have gotten through a single minute of it without you all." She raises her glass, and everyone follows suit. "I love you and am lucky to have you in my life. Cheers."

"Cheers," everyone says collectively before taking a drink.

Just as I swallow the sip of wine, I rise to my feet and set my glass down. Anderson stops talking with Braydon, his eyes on me in my periphery.

One breath at a time. You got this.

I clasp my hands in front of me, twist the ring that has given me strength over the years, and swallow past my nerves. "Hey," I choke out, and all eyes turn my way. My stomach rolls and I silently admonish myself for eating before this.

"North?" Anderson slips his fingers around my wrist. "What are you..."

Inhaling deeply, I peer down at Anderson and smile. I take another deep breath and let his touch settle some of the anxiety rattling my nerves.

One breath at a time.

"Fifteen," I say, my voice shaky. "That's how old I was when I realized I was in love with Anderson."

He sucks in a sharp breath, his hold on my wrist stronger.

Tears well up in my eyes, but I blink them back. "I'd loved him the ten years before, but that love was different. A stepping-stone to something lasting and beautiful." Unclasping my hands, I slip mine into his. "Life threw us curveballs and tore us apart for far longer than acceptable. But not a day passed that I didn't love him."

"Helena..." My name a breath above a whisper as tears trail his cheeks in parallel lines.

"Anderson, you are my definition of love. Every happy memory in my life involves you." I dig into the pocket of my jeans, close my eyes and take another deep breath. "I want every memory with you. Roasted marshmallows and movie nights. Wild adventures in the middle of nowhere and campfires. Lazy Sundays on the couch and steamy kisses in the middle of Main Street."

Hooting echoes through the room and everyone laughs.

"Holidays and all the days in between, I want them all."

He swallows and subtly nods.

"Will you take the biggest adventure with me?" Uncurling my fingers, I hold up the band in my hand. "Will you—"

Anderson bolts up, frames my face in his hands and crushes my mouth with his. Cheers ring through the air as he wraps his arms around me and lifts me off the ground. My arms circle his neck as I melt into the kiss.

"Well?" I faintly hear Lessa in the background.

Anderson breaks the kiss and rests his forehead on mine. Breathes in the moment. Drops a chaste kiss to my lips. Reinforces his hold on me as my feet dangle between us.

"Yes," he whispers, loud enough for only me to hear.

My heart shoots through my chest and I stop breathing.

"Breathe, North."

He brushes my nose with his and I suck in a sharp breath.

"What was that?" Lessa asks, volume cranked all the way up.

Anderson inches back and smiles wide. *Love you*, he mouths.

Love you, I mouth back.

"You're killing us," Logan whines, and everyone laughs.

Turning his attention to the room, Anderson announces, "Yes. I said yes." And then his lips are on mine, sealing his answer with a profound *hell yes*.

EPILOGUE

ANDERSON

Seven Months Later

I nuzzle in the crook of Helena's neck and hum. She tucks a leg between mine, her fingers dancing over my skin as she snuggles closer. I pepper kisses up her neck and along her jaw until my lips meet hers.

"Good morning," I mumble against her lips, my fingers in her hair.

"Morning," she says, the word raspy on her tongue. "Sleep good?"

"Better than good." I drop another kiss to her lips. "You?"

"The best."

Splashes of pink and peach seep through the van windows as the sun crests the mountainside. Leaves rustle in the early morning breeze. Earth and pine and Helena's floral amber scent float in the air. Soft purrs vibrate my pillow, growing louder the longer we lie awake.

Everything about the morning is perfect. And the day will

only get better. In a few hours, today officially moves to the top of my favorites list, all of which include Helena.

"Don't want to get up," I grumble, flopping onto my back. "But know we should."

Helena inches closer and drapes herself over me, keeping me right where I want to be. "Five more minutes."

"Five more minutes," I repeat, wrapping her in my arms.

As if she is our personal alarm clock, Smoky stretches and mewls minutes later. She pads across the pillow, hovers inches from our faces, meows again, then rubs her nose over ours. Her morning kisses are my second favorite.

Groaning, I release my hold on Helena and give Smoky her morning scratches. "I bet you want breakfast, lil' Smoky." She bumps my temple with her forehead and cries louder. Pulling back the covers, I swing my legs over the edge of the bed and sit up. "Mom and I need breakfast, too."

Helena sits up, the sheet pooling around her waist. In only a thin cotton camisole and panties, I resist the urge to stare. If it were any other day, I'd feed Smoky, slip back into bed, and get lost in her.

But that will have to wait. Today, we have other plans.

While I scoop kibble for Smoky, Helena fills the kettle with water, lights a burner, then leaves it to heat. She disappears outside to visit the new camping privy I insisted we get. I laugh, thinking back on our argument in the middle of the outdoor supply store.

"I do not need a literal toilet in the woods."

My eyes scan the faces nearby. A man rolls his eyes. A woman covers her mouth in an attempt to hide her laughter. Others stand by idly, pretending to pay us no attention while they wait to see what happens next.

"I know you don't need *it. Camping is in your DNA. But think*

about winter. I mean, if I'm being honest, I'd like a toilet with an outhouse-style tent when the wind chill is below thirty."

At this, she laughs. Hallelujah.

"We don't have space for it in the van," she argues, and I know she is doing it because conceding now would be too soon.

"It won't be used in the van, North." I spin the box around on the shelf and point to the images. "But how nice would it be to not worry about bugs or plants tickling your butt while you pee?"

She playfully smacks my chest. "Ander," she grumbles under her breath. "People are listening to us."

I shrug, having too much fun with this. "And everyone poops, North."

The laughing woman snorts, and Helena's cheeks pink.

"Look, you don't have to use it. But I plan on it." I rest my hands on her shoulders and look her in the eye. "I'm not saying you can't go in the woods. What I am suggesting is that you don't have to." Without another word, I pick up the box and put it in the oversized cart.

"Fine," she huffs out. "Get the stupid porta-potty. But it's all you."

Our first trip after buying the outdoor bathroom setup, Helena intentionally avoided it. On the second trip, she changed her tune. Waking up in the middle of the night to go to the bathroom is bad enough. Doing so in the middle of the forest is totally different. That was her turning point.

Now, she is team portable outhouse.

Stepping out after her, I return a moment later to her scrambling eggs. While she cooks, I make drinks and cut fruit. Soon, we sit down to breakfast and slowly start our day.

The past year has been a whirlwind. Helena and I coming back together and falling madly in love. Moving in together. Getting engaged and deciding to take this trip to elope. And then finally closing the chapter on my parents—one of the toughest decisions I've made, but one I don't regret.

A couple weeks into January, I sat down with Ales and told her I wanted to give one last try with our parents. I set boundaries, laid out rules, and asked her if she would be the middle person to coordinate lunch at the diner. I wanted Helena, Ales, and Braydon present to not only anchor me but also keep my mother more amiable during the meetup.

Sixteen minutes. That is how long it took for my mother to flip. One second, her faux-loving-mother persona was firmly in place and on display. Smiles and invitations to the house under the guise of being missed. Then, in a blink, she was the woman that knocked me down peg after peg during my youth. Sneer in place, she reiterated how she thought I was making poor life decisions. My career choices. My love choices. The worst part... she didn't care who heard.

I refuse to be her scapegoat. And hours before Lake Lavender got its heaviest snowstorm in years, I exited the booth, told my parents to never contact me again, and walked away with Helena at my side.

Much as I wish my mother would have been more mature and less hostile, she has her own demons to conquer, and it isn't my job to exorcise them. One day, I hope she finds peace. I hope she lets go of all the hurt in her heart and discovers a happier future. Unfortunately for her, that future will not include me.

When our plates empty, I take on dish cleaning duty and let Helena get ready. She moves to the back of the van, opens the doors, and pulls out a garment bag from under the bed. I get momentarily distracted as she strips off her camisole, and the plate in my hand clatters in the sink.

She peeks up. "Eyes on the sink, mister," she teases.

I lift a sudsy hand to my forehead and salute her. "Yes, ma'am."

It's rather difficult to not see the bride in her dress when she has nowhere to hide. But I do my damnedest to keep my attention off her as she gets ready. While she slips on her dress and adds small touches of makeup, I finish cleaning. When she announces she's done, she moves around the van so I can change.

As I fasten the last button on my shirt, leaving the top two undone, the sound of tires crushing leaves and sticks echoes up the trail. A black pickup rounds the bend and parks opposite our firepit.

The doors swing open just before a gravelly "morning" hits my ears. Walking to the passenger side of the truck, Mr. Williams helps his wife down from the truck. Stepping out after her is the ordained minister, an older woman with stark white hair, beautiful brown skin, and a look in her eyes that says she's lived a memorable life.

When Helena and I decided to elope, her parents were crestfallen. Even with the promise of a party when we returned from our trip, her dad wanted to be present during the ceremony. Her mom, too. After an hour of healthy back and forth, we reached a compromise.

Her parents would drive out for the ceremony, be present for our vow exchange, smother us with hugs and congratulations, then return home. It was a small concession, but it meant the world to her parents, and we agreed without protest.

Mr. and Mrs. Williams were always gentle and loving with me as a child. During high school, when they'd expressed concern for Helena and laid down stricter rules, they'd still been kind. Not only had they gifted me with years of happy memories during our annual summer trips, they also loved me as if I was their own. They may not be my family by blood, but they are the family I choose.

"Where's my Bug?" Mr. Williams calls out.

Helena peeks around the front of the van and waves. "Hiding over here," she says on a laugh.

The minister sidles up to me at the rear of the van. Warm brown eyes look me up and down before meeting my blues. "You finished getting ready, son?"

I give myself one last look over, pat my pocket, double-check I have Helena's ring and nod. "Yes, ma'am."

She waves me off. "None of that ma'am business. Call me Opal." Burlap messenger bag slung over her shoulder, she loops her arm with mine. "Walk an old lady to the spot, would ya?"

"I'd be honored, Opal."

In no hurry, we walk the trail Helena and I roamed count-less times in our youth. A mile-long hike with a breathtaking view at the peak. A spot filled with wondrous memories. The place where we'd make more memories today.

Days after Helena proposed, we snuggled on the couch and discussed how we each pictured our wedding day. We both wanted something small and intimate. No church or rigid cere-mony. No colossal expenses or fancy attire. Just us and the love we shared.

It had been Helena's idea to blend the good memories of our past with who we are now. *Something old and something new,* she'd said. Those were the only traditional pieces about today. All I know of her dress is that one of her shop designers hand-stitched the cream-colored fabric. Casually chic is how she describes it and that is how I explained it to the man in the menswear store.

Tucked into dark-brown slacks, the off-white short-sleeve

linen shirt is snugger than I prefer but has wiggle room. My only concern is looking good next to Helena when photos are taken.

A wide smile highlights Opal's face when we reach the lookout. "A beautiful location for a beautiful couple."

I stare out at the water and sigh. This place holds so many memories for us. We became friends here. We hiked trails and shared secrets. As the years passed, this is where we fell in love.

Marrying Helena in Seaquest is us coming full circle. Our beginning and our future blended into one. An infinite loop. Her heart connected with mine. Though we share countless memories outside this place, here is where our favorite memories exist. In the earth and trees, the piney air and warm breeze. Nights by the fire and hand-holding in the woods.

An excited meow snaps me out of my memories and I turn to see Hannah with a leashed Smoky. I shuffle into position and squat down, holding my arms open as she trots in my direction, a cream collar with a tinkling bell around her neck.

"There's Daddy's little girl." I scratch her head and she headbutts my knee. I open my mouth to say she looks pretty with her new necklace on, but don't get the chance. The rustling of leaves has my head snapping up.

Rounding the bend of the trail is Helena on Reginald's arm. *Damn. She stuns me more every day.*

Every night since returning to Lake Lavender, I count my stars. Thank each and every one that I got a second chance with my favorite person, my best friend, the love of my life. Years ago, I was lucky to call Helena mine. Now, it is something greater than luck. Grander than kismet or providence.

Like all true loves, ours didn't come easy. We had hiccups and heartache. Good days and bad. But without them, we wouldn't appreciate and cherish what we have now. An unbreakable bond and irrefutable love.

With tearstained cheeks, we exchange our vows. On whispered I dos, she slips a new ring on my finger and I slide one on hers—an oval halo sapphire in an antique, rose gold setting with diamond chips. The ring reminded me of the nights we stared at the stars and was an instant yes.

"Well, go ahead and kiss already," Opal declares, and we all laugh.

I lift my hands and frame Helena's face, drop my forehead to hers, and hover a breath above her lips. "I'm no longer lost." My thumbs stroke her cheeks. "I have my true North." And then I seal my lips to hers, pledging my heart, my love, and my soul to her.

My North.

BONUS CONTENT
HELENA

Five Years Later

"This is the life," Lessa says, sinking into her camping chair with a glass of wine in her hand.

"Best idea ever," Mags adds as she twirls her skewered marshmallow over the fire.

I snatch the bag of marshmallows and load one on my and Anderson's skewers. Breaking apart chocolate and graham crackers, I set the pieces on a plate between me and the fire, then lower the sugar squares to the fire and wait for the magic to happen.

The guys huddle near the new Airstream Braydon and Lessa purchased last month. This week is its maiden voyage and Braydon is eager to show off all the gadgets and gizmos. Lessa promises to give us a tour when the guys quit fawning over it.

I doubt the guys with give it a rest anytime soon. Until then, I'll hang by the fire, pet Smoky, and eat my weight in s'mores.

A few years back, Lake Lavender had a slight population boom. Still classified as a small town, we gained hundreds of residents when, on the outskirts of town, new homes were built. Many of the late-generation residents complained to the mayor. Decreed the town would lose its appeal and peace. The mayor vowed after this cluster of homes was built, there'd be no new housing for at least twenty years. They grumbled for weeks, but finally conceded.

The boom has been great for the town. Not only did the town and its storefronts see a boost in sales, the town gained more friends. It was a win for the town and residents.

Geoff's architectural firm has been nonstop since the town mentioned adding more homes. Mags started her own practice shortly before the boom. Her love of helping others, especially youth, holds a special place in my heart. She experienced so much heartache when she lost her parents. Her desire to help others overcome pain and heartache is the best gift.

Braydon writes quarterly articles for his father's magazine, Washington's Hidden Gems, but keeps busy with the town paper the rest of the year. Each week, he highlights something new about town—a business, outdoor adventure, or resident. As for Lessa, the coffee shop has never been better. After another expansion and staff increase two years ago, Java and Teas Me serves thousands daily. She also learned to take time for herself. Once a month, she and Braydon take a long weekend out of town and go see some of the places he has written about. The time away has been good for her.

Then there is me and Anderson.

After a full year in Lake Lavender, I worried Anderson would go crazy as he set down roots. Every time he asked what was wrong, I asked if he was happy living in the cramped apartment above a clothing store. And every time he answered the same.

"It doesn't matter where I am. As long as you're with me, I am exactly where I want to be."

To keep his wild heart happy and my adventurous side nurtured, we take week-long trips every few months. Sometimes, we come back to Seaquest. Other times, we explore with no destination in mind. Thanks to the town boom, I have a great staff to hold down the fort when we leave.

Two of our yearly trips involve a little work. Well, Anderson does all the work—pictures and finding the perfect spots to take them—for travel blogs. Smoky and I tag along to traverse new places and snuggle with him at night. It fills more than one well and gives him the fresh air he doesn't get working in the store with me.

Smooshing the marshmallows between the chocolate and graham cracker halves, I add two more to the skewers and set them in the middle of the fire. As they char, I chomp down on my first s'more. Halfway through, Anderson sits down next to me and hands me a mini carton of oat milk.

"Thank you," I mumble, yanking his charred marshmallows from the fire. "For you, husband."

He kisses my nose then takes the skewers. "You're the best, wife."

"And you two are nauseating," Lessa says on a groan.

"I'm sure Braydon would rather be called husband over Care Bear," Anderson teases.

Hand to her heart, Lessa gasps. "Never." But with one look from Anderson, she twists in her chair and hollers, "Care Bear."

Braydon stops talking to Geoff and turns his attention to his wife. "Firecracker."

"Should I start calling you husband instead of Care Bear? I'm getting mixed opinions over here."

I laugh with a shake of my head.

"Hell, no."

"Love you, Care Bear." She turns in her chair and cocks a brow at Anderson. "See. I was right."

Anderson tears off a piece of his marshmallow and shoves it in his mouth. "And I live to mess with you." He blows her a kiss and she flips him off.

Geoff and Braydon join us at the fire. We snuggle into each other and reminisce over camping trips of the past. Tales of sprained ankles and rashes. Bug bites in awkward places and days when the world seemed a little less busy. Mags talks about her parents and how she helped Mrs. Bishop make breakfast at least once each year and learned how to fish because her dad loved it.

"Glad we started coming back here," Anderson whispers in my ear, his front to my back, arms around my middle as we gaze at the fire.

"Me, too." I drop my head back on his shoulder and sigh. "Best decision we made as a group."

Reinstating our annual camping trip had been Mags's idea. A break away from life and a family vacation. Last year, Logan and Owen tagged along. Logan drank too much, and Owen had trouble relaxing. This year, instead of joining us for the entire week, they opted for half the week and will be here tomorrow. Unlike us, they needed to work their way up to such a life disconnect.

Also new... they are both bringing a guest. Wild as he still is, Logan's girlfriend of six months has tamed him considerably. Owen's relationship is still fresh at two months. From what I hear, this trip is a leap into the serious category.

S'mores get eaten and wine is drunk as the fire slowly fades. One by one, our friends head for bed. But Anderson and I aren't ready for bed. Not until we do one last thing.

I scoop Smoky up in my arms and rise from my spot on the blanket. Anderson takes my proffered hand, dusting off his shorts as he stands. He picks up the blanket and drapes it over his shoulder. Lacing our fingers, he leads the way to a place we've been countless times but never enough.

A short distance from the van, he stops and lays the blanket on the earth. He lowers to the ground, lies back, and holds out his hands for Smoky. After I hand her over, I lie at his side and stare up at the sky with him.

Away from all the light pollution and noise and chaos of the world, I get lost in the stars with Anderson. My best friend. My husband. My person.

I may be his North, but he will always be my heart.

MORE BY PERSEPHONE

Depths Awakened

A small town romance which captivates you from the start. Mags and Geoff are two broken souls who have sworn off love. Vowed to never lose anyone else. But their undeniable attraction brings them together and refuses to let go.

One Night Forsaken

One night. No names. No romance. Just fun. Nothing more–at least, that's what she tells herself. Until he appears in her coffee shop months later with that addictive smile. She swore off commitment. He vows to never love again. But the more they fight it, the more life brings them together.

Distorted Devotion

Free-spirited Sarah lives life to the fullest. When a new love interest enters her life, she starts receiving strange gifts and letters. She doesn't want to relinquish her freedom or new love, but fears the consequences.

Transcendental

A musician in search of his muse and a woman grieving the loss of her husband. Two weeks at an exclusive retreat and their connection rivals all others. Until she leaves early without notice. But he refuses to give up until he finds her again.

The Click Duet

High school sweethearts torn apart. When fate gives them a second chance, one doesn't trust they won't be hurt again. Through the Lens

(Click Duet #1) and Time Exposure (Click Duet #2) is an angsty, second chance, friends to lovers romance with all the feels.

The Inked Duet

A man with a broken heart and a woman scared to put herself out there. Love is never easy. Sometimes love rips you apart. Fine Line (Inked Duet #1) and Love Buzz (Inked Duet #2) is a second chance at love, single parent romance with a pinch of angst and dash of suspense.

The Insomniac Duet

He was her high school bully. She was the outcast that secretly crushed on him. More than ten years later, he's her boss, completely oblivious to their shared past, and wants no one but her. More importantly, he doesn't understand her animosity toward him.

The Artist Duet

A tortured hero with the biggest heart and a charismatic heroine with the patience of a saint. Previous heartache has him fighting his desire to be more than friends with her. But she is everywhere, and he can't help but give in. The Artist Duet is an angsty, friends to lovers slow burn.

Broken Sky

Their eyes meet across the bar, but she looks away first. Does her best to give him zero attention. But when he crowds her on the dancefloor, she can't deny the instant chemistry. After one night together, he marks her as his. Unfortunately, another woman thinks he belongs to her.

Slipping From Existence

Would it be so bad to slip from existence? Would it be so bad to give in to the darkness?

Slipping From Existence is a dark poetry collection centered around depression and coping while maintaining a brave face.

THANK YOU

Thank you so much for reading **Every Thought Taken**, book three in the **Lake Lavender Series**. If you wouldn't mind taking a moment to leave a review on the retailer site where you made your purchase, Goodreads and/or BookBub, it would mean the world to me.

Reviews help other readers find and enjoy the book as well.

Much love,
   Persephone

PLAYLIST

Here are some of the songs from the **Every Thought Taken** playlist. You can find and listen to the entire playlist on Spotify!

This Town | Niall Horan
You Are In Love | Taylor Swift
Ghost Of You | 5 Seconds of Summer
Repeat Until Death | Novo Amor
Happiest Year | Jaymes Young
Saturn | Sleeping At Last
Haven | Novo Amor
Bigger Than The Whole Sky | Taylor Swift
Keep Me | Novo Amor
Ontario | Novo Amor, Ed Tullett, Lowswimmer

CONNECT WITH PERSEPHONE

Connect with Persephone
www.persephoneautumn.com

Subscribe to Persephone's newsletter
www.persephoneautumn.com/newsletter

Join Persephone's reader's group
Persephone's Playground

Follow Persephone online

instagram.com/persephoneautumn

facebook.com/persephoneautumnwrites

tiktok.com/@persephoneautumn

bookbub.com/authors/persephone-autumn

goodreads.com/persephoneautumn

amazon.com/author/persephoneautumn

pinterest.com/persephoneautumn

ACKNOWLEDGMENTS

To my wife, daughter, and dad... Thank you for always being there for me when I am not my strongest self. For staying by my side and being the support system I need when my mind becomes my worst enemy. I love you more than I express. You are my rock, my foundation, my reason to keep going.

Ellie and Rosa at My Brother's Editor! I love you both 🖤 Your expertise is invaluable. Thank you for making my manuscript better than it was before I sent it to you. Just when I think I have things figured out, you prove me wrong 😆 Fuck commas! Fuck lay, lie, laid, laying, and lying.

Abi of Pink Elephant Designs! I am so fucking in love with all the covers you made for this series! You took my fumbled ideas and made something brilliant and stunning. Thank you so much for your talent and expertise 🥰

Bloggers!! I would be nowhere without you! Thank you for reading my words, creating magical edits and videos, and promoting my books all over the internet. YOU ROCK!!

ARC readers! If this is the first book of mine you've read, thank you for taking a chance on me. Those that've read me before, I love you more than words! Thank you for reading my books and your continual support. Your reviews are GOLD! Without you, I wouldn't be where I am. Complete gratitude!

Author peeps... I love you! This business is rough and exhausting, but I love how we lean on and support each other. To belong to a community where every person wants everyone to thrive and succeed... I love it and you!

Readers are the best humans! Thank you to each and every one of you for reading my words. For choosing one of my books, thank you times a million. If I could hug you all, my tentacle arms would squeeze you tight.

ABOUT THE AUTHOR

USA Today Bestselling Author Persephone Autumn lives in Florida with her wife and psycho cat. A proud mom with a cuckoo grandpup. An ethnic food enthusiast who has fun discovering ways to vegan-ize her favorite non-vegan foods. Most days, you'll find her with a tea latte or fruity concoction in her hand. If given the opportunity, she would intentionally get lost in nature.

For years, Persephone did some form of writing; mostly journaling or poetry. After pairing her poetry with images and posting them online, she began the journey of writing her first novel.

She mainly writes romance and poetry, but on occasion dips her toes in other works. Look for her non-romance publications under P. Autumn.